IN ALEXA'S SHOES

Captured by the enemy.
Can she triumph over tragedy?

ROCHELLE ALEXANDRA

AUTHOR ACADEMY elite

Copyright © 2019 Rochelle Alexandra
All rights reserved.
Printed in the United Kingdom.

Published by Author Academy Elite
P.O. Box 43, Powell, OH 43035
www.AuthorAcademyElite.com

Paperback ISBN- 978-1-64085-614-1
Hardcover ISBN- 978-1-64085-615-8
Ebook ISBN- 978-1-64085-616-5
Library of Congress Control Number: 2019935712

DEDICATION

This book is dedicated to the memory of my
beautiful grandmother Alexandra.
'My sunshine, my diamond, my heart...'
Who passed away on April 15, 2019
at the age of 92, just a few months
before this novel was published.

...and to the memory of all the many
innocent victims, whose lives were taken
and forever changed during the holocaust
at the hands of the Nazis.

We must never forget!

PREFACE

As a young girl growing up, I knew that my Polish grandmother had endured a harrowing personal experience during World War II. I was told that she had been forcefully rounded up along with her mother, by the Nazis one day and was then taken to Germany for several years when she was a young girl. But that was all that I knew.

I was born and raised in Scotland and only got to visit my grandmother every other summer, during the school holidays with my mother. Our visits together were always happy times. We adored each other and shared only pleasant and enjoyable times and an unconditional love.

It wasn't until 2002 when I visited my grandmother in Krakow for seven weeks, that she finally opened up to me and shared her heartbreaking story. We talked about it many more times over the years when I would visit and each time, she would share some new chapters and experiences from her life with me. She always said that I should write her story down one day for her, as she was now too old. I said that I would, and now I have.

What you are about to read, is her story.

CHAPTER -1-

In September of 1940, Alexa was one week into the start of her new school year. A blisteringly hot summer had finally come to an end throughout Europe and as autumn began, the leaves on the trees were beginning to slowly turn color. Alexa sat close to one of three large picture framed windows in her classroom, which looked out onto a large field at the back of her school. The field was surrounded by a forest at its far edge. Alexa had a front row seat as the seasons put on a natural performance for her. The scenery was ever changing, and although ever so slowly, the trees always entertained her. Autumn was her most favorite season. She loved the vibrant colors and the dance of the leaves. Often accompanying her view, she would hear Vivaldi's four seasons play in her head. He was the composer of whom she was fondest and whose music she knew very well, from listening with her mother over the radio at home. She watched the seasons change with great anticipation and pleasure. As autumn shed its colorful beat, she was in awe of the rich vibrant reds, the golden yellows, burnt oranges and copper rusts on display. Then ever so slowly, day by day, one by one, the leaves would gently fall to the ground. She could hear violins play in her head as they fell swirling, spinning, twisting and turning on their descent before being added to the cushioned pile on the forest floor below. Some days they fell faster than others especially when the elements took over, blowing strong winds that frantically tossed them through the air, detaching the dry leaves from the safety of the branches that once held them securely. Eventually the winds would die down and calmness would be restored. It was nature's way. Everything had its time and its season. Life, death and rebirth. Nothing could stay the same forever. This, however, was the constant safe peaceful place in which she often found herself daydreaming. Alexa was a model student, a smart creative girl who learned fast and worked hard in class, always obedient, always doing as she was told. It was usually only after her school work was completed that Alexa allowed herself the luxury of letting her thoughts drift off.

It was late afternoon on Friday and, as Alexa looked out of the window towards the field, she noticed some sudden movements taking place just at the field's edge where the forest began. There were what seemed to be three dark colored military trucks parked up on the grass verge, with groups of men who were filing out the backs of them. They were German military trucks. They had become a very common sight around Poland since the German invasion the previous year. Alexa looked harder and focused more than she had ever done previously, squinting her eyes until they were almost closed, as she tried to see clearer into the distance. She had never seen any gatherings of people, or group activity there before. The men seemed to be carrying something over their shoulders and every now and then as they moved, the sun would reflect a bright silver glint, as if from metal. The men then disappeared off into the woods, through the trees and were gone from sight.

Alexa lived at home in Lublin, in the East of Poland, with her mother Sophia aged thirty-seven and her eight-year old sister Asha. Their father, Alexander had been older than their mother and had died after a long painful illness when Alexa was only seven-years old. He had been a wonderful man, father and husband who loved his wife and family dearly. He adored

Alexa, and she was named after him even though she was a girl. Being that she was his first-born child, he spent most of his free time playing games with her and encouraging her creativity. He made a habit of sketching and regularly drawing with her, as he tried to teach her and pass on his artistic talents. He was an accomplished artist who had many of his oil paintings displayed in art galleries for sale throughout Poland, as well as in some other European cities. Although he had given up painting commissions for clients and creating new works of art, he took great pleasure in showing Alexa how to mix colors and how to make a blank canvas really come to life. He taught her about the great masters of the past as well as their various painting styles.

He tried to share all the things that he viewed as beautiful and important in life with her, sensing that he only had a short time to live. This contributed to them being such a very close loving family, who were extremely attentive to each other's needs. Sophia's mother also lived with them since the death of her husband and shared in caring for and raising the girls. Sarah was a religious woman, a good Roman Catholic lady who had a real love for God and the Bible. She had shared this love with both of her granddaughters, teaching them as they grew up. Sadly, Sarah had died suddenly, two years before when Alexa was just eleven. It was deeply painful for them all. However, as she had been such a big influence in all of their lives, her good habits, morals and teachings, remained very much alive in their home life and in their hearts.

Alexa had been promised by her mother that she would buy her a new pair of shoes for school that coming weekend in town. Her mother had managed to save hard and now had enough money put aside to finally buy them for her. Alexa was so excited and could think of little else. She had passed by the town square's only shoe shop many times and had peered through its windows often, with her nose pressed up against the glass, imagining wearing several pairs of the pretty shoes inside. There was a royal blue leather pair which had a reasonably sized small square heel, with a side strap and a shiny silver buckle. These were a big favorite of hers and blue was Alexa's favorite color. The black ones were more practical, but she really wasn't too keen on them. Deep down, she really wanted the one pair of shiny red patent shoes in the shop. They were a brand-new style and so eye-catching, but she knew that her mother would never allow her to get those ones. After all, they were also the most expensive pair in the shop. No, her shoes needed to be a practical pair of shoes, comfortable with durability that would last.

As Alexa daydreamed about the blue shoes while sitting in the classroom, her thoughts were brought back to reality when the school bell rang, and Friday's school day came to an end. However, the bell had rung an hour earlier than it normally did, and the confused teacher told the children in her classroom to remain in their seats until she returned. She went off to investigate and wasn't gone for very long, before she came back into the room with a serious expression on her face.

"Children I need you all to quickly put away your books, bring your bags and jackets with you, and follow me hastily out of the building," she instructed her pupils.

The children looked confused but did as they were told. They packed up their bags and followed their teacher along the corridors. As they approached the main doors, they excitedly ran outside to get to the freedom of the open field. But for the first time there were some SS soldiers with large ferocious German shepherd dogs outside of the school building and also standing guard at the gates. Freedom was most definitely not to be found there. The students came to an abrupt stop, while eight armed soldiers motioned the large group of children to line up in twos along with their teachers. A tall German officer, sharply dressed in his grey Nazi uniform and black shiny jackboots, instructed the children in a firm loud voice that under no circumstances were they allowed to go near to, or walk through the field at the back of the school. Nor were they permitted to freely go play in, or explore the woods anymore. They were informed that this area was now out of bounds to everyone except the German soldiers. Instead, they were told to use the main road in the front of the building to the right, to walk away from the school area back towards their homes. It was abundantly clear to everyone that this was an order, not an invitation. There was no personal choice on the matter. The teachers knew better than to ask any questions and immediately motioned the children under their care to quickly walk out onto the roadway. The soldiers told them to keep walking briskly together along the side of the road, to keep to the left and to keep going until they arrived home. "Don't look back or come back here for anything!" They told the children in no uncertain terms. The teachers along with their young pupils, began the long walk together. There was an air of fear surrounding them all. As the last pupils joined the long procession, two of the SS soldiers stood guard outside of the school gate and six armed soldiers followed along behind the march, of around a hundred children and teachers.

"Schnell!" the soldiers shouted.

As the children walked along the road, they displayed a longing for the security of their mothers, which showed in their drawn faces. Alexa had paired up with her best friend Helena, who lived near her. They held each other's hand tightly as they briskly marched on along the road. Alexa silently began reciting her favorite prayer to herself. Her grandmother had taught her a version of the 91st Psalm from the Bible, when she was only five years old and every night before lights out and sleep, she'd say the prayer out loud in rhyme form. Once Alexa had finally learned it off by heart, they would recite it together and this became their bedtime ritual. Even after her grandmother's death, she faithfully continued saying the prayer out loud in the morning and at night. Once Asha was older, she'd recite the Psalm for them both. Now however, Alexa was silently repeating the prayer as hard and as sincerely as she could, with the firm belief that God would hear her and help.

'You are my refuge and my stronghold, Oh God...Rescue me from the bird catcher...Protect me under your wings...You are my Salvation!'

A few seconds later, two of the six soldiers marching them along pulled back, stopping off on the roadway and stood guard with their barking dogs beside them. A few miles further along the road, another two of the soldiers halted, also taking up guard positions along the route. For the first twenty minutes into the long walk, none of the group spoke at all due to the uncertainty of what was going on and the heightened sense of fear which they all felt. Finally, as they reached the edge of town, the last two soldiers pulled back and took up guard positions on the side of the road, just as the other soldiers had done previously. With the teachers now leading the group alone and the soldiers no longer with them, eventually light chatter began amongst the group of children once again.

"What do you think was going on in the woods Alexa? asked Helena, "What's this all about?"

"I don't know, but in school as I looked out of the class-room window across the field, I saw some German army trucks parked at the edge of the forest. There were groups of men getting out of the trucks and disappearing in through the trees."

"I don't like the sound of that." Helena said nervously.

"I know, me neither. Oh, and they were carrying something that seemed silvery over their shoulders, because I saw the sun reflect off whatever shiny metal looking things they were carrying." Alexa added.

They walked a few more minutes in silence, quietly thinking and contemplating to themselves, until a new thought floated in.

"So, what pair of shoes have you decided on, Alexa?"

"Well you know I'd really love the red patent ones, but realistically I think it's going to have to be the royal blue ones, I really love them too and they are so much more practical."

"Well, blue is your favorite color and I'm sure they will look so good on you. Plus, they'll go with anything. Can I try them on when you get them?" Helena asked.

"Yes, for sure! I'm getting them tomorrow morning in town with my Mama, so I'll be wearing them to school on Monday. You can try them on during our lunch break."

"Oh, thanks Alexa, I can't wait!"

"Have a great weekend and I'll see you on Monday at school."

The two best friends hugged goodbye. Helena quickly crossed over the road and headed off towards a side street, close to where she lived. Just before she disappeared out of sight, she turned back, raised her hand high in the air and waved to her best friend. Alexa smiled and waved back blowing a kiss in the wind and then, she was gone.

Alexa's little sister Asha had not been at school that day. Their mother had said that she could stay home from school, as she had taken ill with a sore throat and bad cough. She hadn't slept much through the previous night, so her mother had decided that she'd be better off resting at home. Alexa was now quite relieved that Asha hadn't been at school that day. Asha was quite different from Alexa. She had always been the frailer of the two sisters and she was quite the worrier. Perhaps the early death of her father and grandmother had also had an effect on her character formation at such a tender age. Alexa always took extra special attention and care when it came to her little sister. Always trying her best to protect her from life's cruelties, knowing just how fragile she was. Alexa finally arrived home safely and breathed a deep sigh of relief, as she closed the door behind her.

"Mama I'm home, I'm safe and I'm home!" she yelled out in relief.

Sophia came out of the kitchen and her daughter ran straight into her arms.

"Whatever's the matter my dear child? What's happened to you?" enquired Sophia.

"The SS, the soldiers, they came to the fields at the back of the school in trucks this afternoon. They sent groups of men with what looked like shovels into the woods. I saw them from the window in my classroom. When the bell rang early at 2 pm, they were waiting outside of the school. They ordered everyone to stay away from the fields and the forest and made us all march together along the roadway. We had to take the long way to get home. I was so scared Mama!" Alexa spoke very fast, trying to give her mother all the pertinent facts of what she had just gone through.

"Oh, my darling girl, are you alright? Are you hurt?"

"I'm okay, they never hurt us. The German guards followed behind us with their rifles and their big dogs barking at us, but they didn't hurt us. The teachers were with us and I walked next to Helena the whole way. Oh, Mama I'm so glad I'm home!"

"Me too sweetheart! There, there, it's all okay. You're safe now. Sit down and I'll make you some hot tea. There's some cake left, and the sweetness will help you feel better. Sit darling!"

Alexa sat at the kitchen table as her mother quickly boiled some water on the stove. Alexa kicked off her tight, well-worn shoes under the table.

"My feet are sore Mama."

"Don't you worry Alexa. Tomorrow is Saturday and I'm still taking you into town to buy your new pair of shoes, as I promised you. Your feet will feel great in them and then you'll forget all about today's drama," assured her mother.

"Thank you, Mama, I can't wait! Would it be alright if I got the pretty royal blue pair of shoes with the silver buckle?"

"Yes, my beautiful girl, I knew you would pick the blue ones in the end." Sophia smiled at her daughter as she placed a slice of cake on the table in front of her. Just then they heard Asha stirring who came out from the bedroom where she had been asleep. "Let's not tell your sister about what happened today, we'll tell her before school on Monday," suggested her mother.

Alexa nodded silently in agreement, knowing just how worried it would make Asha. They all sat down at the kitchen table and Sophia poured out three cups of hot tea.

"How are you feeling now, any better?" asked Sophia. "Here, drink some tea, I put lemon and some honey in it for you. It'll help soothe your throat."

"Thank you, Mama, my throat's still sore and I feel so hot," answered Asha coughing.

Her mother leaned over and felt her forehead.

"You do have a bit of a temperature, let's get you back into bed sweetheart. And tomorrow morning when Alexa and I go into town to buy her new shoes, I will ask Magda next door to look after you until we get back. Come on, I'll carry your drink through to the bedroom for you. Now back into bed," ordered her mother.

Alexa said she would go through and read to Asha a little later, after she had finished helping their mother prepare dinner. Asha was happy with that plan. She loved her big sister so much and enjoyed every moment that she spent with her. Alexa was now thirteen and a half years of age and was blooming into quite a beautiful young woman, the very image of her mother. Alexa had soft smooth unblemished skin, and had a golden glow from the summer's sun, which gave her a healthy looking, bronzed complexion. Her eyes were like deep pools of blue sapphires, which drew you into her gaze and held you there for a while. Her hair was a beautiful shade of light golden blonde which shimmered as the sun kissed it. It was soft and straight, its length reaching down just past her shoulders. Her figure was just right for her height. Shapely and perfectly proportioned, which gave the impression that she could have been older than she actually was. She appeared strong, fit and healthy and was indeed a really stunning, beautiful young Polish teenager.

Sophia said she wouldn't be long and went next door to her neighbor Magda's house. Magda was a German woman who lived in the adjoining house with her husband Michael and nine-year old twins, Eva and Peter. Five years earlier, they had moved from Berlin to Lublin not far from the German border. Over the years they had become good friends as well as neighbors. Asha and the twins were friendly and played together often in each other's houses, as well as outside in the garden. Sophia knocked on their door hoping to find Magda at home.

"Hi Magda, I need a favor. Asha is poorly with a sore throat and running a slight temperature and I wondered if you could look after her in the morning for about an hour or two, while I take Alexa into town to buy her new shoes?"

"Yes, it's no problem, I would be happy to watch over her. Just let me know what time."

"We'll leave at 9 am, if that's okay?"

"Yes, Michael will be home, and he can look after the twins."

Sophia thanked her and returned back home to make dinner. After they ate, Alexa read a little to Asha as promised while the hours ticked away as darkness fell. Alexa got ready for bed, brushed her teeth and combed her lovely long blonde hair. Sophia came into the bedroom to bid her girls goodnight, telling them that she loved them, as she always did. Alexa then began their ritual prayer of Psalm 91.

'Anyone dwelling in the secret place of the Most High, will lodge under the shadow of the Almighty.

I will say to the Lord: "You are my refuge and my fortress, my God in whom I trust."

For He will rescue you from the trap of the bird catcher, from the destructive pestilence.

He will cover you with his feathers, and under His wings you will take refuge.

His truth will be thy shield and a protective wall.

Thou shall not be afraid for the terror by night, nor the arrow that flies by day.

Nor the pestilence that walks in darkness, nor for the destruction that ravages at midday.

A thousand will fall at your side and ten thousand at your right hand, but to you it shall not come near.

Only with thine eyes shall you behold and see the reward of the wicked.

Because you said: "God, is my refuge," You have made the Most High your dwelling.

No evil will befall you, neither shall any plague come nigh thy dwelling.

For He will give his angels a command concerning you, to guard you in all your ways.

They shall bear thee up in their hands, less thou dash thy foot against a stone.

On the young lion and the cobra, you will tread;

You will trample underfoot the maned lion and the big snake.

God said: Because he has set his love on me, I will deliver him.

I will set him on high because he knows my name.

He shall call upon me, and I will answer him.

I will be with them in distress.

I will rescue him and honor him.

I will satisfy him with long life, and I will cause him to see my acts of salvation.' -Psalm 91

They all said, "Amen!"

Sophia leaned over and kissed each of her daughters on their foreheads and said, "I love you girls, sleep tight." She exited their bedroom turning out the light, leaving the door slightly ajar behind her.

---

*Psalm 91- see endnote

CHAPTER -2-

Saturday morning arrived with a deep red sun rising up from the horizon. The early morning birds sang a wake-up call as they flew about their daily business. Sophia was first to waken in the household and went about the kitchen preparing breakfast for her and her two daughters. Alexa was first to rise from the girls' bedroom she hugged her mother good morning then sat down at the kitchen table.

"Did you sleep well my darling?" asked her mother.

"Yes Mama. At first, I was too excited to sleep thinking about getting my new pair of shoes today. So, I started counting sheep, but that didn't work so I started counting shoes in my mind instead and must have lost count and eventually dozed off at about 300."

"You're so funny Alexa," her mother smiled as she walked behind her chair and began affectionately stroking her daughter's beautiful long blonde hair. "Was that 300 shoes, or 300 pairs?"

They both looked at one another and began laughing together. They heard Asha coughing from the bedroom, so Sophia began fixing a warm cup of black tea with lemon and a spoon of honey and took it through to her.

"Good morning sweetheart, are you feeling any better today?"

"Morning Mama! No, I feel even worse today I think?" she coughed some more.

"Don't worry my love, I'm sure it will clear up soon. Drink your tea while it's hot. Magda is going to come and sit with you this morning while Alexa and I go into town to buy her new shoes. I'll go into Carl's shop on our way back and get something to help your cough. We won't be away too long!" Sophia reassured her.

"Okay Mama, thanks."

Alexa had finished her breakfast, freshened up and was all dressed and ready to go. "What time is Magda coming, Mama?"

"She said she'd be here at 9 am, so we have about fifteen minutes yet."

Alexa cleared off the table then washed up the few dishes which they had used for breakfast. Sophia reached up into the back of one of the kitchen cupboards and pulled out an old glass jar. Inside, wrapped up in a handkerchief, was the money which she had saved up to buy Alexa's shoes. She screwed off the lid and emptied the contents on to the wooden table. It seemed that there were more coins than notes but after Sophia had counted the amount out, she gave an approving nod, content that she had enough money for what she needed to buy that day. Sophia and Alexa went through to the bedroom where Asha was lying and placed a cup of warm water with lemon and some honey, on the table next to her bed. They asked if there was anything else, she needed before they left.

"No thanks, just come back quickly. I miss you both already!"

"Aww, darling don't worry, we'll be back as soon as possible. Two hours maximum."

"Mama, can I wear your rings while you are in town?" asked Asha, which was something that she often liked to do.

"Okay, darling I suppose it's ok since you're going to be in bed the whole time," reasoned her mother. She took off her gold wedding band along with her engagement ring, which was also gold. It had a raised rectangular cut amethyst stone in the center, which was held securely in place by four gold claws. Sophia still wore them every day, as if her husband were still alive and with her, but Asha often liked to try them on her little fingers and pretend. Her mother handed them to Asha. "Be good for Magda!"

The doorbell rang. Sophia leaned over and kissed her daughter's cheek. "I love you."

Alexa opened the front door to let Magda in, put on her coat then ran through to Asha. She leaned down and kissed her forehead.

"See you soon little sister, feel better."

It was 9 am when Sophia and Alexa closed the door behind them and began the twenty-minute walk into town. The red morning sun had long since disappeared from the sky and it began to get cloudy and slightly overcast. Alexa took her mother's hand as they crossed the road. The town was fairly busy for an early Saturday morning. Many of the locals were out grocery shopping for the weekend at the farmer's market, set up in the town square. Friends were chatting on the streets, while children looked for mischief to amuse themselves in. Most of the local shops were open with customers browsing and buying their desired goods. From across the street, Alexa noticed her friend Carolina walking out of the butcher's shop with her mother and little brother. She waved over to them. They all smiled and waved back. A few more steps and finally they were at the shoe shop.

"Mama we're here!" Alexa announced.

"Okay, let's get your new shoes first. Everything else can wait until after that."

The shop wasn't very big. It had two large framed display windows at its front on either side, with two wide concrete steps up to the wooden framed glass door entrance in the center. Sophia reached up for the handle and opened the door. As it opened, a small brass bell rang overhead announcing their arrival. They both stepped inside and as the door closed behind them, the bell rang once again. Alexa immediately ran over to where the royal blue pair of shoes that she wanted were on display.

"Good morning ladies! Can I help you with something?" asked the shopkeeper, a woman in her late fifties, well dressed, with her hair tied up neatly in a bun and very polite.

"Yes, thank you," replied Sophia. "Could my daughter please try on those pretty royal blue shoes over there with the silver buckle, in her size?"

"Yes of course, let me just get them for her. What size is she? Perhaps a 28?" estimated the shopkeeper.

"Maybe a size 30 would be better? So that she has some room to grow in them. You know how fast these young teenage girls grow, and I want these shoes to last her," Sophia said.

The shopkeeper nodded, "One moment please," then she disappeared off into the back of the shop behind a burgundy curtain to locate the shoes.

Her mother told Alexa to come and sit down on the chair next to her, where she could comfortably try on the shoes when the woman brought them out for her. Alexa took off her coat and placed it neatly on the chair next to her.

"Oh Mama, I'm so excited. You're so good to me, thank you for today." Alexa threw her arms round her mother and kissed her cheek.

"Oh sweetheart, you're so welcome. You deserve them. You've always been such a good and pleasant girl, I'm so happy you are my daughter and no one else's," Sophia said proudly.

Just then the shopkeeper returned with an opened shoe box. "Here we go, size 30 for the young lady to try on." She handed the shoes to Alexa, who gently placed them on the floor. She kicked off her old shoes then, gently slid her right foot into the right shoe first. She pulled over the leather strap and fastened the silver buckle. She had a blissful smile on her face as she next slipped on the left shoe and fastened it in place. She could smell the new leather.

"Stand up darling, try walking in them. They look beautiful on you," her mother said.

"Walk over to the mirror and you can see how you they look on you," the shopkeeper suggested.

Alexa walked over to look in the long ornate mirror, which was freestanding near the back wall facing the shop front. She could see the reflection of the street outside behind her, as the sun briefly peeked through the clouds in between the buildings casting random shadows and shapes onto the ground. She looked down at the new blue shoes on her feet, pointing her toe to the left and then to the right. She turned to the side to see the small heel and then the view from the back. As the daylight hit the silver buckle, it glistened brightly in the mirror.

"How do they feel, are they comfortable?"

"They feel great on. I love them Mama."

"Then you can have them my love."

Alexa walked the entire length of the shop looking down at the shoes on her feet the whole time. Her mother spoke with the shopkeeper and agreed to buy the new shoes for her daughter. They continued to admire them on the young girl while she modeled them with a tremendous smile across her face. All of a sudden and from out of nowhere, there was what sounded like a loud roll of thunder. Alexa's smile was interrupted. All three females appeared puzzled by the noise and immediately found it strange, as there had been no thick dark clouds in the sky that morning and no obvious signs of bad weather on the horizon. Alexa turned around with a spring in her step and walked back over to face the mirror again, but now the reflection that she saw behind her had changed and had changed for the worst. All traces of her beaming happy smile fell from her face in an instant.

"Mama look! The German soldiers are outside in the street!" Alexa gasped her voice full of panic.

Both Sophia and the shopkeeper immediately turned to look out of the window and to their horror, they saw the terror unfolding before their eyes. The thunderous noise which they had heard, was the sound of large army trucks rolling along the cobbled streets of the town square outside. The heavy vibrations made the shop windows rattle in their wooden frames. Fear filled their hearts and panic engulfed every part of them. Sophia pulled Alexa close to her and took a firm grip of her hand. Sophia asked the shopkeeper if there was a back door leading out of the property. But the woman shook her head, 'No'. Through the windows they could see that outside was a line of about five or six large grey colored German military trucks parked to one side, along with a dozen or so military armored cars. On the other side of the street, people were being lined up together by Nazi soldiers with brutal force. The local people were being dragged out of the shops at gun point and forced to stand together in the middle of the town square.

"Mama! There's Carolina...they've got Carolina!" Alexa shrieked.

Sophia held her daughter's hand even tighter. "Don't worry darling, try to stay calm," said her mother. Not really knowing what to say for the best in the situation into which they had now been thrown.

The door of the shoe shop burst open and the bell above, loudly rang a warning sound.

"Get out! Everybody out! Get out onto the street now! Raus! Schnell!" yelled one of the angry German soldiers pointing his threatening rifle at them. He had another soldier with him, holding a vicious barking German shepherd on the end of a long chain. Saliva drooling down from its jaws. Sophia moved hurriedly towards the door, grasping hold of Alexa's hand. There was no time to think, only to do. To do as they were ordered. To go outside with all the others. They spilled out onto the street and lined up with all the other people being forced against their will. The woman from the shoe shop hastily began to protest her innocence aloud, insisting that there had been some kind of mistake.

"Why are we being treated like this? We are not Jews! We are good, honest, hard-working Polish people! There must be some mistake! I have identification papers and I own this shop!" She insisted.

The German SS commander standing closest to the woman and who seemed to be in charge of the operation, let out a loud laugh.

"Good and honest...ha! Now I've heard it all," he laughed sarcastically with his fellow Gestapo officers and soldiers. "Good for nothing more like it and honest liars, she should actually say." The soldiers all laughed again. "Hard workers, eh? Well let's hope so for your sakes. I hope you Poles work harder than the lazy Jews do."

The woman now became hysterical and began begging the commander to let her go. She moved closer towards him in the middle of the street. Her pleas becoming louder and more out of control. Sophia whispered to Alexa to close her eyes, anticipating what would come next. Then quickly the commander reached for his pistol, laughed sarcastically and said to the woman loudly.

"Now you can Go! Go directly to meet your maker." He took aim at her forehead and in a split second, pulled the trigger. The bullet hit its intended target and the woman became limp, collapsing to the ground in a heap. And just as fast, the life left her body. As her head connected with the cobbles it made a loud cracking noise. Then a slow stream of deep red, began to fill the channels between the stones, her blood staining the mortar. A few screams could be heard from the group, mainly from some of the women and children. Several of the men gasped a deep breath in shock at what was taking place before their eyes. The commander blew on the tip of his pistol, then returned it to his holster. "Now! Let that be a warning to you all, to shut up and follow orders! Don't speak," ordered the commander.

Sophia's heart was pounding, and she could feel Alexa's body shaking and trembling with fear. She again squeezed her hand. The hand that she hadn't let go of since they were inside of the shop, only tighter this time. Other children in the lineup could be heard crying out of fear hysterically.

When the commander turned his back on them, Sophia whispered to Alexa, "Don't let them see that your scared. Concentrate darling. Look down at your shoes and say your prayer over to yourself."

Alexa instantly looked down at her new blue shoes and fixed her stare upon the silver buckle. She closed her eyes then began reciting the 91st Psalm that she knew so well, silently to herself and ever so gradually her trembling reduced. *'You are my refuge, my God in whom I trust. Cover me with your wings, shield me.'* She all of a sudden became still, with a calmness which strangely began to spread through her whole body and when she opened her eyes, she spotted her friend Carolina also in the lineup holding her mother's hand with her little brother. Alexa was relieved that the family were together and as their eyes met, through their fear, they gave a very slight smile of hope to one another. Just then, the clock tower in the market square rang out loudly chiming its bell. It was 10 am. Alexa suddenly became overwhelmed with thoughts of Asha who was back at home with Magda, and her heart began to beat even faster. How were they going to get home to her now? She was filled with a heightened sense of fear and with each chime that echoed out loudly through the town square, it also echoed through her entire body to her very core. She wished desperately that she could stop time, or indeed rewind it. Back to before she had left her home that morning with her mother. But such thoughts were futile. Like chasing after the wind.

The commander gave orders in German to half a dozen of his officers and more than two dozen other soldiers who gave him their full attention, then he sent them off to their given positions. They quickly began selecting all of the men from the lineup who were over fifty years of age and ordering them to run over to the first parked truck. There were about fifteen of them in total.

"Leave your bags and packages on the ground, you will get them back later," commanded one of the officers in Polish.

Next, they ordered all of the women over fifty to run over to the first truck, where the older men were already standing. In total there were about forty-five people in that group. Next, they ordered all of the younger men aged from sixteen to fifty, to go and stand behind the second truck. Half of the soldiers held loaded rifles in their hands aiming them directly at the men. The remaining soldiers carried solid wooden batons in their hands and used them to restrain the group with brutal force. They fired a few warning shots up into the air and swung their batons haphazardly. The young men reluctantly began making their way over to the second truck. There were about twenty-five of them in that group.

Terror spread through every fiber of Sophia's being as the officer next ordered all the women who were aged from sixteen to fifty to go and stand next to the third parked truck. Her daughter wouldn't be included in that group with her, as Alexa was only thirteen and a half. She couldn't let go of Alexa's hand. Just as many of the other mothers in the street couldn't willingly separate from their own children either. Some soldiers rushed over to them with their wild barking dogs snapping and snarling at them and forcibly pulled the children apart from their mothers, while swinging their batons to divide them and break the tight clasp of their hands. Sophia reluctantly let go of Alexa's hand and was speedily rushed over to the third truck with the other women and mothers who were forced to abandon their children. There were about thirty of them in total. All the while Sophia stared back at Alexa who had tears slowly trickling down her cheeks. Sophia didn't make a sound but inside she was silently screaming. Tears brimmed in her eyes, but she didn't allow them to fall. Alexa glanced to her left and saw her friend Carolina standing with her little brother, grasping his hand tightly, with her other arm wrapped around his shoulder. She too had tears rolling down her face, without her mother standing beside them.

Next, the officer ordered the children who were under the age of eight to go and stand next to the fourth truck, the smaller children were left abandoned on the ground. The soldiers pushed and dragged them over themselves, about twenty of them all together. Carolina and her little four-year old brother were now forcibly pulled apart and separated. He along with the other small infant children, were violently pulled by their arms across the square, then the soldiers threw them up into the back of the fourth truck. As that happened, spine chilling screams curdled through the air from the help-less parents as they looked on in horror. At that point one of the SS soldiers fired his rifle up into the air multiple times as a reminder to keep themselves in check. The children could be heard screaming and crying hysterically from inside of the truck. The wild German shepherds continued to bark viciously and growl at each group, trying ferociously to break free from their leashes as they were put on guard, merely inches away from the terrified people. These were blood hungry hounds and their presence was terrifying.

Now all who were left in the lineup were the terrified boys and girls who were aged from eight to sixteen years, totaling about eighteen all together including Alexa. They were told to run over and stand next to the fifth parked truck. The commander in charge then made his way down the street to the first truck and ordered all of the older people, male and female to climb into the back of the truck. He walked to the second truck and ordered all the men to get into that truck.

At the third truck he told all the women to get inside. Then he passed by the forth truck, which was already loaded with the smaller younger children who were crying hysterically calling out for their mothers and fathers in vain.

As he got to the fifth truck, he looked each child up and down from head to toe, examining their appearance as well as their physical build. When he got to Alexa, he seemed quite surprised. He looked down at her shoes for a few seconds then continued on upwards to her sapphire blue eyes. Alexa suddenly became filled with feelings of guilt and thought to herself, *'Oh No! We didn't pay for the shoes!'* He stared into her eyes intensely, which made her even more nervous. So, she shifted her eyes and looked away, down towards the ground. The commander took his baton and placed it under her chin. "Look up girl, lift your head, look at me," he demanded.

Alexa did as she was told, then with the end of his baton he lifted up her chin, then turned her head to the right and then to the left. Next, he ran the baton slowly down the length of her long blonde hair, then stepped backwards. He walked over to one of the officers who was standing at the front of the fifth truck and pointed to Alexa, then he said something to him. Alexa was still looking down, then she turned to her right and could see the third truck down the line onto which the women were now being loaded. She just managed to catch a glimpse of her mother's blonde head as she was being forced into the back of the truck.

"Alexa! Alexa!" Her mother cried out unable to keep silent any longer. She locked eyes with her daughter and began waving her hands frantically in the air. She now sensed that they were saying goodbye and a grey shadow fell over her face as the blood drained from it.

"Mama!" Alexa yelled back. "Mama!" She screamed.

"My Alexa!" were Sophia's final hysterical words, as she disappeared out of sight, while being pushed into the back of the truck. The children and teenagers were loaded into the back of the fifth truck.

Almost simultaneously, all of the military trucks engaged their engines and revved up. The air was filled with diesel fumes and the sounds of loud angry growling engines. A chorus of random names being called out in desperation and sheer anguish could be heard. Parents for their children. Children for their mothers. Blood curdling screams. Wretched cries and frantic despair, all echoed a hopeless choir of grief-stricken panic. Two heavily armed soldiers climbed into the back of each truck, along with two blood-thirsty barking German shepherds. This added even more alarm to the groups while they were being ordered to keep quiet or threatened that they would be shot and have the dogs set upon them.

The commander ordered two of his soldiers to remove the dead shopkeeper whom he had shot earlier in the square and for her to be loaded also into the first truck. The soldiers obeyed immediately, dragging her off of the cobbled street, throwing her lifeless body up into the back of the truck with the older men and women in it. The dead woman's lifeless body landed with a heavy thud, like a sack full of wet sand. The men and women in the truck stepped backwards in shock. Sheer terror was visible on their faces, along with an overwhelming sense of hopelessness. It served as a warning to them to remain quiet and follow orders or they would suffer the same consequences. The soldiers appeared to be unaffected by the anguish of their prisoners and dropped the rear canvas covers of their trucks down so that no one could see in. But it also meant that no one could see out either. The clouds got darker in the sky. It began to rain.

On the street two gaunt looking Jewish prisoners in dirty old raggedy clothing, with yellow stars of David sewn onto armbands on their jacket sleeves appeared. They had been ordered to collect all of the bags and packages left behind by the locals from off of the ground and to pile them onto a nearby wooden cart. An armed soldier then instructed them to load all of the items into the rear of an empty military vehicle, before they too were told to climb inside and placed under his guard. The prisoners inside of the trucks, wouldn't be getting their belongings back later, after all.

The last truck with the youths loaded on to it, joined the convoy and began to drive off. The first truck carrying the older men and women headed towards the edge of town and then, turned in an Easterly direction being led by an armored car at the front and the rear. The second and third trucks carrying the younger men and women also headed out of town, each with an army vehicle escort, heading for the railway station. The fourth truck with the youngest children in it followed the route of the first truck and went East. It was also escorted by armored vehicles. The fifth truck with the youths in it hadn't pulled off yet, but they could sense that the other trucks had pulled off already and were no longer near to them, as the engine noise reduced. Alexa was huddled at the back of the truck with her friend Carolina. They didn't say anything. They just hugged each other tightly in fear as they waited to learn their fate. Alexa said her prayer silently over and over again to herself. Soon the truck began to roll forward towards its destination. Picking up speed, it reached the edge of town and headed towards the railway station.

CHAPTER -3-

T
he rain had started to fall lightly at first, but fairly rapidly it became torrential. The first truck, carrying both the males and the females over fifty, had been driving for approximately fifteen minutes when it pulled off from the tarred roadway onto softer, more uneven ground. The heavy black rubber tires were now rolling through wet mud, trying to hold their grip as they drove along the edge of the field where it met the forest. Finally, the truck came to a stop and its engines were shut off. The prisoners inside remained silent, apart from the sound of their nervous heavy breathing. The rain fell on the canvas roof and poured small streams of water into the truck through the little holes above them. Having no view outside of the vehicle, the prisoners remained in the dark as to where they had been driven. Outside of the truck they could hear soldiers squelching in the mud, along with male voices of German soldiers and dogs loudly barking, all to the background noise of the heavy falling rain. Suddenly, the two soldiers in the back of the truck pulled up the rear canvas cover, securing it open, allowing daylight to somewhat illuminate the interior of the vehicle. They jumped down onto the muddy wet ground with their dogs and held their rifles pointed at the prisoners. Another soldier ran to the rear of the truck and put in place a large empty wooden crate which would serve as a step down for the people inside, in order to speed things up.

Along the side of the roadway appeared the fourth truck which was carrying the twenty youngest children under eight years of age. It had also traveled in the same Easterly direction. It likewise pulled off the road at the edge of the field where it met the forest and forced its path through the grassy mud, just overtaking the first truck. It came to an abrupt stop next to an opening in the trees and its engines were turned off.

Next, the officers ordered the older men and women in the first truck to get out. The men exited first.

"Everybody out, quickly!" yelled a German officer, "Schnell!"

The men moved as fast as they could, trying to assist the older women to get down with some difficulty. The group comprised of forty-five people, who had rifles aimed at them the entire time as the rain pelted down on them.

"Move up ahead of the first truck! All of you! Do it now!" shouted the officer, "Schnell!"

The canvas cover was pulled up on the rear of the truck containing the twenty youngest children and as they were callously lifted down by the soldiers, they could see where they now were. Just up to the left beyond the field, was the familiar school building. The children were lined up in front of the older men and women and all stood in the rain together at the trees' opening.

"Attention!" shouted one of the German officers, "All of the adults will hold the hand of the child in front of you. Do it now!"

They all did as they were instructed, with the elder ones taking the lead, picking up the infants in their arms. Not everyone had a partner to themselves.

"Good! Now everyone will follow the soldiers into the woods, where we can get out of the rain and have some refreshments. Go now, quickly," ordered the officer.

A soldier led the way in front and the group of about sixty-five adult and children prisoners walked off into the woods as instructed, taking some comfort from the hands of a stranger. They walked for at least ten minutes until they reached a wide opening in the forest. At that point, they could see just up ahead through the rain and trees, what looked like a row of about ten Jewish prisoners all wearing yellow Star of David armbands. They all stood lifelessly staring down at the wet muddy ground at their feet. As the group got closer to where they were standing, a large deep ditch became visible between them, like a huge crater in the earth. The young Polish children seemed oblivious as they held on to the hands of their elderly chaperones, but the adults became filled with even more terror than they had felt before, as they began to figure out in their minds the nightmare which was about to occur.

Like lambs to the slaughter, there was no way out for them.

They squeezed the hands of the children tighter and pulled them closer, in a nurturing and protective manner. Then came the commander's voice.

"Walk up, right to the edge. It's time for you to leave us now!"

Some of the adults quickly picked up the smaller children into their arms and held them close to their chests, hiding their innocent faces. Behind the last people at the very back of the group, a line of German soldiers with automatic rifles had formed a firing squad. They took aim at the helpless crowd in front of them and once the order was given, began firing their weapons at full blast.

A murder of crows flew out of the treetops, as though even they couldn't bear to watch.

One by one, the human bodies became limp corpses. Their legs buckling underneath them, before falling on the cold wet mud. Most of the adults who were shot first, were at the back of the group. But quickly, the bullets reached the children near the front, drowning out their blood-curdling screams. Finally, a mass pile of death lay at the edge of the ditch and the continual rapid gun-fire eventually stopped.

The Jewish prisoners were then called to action and ordered to quickly start throwing the remainder of the sixty-five dead bodies down into the ditch. While they did so, the German soldiers stood around smoking their cigarettes and drinking shots of schnapps together. Into the ditch of death, two soldiers began firing shots from their pistols randomly at any of the victims who showed any remaining signs of life still left in them.

After the last body was thrown down into the death pit, two of the Jewish prisoners, escorted by an armed soldier, were ordered to go back and remove the body of the dead shopkeeper from the rear of the first truck. They struggled to drag her through the muddy forest floor in the pouring rain, then finally threw her limp body down onto the mass pile of dead corpses. The Jewish prisoners were then each given a silver metal shovel and ordered at gunpoint to fill in the ditch with the surrounding earth and the wet mud. The massacre and mass burial was over within two hours, with the evidence well covered over and hidden out of sight. The soldiers walked out of the forest, unphased by the events which they were in charge of. They marched their forced labor digging-crew into the back of an empty truck, then loaded their dogs in to guard them. With their weapons and tools loaded onto a separate truck, they got into their vehicles and drove away from the scene of the crime as if nothing had ever happened there.

* * *

Magda looked up at the clock again and now it was almost noon. She tried not to show how anxious she had become, but it was apparently obvious as she looked at the clock every ten minutes or less. She had looked out of the window several times and had regularly stood at the front door, staring down the street for signs of Sophia and Alexa's return. Magda could think of no more excuses to tell Asha to ease her worried little mind. Something was obviously very wrong. Magda told Asha to get dressed and that she would take her next door to her house to wait there. Asha was very reluctant at first and began crying, becoming very upset.

"I don't understand. Where's my Mama and Alexa?" Asha sobbed. "They, they said they'd only be an hour! I need my Mama. Why can't we stay here in my house and wait for them to come home?" Asha began coughing uncontrollably through her tears.

"Look Asha, I don't know what's happened to them, or why they are so late. I just think it's best that we go next door to my house for now. There you can play with Eva and Peter. I will take the key and lock the door. So, you see, your Mama will have to come next door to my house to collect you so don't worry, when they get home, we will know," explained Magda.

The concerned neighbor took Asha next door to her house, hoping that the distraction of playing with her young twins would take the girl's mind off from worrying for a while. The children all went into the twins' bedroom and began to play. Magda began preparing lunch in her kitchen. She closed the door and spoke quietly to her husband so that the children wouldn't overhear her.

"Michael, something is very very wrong. I just know it! Something bad has happened to Sophia and Alexa. There's no way they would take this long to go into town and back, with Asha lying in bed ill. It's been over three hours." Magda expressed her concern to her husband.

"I know it doesn't seem right to me either. Look, you stay here with the children and I will go into town and see if I can find them near the square. I will ask at the shoe shop and see if anyone knows anything,"

"Okay darling, just please be careful, take your German identification papers with you just in case,"

"Alright I will, I'll try not to be long."

"Okay, but please come straight home. I can't be worrying about you as well."

He gave his wife a tight hug, kissed her on the cheek and headed out the front door into town.

*   *   *

The second and third trucks traveling in the convoy together hadn't been driving on the road for very long, perhaps only ten minutes. The first of the two military trucks soon approached the town's train station and drove along parallel to the railroad tracks. The truck carrying the twenty-five men aged sixteen to fifty, had not had a smooth ride. Two of the men had loudly protested during the journey, voicing their anger over the whole ordeal and of not knowing what was happening to them or their families, or where they were being taken to. The soldiers couldn't let that go unpunished, and when the men had started to make threatening moves by advancing towards them, the soldiers took aim with their pistols and shot them. One was lying injured after receiving bullet wounds to his right thigh and side. The other was lying dead on the floor of the truck with various bullet wounds in several places. One of the soldiers had lengthened out the chain attached to the leash of the dog under his control and the ravenous animal, tore into the flesh of the corpse on the floor. The remaining men still had a strong will to live, to be reunited with their families again, to get out of that death truck in one piece. Therefore, they remained as controlled as possible, restraining themselves and obeying the orders given to them and stood well back. Huddled together with strangers.

The third truck, carrying the younger women in it, had continued to follow the men's truck as part of a smaller convoy, accompanied at the front and back by armored cars. Inside of the truck, Sophia had managed to position herself next to Carolina's mother and they sat holding hands together on the floor. The majority of the women were still terribly upset, especially the mothers in the group who were distraught over not knowing where their children were, or when they would be reunited with them. Or indeed, if they would ever be reunited with them again. A few had fainted, falling in and out of consciousness on the floor of the truck. Sobbing and whimpering could be heard from amongst them all.

Sophia's mind kept running back to thoughts of Asha who was still at home with Magda waiting for her return. *'How would her fragile daughter cope? Who would look after her?'* Then her thoughts turned to Alexa who'd been loaded onto the fifth truck. *'Was she in the next truck in their convoy? Was she still with Carolina? Were they all going to the same place? Would she ever see either of her girls again?'* She thought she would go mad. Then she began to pray the 91st Psalm silently to herself. Finally, the truck slowed down, took a sharp turn and then came to an abrupt stop. The soldiers jumped out of the rear of the trucks first, but left the dogs chained on guard inside. German voices could be heard talking outside to the background sound of heavy falling rain but everyone inside the trucks spoke only Polish, so they were no wiser as to where they were or what would happen next.

* * *

The fifth truck, carrying the youngsters and Alexa, had been on the road travelling on the same route to the train station for a relatively short time, when the truck made a sharp turn then drove along the same side of the tracks as the other two trucks. In the station was a large steam engine train with at least ten cattle wagons, designed to carry livestock attached to them. Some of the wagons already seemed to have been fully loaded, but not with animals. People had been crammed inside of them with their doors firmly bolted shut.

The rain was still pouring down heavily under dark clouds above which made quite a noise as it pelted down, landing on the hard roofs and the stones on the ground. There were more armed German soldiers at the station than there had been in the town center. They stood in a line leading from the trucks to the empty transport wagons. Every fourth soldier held a vicious barking blood-thirsty German shepherd dog on a chain, while all the others held either pistols, loaded rifles or machine guns.

Two soldiers headed over to the truck with the men inside and pulled up the rear canvas cover, allowing the daylight to enter the vehicle. They yelled at the men to jump down and get out of the trucks at speed, while the entire time they aimed their guns at them. The prisoners began jumping out of the truck. Some fell as they landed but wasted no time in getting back up, as they felt the barrels of the soldiers' guns closest to them strike their heads and backs. They were rushed along the gauntlet to a vacant boxcar and could see for the first time the train in front of them. From some of the other locked boxcars, hands of some people inside were grasping up onto the small railings near the roof where there was a small open gap, as they attempted to see outside. The men showed fear and panic, caused by the chaos of the situation being created by the angry SS troops and their hungry hounds, who rushed them into the wagon reserved for them. Lastly the bodies of the two shot prisoners were dragged from out of the truck and thrown into the wagon. The deceased man's half chewed bloody body landed with a lifeless heavy thud, like a sack of heavy mud. The injured man who was still alive, let out an excruciating painful yelp like a wounded animal, as though wishing he too was dead. He was thrown violently into the wagon and landed at the feet of the other prisoners all crammed in together. Once all were loaded inside, the doors were quickly and firmly bolted shut.

Sophia and the other women in the second truck could hear the frightening cries from outside and terror continued to consume them. Sophia and Carolina's mother held each other's hands even tighter than before as they trembled with fear. The train's engine let off a blast of white steam and just then, the canvas cover of their truck was opened by two soldiers. The gauntlet of German soldiers now awaited them as they were ordered to get out of the truck and head into the empty boxcar awaiting them less than one hundred yards away. With rifles aimed on them and the hounds wildly barking and snapping at them, the women ran towards the wagon through the pouring rain. Sophia tried to look around as she ran, hoping to catch sight of Alexa but with too little time to scan the area properly, there was no visible sign of her daughter. Once the women were all pushed inside, the wagon door was slid shut and firmly bolted. Although there was still lots of daylight outside, inside of the locked wagon was dark. Carolina's mother stood next to Sophia and grabbed hold of her arm then said through her tears: "The children will probably be in one of the other wagons and we will be able to see them when the train finally comes to a stop and we all get off!"

"I pray to God you're right. Please God let them be alright!"

After about ten minutes, the soldiers opened up the canvas at the rear of the final truck, carrying the eighteen youths aged eight to sixteen and let the barking dogs out first. Alexa had already deduced that they were at the train station and that now it would be their turn to be loaded on to an awaiting train, but she was convinced that they would not be going to a good destination. She had a bad feeling, like the kind you get down in your bones when you sense bad weather is coming. But the weather already was bad and the feelings which she felt terrified her deep in her heart. There were slightly fewer soldiers now standing on guard, but they had the same mission at hand: to empty the children quickly from the truck and load them into the boxcar. In a fast and uncaring manner. One of the soldiers began to lift the younger children down from the back of the truck while another, very brutishly lifted them up into the boxcar almost throwing them in. Once the petrified children were loaded inside, the door was slammed shut and firmly bolted. At least they now felt a little safer away from the ferocious dogs and the soldier's guns. However, being confined in the dirty, foul stench of the boxcar, along with the uncertainty of the journey ahead, brought them no comfort at all.

The train slowly pulled out of the station, blowing off a large blast of white steam into the air, causing large clouds to form up into the air. The trains whistle sharply pierced the air. As the barreling train picked up speed, the loud noise of the steel rails underneath roared loudly and continued a four-beats to the bar rhythmic tune which became almost hypnotic. For the remainder of the journey, Alexa and Carolina huddled together sitting in the corner of the boxcar on the cold, filthy floor. They didn't say much to each other but took a little comfort from just being together. It was dark inside and cold winds blew through small gaps in the boxcar's exterior, as the train sped on its journey. Feeling the cold pierce her skin, Alexa wished that she still had her navy blue coat on, which she had left behind in the shoe shop. Alexa silently began to pray. *'I shall not be afraid by the terror of night, nor the pestilence that walks in darkness. Give your angels a command to guard me.'* For all she knew, they could have been traveling to the far North of Poland but in reality, that couldn't have been further from the truth.

After an almost seventeen-hour journey, the train transporting all of the locals rounded up from Lublin's town square, finally arrived at its destination near Munich. It slowly ground to a halt. The rain had stopped falling but the sky was dark. It was 3:30 am, and suddenly flood-lighting shone on the train, illuminating the tracks and the area around them. The door to one of the wagons was unbolted and slammed open with a loud crash. Nazi troops first ordered the fatigued children to come out and to jump down onto the ground below. Next, all of the other heavy cattle wagon doors were also thrown open and everyone inside was ordered to quickly get out. There was nothing calm about the manner in which this was executed. Once again, the Nazis with their tumultuous shouting, threatening voices and their wild bloodthirsty barking German shepherd dogs, automatically spread fear through the souls of those helplessly forced to stand in front of them. The soldiers could taste the fear of the prisoners under their control and they binged on it, with all trace of humanity absent from their faces. A line of soldiers kept their loaded rifles aimed at the crowd of new arrivals, while army officers wielding heavy batons, moved through the crowd as if making assessments and sizing up each individual.

Now that the prisoners were finally out of the train wagons, they began frantically scanning the crowd for any trace of their children and other family members. Some mothers had already spotted their children and had immediately reclaimed them, pulling them in close to their bodies, holding them tighter than they had ever done before. However, for the majority, they would never find their infants, their youngest children, nor would they ever learn what had happened to them. As was the case with those adults in the group looking around for their mothers, fathers, grandparents - there was no trace of them, and no explanations were offered as to their whereabouts. All who now remained from the Lublin square roundup, were the youths and the adults up to fifty years of age. Carolina's mother had found her daughter, but frantically searched around them looking desperately for her four-year old son. She would never find him. Sophia had begun scanning the crowd as soon as she had jumped down from the wagon and had spotted her Alexa within a split second of her feet landing on the ground. Without a thought for her own safety, her motherly instincts immediately kicked-in and she moved speedily to where her daughter was, grasping her hand once again tightly. As they hugged, they both breathed a sigh of relief and seemed to have a renewed energy and resilience, just from being reunited again and knowing that the other was safe. She did not want to let go of her daughter's hand again.

"Attention!" yelled a commandant taking the lead, "Everyone face forward and pay attention to me!" The prisoners did as they were told and listened nervously for his next words. He had their attention. "You have now arrived at Dachau. This is a labor camp and here you will all be put to work, working hard for Germany and for the fatherland. The officers will tell you where you are to go, either to the left, or to the right. Do as you are told and follow orders quickly, if you want to stay alive."

At that point a few of the officers worked their way through the group of prisoners with their batons, selecting and directing them which way they were to go. Hurriedly the wretched people began to run, spurred on by violent random strikes from the swinging batons. Sophia and Alexa were directed to go to the right and wasted no time in running over there, still with their hands tightly locked together. Most people were instructed to run to the left and stand outside of a windowless brick building, where a soldier seated at a small desk began recording everyone's name and age on sheets of paper in front of him. As Sophia turned to look over in the opposite direction to the left, she could see the other prisoners from their transport start to undress, being forced to remove their clothing and jewelry at gunpoint, out in the cold air. Sophia placed Alexa in front of her, so as to shield her daughter's innocent eyes from seeing the things behind her. But it was too late, as Alexa's face displayed an expression of sheer horror.

They were lined up in front of another desk, where two soldiers asked for their full names and dates of birth, their town of birth and their religion, as well as any special skills or talents which they possessed. Next the adults were told to remove their jewelry and watches and to empty their pockets, handing over any money or items that they still had on them. Sophia felt quite relieved that she was not wearing her wedding rings as she always did and felt inwardly grateful that Asha had asked to wear them before she had left the house the previous morning. The soldier motioned them forward to a large barracks without checking Alexa.

"Move now! Everyone inside!" ordered a female Kapo for that building.

Their selected group was made up of women and young girls and all of them had something very obvious in common. They all looked the same. They were all blonde-haired and blue-eyed. The group of twenty-eight females ran into the building in front of them as instructed, not knowing what they'd find inside. Once they were all inside, the door was bolted shut behind them and no further instructions were given. They were now inside of what appeared to be a long narrow barrack style wooden hut. On either side of both walls were crammed sleeping bunks built out of old wood and stacked three levels high, already packed full with other women and teenage girls on them. There was also another row of three-tier bunks which ran down the middle of the hut, purposely built for maximum capacity. There were no pillows, no blankets and only a flimsy sack with some loose straw stuffed into it, supposedly a substitute for a mattress. There was no furniture in the hut, no tables or chairs, nowhere to sit. It was a most inhospitable place. Some of the new arrivals began looking for empty bunks but they were all filled already. Some had less people crammed on them than others, so some females took the initiative to squeeze in and lay claim to their spots early on, next to random strangers.

A few of the women seemed to treat the newcomers with a resentment that came across as unwarranted. They were, after all, in the same desperate situation. No one was there by choice or of their own free will.

Sophia spotted a bunk with only one woman on it and told Alexa to climb on the end, once she herself had gotten positioned next to the woman. That way she'd be the buffer between her daughter and the stranger. But the woman became difficult and spread herself out, selfishly taking up all of the surface space on the bunk.

"Please can you move over so my daughter and I can lay down here?"

"No! There's no room here for two more people. Go try somewhere else."

"But if you just moved over a little bit…"

"Who are you to tell me what to do? You've only just arrived. Get lost." The woman became more aggressive and hostile, so Sophia took a few steps back still grasping Alexa's hand tightly.

Just then, a voice called out to Sophia from one of bunks two rows down.

"Sophia come over here. You can share this bunk with me."

The invitation had come from a younger woman who knew Sophia. She had worked as a nurse in the local hospital in Lublin and had attended to and had nursed Sophia's sick husband Alexander, before his death.

"Come. There's enough room here for you both. Climb in."

Sophia and Alexa headed over to where the young woman was and climbed onto the bunk with her.

"Thank you so much Angelica. I don't know what we would have done next."

"I'd much rather be next to someone I know, than a complete stranger anyway so it's a better solution for all three of us. I think we are going to need all the friends we can get in this God-forsaken place."

"Yes, I think you're right."

"Mama I'm so hungry. Can we get anything to eat or drink here before we go to sleep? "

From the bunk above them a woman overheard Alexa's question and mouthed out,

"Ha! Get real child, where do you think you are, a hotel?"

"Sorry my darling, not tonight. But in the morning, I'm sure when we wake up, we'll get something. Just try and sleep for now."

Sophia desperately wished that she could supply her daughter's needs. She was well aware that she'd had nothing to eat or drink since breakfast the previous morning but everyone there was in the same boat. There was nothing available to kill the hunger or to quench their thirst. Not a stray crumb, nor a droplet of water to be found anywhere. She cuddled in close to Alexa with her arms wrapped tightly around her, in an attempt to comfort and try to make her feel a little safer. Alexa's empty stomach rumbled, while her mother stroked her long blonde hair, trying to soothe her nagging hunger.

"No talking! "ordered the stern Kapo in a loud voice. All of a sudden, the lights went out and the large dormitory was shrouded in darkness.

Even the shadows hid in the sanctuary of blackness, sensing evil in the air.

It was after well after 4 am and, as the night went on, time passed by very slowly. Sophia consciously tried to stay awake and alert to guard her daughter, while desperately searching her mind for a way out of the hellhole that they were now in. After a long time, Alexa finally fell off to sleep in her mother's arms.

Sunday morning gave way to daylight as the sun shone and roll call was announced at 8 am. The newest females to arrive at the barracks followed the lead of the women who had been there longest and who knew the routine already. Everyone crawled out of their sorry excuse for a bed and quickly stood forming a line on both sides, in front of their bunks. Their names were called out by the Kapo to whom they all had to answer loudly and make their presence known. There were no further orders given at that point and the Kapo abruptly exited the barracks, closing the wooden doors firmly behind her. Most of the women climbed back into their bunks and lay down. Some ventured to make use of the desperate unsanitary latrine provisions at the end of the barracks which consisted of two buckets. Unable to hold their bladders anymore, a few reluctantly swallowed their pride and relieved themselves as best as they could, while gagging from the stench of the foul odor surrounding them. Alexa and Sophia lay back in their bunk with Angelica, with few words shared between them. There wasn't much to say but they took comfort from being together.

Just before midday, the Kapo returned to the barracks with two male armed Nazi soldiers. She began taking a second roll call at which everyone jumped out of their bunk and stood to attention on the ground, answering when their name was shouted out. Once completed, the Kapo began calling out a second list of names and telling those ones to go immediately and stand outside once they heard their names. One by one, the young girls were being selected, rounded up together and forced to run outside of the barracks. Sophia clenched onto Alexa's hand in fear, sensing that her daughter might soon be next.

"Alexa Szewczyk," was the next name called from the list and Sophia's heart stopped mid-beat.

"No! Please don't take my daughter!" She pleaded out loud.

The Kapo ran over to Sophia without hesitation and swung her baton unannounced with full force towards the side of her head. It was a perfect aim and made a loud crack as the hard, wooden object, struck Sophia's temple area and she suddenly collapsed to the floor. Alexa still had hold of her mother's hand and knelt down on the ground over her mother's unconscious body in shock and dismay. Sophia's head was cut and blood began streaming from the deep gash. The Kapo again used her baton again, this time to hit Alexa's hand with excess force, causing her to reluctantly let go of her mother's hand. One of the armed soldiers came running over and grabbed hold of Alexa by her hair, then began dragging her outside of the building to join the other youths already selected and gathered there.

"Mama!" She yelled, "Mama!"

But her mother remained unconscious on the cold hard floor, unaware of her daughter's desperate cries for help. Tears of pain streamed down Alexa's defeated face which she was unable to control. The fierce soldier dragged her off her feet, threw her to the ground outside and ordered her to shut up.

Some young boys had also been rounded up and forcefully taken from inside of the next barracks. The selected group of mixed youths now numbered about twenty-six. They were ordered to climb into the back of a waiting military truck, while two SS soldiers sat in the back of the truck with their wild German shepherds and pistols aimed at their young captives. The young prisoners all sat on the floor and said nothing, their pupils enlarged with fear. Terror filled their young hearts as the soldiers callously lit cigarettes and while smoking, kept their evil eyes and their vicious dogs, trained on them. They reeked of violence and displayed an eagerness to display it. This kept their young prisoners at bay who were almost riveted to the floor where they sat, too afraid to move. The children still had an instinct for survival and as the pangs of hunger continued to rumble and rage inside of them, they obeyed the soldiers' commands in the hope that they'd soon be given some food and water. Eventually after a four-hour journey, the truck reached its destination and finally came to a halt inside the gated courtyard of a large ornate grey stone governmental looking building. It was decorated and draped with large Nazi flags. The unmistakable bright blood red backgrounds, with centered white circles and bold black swastikas were proudly on display. Alexa looked at the other children fearfully, but unlike her last truck journey, she had no friend's hand to hold on to this time. Carolina hadn't been loaded into the truck with her and for the first time in her life, she really felt what it was like to be alone.

The two soldiers lifted up the rear canvas cover of the truck and let both of the dogs jump down first. They ordered the youths to get out and line up in a row in order of their age, starting from those who were eight-years old up to the sixteen. Alexa stood sandwiched in between three other thirteen-year old Polish girls in the center of the lineup. Two of them were also blonde like her and the other was dark haired, carrying a little more weight on her than the others. While they all stood to attention, a German officer came out of the building and marched over to where they were all standing and began looking them over from head to toe.

"If I tap you with my stick on your shoulder, go over to the left immediately and stand next to the soldiers waiting at the bottom of the stairs."

He continued down the line of youths and tapped the shoulders of only fourteen of them. He tapped Alexa on her shoulder, and she ran over immediately to stand at the foot of the stairs. She assumed that the other three girls standing next to her would follow her over, but that never happened. Only two of them were chosen, the two blonde teenage girls, the dark haired heavier one wasn't. The selected children were then ordered to run up the stairs and guided through a large iron door. Alexa glanced back over her shoulder as she got to the top of the stairs and saw the dark-haired girl along with the other similar-looking children numbering twelve, being marched off in a different direction. The large heavy iron door slammed shut behind them.

The fourteen children were taken to a large room, where four female German soldiers were waiting for them. It was their job to make the children presentable and look at their best. First, they gave them all a glass of milk and a piece of buttered bread which they all scoffed down. Alexa hadn't had anything to eat or drink since breakfast the morning of her capture and was famished. The starving children didn't hesitate to swallow down the food they were given. Although it hardly made a dent in their hunger. The female soldiers separated the eight girls and the six boys, and each took a few children to place their attention on. They began to wash their faces rather forcefully and towel-dried them just as roughly. Next, they began brushing their hair. The boys were fairly easy as their blonde hair was short and fell into place with little fuss. The girls however had some tangles in their long blonde hair, so the women worked quickly at detangling them forcefully with metal combs. Alexa's hair was smooth and untangled as she always took pride in her appearance and so didn't need as much attention as the others were getting. She was quite relieved about that as some of the others showed visible signs of pain. Next up was their clothing to be inspected. Again, Alexa was dressed very smartly and needed no changes made to her outfit. She had deliberately worn a blue skirt, white shirt and matching blue cardigan, all to go with the new royal blue shoes that she was going to buy with her mother the day before at the shoe shop. She still had the new royal blue shoes on her feet but in her heart, she now wished that they had never gone into town that day to buy them.

'If only we had stayed home…if only I'd have kept wearing my old shoes…if only.'

A few of the other children were given some smarter cleaner clothes to put on than the ones that they had been originally wearing. Then finally, they were all taken to use some toilets and told to wash their hands well afterwards. As Alexa unbuttoned the top button of her blouse and began to wash her hands, she looked into the mirror over the sink and noticed her necklace hanging around her neck. It was a gift from her mother and had once belonged to her grand-mother, who had always worn it. A long silver chain with a small silver cross on it. She was grateful that the soldier at Dachau had missed it when checking all the others. She hadn't made much reference to it in the camp or in the truck, as she was afraid it might be taken from her. The female soldiers now hurried them all along to another larger room and the fourteen children were placed in a line-up and told to look forwards. They stood relatively stationary for at least five minutes staring ahead before getting distracted and finding their eyes looking elsewhere, as children always did. They were quickly prompted by the soldiers to pay attention and look straight ahead once again.

The tall wooden double doors opened and on the shiny wooden floor, sounded the echo of multiple heavy footsteps in both heels and boots. Fourteen Gestapo officers and their wives were led into the room and one by one they began inspecting all of the children down the line-up. One of the wives seemed very interested in Alexa, who had caught her eye and she walked over to her motioning her husband to join her. He stood looking at her in his SS uniform, which made Alexa nervous, so she dropped her eyes to the floor away from his direct stare. The wife said something in German to her husband and then raised her hand over to Alexa's neck. She moved the collar of her white blouse and then pointed to Alexa's necklace.

"Are you Catholic?" The woman asked in German.

Alexa couldn't speak much German, but she understood the word Catholic and nodded her head yes, as the woman reached for the cross around her neck.

"Good, then you'll come home with us," announced the wife, "We'll take this one!" The Gestapo officer spoke to the head officer in the room for a moment, signed some papers at his desk and then joined his wife again. "Come now girl, you will leave with us!"

The other children also began to be selected by the remaining couples and as Alexa left the room with her new keepers, she finally figured out what the fourteen children all had in common. They were all blonde-haired and blue-eyed, very attractive, healthy and fit-looking. They almost looked as if they could pass for perfect Germans. *'That must be it,'* she thought - like the Aryan race that she had heard stories about in school. The other girl in the courtyard had black hair and was a little overweight, that's why she wasn't selected to be in this group she reasoned to herself. Some others had brown hair too and didn't look as fit as those ones chosen in her group.

'That definitely must be why. We are all blonde, blue eyed and Aryan looking. We could almost pass for real Germans.'

The Gestapo officer led his wife and Alexa down the stairs out of the building towards the courtyard, then over to his black Mercedes Sedan 260D. He told Alexa to climb in and sit in the back seat as he took off his long black leather coat and threw it over on the seat next to her. Then he and his wife got in the front seats and he started the diesel engine, revving up his powerful chariot. As Alexa looked out of the side window next to her, the car loudly vibrated as it pulled out of the gates and rolled along the cobbled stones onto the streets of Frankfurt. The streets were not familiar to Alexa - she had never been out of Poland before, but somehow, she could tell that she was now far, far away from home.

"What is your name?" asked the wife, turning her head back to look at the girl in the rear seat.

"My name is Alexa." she replied with a nervous quake in her voice. In school Alexa's class had been learning some basic German, so she understood the question and tried to answer in her best German. The wife then told her that her name was Emilie and her husband was named Fredrick, but that she should call them Herr and Frau Klauss whenever she addressed them.

"Ja Frau Klauss." Alexa affirmed.

CHAPTER -4-

Alexa wanted to breakdown and burst into tears, both out of fear and due to the total heartbreak, which she felt over being separated from her mother and sister. But as hard as it was, she managed to hold it in, remembering what her mother had whispered to her back in the square. 'Don't let them see that you are scared...Keep strong!' She therefore did her utmost to remove the overwhelming and telling emotions from her face, thinking instead of how proud her mother would be of her for not showing her real emotions.

The long car journey took roughly three hours to reach their destination which was on the outskirts of the city of Bitburg in the far West of Germany. The car drove along the dark country roads and then eventually pulled off onto a long private driveway which led up to a large remote farmhouse. Alexa had dozed off in the back seat at some point and was awoken by the sound of Herr Klauss saying her name.

"Alexa, wake up. It's time to get out of the car. We are home."

Alexa awoke suddenly with a jolt, opened her eyes and quickly got out of the car, while the word 'home' echoed in her head. However, as she looked around, she saw nothing familiar and quickly became aware that she most definitely was not at her own home.

"Come! Come here with me," ordered the Gestapo officer's wife.

Alexa followed her into the farmhouse, and they headed down a long hallway straight for the kitchen. Once in the large kitchen, her husband appeared behind them a few seconds later with another German soldier.

"Explain to the girl!" ordered the Gestapo officer and handed the soldier a sheet of paper to read out to her.

"First of all, you must not think or talk about Poland anymore. Nor will you speak in Polish. From now on you will learn all things German. You will learn to speak only in German. This will be your German home. You will live and work for the Klauss family here in Bitburg," the soldier said to her, ironically in Polish.

"You will begin work at 4 am, milking the cows, collecting the hens' eggs, mucking out the barns etc. Then you'll bake fresh bread daily and will prepare breakfast for Herr and Frau Klauss by 6:20 am each morning. You will attend to all of the family's clothing needs, laundry, ironing and mending. Then you will waken their three children at 7 am. Richard aged nine, Anna aged seven and Rudy aged four, getting them washed and dressed and then preparing their breakfast by 7:45 am. The older children will go to school at 8:30 am, while you will look after Rudy here at home. You'll be expected to clean the entire house except for the study. You must not enter Herr Klauss's study at any time, for any reason. This will be the only room in the house that you will not be allowed to clean. You will prepare dinner for the family and attend to all chores required of you. The cows need to be milked twice a day, so you will milk them in the morning and once again in the afternoon. You will be expected to work in the field ploughing and planting and taking care of the vegetables in the greenhouse. When the children arrive home at 3 pm you will give them a sandwich to eat, make sure that they complete their homework and reading assignments and then have some playtime before dinner. You will cook every meal and serve dinner at 5 pm on weekdays, earlier on holidays and weekends, and after dinner you will bathe the children and make sure they are ready for bed. You will make sure that the kitchen is clean and tidy as well as the rest of the house. Their parents will read a story to them and kiss them goodnight at 9 pm, Rudy at 8 pm. At this time, you will clean out the animal barns, feed the animals and put down fresh hay. You will also check that Herr Klauss's Mercedes is clean and polished, ready for him to drive off in each morning. Do you understand all of what I have told you?" asked the soldier.

"Yes, I do!" Alexa answered.

"You will not leave this farm alone, unless you have Herr or Frau Klauss's permission! Do you understand?"

"Yes!" Alexa replied.

"You will wear a letter 'P' sewn onto your outer jacket for the times that you are permitted and instructed to leave the farmhouse and be outside. You will have no days off, nor holidays and your work day will finish at 11 pm, unless you have completed everything before then and have been dismissed by Frau Klauss. In which case you can retire to your bed earlier. Is this all clear?"

Alexa's heart sank a little more with each job description that the soldier had read out from the list of chores and just when she thought it couldn't sink any lower, she heard that she was expected to work every day without let up.

"Yes, I understand," uttered her broken voice.

"Good! You will not eat with the family. Only after they are finished eating, may you fix a small plate of left-overs for yourself and eat it in the kitchen pantry after your chores are completed. Here is a sandwich, an apple and a cup of milk, pick it up and follow me. I will take you to your room now. You will start work tomorrow at 4 am sharp!"

The soldier then turned to the husband and spoke in German to him, to confirm that he had told Alexa all that was expected of her from the long list he had been given.

Herr Klauss answered him back very matter-of-factly and then dismissed him. The soldier saluted him with a "Heil Hitler," then turned sharply on his heels and walked out of the kitchen door, motioning for Alexa to follow him. He led her up to the top of the stairs and pointed out which were the children's bedrooms and the parents, then led her through a little door and up some more stairs into the attic. At the rear corner of the attic was another door into a tiny windowless room and inside of it was a small bed with a plain wooden side table, an old lamp, a wooden chair, a dresser and some coat hangers, hung on a hook at the back of the door.

"This is your room where you will sleep. There are some clothes that might fit you in the drawers and whatever else you find in this room you can use. Be ready to go downstairs to the kitchen at 4 am to start work. The woman whom you are to replace, will come for you in the morning. If I were you, I'd follow her routine closely and learn your duties very quickly, as she leaves here on Friday. Any questions?"

"Only, where can I use the toilet please Sir?" Alexa shyly asked.

"There is a bucket in the corner, use that and empty it in the morning. There's a well outside near the barn if you want water to wash yourself in the morning. Now I must go," he turned un-empathetically and left the room, closing the door behind him. Alexa then heard a key go into the door and it being locked from the outside, confirming to her that she had no way out.

Alexa was totally disheartened and completely demoralized. She felt as though she were falling deeper and deeper into a never-ending nightmare. *'How can this be happening to me?'* She sat down on the bed placing the cup of milk and sandwich in her shaking hands onto the table. She placed the piece of fruit on the edge of the uneven table surface which began to roll, falling off and then rolled along the dirty floor coming to a stop against the leg of the dresser. As hungry as she was, her appetite was completely gone. The tears began to stream down her face now that she was finally alone and could cry her heart out. Alexa buried her face into the pillow and cried uncontrollably. She hadn't cried like that since her grandmother had died. '...*Now I'm in the bird catcher's trap! Now the bird catcher has me! How can I ever escape from here?*' she bleakly thought to herself. After some time, she eventually cried herself to sleep, curled up in a ball on top of the bed in the lonely dismal attic room.

Some hours had passed by, but Alexa had no concept of the time. It was around one o'clock in the morning and after being asleep for about four hours, she opened her eyes from her long nap. At first, she had no recollection of where she was. Immediately panic engulfed her, fearing that she had spent another night on one of the shared bunks of the horrific work camp at Dachau. However, she quickly realized that her mother was not next to her and her new reality set in fast. As her eyes adjusted to the light, she became all too aware that she was not in the comfort of her own bed either. She was not in her pretty bedroom that she shared with her little sister in their family home. Not resting her head on her comfortable feather pillows, nor tucked up warmly under her pink feather quilt that her mother had made for her. Reality quickly set in as she recalled the soldier locking her into her dismal new bedroom earlier that night. It was a stark contrast to what she was used to. The bed was metal and hard, with no soft mattress. There was a thin grey woolen blanket on top and below it, were two thin, old scratchy sheets. They didn't match the pillow, which was more of a cushion really, an old stained cushion and rather fusty and stale smelling. Certainly not the kind of place where a cared for young girl would sleep.

Alexa's eyes caught sight of the cup and sandwich on the table next to her. She suddenly became aware of the hunger pains in her stomach. She recalled that she hadn't eaten anything since she had been groomed for selection with the other blonde children, when they were given some bread to eat and milk to drink. Alexa reached for the cup and drank half of the milk. She picked up the plain looking sandwich which was made of two thick unevenly cut slices of bread, spread thinly with some butter and four slices of German sausage placed in between. Alexa opened the sandwich and split it in half, laying two pieces of sausage on each slice of bread. She ate the first half, then drank some more of the milk. It didn't taste so bad, so she quickly devoured the second half and her hunger slightly subsided.

Alexa remembered the soldier telling her that there was some clothing in the dresser that she could wear. She lifted her feet off of the wooden floor and looked at the pretty new royal blue shoes that were on her feet.

'...I never thought in my worst nightmares, that I'd walk in my dream shoes to a place as horrid as this!'

She moved off the bed and walked over to the wooden dresser which had two large drawers in it. Opening the top drawer, she found inside two plain white blouses, two white cotton vests, three pairs of white socks and three pairs of underwear. In the bottom drawer was one grey plain dress, a grey skirt, one grey woolen cardigan and a pale blue nightgown. Underneath the dresser on the floor, was a plain pair of wooden clogs. Alexa didn't like the look of any of the clothing that she had found, and she certainly didn't like the look of the clogs. *'...I hope I don't have to wear any of these clothes... and definitely not those clogs...now I'm glad I have my new shoes!'* As she looked down at the floor, she found the apple that she had dropped earlier and picked it up. She sat back down on the bed and cleaned it off by rubbing it against the grey blanket and took a bite. The apple was sour and not to her liking, so she placed it up on the table next to the bed but soon after, reached for it once more as hunger got the better of her and won over her tastebuds. Alexa felt a chill, so she pulled up the grey blanket and crawled underneath it. She lay her arm across the cushion so she could rest her head down on her sleeve without her hair touching it.

"I really don't want to be here, please God do not let it be for long! Please God rescue me from the trap of the bird catcher. Remove the terror of this night...Please guard and protect me. Please protect my sister and Mama too wherever they are right now. Rescue me dear God!" Alexa prayed aloud and ended it as always with an, "Amen!"

Alexa's thoughts became filled with her mother's condition after she had received such a violent blow to her head that morning. How would she ever know if she had recovered and was still alive? How would her mother ever know where she now was? The nightmare held and consumed her, giving no solutions or hope to cling to. Eventually the shattered teenager drifted off to sleep.

*   *   *

Magda's husband returned home about an hour or so after he had headed off into town to look for Sophia and Alexa. Magda remained at home with Asha and her twins, waiting anxiously to hear some news. The front door opened, and Magda went to meet her husband. He gestured to her to go through to the privacy of the kitchen where they closed the door behind them.

"Darling, it is not good news," announced her husband Michael with a look of despair across his face.

"What do you mean? What has happened?" Magda asked in a worried voice.

"Well when I got near to the town square, it was unusually quiet. Eerily quiet, almost deserted, but the market stalls were still set up and the two blocks of shops on Slawka street were completely empty of people."

"What do you mean? Where was everyone?"

Michael walked back over to the kitchen door and looked out to make sure that the children were not within listening distance, then closed the door tightly. He walked over to his wife and placed his hands on her shoulders.

"There were some small abandoned food packages lying on the streets around the square – broken eggs, spoiled cake, shattered glass, even a children's doll and some of the shop doors were left wide opened, but there was no one in sight. It was hauntingly quiet and there were a few German army barriers placed at either end of the street surrounding the town square."

"Didn't you see anyone?"

"As I was heading away from the market square and back towards home, I spotted Jack and asked him what had happened. He said that half a dozen Nazi trucks had driven into town and soldiers had started pulling everyone out of the shops at gun point and rounding everyone up."

He held his wife closer as Magda buried her head into his chest.

"Jack said that everyone was separated into groups, men, women, old, young and children and then loaded off into trucks and driven off."

"Oh, no, say it is not true!" Magda begged.

"Jack said he thinks that they were perhaps taken to a labor camp, or to Germany, but he didn't know for sure."

"No!" Magda cried.

"Quiet Magda, the children will hear you!"

"Not Sophia and Alexa, no it can't be true! And not everyone who was shopping in town, I can't take it all in."

Magda began to shake as tears ran down her face, while she tried to absorb the information she had just heard. Michael sat her down at the kitchen table. He walked over to their kitchen cabinet and took out two small glasses, then reached for a bottle of brandy pouring two small amounts. He carried them over to the table and handed one to Magda.

"Here drink this down quickly, it'll calm you."

They both drank down the brandy in one swift gulp and Magda composed herself as best as she could. She picked up the glasses and placed them in the sink then turned to face her husband.

"What should we do now?"

Michael pulled her close and hugged her, "We will say nothing to the children just now and we'll keep Asha here with us until we know for sure. Try and act as normal as possible, I know it won't be easy, but we must try." He hugged his wife tighter, then said he'd go check on the children.

Magda had a really bad feeling in the pit of her stomach, she knew something awful must have happened, but she had never thought of such a terrible outcome as this was. She began to imagine the horrific scene of Sophia and Alexa being dragged out of the shops with all the others. How terrifying it must have been for everyone. Who else was taken that she knew from town? Were they taken just because they were Polish? Then for a moment she felt relieved she was German, but then in a split second she was disgusted that she herself was actually a German. How can my own people be so cruel, so wicked and so evil? She searched her powers of reason, but no answers came. There was no reasoning. She could not fathom how any human beings could be that evil to their fellow humans. Magda began to pray.

* * *

Morning arrived and the time approached 3:50 am when a key began turning in the locked door of Alexa's room. She was still asleep but awoke to a female's voice in German ordering her to get up. As Alexa opened her eyes, she saw an older woman in her fifties standing next to her bed. She had a large white stained apron on that covered most of the dress she was wearing underneath, looking almost nurse-like.

61

The woman opened the drawers and selected clothes for Alexa to put on and then motioned to the girl to get dressed quickly. Alexa did as she was told with no argument until the woman pointed down to the clogs and told her to put them on. Alexa didn't want to take off her new blue shoes and sat back on the bed, shaking her head no. The woman picked up the clogs and dropped them on the floor in front of the girl and again Alexa shook her head no. The woman appeared angry at the girl's disobedience and with a lift of her right arm, slapped Alexa across her face. Alexa had never been hit like that before. She was always a well behaved, obedient and pleasant child who did what she was told when asked but she really didn't want to take off her new shoes. She hadn't even removed them when she had gone to sleep the previous night. In fact, they hadn't been off her feet since she had first put them on in the shoe shop. The woman reached for her left leg and pulled off the left shoe forcefully from her foot, she then grabbed the clog and pushed her foot inside of it. She was about to do the same with the other leg, but Alexa quickly reached down to her right foot and slid off the shoe herself, then placed her foot into the other clog. She could see that this woman had no patience and was not playing with her. Her own clothes were left on the bed and her new blue pair of shoes lay abandoned on the floor. The woman motioned to Alexa to stand up and she stood behind her. She took hold of her long blonde hair, pulling it all together tightly in one hand and then with her other hand, she tied it up using a thick rubber band. She twisted it up into a bun and fixed it in place so that it was up out of Alexa's face.

"Come!" The woman said then she led Alexa out of the attic down the stairs all the way to the kitchen. Alexa's first day as an unpaid slave was about to begin.

CHAPTER -5-

The large clock in the kitchen showed 4 am. It was now Monday morning, but it was still dark outside and the sun had not yet risen. Alexa was given an apron to wear by the woman and told to put it on, which she did. It was the woman's responsibility to teach Alexa all of the many daily jobs and duties that would be expected of her, and to teach her them quickly. The woman would be leaving the Klauss's home on the Friday for good and Alexa would be her full-time replacement, so she had to learn fast. First, the woman handed her a pencil and notepad then showed her over to the gas stove. She turned the oven on setting the dial to two hundred and fifty degrees then, lit the two back burners. She filled a large pot with cold water placing it on the stove, then filled a large iron kettle with cold water and placed it on top of the second burner. Alexa thought to herself that she would never be able to carry even one kettle full of water by herself and was already thinking of a way that she could fill them up on the stove, by using a smaller pot and making several journeys over to the sink.

Next, the woman led Alexa outside to the barn where the animals were kept. She handed her a basket and showed her where to collect the freshly laid eggs from the hens. They collected twenty fresh eggs before Alexa was instructed to put them on the table in the kitchen and then come straight back out to the barn. After that, the woman grabbed a metal bucket along with a small wooden stool, which she set up next to one of the five large cows. She motioned to Alexa to come closer so that she could see and learn how the milking was done. The woman placed both hands underneath the cow, with her fingers and thumbs on the udders, then began to gently squeeze the teats and milk the first cow. Alexa had never been on a farm before. She had never been up close to such a big animal before and so was understandably apprehensive. The woman was very well built with large muscly arms and a very full figure. It took her about eight minutes to milk the first cow then, after the woman was finished, she stood up, moved the bucket over to the next cow and pointed to Alexa to bring the stool over. This time she motioned to Alexa to sit down on it. Now it was her turn to milk the cow. She wasn't looking forward to the task but feared that the woman might slap her again or worse, if she didn't do what she was told. Alexa sat down in position just as she had been shown and placed her fingers around the two front teats. She began to gently pull, but nothing came out. She was scared and getting more nervous with the woman behind her watching her every move. The woman leaned in and squeezed Alexa's fingers harder, pulling in a firmer manner, then the milk began to slowly squirt out. Alexa gradually got the hang of it after much practice, but it took her much longer than it had taken the woman. Alexa was told to milk one more of the cows. Alexa's small soft hands and arms were hurting. It was hard work milking the cows. She didn't have big muscles like those of the woman, but she did as best as she could. The woman stopped her and lifted the stool away while instructing Alexa to bring the bucket and carry it into the kitchen. She then showed her to where the milk had to be cooled down.

It was now 4:45 am and the woman next lifted a tin of flour onto the large wooden table and reached for a large mixing bowl. Alexa was watching everything closely while trying to write it all down in her notes at the same time. Into the bowl went several measures of flour, some salt, yeast, warm water and oil, then the woman mixed it all together vigorously with her hands. After five minutes she had Alexa wash her hands and knead the dough for a further five minutes, then she covered the bowl leaving it to sit for an hour and a half near the stove. Alexa was given the milk to strain through some cloth into one of two large milk jugs and told to put them into the fridge. After that, they were back outside again filling a bucket of coal and gathering logs of wood. The coal was shoveled into a door opening at the bottom of the stove and the logs were brought through into both the lounge and dining room, then put in the fireplace. Next the woman scrunched up some old newspapers placing them in between the logs with some dry twigs, then she took a box of matches from a pocket in her apron and carefully lit the paper. Slowly the twigs began to light on fire and the flames gradually spread to the logs. The woman placed an iron guard in front of the dining room fireplace and told Alexa to start lighting the one in the lounge, just as she had done. Alexa had never lit a fire herself before, but she did just as she had seen the woman do and had the fire going well in a relatively short time.

Her next chore was to set the dining room table for breakfast. Tablecloth, china plates, bowls, egg cups, glasses, cups and saucers, cutlery and napkins for five people. This she managed with little trouble as she had often set the table at home in her own kitchen for the family meals, although they were only three people. Back into the kitchen again and the clock showed 5:10 am. The woman told Alexa to empty out the fresh eggs from the basket into separate cartons and to wash out the empty milk bucket and take it back to the barn, as she now had the other two cows to milk. One of the cows seemed to catch her attention more than all the others. All of the cows had names. One cow in particular was named 'Bloomshen' which translated to 'Little Flower.' For some strange reason Alexa felt that the cow was being sympathetic to her situation, as if the cow knew how she was feeling. It stared at her most of the time and seemed to shed a tear from its sad looking eyes. Alexa thought she must be imagining it and that she was just feeling sorry for herself. So, she finished up and moved on to the last cow. The woman next showed Alexa how to lead the cows out to the field to graze, and how to open the rear gates. This chore went a little easier this time for Alexa who then took the bucket of fresh milk back into the kitchen and washed her hands. Now the clock showed 5:45 am. The woman took the dough mixture from before, uncovered it and shaped it into a metal baking tin. Then, she opened the oven door and placed it inside on the middle shelf, firmly closing the door afterwards. As Alexa was writing all this down in her notebook, the woman took the pencil from her and wrote the number thirty. Thirty minutes was how long the bread was to bake for. She then took out from the fridge a selection of cold meats and sausages and began slicing them thinly, placing them neatly onto a small platter. Next, she took some tomatoes and cucumbers and began slicing them. They too were added to the platter. Cheese was next to be sliced and it completed the platter, ready to be served.

It was now 6:10 am and the woman brought a carton containing eight eggs to the table. Six of the eggs she cracked into a bowl, added salt and pepper, some milk and then she began to beat them quickly. She fetched a metal saucepan and into it put a tablespoon of butter, then placed it on top of the stove, lighting one of the front burners. She poured the egg mixture into the pan cooking it on a medium heat, while stirring them continually. Alexa continued watching and writing everything down. The woman then took the two remaining eggs, dropped them into the pot of boiling water, then held up three fingers to Alexa, meaning three minutes cooking time and told her to write that down. Both kinds of cooked eggs were ready at the same time and the woman used a large slotted spoon to retrieve the boiled eggs setting them down on the table. The scrambled eggs she removed from the heat and placed a lid over them.

Next, she got a teapot and filled it with boiling water from the kettle then spooned four teaspoons of loose tea leaves into the pot and placed the lid on it to brew. She next did the same with a coffee pot, making it strong and black. As the clock neared 6:15 am, the woman opened the oven and carefully removed the freshly baked bread, sitting it to cool on top of the kitchen table. On a tray she placed a butter dish, a jug of fresh milk, sugar bowl, salt and pepper, sliced lemon, then had Alexa carry it through to the dining room table. She prepared another tray with the meat platter, two kinds of eggs and the freshly sliced loaf of warm bread then carried it through to the dining table. She told Alexa to go and get the tea and coffee pots while she set the items in place on the table. As Alexa came back into the room, Herr Klauss appeared through the door behind her with his wife at 6:20 am sharp.

"Good morning," he said in German.

"Good morning," said the woman, as she motioned to Alexa to answer him also.

"Good morning Herr and Frau Klauss." Alexa said.

The woman asked if she could get them anything else then she left the room with Alexa, returning towards the kitchen. Alexa was pretty tired already. She had only been working for a little over two hours. But she had already filled up six pages of work notes in her notebook. The woman handed Alexa a piece of thick bread with a slice of meat and cheese on it, along with a small glass of milk. Alexa was feeling quite hungry and was grateful for the food. She thanked the woman and began eating and drinking quickly.

It was now time to go upstairs to the first floor. They went into the largest bedroom first which belonged to Herr and Frau Klauss and began making up their bed. They collected their already worn clothes from the previous day which lay scattered around the room and placed them in a pile for the laundry. Then they headed into their bathroom, collecting the used towels from the floor, cleaning off the excess water around the bath tub and mirrors and wiping down the surfaces. Gathering all the laundry, they headed back downstairs then, walked through a rear door in the kitchen where there was a utility room. The woman separated the white articles into a pile and left them to soak in a sink full of hot water. They walked back into the kitchen while Alexa continued writing down all the chores in order. The woman walked back into the dining room, placed a newspaper at the right side of Herr Klauss on the table and asked the couple if they would like anything else, but they were quite satisfied with all that they had before them.

The woman collected Alexa from the kitchen then took her back upstairs to waken up the children. First, they went into Richard's bedroom. The woman opened the curtains letting the sunlight pour into his room.

"Good morning Master Richard, time to get up," she said.

Richard rolled over in his bed, then sat straight up. He saw Alexa standing in his room.

"Who are you?" He asked. But Alexa didn't understand him.

"Her name is Alexa, she will be living and working here from now on," the woman told him.

"Oh yes, my mother told me about her. But isn't she too young? I mean she doesn't look much older than I am."

"Don't you worry about that master Richard. She will be able to do all the things I do for the family and more. She will be my replacement when I leave on Friday."

"Yes, but will she be as good as you Olga?" Richard asked.

"Well it's too early to say, let's just get on with today, shall we? Now let's get you out of bed and dressed young man. Your casual clothes are laid out on the chair ready for you to wear. No school today it's a holiday," she smiled.

That was the first time that Alexa had seen her smile all morning. Now she also knew her name. Olga. She seemed a little bit more human by actually having a name and the ability to smile. They walked out of the door into the next bedroom which belonged to the daughter Anna, who was the Klauss's seven-year-old. Olga opened the curtains, walked over to the young girl's bed then placing her hand on her shoulder, she gave her a little shake.

"Good morning Anna, time to wake up." Olga said.

Anna was harder to waken than her older brother and pulled the covers over her head.

"Come on, it's a brand-new day outside. No school today it's a holiday, let's get you up and dressed in some fun clothes," encouraged Olga, "and there's someone new here to meet you."

That sparked Anna's attention and she peeked out from beneath her blanket to take a look.

"Who is she?"

"This is Alexa, she will be living and working here in the house from now on."

"Why? Doesn't she have a house and family of her own?"

"Anna don't be difficult, just get up out of bed and stop wasting time."

Olga and Alexa left the girls' room and went into the last bedroom where young Rudy aged four slept. Olga again began by opening the curtains, but the boy was already awake.

"Good morning Olga, I'm already wakened."

"Yes, I see that Rudy. Let's get you dressed and ready for breakfast. This is Alexa, she will be living and working here every day from now on."

"Oh good, someone new to play with." Rudy said excitedly.

Rudy hopped out of bed and walked over to Olga, who was taking out some clean clothes from his dresser for him to wear. She motioned to Alexa to make up Rudy's bed and gather his dirty clothes for the laundry pile, while Olga removed the boy's pajamas and began dressing him. Then she took him through to the hall bathroom to wash his face, brush his teeth and comb his hair. The other two older children were dressed already, and Olga then proceeded to brush and style Anna's hair, while Alexa made up both of their beds and gathered their clothes worn from the previous day. Once presentable and ready, they all headed downstairs together into the dining room for their breakfast.

Herr Klauss had finished his breakfast already and had gone into his office, locking the door behind him. Frau Klauss was still in the dining room and welcomed her children like a mother hen.

"Good morning my little angels," she said as she kissed them all on their foreheads one at a time.

Alexa's mind drifted off to memories of her own mother who was always so happy to see her and her sister Asha first thing in the morning and how happy they both were to see their mother too. By the way Sophia would hug her girls and kiss them affectionately, they always felt their mother's unconditional love. Olga grabbed Alexa's arm and interrupted her reminiscing, taking her from the dining room through to the kitchen. They now had breakfast for the children to prepare. Three boiled eggs and some scrambled for them to choose from. Olga beat the eggs together quickly in a bowl while she motioned to Alexa to quickly fetch the laundry pile from upstairs and bring it down to be washed. Alexa did as she was told then caught up on the note-taking of her chores so far, adding the children to her list. Olga placed some more sliced bread, sausage and cheese to a plate and carried it along with the bowl of eggs through to the dining room table for the three children to eat. She then poured out two large glasses of milk with a smaller one for Rudy and placed them next to their plates. At that time their mother left the room. Olga peeled the boiled eggs from their shells, then dished out the scrambled eggs onto their plates, followed by some meat, cheese and bread.

"Now eat up children, I will be back in a few minutes," she said, then told Alexa to follow her.

Alexa was rather tired after her four hours of continual manual labor. Her feet were sore, as she hadn't quite mastered how to walk comfortably in the clogs she was forced to wear. She couldn't imagine they'd ever become comfortable to wear. *'If only I had on my new blue shoes, I could walk faster and work better.'* She just wanted to crawl back into bed, but not the strange horrible one that she had slept in the night before, she wanted to climb into her own warm cozy inviting bed in her own bedroom. To be in her own home, with her own family, eating breakfast prepared by her own mother, at their own family table. However, she was all too aware that such thoughts were just wishful thinking. This instead was her new reality which she'd just have to accept and get used to.

Olga went back into the utility room with a large stick where she stirred the water with the white laundry in it. Then she showed Alexa a bar of laundry soap and a scrubbing board, while she pointed with her hands for Alexa to roll up her sleeves and start scrubbing. She did as she was told. She had no choice. Alexa had never done laundry before. Her mother and grandmother had always taken care of that, but she had seen it done and did her best to get the clothes cleaned. Olga left her alone in the small utility room, but left the door opened so she could still keep an eye on her from the kitchen. She checked on the children who had finished eating their breakfasts then she dismissed them from the table to their playroom, while she began clearing their plates, carrying them through to the kitchen. She called Alexa and had her come to help clear the dining room table of all the remnants of breakfast, then had her wash the dirty dishes in the kitchen sink while Olga covered the left-over food and placed it into the fridge. Alexa then returned to continue washing the laundry by hand.

'Will this day ever end?' wondered Alexa.

CHAPTER -6-

H err Klauss had not ventured out of his study that morning since he had gone in just after breakfast. He had closed the door firmly shut and locked it behind him and presumably, had important work to attend to. He was not to be disturbed, which was clearly understood by the entire household and was a rule that was strictly adhered to. Alexa wondered to herself if this was a daily occurrence, or just his Monday ritual. As the clock neared noon, he finally came out of his study closing and locking the door once again behind him. He called for Olga to bring him some fresh coffee which she began making immediately. Alexa was also in the kitchen and set about arranging a tray with two cups, saucers, teaspoons, cream and sugar. Then Olga handed her a plate with a selection of premium Belgian chocolates which were also to be placed on the tray. Alexa looked down at the plate with envy. Her mouth began to water as she salivated over the delicious looking chocolate temptations in front of her. She would have loved to have had, even a tiny taste of just one of those fine delicacies. After all, she did have quite a sweet tooth and a childish love for chocolate. But she daren't even take so much as a corner from one of them. Just then, Olga added the fresh pot of coffee to the tray and just as quickly lifted it with both hands, turned and carried it away through to the lounge where Herr Klauss was patiently awaiting its arrival with his wife. This was a regular occurrence for the couple on holidays and weekends and Olga motioned to Alexa to make a note of it in her book. ...12 noon coffee and Belgian chocolates for Herr and Frau Klauss in the lounge, she wrote.

Olga next pointed out to Alexa that it was time to prepare dinner for the family. The older children had been playing out in the courtyard on their bicycles since after breakfast, while young Rudy had spent most of the morning with his mother in the children's playroom upstairs. She was keeping him occupied so that Olga could concentrate on teaching Alexa her long list of new chores and duties. Olga took Alexa out to the rear of the farmhouse, across the courtyard to where there was a large glass greenhouse. She proceeded to show the girl what was growing there - some fresh lettuces, several tomato plants, cucumbers, spring onions, radishes and green beans. They picked some of each then placed them in a wicker basket. They headed outside to a small vegetable plot of land which was farmed with various vegetables growing in it. Olga began selecting some fresh carrots and with a digging trowel, she chose some large potatoes from the patch and pointed out to Alexa where the cabbages, onions, beetroots, peppers, and broccoli were grown. Alexa continued to make note of everything she was being shown, both mentally and in her notebook. It was a lot to take in and although she had spent nine hours working there so far, she could sense that she'd have a lot more work to do before the day was over. There were no signs of her load lightening up anytime soon.

As they headed back into the farmhouse with the vegetables which they had gathered, they passed Anna and Richard playing in the courtyard on their bicycles. Coming up the driveway, appeared a black car. When it came to a stop at the farmhouse, out stepped two Gestapo officers, sharply dressed in their uniforms and shiny black boots. Olga told the children to put their bikes away into the shed and to come inside the house, after they had saluted the officers. She told Alexa to go with them up to the playroom and to stay there out of the way, while the officers were in the house. Herr Klauss walked out to meet them. They all gave a "Heil Hitler" salute raising their open right hands upward, extending their arms out straight, while clicking their heels loudly together behind them. One of them carefully lifted a large rectangular sealed wooden narrow box out of the car. The other carried a square shaped similar wooden box in his hands. They were led into Herr Klauss's study, then he closed the door firmly behind them.

Alexa did as Olga had told her but was naturally nervous after seeing the officers arrive in their uniforms at the farmhouse. It was, after all, only two mornings before that she had been forced out of the shoe shop with her mother, by men dressed in those same kinds of uniforms. It was men like them who had separated her from her mother in the street, who had loaded them forcefully onto trucks and trains and then drove them far away from their home. She couldn't help but think that they had come for her again. She immediately thought of hiding.

"Let's play hide and seek!" Alexa suggested. She took little Rudy's hand and hid behind a curtain with him. Then out loud she began to count to ten in German, the best that she could. Rudy corrected her on her pronunciation and filled in the numbers which she got wrong. Richard and Anna had been preoccupied while they hid, so they hadn't seen exactly where they were concealed in the large playroom. They both began seeking and in a relatively short time, Richard pulled back the long green velvet lined curtains to the side of one of the windows, to reveal Alexa and Rudy.

"Now it's our turn to hide," said Richard, "Close your eyes and count to twenty."

Alexa continued the game and began to count in German, even though she had only learned up to ten in school. The three children hurried about looking for the best place to hide in the spacious room.

"Eighteen, nineteen, twenty, here I come," Alexa said, counting the teen numbers in Polish.

She deliberately took her time to search out the two boys and the girl, wanting them to be as quiet as possible for as long as possible, so she delayed their discovery.

Rudy being the youngest at four years of age, did not have a great deal of patience and as Alexa passed by near his hiding place, shouted out, "You missed me," and jumped out from behind a chair where he was hiding. Alexa tried to act surprised, so as not to let on that she knew where he was all along. Rudy then announced that he would help her to find his sister and brother, then proceeded to look in all of their good hiding spots that he could think of, dragging Alexa with him. The game continued for thirty minutes or so with Alexa always doing the counting and seeking, before Olga opened the door and entered into the playroom.

"What are you children doing?" Olga asked, "Or rather, what have you done with the children Alexa?" The three of them were nowhere in sight.

"They are hiding." Alexa answered.

All of a sudden Rudy jumped out again.

"Boo!" He yelled, "She's not very good at this game - it's taking ages for her to find us."

Olga had left the door ajar and, from downstairs, Alexa could hear that the men were talking in the hallway. The voices became faint as they left the house and headed back out to their car. The engine started up and the car drove off with the two officers inside. Herr Klauss returned to his study and locked the door behind him.

Olga left the children to play upstairs and took Alexa with her to the kitchen. They now began the task of making dinner for the family. Potatoes and carrots all had to be peeled and chopped then placed in pots to be boiled or steamed. Olga took chicken pieces out of the refrigerator, first tenderized the meat then dipped them in flour, eggs and breadcrumbs ready to be fried. She put a chopping board, bowl and knife in front of Alexa and had her prepare a salad with the fresh lettuce, tomatoes, cucumber, onion and a carrot. Olga took the boiled potatoes and proceeded to mash them together adding some butter, milk, salt and pepper. She then fried the chicken pieces in some hot oil in a pan on the stove and steamed the carrots. Alexa took note of it all and, as the aroma of tasty food filled the kitchen, she felt herself getting hungrier by the minute. It was approaching 2 pm when the meal was finally cooked and Olga gathered five dinner plates, bowls and sets of cutlery then had Alexa place them through on the dining room table. The family came into the room and sat down at the table. Olga placed a glass of milk in front of each child then served their meal. After she was content that she hadn't forgotten anything, she left the room. Herr Klauss opened a bottle of wine and poured two glasses, one for himself and one for his wife.

Olga told Alexa to continue attending to washing the family's clothes in the utility room. The poor girl was so tired and longed to take the weight off her feet. To take her feet out of those most uncomfortable clogs. But she had to carry on with her demanding chores. Olga handed her a book and pointed to the words on the cover a few times. 'Learn German' it read. Alexa knew that German would be replacing her own Polish language and that the sooner she learned it, the better it would be for her. However, she did wonder at what time of day she would be able to look at the book and learn German, as she hadn't even had five minutes to herself so far.

It was now three in the afternoon. Alexa had completed the washing of the laundry, had rung out the excess water using the old hand-turned clothes wringer and had it all hanging outside to dry. Olga made her clear the dining room table after dinner. It was also her job to wash all of the dishes, cooking pots and pans and to clean the kitchen. Her young delicate hands were red and sore by now, but she carried on until everything was clean and put away where it belonged. To Alexa's surprise, Olga placed a small bowl of left-over food from dinner in her hand with a spoon and pointed to the utility room where the girl was to go and eat her cold food. Alexa, being so hungry, said thank you and took the bowl into the small room where she had done all of the laundry and, for the first time since milking the cows in the morning, she finally got to sit down. She slipped her feet out of the heavy, extremely uncomfortable clogs that she was wearing and placed her throbbing feet on the cold stone floor. She quickly began devouring the food she had been given and could almost feel it land in her empty stomach. She wasted no time, as if the bowl could be snatched away from her at any moment. After a few minutes, Olga approached her with the metal milking bucket and told her that it was time for the cows' second milking of the day. She led Alexa back out to the barn and opened the rear gate out to the field where the cows were grazing. She began leading the cows back into the barn, and said the word "Five" in German, pointing to the cows, meaning that all five cows were to be milked again. Alexa placed the stool under the first cow to begin the process again. Olga watched over her as she milked the first cow, then she walked out of the barn closing the large doors behind her, sliding the locking post securely into place. Alexa continued to milk the cows one after another and as she got closer to 'Bloomshen' again she noticed the cow staring at her continually, with its sad eyes and lowered head. As she began milking 'Bloomshen', she began to speak to it in Polish. "I hope you can understand Polish. Why do you look as sad as I feel? Are you sad for yourself, or just feeling sorry for me?"

She continued to milk the cow and when she next looked up, she could see a visible tear rolling out of Bloomshen's left eye. She looked round to her right eye and it too had a tear trickling down from it. *Well I never! I think this cow's crying for me.'* Alexa stood up and gently placed her hand on the cow's head, softly stroking it.

"Don't cry Bloomshen, we will be good friends and then I won't feel so awfully alone in this place. I can talk to you secretly every day in Polish and you will help me not to forget my own language."

She finished milking all of the cows then heard the barn door opening. She shared a silent glance with Bloomshen then Olga came back to the barn with Alexa's next chore, after the milk was removed to the chilling area. It was her job to guide the cows back out to the nearby field for grazing then to securely bolt and lock the gate. The cows set off while Bloomshen kept her head raised up, staring at Alexa until she was out of sight.

Olga then had her come out to one of the sheds on the property where there were several large baskets of apples being stored. She collected about two dozen and, on their way back into the kitchen, Olga pointed out to Alexa where the apple trees were in the garden. Alexa figured out that she'd probably have the job of climbing up and picking the apples when they were ripe - more manual labor. They took the apples back into the kitchen and Olga told her to wash her hands then handed her an apple peeler and a large bowl, instructing her to start peeling. Once peeled, Olga cored and sliced them thinly then began preparing the ingredients to make an apple pie. Alexa wrote down all the steps including what temperature the oven was set at to bake the pie.

Before the pie was ready, Alexa was taken out to the barn where the animals were, and Olga showed her how to rake the soiled straw and replace the barn floor with fresh straw and hay. The cows were still out in the field grazing. Then they added fresh hay to the sty where the pigs were kept. The day's leftovers were poured into the pigs' trough for them to eat. In total there were four pigs with six piglets. After that it was the chicken coop that was to be cleaned out. There were eight chickens in total, seven hens and one cockerel. They were not kept in the coop during the day and instead, freely roamed about a fenced-in area at the back of the barn. Alexa couldn't help but think that, in comparison, the animals had a lot more freedom than she did. Next up was the stable which was home to two horses. Only one was in the stable. The other, Herr Klauss had saddled up and taken out for a ride after dinner. Olga pointed to a shovel for Alexa to pick up and lift the horses' mess into a nearby wheelbarrow. Then she was to rake the straw and hay that was on the ground and replace it with fresh, along with a bale of hay for the horses to eat. After that, the water for the horses needed to be refreshed, along with all the other animals' drinking water which Alexa had to draw from the well out in the courtyard and carry by the bucketful. After that chore was completed, it was time to check on the apple pie. Its aroma filled the kitchen and Alexa's mouth watered as Olga removed it from the oven, carefully placing it on a metal rack on top of the kitchen table. She motioned to Alexa to wash her hands after she had cleaned hers, then told her to get five bowls and desert spoons out and to go place them on the dining room table. Alexa did as she was told, as she had done all day. It was now 5:30 pm, they could hear the voices of the children who had gone for a walk with their mother after dinner, now returning to the house. Olga served the warm apple pie with cream to the family and stoked the fireplace with a steel poker, adding another log or two of wood to the pile. Then she collected a large jug of fresh fruit compote and five glasses from the kitchen and poured everyone a refreshing drink.

By 6:30 pm the family had finished their dessert and had left the dining room. Alexa cleared the table and carried the dishes through to the kitchen sink where she began washing them. Olga followed her through with the glasses placing them at the side of the sink. While Alexa put all the clean dishes away. Both parents had retired through to the lounge to relax and their children followed them. The family usually spent some time together in the evening before the children were taken upstairs to get ready for bed. Meanwhile, Olga took Alexa upstairs where they prepared the children's bedrooms, putting on lights, getting out pajamas, pulling back their bedding and running warm bubble baths, beginning with Rudy's. Once Rudy was all clean and dry, Olga got him dressed in his pajamas ready for bed. She then ran baths for both of the other two children setting out fresh pajamas and a nightgown for them. Anna being seven, still needed assistance bathing especially in washing her pretty long blonde hair. But Richard was nine and insisted on privacy in the bathroom. He bathed and got himself clean, becoming quite the independent young man. However, he had no interest in picking up after himself, or cleaning up the mess he left behind him. That he left for Olga. That was Olga's job and now it would be Alexa's. Richard's parents had ensured that he joined the German Youth movement and it was becoming obvious from his words and actions, that the classes were having a major influence on the young boy who was over-filled with nationalistic pride. Olga told Alexa to clean up the bathroom after the children were finished, collecting all the wet towels and soiled clothes and take them downstairs to the utility room where she was to begin washing them. It was after eight o'clock and the night had already turned dark outside. Alexa went outside to collect the dry laundry and began folding it into piles.

The parents came upstairs to say goodnight to their children. Rudy was first to get some attention. His mother sat on his bed to read him a short story, after which his father kissed his forehead and left his room. Herr Klauss was carrying a large book and next went into his older son's bedroom, closing the door behind him. After Rudy's mother finished reading his story, she tucked him into bed pulling the blankets up below his chin then lovingly, kissed his cheek. She turned out his bedroom lamp, pulled over his bedroom door behind her, leaving it slightly ajar. She then went through to her daughter's bedroom where Anna was waiting with her book of choice. First of all, her mother took a soft brush and began gently brushing her little girl's hair, then she read her story. The parents spent about an hour with their children before kissing them goodnight and heading back downstairs.

Once Alexa had completed hand-washing all of the families' laundry, she hung it up to dry. Alexa was beyond exhausted at that point. Olga took her outside to the field and showed her how to bring the chickens into their coop, then the cows into the shed. Thankfully this was Alexa's last chore of the day, the poor young girl could hardly stand. Her feet throbbed in the wooden clogs. As she walked back into the kitchen, she could feel them blistering. Olga cut two slices of the left-over apple pie into two bowls, one bigger than the other then covered them over with the cream, taking one for herself and giving the smaller one to Alexa to eat. She poured them a glass of fruit compote to drink. Once they finished and cleaned up, Olga then led Alexa out of the kitchen, upstairs stopping at the children's bathroom, where she motioned her to go in and use the toilet. Then she took the girl upstairs again to the attic and over to the small room in the corner where she had slept the night before. It was now 10:30 pm. Olga told her she'd be back for her in the morning at 4 am. Olga switched on the lamp and closed the door behind her, locking it with her key. Alexa kicked off the clogs and collapsed onto the bed in sheer exhaustion. Then she thought of her new blue shoes. She hadn't seen them all day. She got off the bed and searched the small room for them, but there was no sign of her new shoes. Her little heart sank. They were gone. Alexa recalled her last conversation that she'd had with her best friend Helena as they had walked home from school on that last Friday only three days before. Now she'd not be able to keep her promise to let Helena try on her new shoes. Nor did it look like she herself would get to wear them ever again either. She thought how disappointed her mother would be at her losing them. The tears began falling from her eyes as she climbed into the uncomfortable bed, feeling totally alone. She said her prayer, reciting her Psalm, then said "Amen" at the end. She buried her head in her exhausted arms and drifted off to sleep, while her tears continued to trickle down her cheeks.

CHAPTER -7-

As time went on, Alexa's list of chores for the Klauss family became like second nature to her. Olga had taught her well during her final week there before leaving the Klauss's farm. Alexa was a quick learner. She became very familiar with the families' routine, their likes and dislikes and soon she had the household running very smoothly, like a well-oiled machine. Alexa kept telling herself that her situation was only temporary and would come to an end. That she would be reunited with her mother and sister again one day soon and be able to go back home to the life that she knew and loved. However, no matter how many times she told herself that, there was still a small part of her which didn't fully believe it. But she kept her hope alive choosing to ignore her doubts and instead fuel her positive thinking. She knew she wasn't free to physically leave whenever she wished, being kept against her will. *I'm basically a slave, she reasoned, I'm as good as a prisoner here. But I still have my mental and spiritual freedom,'* and that she would consciously preserve. In her mind as well as in her thoughts, she could be free. There, she could escape from the pain, suffering and separation which she felt so deep in her heart. There she could be her own liberator and dismantle her prison walls, brick by brick. She would choose to be happy, rather than depressed. She'd choose to be hopeful, over being miserable and bitter. She realized that it was her choice, and she choose joy and freedom of mind. She would muster the needed courage to allow the worst situations, to bring out the very best in her. She reminded herself daily, that this was only temporary. *'I will survive today and tomorrow, I will be free. As long as I still have hope, I will live. I will survive this.'* These thoughts sustained her and helped her to endure through her most difficult days.

Her father had always taught her when she was little, that if a job was worth doing, it was worth doing well and so no matter what task was laid before her, Alexa did the very best job that she could. In time, Herr and Frau Klauss could see that she did a great job of each chore that was placed before her and that she was especially good with their children, with sincerity and real affection which showed through in her nurturing manner. The three children quickly grew very fond of Alexa and they enjoyed spending time with her. Alexa shared her love and talent for art with the Klauss's children, creating little masterpieces to amuse them with and art projects to involve them in. Just as her father had done with her when she was a child. The parents saw that she was trustworthy and honest so as time went on, began to give her certain privileges.

The very first was that she no longer had to sleep up in the tiny back attic room which was dreary, dark, dismal and more like a dirty old cupboard with no windows. Instead she was moved into a real bedroom in the house on the floor below. Of course, it wasn't as nicely decorated or as beautifully furnished as the three children's rooms were, but it was clean, bright and more spacious than the farmhouse attic. Furthermore, she didn't get locked into this room at night. It had a proper bed, with clean bedding, pillows and a warm feather quilt. On the opposite wall from the bed was a small window which gave a good amount of natural light, although Alexa was always busy working during the daylight hours, she never really got the pleasure or benefit of it. Her room faced onto the greenhouse and over the fields that were at the rear of the farmhouse, which reminded her of the view from her old classroom window where she used to sit at school. She recalled how she and the other children used to dream of being free from that classroom most days, away from all the hard work that was given to them there. But now she wished more than anything, that she could go back to the safety of that school classroom. She would have given anything to trade in the incredibly hard work that she was now being forced to do each day, for those few hours of daily education, Monday to Friday from her teacher. *'To be able to do maths, science, reading, indeed any subject would be better than this,'* she thought.

The war battled on year after year, with no sign of any immediate let-up and Alexa's daily chores for the Klauss's continued without any slackening. However, Alexa quickly became an expert at her job and the set of individual skills which she developed, had become very refined and professional for such a young teenager.

The Klauss's farmhouse in Bitburg was only a few kilometers from the border with Luxembourg and when Alexa was roughly sixteen and a half, the Klauss's decided she could be trusted to make the journey on foot to run a new errand for them - an errand that would extend their trust in her. Just over the border was a little village called Vianden and in it was a small shoe shop where the Klauss's would place orders and have their shoes custom made. Previously Herr Klauss had always sent an officer to collect them by car but this time, his wife convinced him that it would be good for Alexa to go alone and that she could indeed be trusted. They gave Alexa straightforward directions telling her how to get to Vianden. They said that once she crossed the nearby border, she was to go over the wooden bridge crossing the river, then just adjacent from the large white church, she would find the quaint little bespoke shoe shop roughly an hour away. They gave her the necessary documents in order to collect the shoes, along with the money to pay for them. Then she put on her jacket with the letter 'P' on it, identifying her as being Polish and off she headed on the hour's walk to Luxembourg, unaccompanied for the very first time.

Alexa felt a mixture of emotions on her journey. On the one hand, she felt very trusted by the fact that both Herr and Frau Klauss had believed in her enough to allow her the freedom to go so far and come back alone. But on the other hand, she couldn't help but have feelings of wanting to take advantage of her short window of freedom. Her first real window of opportunity which she'd had. She thought over in her mind of how this could be her chance to escape - perhaps her one and only chance to ever escape. *'I could run away and just keep running. It would be hard to find me'*, she thought. But then more realistic thoughts came to her mind. *'Where would I run to? How could I even run anywhere far in these stupid clogs? What would I survive on? Where would I live? I have no food and the money wouldn't last long! What if someone else captures me?'* Alexa came to the conclusion that she'd be better off to just collect the shoes as she was instructed, then take them straight back to the Klauss's farmhouse. Her thoughts then drifted back to the last time that she had gone to buy new shoes with her mother in Lublin, and what a horrific event that had turned out to be. It couldn't have been any worse and she began to worry that this journey to the shoe shop might also be a bad experience. As the flashbacks went off in her mind like fireworks, she began to pray her familiar Psalm 91.

'You are my God and my stronghold, in whom I trust. Let me not fall into the trap of the bird catcher. Let me take shelter under your wings. Have affection for me and rescue me my dear God. That I will see your acts of salvation. Please keep me safe, Amen'

Alexa crossed the river over the bridge and eventually neared the large church just like she had been told and there in front of her was the small shoe shop. Alexa walked into the store and approached the woman behind the counter.

"Good afternoon, can I help you?"

"Good afternoon, I have this card to collect a pair of shoes."

"Ah! So, you are Polish I see, we never see any Polish people. What are you doing in Luxembourg?"

Alexa found the woman to be very endearing as she engaged her in conversation. She had a kind face and genuinely seemed to be interested in Alexa. She began to explain her situation to the woman and while listening, all of a sudden, the woman said, "Oh no! In that case, you are not going back to slave away for the mean Germans any more child. I have some really lovely cousins in Belgium, I will arrange for you to go and stay with them tomorrow. My husband is a politician and he can drive you there in secret in his car. You don't ever have to work for the Germans anymore. How dare they!"

Alexa liked what she was hearing but was still very anxious over what the consequences might be, of her not returning to the Klauss's home that night. The woman closed up the shop early and took Alexa to her large family home in the nearby mountains where she could spend the night and decide what she wanted to do. She told her that her name was Alice, then introduced her to her family. She made Alexa a tasty meal to eat with some fresh fruit compote to drink. Alice encouraged Alexa to tell her story of how she had ended up in Germany and was visibly moved with empathy as she listened intently to Alexa's every word. It was late in the evening and dark outside, so Alice showed Alexa to one of her comfortable spare bedrooms where she was invited to sleep for the night. Alice gave her a clean, fresh nightgown to wear and some fresh towels to use, while she ran her a warm bubble bath and made her feel as much at home as possible. Alexa settled into the comfortable bed with ease that night. It reminded her of her childhood home and of her own pretty bedroom in Lublin which she'd never forgotten. She wished more than anything that her mother would walk through the door and come to tuck her in, kissing her forehead, saying their nightly prayer together before turning out the light. But no matter how hard Alexa stared at the door, she knew her mother would never walk through it. She turned out the light herself, pulled up the covers around her neck and said her prayer by herself, thanking God for the kindness of strangers.

In the morning Alexa was awoken by loud voices and some commotion coming from outside. There was heavy arguing and Alexa could hear Herr Klauss's angry voice shouting. Alexa made her way downstairs.

"Look I know the girl is here because we sent her to your shop yesterday and she had nowhere else to go and didn't come home last night. I have come to collect her and if you don't produce her immediately, I will report you to the German army then they will have you, your family and Alexa all arrested and sent off to a work camp. Is that what you want?"

"Look, please let's all calm down and go inside the house, I'll make some fresh coffee and we can talk about it. I'm sure there is a simple solution to all of this."

Alice calmed things down slightly with her invitation. Perhaps it was all those years of her husband being a politician that helped her defuse the situation. So coffee was made, and they all drank some together. Calmer discussions were then had, until a mutual agreement was finally reached and agreed upon.

"Alexa will go back to Bitburg to work for your family from Monday to Saturday, but on Sunday's she will be allowed to come freely to Luxembourg, where she can relax with us, eat good food and enjoy fine company every Sunday, as her day of rest," established Alice's husband.

This was finally agreed upon by Herr Klauss who knew Alice's husband since they were young boys. Being a politician,

Herr Klauss had called on him for special favors over the years and so obliged him by granting his request regarding Alexa. They returned to the shop to collect the new shoes which Alexa had originally been sent for, and then she returned to Bitburg with Herr Klauss that morning in his car. The following Sunday, Alexa took the walk to her retreat in Luxembourg as agreed upon, where she was welcomed warmly and got a taste of normality with her new-found friends. It gave her something to really look forward to all week and she cherished her visits with Alice and her family along with the freedom which she felt when with them. When she left after her second Sunday visit, the woman gave her a new pair of shoes, which they had made as a gift, to be given to the Klauss's oldest son. When the Klauss's received them, they were very pleased so the following Sunday, they sent Alexa carrying a parcel full of fine cheeses, and fresh meats for them in return. Then on her way back, the shoemakers gave shoes for young Anna as a gift and the following week a pair for Rudy, then a new pair of shoes were made for and given to Frau Klauss. The Klauss's continued to show their appreciation and never allowed Alexa to visit them empty handed. They always sent her off with a bag full of gifts in return. Alexa spent almost every Sunday in Luxembourg relaxing with Alice and her family for an average of four hours, which allowed her to unwind giving her the endurance she needed to carry on working for the Klauss family. After the first month of getting to know her, Alice and her family presented Alexa with a beautiful pair of new black shoes which they custom made just for her. Alexa was overcome with emotion and gratitude. The kind gesture made her feel special. These became her Sunday shoes and the Klauss's allowed her to take off her clogs leaving them behind at the farmhouse for the day while she wore her beautiful new comfortable shoes instead, for her walk to Luxembourg and back. Alexa had a youthful spring back in her step once more.

CHAPTER -8-

Roughly five hundred and fifty kilometers away from Bitburg was the city of Munich, Germany. There were large numbers of Gestapo officers' in many of the big, bustling cities, with their offices in various locations. Munich was one of the largest. Since the events of 'Crystal Night' back on November ninth of 1938 and continuing on into the next day throughout Germany, the Nazis had conducted an all-out attack which made it impossible for the Jews to live a peaceful, normal existence anymore. Hundreds of their synagogues were torched and left to burn to the ground while German fire fighters standing nearby were instructed not to save the synagogues, but instead only to fight a fire if it threatened to spread to an Aryan-owned building. Jewish businesses were severely vandalized and glass-fronted stores were smashed in the Pogrom. Local German police officers had joined in on the horrific events arresting thousands of innocent Jewish men both young and old, sending them off to labor camps or worse, never to return to their homes or families again. The Germans continued segregating the remaining Jewish population and setting harsh, almost impossible boundaries for them to live by. Rapidly, the hate for all things Jewish had spread like wildfire from the busy cities to the small country-side villages. The German youth movement recruited many youngsters teaching them to hate all Jews from childhood, even if they had young Jewish friends a few years earlier at school or as neighbors. They were now to be despised. To be hated at first sight. The majority of adults who were once friends with Jewish work colleagues and neighbors, now betrayed and turned their backs on them. The Nazi regime made Jewish life and survival virtually impossible in Germany, while hate for them spread like wildfire.

Life rapidly became harder for the Jews throughout Europe but especially in Germany and Poland. Their stores were boycotted, attacked and vandalized so that making a living became near impossible. Many highly qualified professional and intellectual Jews were no longer permitted to work or practice in their chosen fields. Their children were no longer permitted to attend regular schools and further education was out of the question. They were treated as less than second-class citizens, forced to wear a yellow 'Star of David' made out of material, visibly sewn onto their outer sleeve jackets and coats to identify them clearly as being Jewish. A visible label that they couldn't avoid. These stars were also painted on their few remaining businesses, homes and windows. It wasn't long before Jewish people were being removed from their homes by force during night raids and being transported to work in concentration camps while having their valuables confiscated by the Gestapo and Nazi army.

Those wealthiest Jews who had the finances, connections and the foresight early on, obtained visas and bought tickets for their families to leave Germany. Those lucky ones could escape and go to stay with other family members or migrate to other countries further away by any means possible. These arrangements were usually made very hurriedly, as families would disappear in the cover of night carrying very few belongings or valuables with them, which meant that there were many homes with valuables left behind. Priceless works of art, famous paintings, valuable antiques and jewelry, all left with no guardians. Of course, the Nazi party needed no invitation or permission to take possession of these valuables.

They took their fill of the abandoned bounty. The German museums had already been pilfered and stripped of their greatest assets, antiquities and masterpieces. The Gestapo raided private collectors and Jewish homes alike, taking their plunder. Their hoards became massive as they took their choice of priceless art from across Europe which they stashed in a variety of safe locations all over Germany and occupied Poland

Herr Klauss travelled to Gestapo HQ in Munich once a week and on a daily basis to the Frankfurt offices which were closer to where he lived. There he oversaw operations locating the desired masterpieces and artworks which the Gestapo were still trying to locate and acquire from their secret 'List'. The 'List' was just that, a very extensive and lengthy list of hundreds of thousands of priceless paintings and famous works of art, along with their titles and the artists' names who had painted them. 'The List' noted the artist, the date and country of the painting's completion, the last known location and owner of the works of art along with a full description of the actual paintings including, colors, mediums, frames, settings, scenery and characters. 'The List' was continued in book after book, all numbered in sequence methodically, within large black bound leather ledgers full of Hitler's ultimate collector's wish-list. They consisted of several million paintings and sculptures in total, which the Gestapo kept meticulous records of.

Herr Klauss had an intense passion for art. He took his position and responsibility very seriously with an enormous amount of pride. His job was to maintain 'The List' as top secret, privacy was paramount. He was head of his office in Frankfurt, having six senior officers under his command and direction, who subsequently had a few dozen Nazi foot-men under their control, whom they would order out on reconnaissance and retrieval missions. Three years into the Second World War, they already had three quarters of 'The List' successfully gathered and safely stored out of reach, in secret locations across Europe. Herr Klauss had several dozen personal favorites which he had always loved, but there were still some of his own favorites that he was yet to trace and lay his hands upon for the Fuhrer. He was committed to the cause and it was his duty to help attain them by any means possible. Eventually all the individual pieces of art would be homed in a new enormous German mega-museum to be purpose-built for the Fuhrer in Berlin. It would be the greatest museum the world had ever seen, and Herr Klauss and his officers took tremendous pride in their part, working towards its creation.

Herr Klauss was a popular man and was well respected by his peers. He was well known in German society and with the local towns people where he lived. The Gestapo uniform he wore gave him another dimension to his personality, an added air of authority and inevitably many people feared him just by sight. However, although he was a highly decorated SS officer, he had a certain quality of kindness to him that shone through and when in a good mood, he was quite approachable and pleasant. He viewed himself as a good Christian man. He and his family were Catholics and every two weeks his first cousin Edgar, a Catholic priest, would come and visit with him at his farmhouse. This always made him feel that he was approved by God in some way. As if God somehow approved of him.

From the German point of view, the war was going quite well. However, for the millions of Jews and innocent Europeans caught up in the crossfire, the same could not be said. Towards the End of 1943, Herr Klauss had the idea of entertaining groups of officers at his farmhouse and hosting private parties to boost the morale among his junior officers, soldiers and staff. His wife thought this was a wonderful idea and took charge of inviting several young local women whom she knew, as well as some of her attractive single female friends. There would be music and dancing, tables of fine foods, delicacies, wines, vodka and cognacs for all to enjoy. This was just the very distraction that the Klauss's needed as the war roared on.

Alexa was now seventeen and was blossoming into a beautiful young woman, quite the head turner although she was completely oblivious to her attractiveness. She still worked almost every hour of the day except from eleven at night until four o'clock in the morning when she got to take the weight off of her tired feet, from walking all day in the heavy clogs. It was no wonder she so looked forward to her Sunday afternoons and some much needed, respite with Alice and her family. Apart from her chores being so mundane, monotonous and demanding, Alexa became the perfect housekeeper, an excellent cook, meticulous cleaner and wonderful child care provider. She was hard not to like and almost everyone who met her took an immediate liking and warmed to her. From some of the other nearby farmhouses, Alexa had met a few other young European girls who had also been taken from their homes and families in a similar and horrific manner. They too had been made to work as house slaves for other Gestapo officers and their families nearby. Sometimes they would be dropped off at the Klauss's farmhouse with the children whom they looked after, so that the young ones could have some supervised playtime together. This gave the opportunity for Alexa to make some friendships with a few of the other girls. These moments in time, would be amongst the most enjoyable ones of her years of captivity and forced labor. Alexa was now fluent in German and could communicate very well indeed as though it were her mother tongue, so there was no language barrier with the other girls who had also been forced to learn German. She was especially fond of Eva who was originally from Luxembourg and Elizabeth who was Belgian.

Frau Klauss gave Alexa the details of what she wanted for the upcoming party. It was Alexa's job to decorate the main barn for the dance, as well as to prepare all of the food which was on the list that she had been given. A day before the event, an SS truck delivered stacks of chairs, folding tables, several crates of soft drinks, fine wines and beers. The party was coming together nicely, and Frau Klauss told Alexa that she too was invited, along with Eva, Elizabeth and some of the other local girls. Much to Alexa's surprise, she was given a beautiful new powder blue dress to wear for the night of the party by Frau Klauss and, all of a sudden, as she became overcome with joy and genuine excitement, she threw her arms open and hugged the lady of the house thanking her. Frau Klauss was quite surprised by her reaction, but her motherly instinct naturally kicked in for a split second and for the first time she showed some genuine affection for Alexa putting one arm around her, patting her shoulder. She then gave her a pretty blue velvet bow for her hair and told her to take them both upstairs to her room out of the way until the party the following evening.

The day of the first party finally arrived and Alexa's morning began as had all her other days at the Klauss residence at 4 am. She set about attending to her many regular daily chores as always but also began preparing the food which she'd be making for that evening's event. Frau Klauss had told Alexa to cater the party for sixty people, which was a new challenge for the seventeen-year-old girl. She had never cooked for more than twelve people at the one sitting before and so the task was very daunting, but as always, she did her very best. As the day went on, Alexa continued working tirelessly as her imagination drifted off into thoughts of how much fun the party would be that evening. The prospect of having interactions with new people and getting to spend some time with her few friends from the surrounding farmhouses, when they wouldn't be working either, excited her. She wondered what Eva and Elizabeth would be wearing to the party, if they had been given a new dress to wear, as pretty as hers.

These girlish thoughts helped the hours fly by and her pile of chores reduced rapidly too. With all the food prepared, glasses out on tables and the barn decorated and set up ready for the guests to arrive, Alexa was excused from further duties and allowed to go upstairs to get dressed up and make herself look pretty. She looked in the old mirror in her bedroom as she let down and brushed her lovely long blonde hair, then began positioning the blue velvet bow in place. It took her several tries, as she had worn her hair in the same clinical style every day for the past four years, tightly pulled back and tied up in a bun out of the way. As she stared at the reflection looking back at her, she couldn't help but notice that there was a similar resemblance to her mother Sophia when she was that age. Alexa specifically remembered a black and white photograph of her mother, that used to hang in a picture frame in their old house. In the photograph Sophia's hair was long, straight and blonde which seemed almost identical to how Alexa's was now, as she peered back to the memory in her mind's eye. There was a knock on Alexa's door and then Frau Klauss entered her room.

"You look very pretty Alexa."

"Thank you."

Frau Klauss had a folded over, brown paper bag in her hand and handed it to Alexa.

"Here open this and put these on, then come downstairs," she said, then exited the room.

Alexa took the bag, opened it and reached her hand inside. To her complete and utter surprise, she pulled out a pair of shoes. But these were not just any pair of shoes, these were the very same pair of brand new royal blue shoes which she had arrived in four years earlier. The very shoes which she had been shopping for with her mother in Poland that fateful day in the town square. The same shoes she was taken away in. The shoes that she had arrived at the Klauss's home in but had never seen again since that first night until now. The only

96

shoes that Alexa was given to wear at the Klauss's were the big restrictive wooden clogs and it became clear to her what the reason for that was as time went on. All of the captured young foreign girls forced to work in the farmhouses locally, were all made to wear them so as to deter any attempts to escape. Running away wouldn't be a wise choice on foot in large clogs being that they were so uncomfortable. Definitely not a shoe for gaining speed or distance in. However, none of that mattered now to Alexa, she had her shoes back and a wave of comfort and overwhelming emotion flooded over her. She quickly took her feet out of the ugly clogs and one by one slipped on her own pretty royal blue shoes. To her amazement, they still fit her feet but only just. There was no extra room left to grow. Her mother had chosen the size wisely that day in the shoe shop, when she said that it would be better to allow Alexa's feet a little room to grow. Alexa had to loosen the straps of the silver buckle two holes lower down, so that they weren't as tight on her, and then she could get away with wearing the shoes just and no more. But she didn't care that they were snug on her. As she looked down at them on her feet, they were the perfect complement to go with her blue dress and they were still in brand new condition. For the first time in four years, the young girl felt attractive and comfortable in her own shoes. She closed her bedroom door behind her and walked downstairs with a spring in her step and joy in her heart.

In the courtyard were a few parked cars already and more were making their way up the driveway. The lights in the barn were lit and music was playing on a record player housed in a stand-alone wooden console, which was positioned against a wall in the middle of the barn. Herr Klauss was welcoming his friends and colleagues as they arrived at the party and told Alexa to take the coats from their guests and hang them up. Junior officers were placed in charge of the music and also of the serving of drinks for everyone. The food was laid out for all to freely help themselves in a buffet style and the party was underway. Herr Klauss was the first to take to the dance floor, as he took his wife's hand leading her in a waltz. There erupted a round of applause and gradually some other married couples joined them on the dance floor getting the party off to a fine start. Eva and Elizabeth arrived, and Alexa made her way over to greet them. They were both in pretty dresses also and it was the first time that they all looked like normal attractive young females, freely enjoying life without the burden and yoke of forced labor around their necks.

Frau Klauss had allowed her two older children, Anna and Richard, to say hello to their guests and spend half an hour at the party. But the agreement was that they then had to go upstairs to their bedrooms afterwards to join Rudy who was already tucked up in bed. The children were reluctant to leave but Alexa led them out of the barn and into the main house where she got them ready and settled for bed. After about twenty minutes, Alexa returned to the party where most all of the guests had now arrived and were enjoying their evening together. Both Eva and Elizabeth were up dancing with two young handsome soldiers in their smart uniforms. Alexa looked on and seemed quite happy for the attention her friends were getting. There was a mix of single German soldiers at the party and several of them had also selected a dance partner from the young attractive foreign and German girls who were there. The soldiers seemed quite interested in their dance partners and were visibly enjoying having a pretty young female close in their arms. Once the music had ended, the girls began to make their way from the dance floor back to their seats, but the soldiers pulled them back for another dance. Both Eva and Elizabeth appeared to be enjoying the male attention that they were receiving however, there was also an air of unease about the situation. They were, after all, dancing with German soldiers, the very people who had ripped them away from their homes and families, from the lives that they had once lived. They were responsible for robbing them of their freedom and forcing them to work as unpaid slave girls. However, even with that knowledge, the young girls were both still rather enamored and quite swept away with all the interest and male attention being shown towards them. Being asked to dance by the handsome soldiers, after being treated and regarded as nothing, as less than a second-class citizen for so long, gave them a feeling of being special, of being worthy of not only the attention of a man but of the attention of a German man and a soldier no less.

The girls left the dance floor when the music ended and headed back over to their seats where they had been sitting before their dance. Alexa was now there sitting and had enjoyed watching her friends happily glide across the dance floor with the young men. Both girls were giddy with excitement and, as young girls do, they quickly shared their thoughts and feelings about their dance partners. They commented as to who was the most handsome and who held whom the closest. The soldiers had returned to their seats across the room, where they were sitting with their fellow soldiers and were also sharing comments about the girls with each other over a few steins of beer. However, their eyes shifted from their two dance partners, onto someone else who had caught their attention. One of the other soldiers jumped up to his feet making his way over to where the three girls were sitting together, then suddenly his two friends who had danced with Elizabeth and Eva, hurried up to join him. Eva turned to her friends and said, "Here come the good-looking soldiers again and look, there's one for you too Alexa!"

Alexa looked up and, as the three soldiers arrived at her seat, she became suddenly aware that the soldiers were directing their attention completely at her. The soldiers all had large flirtatious smiles on their faces and couldn't seem to take their eyes off Alexa. The first soldier approached Alexa and asked, "Would you like to dance with me?"

Next the soldier who had danced with Elizabeth said, "No don't dance with him, dance with me!"

The excited smile quickly disappeared from Elizabeth's face, who now wore a puzzled expression showing visible signs of disappointment.

"He can't dance," voiced the soldier who had been dancing with Eva, "Don't waste your time with him, come and dance with me."

Then just like Elizabeth, Eva's mood changed as she showed signs of displeasure at what she was hearing. Alexa could sense and clearly see that her two friends were getting upset and angered by the attention which she alone was receiving. So, she politely thanked the soldiers for their dance invitations and turned them down.

"I'll dance with you." Elizabeth said to the soldier with whom she had already danced with. But he rather abruptly declined her offer and once again asked Alexa onto the floor. Alexa was now feeling extremely uncomfortable and really didn't want to dance with any of them, so she stood up, declined once again and excused herself from the group. The soldier who had first asked her to dance, forcefully took hold of her hand as she attempted to walk away, pulling her close to him trying to hold her in a waltz position, but Alexa tried to break free. Then he became a little more forceful and using more strength, he wrapped his left arm around her waist firmly taking hold of her right hand, pulling her in close to his chest and began waltzing with her to the melody of the music. Alexa was overpowered and realized that it would be better for everyone there if she just went along with him, so she stopped fighting it and followed his lead across the dance floor. The other two soldiers took Eva and Elizabeth back onto the dance floor but, as they danced with them, it was blatantly obvious that their eyes were fixed on Alexa. Once the music ended and Alexa was free from the soldier's grip, she swiftly moved out of the barn, across the courtyard and ran into the farmhouse where she closed the door behind her and headed straight upstairs to check on the children. She used that as her convenient excuse and stayed there for the remainder of the evening. Her absence was noticed by the three soldiers who eagerly waited and anticipated her return, only to be disappointed. However, Alexa's friends were well aware that she had left the party. But, on the other hand, they were very pleased as it meant that they would get the full attention of their soldiers and dance partners again for the rest of the evening.

Alexa had shown wisdom in her decision. Sensing that her two girlfriends were getting upset by all the attention that she was receiving, she had deliberately declined the advances of the German soldiers so as not to anger Eva and Elizabeth. Her lasting friendships with the girls were far more important to her than any short-term physical interest that the young men might have had in her. For her the best option had been to remove herself from the situation so as to not upset her friends further. This also meant that she would avoid any further uncomfortable and awkward situations. Alexa went to her room and took off the pretty dress, hung it up in her wardrobe, then she put her work clothes back on and tied up her hair gathering it in a bun. However, she couldn't bring herself to take off her blue shoes, so she kept them on. As the clock approached midnight, Alexa knew that she would still be required to clear up and remove the leftover food from the tables, so she headed downstairs and back over to the party.

The music had finally ended, and some of the invited guests had already started to leave. Next to an armored car, Eva and Elizabeth were talking and laughing with the soldiers whom they had danced with and were getting pretty close with them. Or rather, the soldiers were getting up close to them. Alexa began the clear up and collected the food that could be saved, to store away in the kitchen. The party had been a great success and the Klauss's were very happy with the event's turnout. From then on, they made the dances at their farm a regular thing every month. And every month Alexa kept her wits about her and excused herself early on and at certain points throughout the evening with various excuses as a rule, so as not to be compromised, or upset any of the other girls there.

CHAPTER -9-

The war had roared on in Europe unmercifully for almost six years at the power-hungry hands of the German army, under Hitler's brutal and inhumane command. Millions of Jews from many countries had been murdered as part of the Fuhrer's final solution and along with those victims, were also many European non-Jewish prisoners who were captured for simply being in the wrong place at the wrong time or having the wrong political, religious or sexual preferences. It had been a particularly cruel and evil war, full of much violence and devastating destruction and as the Allied troops from Russia, Britain, France, America and other countries finally came closer to bringing an end to the German tyrant's reign of terror, there was much movement going on.

Now aged eighteen, Alexa had spent the previous five years forced to work in the farmhouse of the Klauss's as their unpaid slave attending to all of their families' needs. Although this was not of her free will or choice and considering that Herr Klauss was a Gestapo officer, Alexa had actually been more fortunate than some of the other young Christian girls who had also been taken captive. She had never been sexually or physically abused, nor was she ever beaten by the Klauss's, which was not something that could be said by many of the girls in similar circumstances. Early on when Alexa had first arrived at the Klauss's farmhouse, Fredrick's cousin Edgar the

Priest had reminded them that they were baptized Christians. That they had a Christian duty as good baptized Catholics to take care of Alexa. That she was in fact an orphan with no mother, or father, or family of her own to care for her and so it was their responsibility to make sure that no harm came to her under their roof, or on their watch. Edgar's reminder was effective and stayed with the Klauss's, while they were Alexa's keepers.

After the first year of Alexa's enforced labor, the family had grown rather fond of her and had given her some privileges, like being allowed to eat with them and the children at their table on the weekends and during the celebrations of various holidays. They had even given her small presents at Christmas time. Of course, this was by no means where she wanted to be and not a day went by when she didn't think of where her mother and little sister were and when she might be reunited with them once again on her return to Poland. She kept her faith and hope alive that the day would eventually arrive. She continued to recite her prayer of Psalm 91 which she could now say in perfect German. Anyone meeting Alexa for the first time would easily have been convinced that she was actually a natural born German citizen. She spoke German fluently and along with her beautiful appearance, blue eyes and lovely long blonde hair, she looked the part too.

In the final months of the Second World War, there were many bombing campaigns across Germany as certain targets were hit and the Allies tried to take out as many of the main German army positions as possible. Of course, there were many stray bombs as well and inevitably many innocent Germans were caught up in and killed in the crossfire. Many properties were destroyed, and buildings leveled in the quest to regain power.

One cold day in early December of 1944, Herr Klauss and his wife called Alexa into his office. Alexa had never been permitted to enter his office before in all of her time at the farmhouse, as Herr Klauss had always kept the door locked when he wasn't in it. It was the one room in the house that Alexa had never been allowed to clean, and she never knew why. As she stepped into the room she looked around, but there didn't seem to be anything unusual about it that warranted it being kept under lock and key all of the time. There was some matching wooden furniture, a desk, a bureau, bookshelves with a large collection of books and a black leather chair. Hanging on the walls were an assortment of paintings. Alexa figured that there must be a very important matter to be discussed for her to be invited into the Herr Klauss's study. However, she could never have guessed the words which were about to be spoken to her. With his wife standing behind him, Herr Klauss sat at his desk in his uniform and in a very serious voice said.

"Alexa, the war is ending, and we are giving you back your freedom!"

Alexa couldn't believe her ears! She heard the words, but she couldn't quite take them in. She looked at the Klauss's with a puzzled expression on her face and said nothing.

"Did you hear me Alexa? Did you understand what I just said to you?"

"Yes, I think so."

"The war is almost over, and you can go home now!"

Alexa opened her mouth and out came the words, "But I don't know the way. I don't remember how to get back to my home."

Both the husband and wife looked at each other for a few moments in silence, then Herr Klauss addressed Alexa again.

"Don't worry, we will help you to get back to your home. I have arranged for some fake German papers for you to use so that you can travel within the country as a German citizen. If anyone asks, you are a German. Once you cross over the border to Poland of course, you can dispose of them." He opened his desk drawer and pulled out the documents he was referring to then showed them to Alexa. She took them in her hand and examined them still in disbelief.

"Thank you."

Frau Klauss moved around the desk and took a look at them, then she handed them back to her husband who placed them back into his drawer.

"You will leave on Friday afternoon!" Herr Klauss announced, "I will buy you a train ticket tomorrow towards Berlin and then I'll tell you all the pertinent information that you'll need to know for your journey."

It was already Wednesday evening and Alexa was suddenly filled with great excitement at the realization that so soon now, she would actually be making her way home and was facing the prospect of finally being reunited with her mother and sister again after so long. Freedom was finally within her reach. The day that she had hoped for and dreamt of for five years was so very near to her now and consumed her every waking moment, her every thought. Alexa still had chores to attend to, but they now seemed so much lighter to her since the knowledge that her captivity was soon coming to an end and her release was in sight. This made everything seem less burdensome. She could almost taste her freedom and it was sweet.

Throughout the evening and into the early hours of Thursday morning, there were many bombing campaigns that rumbled loudly through the cities and towns. Dresden and Leipzig were almost completely annihilated in the Allied attacks. Meanwhile through Gestapo intelligence, the word had gotten out and spread, so, many officers took to removing records of their crimes and attempted to destroy all incriminating evidence of their pillaging. Frankfurt was another Center of Nazi activity which was heavily targeted by Allied bombing campaigns. Hitler's art collection was nearing completion, but there were still some masterpieces on 'The List' which had escaped the reach of the Gestapo. Very late that night two army trucks had arrived at Herr Klauss's farmhouse and in the dark cover of night, some accompanying soldiers took to emptying their contents into the smaller of the two barns. There were various crates and wooden boxes of different sizes. The larger ones went into the barn and the smaller ones were stacked carefully and placed next to them. Finally, after all the crates were stored in the barn, two soldiers carried three smaller numbered wooden crates into Herr Klauss's office. He held a leather-bound notebook in his hand and seemed to be checking off all the items that corresponded to numbers on his list as they were brought to him. Once the task at hand was completed, the two empty trucks relieved of their precious cargo, left the farmhouse, but not before Herr Klauss handed a black leather briefcase full of German marks to one of the soldiers taking the lead. The soldiers climbed into their empty trucks, started up their engines and drove off down the long driveway and turned out onto the road away from the Klauss's farmhouse.

Herr Klauss locked up the barn and then disappeared into his office, locking its door securely behind him. There before him, in his own office, lay his heart's desire. He now had in his possession, some of his ultimate masterpieces. Three of his most favorite works of art were now finally his. He had saved a special bottle of the most expensive and rarest red wine, especially for this precise day. An 1869 'Chateau Lafite'. He carefully opened the bottle and gently popped the cork, then left it to breathe. Next, he took a chisel and carefully began prying open the lid of the wooden crates which he had directed to be placed in his office. These were the ones that he had personally bought with his briefcase full of German marks. These were now his, separated from the many other listed paintings in the barn. The barn ones were all still listed and accounted for and even had documentation as to where they had been moved to for safe storage that night. But the three stolen paintings that Herr Klauss had paid for, had been listed as missing in action, destroyed or burned and all trace of them had gone cold before leaving the Frankfurt office. He eased the lid off from one of the wooden crates slowly and to his sheer delight inside sat one of his most favorite paintings. He carefully placed it onto an empty easel which he had set up and, after centering it in place, he stepped back. He walked around his desk and sat down in his black leather chair. He reached for the priceless bottle of wine and poured out a generous measure into one of his finest crystal glasses. He breathed in the aroma as he swirled the rich red liquid around inside of the glass, then finally took a sip of his priceless matured wine and drank in the vision that lay before him. *'It's magnificent!'* He thought, *'and it's mine!'* Finally, after an hour he got up from his desk and began opening the two other crates to reveal the other two wonderful masterpieces which he had paid for, by dishonest means. Even long after daylight had broken, he remained in his office with his treasure of three priceless paintings and his bottle of 'Chateau Lefite'.

* * *

It was now Thursday, and Alexa was eager to get her day's chores completed. She got the three Klauss children ready and off to school, then prepared the day's food for the household. Herr Klauss left the farmhouse in his car at 2 pm and was gone for several hours. Frau Klauss found Alexa in the kitchen and told her to come through into the lounge with her.

"Here is a small suitcase that you can use for your journey home. There is no need to take everything you have, just enough for an overnight stay. That way you won't attract too much attention to yourself." Frau Klauss told her.

"Okay, thank you Frau Klauss, I will do just as you say."

Alexa didn't actually have a lot of possessions to her name. She had never received a wage for any of her hard work, so it wasn't as if she had ever been able to buy things she liked. She didn't even know what she liked. She very rarely left the Klauss's farmhouse, so she never really had the opportunity either. All she had, was what she had been given. But the few things that she did have, she had taken good care of and valued them. She had a few outfits mainly for working in and one which was smart and dressy which she'd wear on special occasions only, along with a pretty dress for the dances. Since the night of the first dance at the Klauss's she was allowed to keep a hold of her blue shoes and these she treasured very much, even though they didn't fit her anymore. They were more of a comfort item which she associated with her mother. She had her Sunday shoes from Alice. She had also been given a German Bible by the Klauss's one Christmas which she read often and cherished very much. Beyond that she had a hairbrush, some bows, a few hair combs and a scarf. Not much to show for the life of a young eighteen-year old female. The only good thing was that it made her small suitcase easier to pack.

Frau Klauss then went on to instruct Alexa not to tell the children that she would be leaving, saying that it was something that she would rather tell them. Alexa agreed, but inside felt rather sad about it as she had grown very close to the children over her five years caring for them. But it wasn't something she was going to argue about. Her main concern was to return back home to her own family. That was her priority now.

Herr Klauss returned home just after dark and while Frau Klauss kept the children busy upstairs, he called Alexa into the dining room. "Alexa, I have your train ticket. You will leave on the 1 pm train to Berlin, I bought you a first-class seat in the first carriage. It's important that you get on carriage 'A' and your seat is number 18. 'A18' Do you understand?" Herr Klauss asked.

"Yes, Herr Klauss I understand A18," she answered while thinking it was easy to remember, A for Alexa and 18 was her age.

"Good. Speak only if someone speaks to you. Answer only in German and keep it short. Don't give too much information. If anyone asks, stick to the story that you are traveling to visit your sick aunt for the weekend." He waited for her to reply.

"Yes Herr Klauss, I understand."

"You will be on the train for just over five hours. Then you will get off at the Potsdam crossing which is just before Berlin where you will take the road towards the left. You will then need to walk for another five hours leaving the roadway, going off through the woods on foot instead, until you reach the town of Kreuzberg. There you will find a convent where you will stay for one or two nights. They are expecting you." Herr Klauss walked over to his drinks cabinet and poured himself a large brandy into a crystal glass. He raised it to his mouth and took a large sip.

"From there you will then need to walk or find transportation towards Ahrensfelde. After that you can use the money that I'm giving you to buy a bus or train ticket to get from there to make the connection to travel to your home town of Lublin, where you will hopefully find your home and your family waiting for you." After he had finished speaking, he took another large sip of his brandy.

"I have written down all the instructions and directions for your journey on these pieces of paper. You must memorize them and then throw away the papers before you leave here tomorrow. Throw them into the fire in the morning. Don't take the papers with you, understand?"

"Yes, Herr Klauss I understand, I will memorize them tonight. Thank you."

He then handed her the papers with all the directions written down on them and her new German identity papers.

"I will give you your train ticket to Berlin and the money tomorrow. Leave your packed suitcase in the wardrobe in your bedroom well out of sight. Don't let the children see it."

"Yes, Sir I will do exactly as you have told me and thank you for letting me go home."

Herr Klauss took one final large gulp and finished his brandy then looked at Alexa and said, "You have always been a hard worker and have taken good care of my home and my family. You have earned your freedom. Be ready to leave at 12:30 pm tomorrow. My cousin Edgar the priest will drive you to the station in my car." He then turned and headed out of the dining room door, disappearing off into the privacy of his office.

Alexa put the papers which Herr Klauss had given her safely into the pocket of her apron out of sight, then headed upstairs to run baths for Rudy and Anna. Richard was almost fifteen-years old now and ran his own bath when he wanted before going to bed. Alexa knew it was her last evening with the family and it brought her mixed emotions. She tried to act as normal as possible with the children. It was something that she had mastered well over the past five years since she was taken - the art of masking her true feelings. However, she was still human and felt very much from her heart. She knew that she'd miss the family but not the laborious never-ending chores along with the hard work of looking after all their demanding needs. Finally, her chores were done for her last evening with the Klauss's. She cleaned up the kitchen, turned off the lights, then headed upstairs to bed. She closed her bedroom door quietly and tightly behind her. In the bottom of her wardrobe was the small black suitcase which Frau Klauss had given her. Alexa began selecting the few items that she would take with her on her journey. First into the bag were her royal blue shoes which she placed at the bottom. Even though they didn't fit her anymore, they were of great sentimental value to her and, apart from her grandmother's silver cross necklace, were the only things she had from her past. She wanted to show her mother how well she had taken care of them for all those years, once they were reunited. It didn't take her long to pack the case with her few possessions - her Bible, a pair of pajamas, a change of clothes, her hair brush, some clean socks and underwear. Then she closed the suitcase and placed it back in the bottom of her wardrobe. She hung the good outfit that she would wear on one hanger inside of the wardrobe, ready to be worn before she left for the train station in the afternoon. Finally, she climbed into bed taking the white pieces of paper that Herr Klauss had given her with the travel instructions on for her to memorize and then began reading them intently, over and over again until she knew them off by heart. She then recited her prayer of Psalm 91 emphasizing certain parts with deeper feeling, tailoring it to fit her needs.

'You are my fortress, my refuge, my God in whom I trust. Rescue me from the bird catcher. Shield me with your mighty wings. Let me not be afraid and let evil not come near me, nor disaster befall me. I beg of you to protect me dear God almighty, on my journey home. Amen'

Alexa anticipated her great day of release ahead with excitement, then she finally fell asleep.

CHAPTER -10-

The cold winter's morning broke through the cover of darkness with the birds singing their morning welcome. Alexa was wide awake before 4 am on that, her very last day serving the Klauss's. She made her way downstairs and began her chores just as she had done every morning for the past five years. But this morning was different, her approach and attitude were far more joyous than ever before. She recognized the finality of the tasks before her - the last time she would milk the large smelly cows, collect the hens' eggs, clean out the mucky barns and stables, shovel the manure. No more would she have to do all the laundry for the household, clean the farmhouse, work the land nor cook the family's meals. She now thought only towards the joy she would have of being able to cook for her own mother and sister and of how proud they would be of her, at tasting her delicious dishes.

The morning eventually gave way to sunrise, but it was a red sky that the clouds highlighted with a shepherd's fore-warning of unpleasant weather conditions on the horizon. There had already been a significant amount of snowfall early on during that month of December and the signs of it were still visible on the ground. Alexa made her way over to the barn where the animals were to begin milking the cows. She went over to Bloomshen first and reached her hand up to gently stroke her head.

"I'm going to miss you my friend, today I leave this place and won't ever see you again." Alexa said in Polish, "Herr Klauss is letting me go home. I'm finally going back to Poland to find my Mama and sister."

A tear trickled down from Bloomshen's eye as she continued to stare at Alexa, as if the cow really understood what she was being told.

"You've been my best friend and my confidant through these difficult years, and I'll never forget you." Alexa finished milking the other cows then gave a final farewell to Bloomshen as she wiped a lone tear from her own eye.

The hours passed by quickly for Alexa, as she kept her mind thinking about her journey home. After breakfast Herr Klauss took the children off to school and that was the last Alexa saw of them. She had wanted to hug them goodbye, but she knew that she mustn't let the children know of her planned departure, so she refrained and watched them leave from behind a curtain of one of the windows, as tears brimmed in her eyes. She cleared up the remains of breakfast, made the beds in the household, did some loads of laundry and prepared dinner for the family. Alexa prepared a few sandwiches for herself and wrapped a slice of cake in some paper to take with her on her journey. Then, at noon, she went upstairs to her bedroom for the last time and dressed in her good clothes which were neatly hanging inside her wardrobe. She put on a warm woolen sweater and brushed her long blonde hair then, took one last look in her mirror.

"It's time! I'm coming home Mama!" Alexa said out loud, then she turned and walked out of the bedroom for the last time. When she got downstairs, Frau Klauss called her into the dining room. Alexa went to her and to her surprise, the woman told her to take off her clogs.

"We can't have you traveling in those, it would be too obvious and give your identity away. Here put these on, I think they will fit you."

Alexa removed the heavy wooden clogs that she was wearing and tried on the black shoes that Frau Klauss handed to her. They were not brand-new shoes, but they were in fairly decent shape with only a little wear and tear. They seemed to fit her quite well and they completed her look - that of being a normal young German woman. Alexa was so relieved to be freed from the burdensome clogs which had been like shackles to her. It felt very liberating wearing normal shoes on her feet which to her, were like new shoes. She thought of the parallel of the first time she had gotten her new pair of shoes with her mother in Lublin - that dreadful day which had led to the long journey away from home and a whole new nightmare chapter in her life. This pair of shoes would take her on another long journey, but this time back home again and begin a brand-new chapter, with her family being reunited. Alexa was filled with excitement but also with much anxiety and fear too. Then she thought of the wonderful gift of the new handmade pair of shoes that Alice had given her two years earlier in Luxembourg, even though they didn't fit her anymore. That had been a wonderful unexpected surprise and theirs had become a beautiful friendship. Alexa was sad that she wasn't able to tell Alice in person that she was finally going home. But she couldn't say goodbye to her, there wasn't time, she had to go, and Sunday was two whole days away. Optimistically, she reasoned that these shoes from Frau Klauss could lead her on a positive journey, this time with a happy outcome.

Herr Klauss came out of his office at 12:30 pm with Edgar and told Alexa that it was time to go.

"I'm ready sir!" Alexa said as he stood in front of her.

"You'll not last very long out there without a warm coat and especially not with one that has a letter 'P' on it! Here take this one," Frau Klauss said and handed Alexa a long black woolen coat to put on. "There are a pair of gloves in the pocket, you'll need them, it'll be cold on your journey."

Alexa put on the coat and buttoned it up. Frau Klauss then wrapped a woolen scarf around her neck and said,

"Now you are all ready to go home, Alexa."

Alexa leaned forward and hugged the woman, thanking her for the kind gestures and out of the pure gratitude which she now felt over them willingly freeing her. Alexa knew that they didn't have to do that.

"Okay, now you must leave." Herr Klauss announced and headed out of the door to his car, with Alexa and his cousin Edgar following behind him.

"Sit in the front seat."

Alexa picked up her suitcase, walked outside and got into the black Mercedes. With the door still opened, Herr Klauss turned towards her and handed her some German marks and her train ticket.

"Did you memorize all the instructions I gave you on the pieces of paper?"

"Yes Sir, I did and then I tore them up and threw them in the fire this morning."

"Good! Edgar will let you out of the car a few minutes walk from the station and you will go for the train by yourself and don't forget to sit in the first-class compartment, at seat A18!"

"Yes Sir, I will, I understand." Alexa confirmed.

Herr Klauss closed the car door and Alexa took one last look out of the window as the car drove off down the long driveway and out of the farm along the country roads. Alexa could taste her freedom and tried hard to control her emotions. The clock on the car's dashboard was just leaving 12:45 pm as Edgar pulled the car over on the roadside and stopped underneath the railway bridge. He instructed Alexa to get out with her suitcase and continue on foot towards the station, which she could see just off in the near distance.

"Your train is departing at 1 pm, so hurry along to the platform and remember to follow Herr Klauss's instructions exactly. I sincerely hope that you have a safe journey back home to your family Alexa. Now go and may God bless you child."

Alexa said thank you and closed the door. The car drove off and Alexa took a deep breath. Her first real breath of freedom. Now she belonged to no one. She quickly began walking along the road towards the small station and within a few minutes, she made her way onto the platform. The sky had become grey and it looked like more snow was on the way. There was a smartly dressed elderly man wearing a hat with his wife sitting next to him on a bench on the platform awaiting the arrival of the train, but no one else. Alexa sat down on another bench placing her suitcase on her lap as she waited. She stared blankly down onto the train tracks before her and at the cold hard steel rails which were firmly bolted down to hold the wooden sleepers in place. It made her think back to when she was first loaded into the boxcar in Poland and transported to Germany. Alexa vividly recalled being loaded into the wagon with the other youths, herded in like livestock for the long uncomfortable overnight journey to Dachau. At least this train journey was guaranteed to be a far more comfortable one, being that she had a first class ticket this time. She wondered where her mother was at that moment in time. If she had gotten moved out of Dachau, as she had been. Maybe she had managed to make her own way back home to Poland already and was waiting for her there. As Alexa's eyes followed the train tracks, she became aware of how the parallel lines of the two steel rails although separate, seemed to join and meet up again in the distance. She made her own parallel in her mind, of how she and her mother had been separated, but would again meet up further down the line.

On the station wall hung a large clock which showed the time as approaching 1 pm and just then, the faint sound of rumbling could be heard vibrating on the steel tracks, becoming louder as the train got closer. Then the sound of the train's whistle let out a double blast announcing its imminent arrival into the station, followed by the screeching sound of the brakes gradually slowing down the long and powerful train to a full stop.

The elderly couple got up from the bench and walked along the platform looking for their carriage. Alexa picked up her suitcase and headed over towards the first carriage which was marked 'A' for first class. She reached her hand up onto the door handle, pulling it down to open the train door. She climbed up the three steps then pulled the door firmly closed behind her. She turned to her right, took a few steps forward and approached the door marked 'A' leading into the first-class carriage. She turned the door handle and stepped inside.

As Alexa looked up, she became frozen with fear and was sure that the shockwaves shooting through her body would surely stop her heart. In a split second, her survival instinct kicked in and her brain engaged the well-trained skills set which she had developed, those of masking her true feelings and emotions to become the character she needed to be at any given time, for the situation she found herself in. Now she was indeed, in a situation.

Alexa closed the door behind her, then walked through into the carriage which was full of Gestapo officers and male German army soldiers, who occupied almost every seat. By now they had all seen her walk in through the door and were staring at her intently. Alexa looked at the seat numbers praying that hers was vacant and finally, she reached number '18' and found that it was. Number '17' had no one sitting in it but there was an army jacket and hat resting on it. Alexa slowly eased herself into seat number 'A18' and sat down, placing her suitcase on her lap in front of her and gave a general smile, but to no one person in particular.

"Good afternoon Fraulein," said one of the Gestapo officers sitting diagonally across from her.

"Good afternoon." Alexa replied in her best German accent with all the confidence that she could muster. She then turned her head with confidence and looked out of the nearby window. Inside she was stricken with panic and fear, but on the outside no one could tell. The station master blew his whistle from the platform waving his flag and the train slowly pulled off from the station. Snowflakes began to fall.

There were about thirty German soldiers and SS officers all together in the first-class carriage. Several of the soldiers were playing card games and gambling on the tables in front of them which they returned to almost immediately when the train started moving again. Others were reading and smoking, some chatting while drinking schnapps and beers, which they ordered from the small bar at the end of the carriage. However, there were still about ten or twelve of the men who continued to fix their stare on Alexa, which made her feel even more uneasy and very uncomfortable although she never showed it. Instead, she began saying her silent prayers and repeating her familiar Psalm 91 over and over again. Sometimes she would close her eyes too, which prevented her from having to make direct eye contact with any of the soldiers.

The door on the opposite side of the carriage opened and in walked the train conductor. He quickly became aware that there was now a female civilian in the compartment with all of the German soldiers and officers and immediately walked over to where Alexa was sitting.

"Let me see your ticket please!"

Alexa reached into her pocket and took out the train ticket that Herr Klauss had given her and handed it to the conductor. He took the ticket from her, looked at it then suddenly became enraged and began shouting at Alexa.

"What are you doing sitting in this seat? This is not a first-class ticket. You shouldn't be here! This is a first-class seat!"

"I'm so sorry Sir! The ticket was bought for me and I was told it was for first class! I'm so sorry!" Alexa tried to reason.

By now all of the soldiers were looking over towards the commotion between Alexa and the conductor who was now furious but seemed to have a valid point, as well as being concerned over his own job.

"You cannot stay here! You'll have to leave this carriage! Get up!" The conductor shouted at her.

Alexa's face turned red with embarrassment. She didn't know what to do next for the best. Just then, the Gestapo officer who was sitting diagonally across from Alexa, stood up and walked over to where they both were.

"What seems to be the problem here?" He asked the conductor, who was now showing signs of fear himself.

"My apologies Sir, but this woman should not be here in this compartment, she does not have a first-class ticket! I shall move her out of your way immediately."

"Tell me, how much will it cost for her ticket to become a first class one, so that she can continue to sit here in this seat?" Asked the Gestapo officer.

The conductor seemed puzzled at the question, but he was becoming filled with more fear himself over the ticket discrepancy as the seconds went by, as if he were to blame in some way.

"It would cost another eleven marks," the conductor answered.

At that, the officer reached into his rear pocket and pulled out his wallet. He took out eleven marks and handed them to the conductor.

"There's the additional money. Now give the pretty young lady a first-class ticket and apologize for shouting at her," ordered the officer.

The conductor took out a new first-class ticket which he handed to Alexa and said that he was sorry for shouting at her, while his own voice now quivered a little.

"Okay, now you can leave our carriage and don't come back here until we have left the train. Do you understand?"

"Yes Sir, I understand! I'm sorry Sir to have bothered you." He then turned and hurriedly left the carriage out of the same door that he had come through.

"I'm sorry that he was so rude to you Fraulein but now you can sit here for the rest of your journey," said the officer.

Alexa had thought that her cover was surely going to be blown but kept her composure.

"Thank you, Sir, that was very kind of you. I'm terribly sorry for the misunderstanding."

"Where are you traveling to?"

"I'm getting off at the stop just before Berlin Sir, at Potsdam. I'm going to visit my aunt for the weekend."

"Well, it should be about five more hours roughly until then," he informed her as he looked at his pocket watch. He smiled, then returned back to his seat.

Some of the other soldiers were still looking over in her direction, puzzled at why one of their senior officers had just paid the rest of the young lady's ticket to keep her in the same carriage with them. Some derogatory comments were made by some of the soldiers. She was after all a very beautiful young blonde woman, unaccompanied and alone in their midst. Alexa tried to figure out in her mind what had just happened. *Why had Herr Klauss given her an incorrect ticket? Why did the officer insist that she stay in first class? Why did he pay the rest of her ticket? What did it mean? Did she now owe him? Why were all these German soldiers staring at her? What were they going to do with her? Could they tell she was Polish?* All these thoughts spun round and round in her head until she thought she would go mad.

After an hour had passed, Alexa stood up and placed her suitcase onto her seat along with her gloves, excused herself and made her way to the small toilet which she had passed on her way into the carriage when she had first boarded the train. Several of the soldiers followed her with their eyes, then returned to their business at hand. She closed the toilet door behind her and locked it. *'Oh, dear God above, please give me the strength beyond what is normal to endure the rest of this journey and to make it off this train alive and in one piece. I beg of you, help me get home safely! Amen!'*

Alexa turned on the tap over the small sink and splashed some cold water onto her face. She rinsed off her clammy hands and dried them with the towel. She took some deep breaths and felt safe, alone in the privacy of the small space with the door locked. She didn't want to leave. She had been in the toilet for about fifteen minutes, but she knew that if she stayed there much longer, she would attract unnecessary attention from the soldiers. She flushed the toilet then straightened her hair in the mirror. She reluctantly unlocked the door and stepped out into the hallway, then confidently made her way back into the carriage and back to her seat. A few of the soldiers smiled at her while a few of them carried on their intense staring in her direction, while the rest drank schnapps and made her the brunt of their jokes.

When she sat back down, she avoided making eye contact with the soldiers again and stared out of the train window, looking at nothing in particular. The train moved at speed through the countryside and the trees nearest to the tracks sped by as a blur with their individual leaves and branches indistinguishable. The noise of the train hurrying along the tracks had an almost hypnotic sound and Alexa found herself lost in the rhythm. After a while she opened her bag and took out her Bible and began to read the book of Psalms from its beginning.

The train continued on its journey getting closer to its destination and it seemed as though the soldiers were no longer paying much attention to Alexa which made her feel a little more at ease. Of course, for as long as she was still alone in the carriage with all the German soldiers and Gestapo officers, anything could happen to her and of that fact she was all too aware. Some of the soldiers were readying and repacking their bags and loading their guns and pistols with ammunition, which brought home to Alexa just what a dangerous situation she really was in. If they even had the slightest suspicion or inclination of her true identity, that she was actually a released Polish slave trying to return home after five years of capture, she knew they'd shoot her or even worse. Alexa knew she had to hold it together for just a little bit longer.

The train blew its whistle as it was approaching the Potsdam crossing, the last stop before Berlin. This was where Alexa had been told to get off the train by Herr Klauss. She closed the book and placed her Bible back into her suitcase. Then she buttoned up her coat, tucked in her scarf and stood up from her seat. Most of the soldiers noticed her getting ready to leave the carriage and followed her with their eyes. Alexa walked along the carriage towards the door at the far end, then placed her hand on the handle to open it.

"Stop!" came the voice of the Gestapo officer who had been sitting diagonally across from her during the journey.

Alexa froze on the spot and slowly turned around to search out the voice. She could feel her legs shaking beneath her and was sure that she'd collapse out of fear. The brakes of the train were applied and began to screech, gradually slowing the train down and, as it jolted, Alexa had to steady herself on the back of one of the soldier's seats. She then looked up at the officer with hopelessness written across her face.

"You forgot one of your gloves. It's there on the seat," said the officer.

Alexa couldn't believe her ears at first but automatically began walking back towards her seat while one of the other soldiers picked up the glove and handed it to her.

"Thank you, Sir. Thank you very much indeed," she said. Then taking the glove, she turned and headed for the door once again then stepped down from the train onto the snow-covered ground below. There wasn't much of a station at Potsdam. It was more of a level crossing train stop without a platform.

The snow was coming down quite heavily and several of the officers and soldiers had stood up from their seats and moved towards the windows. Alexa could see them from the corner of her eye and began walking away in the opposite direction from the train. From behind her, she could hear the windows lower from the first-class carriage that she had just been in with all of the soldiers. She tried not to look back, but she thought to herself, '*...if I'm going to be shot, I won't be shot in the back of the head, I won't make it easy for them, they'll have to see my face and look me in the eye*s.' She looked back in defiance and sure enough, several of the officers were staring at her out of their open windows as she walked away. Alexa couldn't see any of them taking aim at her, so she continued putting one foot in front of the other and continued walking alongside the railway tracks towards the roadway.

'Dear God, please protect me!' She repeated over and over again to herself.

The train slowly began to pull off and Alexa took one last look back at the carriage. The soldiers still had her in their sights until the train picked up speed and finally disappeared out of view.

Alexa let out a deep breath of relief mixed with sheer disbelief. She had made it. She had survived the train ride, from right under the nose of all those German Nazi and Gestapo officers. Despite not even having the correct ticket, she had managed to convince them that she was a real German woman. A German citizen. She immediately became convinced that God had heard her prayers, and in her mind, he had indeed answered it, by keeping her safe. She offered a sincere prayer of thanks and continued walking along the road until it met up with the forest.

CHAPTER -11-

The fresh new powdery snow continued to fall steadily which added to the accumulation of the older snow which already lay frozen on the ground beneath it. The time was approaching 6:30 pm and the winter's sky was already dark. Alexa had memorized the list of instructions that Herr Klauss had given her, but she couldn't help but wonder if he had got the next part wrong also, just as he had with the mistake over her first-class train ticket. However, having no other options available to her, Alexa followed the directions which she had been given and memorized in her head.

At the end of the road leading away from the Potsdam train crossing was an adjoining road. It led off to a main intersection, then veered to the right as it followed the edge of a deep forest and the line of the trees. Alexa had been instructed to go to the left, but she was also told not to walk on the roadway. Instead, the pages of notes had said that she was to walk into the woods for about three quarters of a mile so that she could still see the roadway through the trees, but that the forest would hide her from the traffic traveling along the road. The roadway didn't seem very busy to her, but she trusted that there must be a good reason for the instructions and headed off into the woodlands, away from the road's edge.

The terrain was very hard going on her feet. Not only was there the forest floor to deal with, full of uneven tree roots, sharp branches, jagged bushes and thick undergrowth, but it was covered and hidden under deep snow upon which it was hard to get a firm footing. It crunched and cracked under her feet. After she figured that she was far enough into the forest, Alexa began her long lonely walk, keeping an eye on the roadway through the trees.

The natural daylight was long gone, and the cloak of darkness made her journey all the more strenuous and arduous. The full moon above illuminated the sky. It poured down between the pine trees and lit some of the terrain ahead of her, as well as casting long dark shadows across the frozen forest floor. The tall bare birch trees looked silver in the moonlight and, having been stripped of their foliage, looked like tall lightening-rods to Alexa. After about an hour of painful walking in the freezing cold, she chose a large tree to sit against to take a much-needed rest. She opened her suitcase and first of all took out the extra pair of socks that she had packed and put them on, doubling them over the ones she already had on, pulling them as far up her legs as they would go. Next, she took out her pajama bottoms and climbed into them, tucking the legs down into her socks. Her scarf she loosened from around her neck and instead pulled it up over her head covering her blonde hair, then crossed the two ends under her chin and tied them at the back of her neck. She pulled up the collar of her coat and did up the very top button. She smiled to herself and thought how glad she was that no one could see how ridiculous she must have looked. After she had layered on some warmth and a little protection from the harsh freezing elements, Alexa reached into her suitcase and took out the sandwiches which she had made earlier and unwrapped them. Then she sat against the tree and began to eat a half. She couldn't see very well, with all traces of daylight long gone but as she looked through the trees in the direction of the roadway, she could see the distant headlights of army trucks and cars randomly coming and going in both directions along the roadway. She finished off the other half of the sandwich, then ate the sweet piece of cake that she had brought with her. She wished that she had brought something to drink with her also, as she felt a real thirst in her dry throat, but she had nothing to drink. Then Alexa had an idea. *'There's all this fresh snow around, I'll just have some of that'*, she thought and as cold as it was, it quenched her thirst as she took handfuls of fresh fallen snow and let it melt on her tongue inside of her mouth. She also thought that the aid of a tree branch as a walking stick would assist her in her journey and looking around the forest floor, she soon found the perfect one, which was just the right length for her height. After a fifteen-minute rest, Alexa gave both of her feet a good rub to warm up her circulation then climbed back into her shoes, closed up her suitcase and put her gloves back on to continue her strenuous walk through the night forest.

The night air was full of an array of familiar and unfamiliar sounds. In the far-off distance Alexa could hear the dull noise of explosions, as bombing raids by Allied forces targeted various prime targets in and around Berlin and other surrounding areas. Alexa could hear faintly the sound of engines and tanks as they drove along the roadway at the edge of the forest. Occasionally the hum of a bomber's engine could also be heard flying overhead. With every step that Alexa took, twigs and branches snapped under her feet along with the crunch of the frozen snow just below the newly fallen fresh powder. From high up in the trees the hoot of an owl could be heard echoing through the forest. Then another in reply from further away. The cries of crows and the various whistles of other birds made their presence known. Nature's wildlife, the creatures of the night were awake. Alexa suddenly wondered if there were wilder, more dangerous animals in the forest around her like foxes, wolves and bears. Her familiar prayer came to mind, especially the parts of Psalm 91 which petitioned for protection from the bird catcher and the snare of the fowler, from the terror by night and the pestilence that walks in darkness, for the foot striking against the stone, also from the maned lion and the snake under foot. She was quite sure that she didn't have to worry about any lions, but she couldn't have the same confidence that there were no bears. As she meditated and pondered on the phrases in the verses she knew so well, she gained comfort and had faith that she would be protected. However, walking in the dark through such harsh terrain for so long did cause Alexa some pain and her legs received cuts on them from brushing against the sharp branches and prickly thorns. After she had been trekking for over two more hours, she decided to take another break to tend to her wounds, rest a little and eat the other remaining sandwich. She found a tree with a low thick branch and sat down upon it, slipping off her shoes one by one to examine the damage. The shoes weren't holding up very well at all. There was a cut in the sole of the right shoe which was letting in cold water and soaking through to her sock. Her legs were very cold, almost frozen, and she could feel the sting of cuts as a few of her open wounds were exposed to the cold air. One cut in particular, on her left leg just above her ankle, seemed to be the worst. Alexa lifted up her pajama leg and could see the blood still seeping from it, so she took some fresh snow and rubbed it against her leg to clean it with, then took her cotton handkerchief and tied it tightly around it. She pulled down the trouser leg and tucked it back into her sock, then cleaned off her hands in the fresh snow. She took some more handfuls of fresh snow to quench her thirst, all the time shivering down to her very bones.

Alexa estimated that she must have been walking through the forest for about roughly four hours by that point and that she probably only had one more hour or so left to go until she could finally exit the woods and get back onto a road again. Her destination that evening was a convent on the outskirts of the small town of Kreunsberg. She had been told that they were expecting her there. Herr Klauss's instructions had said that after walking through the forest for five hours and following the line of the roadway, the trees would stop and there would appear a large opening like a field that she would have to walk across. Once she crossed the field, there would be another road in front of her which she would have to cross over and this time, she was to walk to the left which would take her in a Westerly direction for about ten minutes until she reached an intersection.

The snow finally stopped falling. She stood back up and continued walking for at least another hour. Finally, the trees stopped, and she could see the field that she was told to cross through. After reaching the roadway, she walked on it to the left continuing on for about ten minutes as she had been instructed to do. Suddenly she heard the dull sound of engines coming nearer and getting louder and could see some headlights off in the distance, so she threw her suitcase into the ditch and jumped down off the road laying as flat as she could, out of sight. A convoy of large SS military trucks drove by along the road just above where she was hiding. But soon they had passed by and the sound of their loud engines became a dull hum again, then disappeared off into the night. Alexa's heart was pounding, and the young girl's nerves were shattered. She threw her suitcase back up onto the roadway and climbed carefully out of the ditch. Wiping herself down, she composed herself then continued on along the roadway once again.

There was a full moon in the night sky which was clear, and Alexa appreciated it illuminating the road which lay before her. She could see in the distance that she was approaching the intersection. But she couldn't remember in which direction she was to go. With each step that she took, she tried harder and harder to recall which road she was instructed to take but the answer wasn't coming to her. The road was dark and deserted, there were no signs to read, no houses to enquire at, no people to ask, she was all alone and now she was lost. The intersection ahead of her had three options. She could either take the road to the left, go straight, or follow the road to the right. But only one of the options would lead her to the correct destination. Alexa stood looking at all of the three roads, but it was no use, she couldn't recall which one she was to take and besides, they all looked the same. The young girl was physically exhausted and felt totally alone and defeated but as always when feeling alone and fearful, she began to pray.

'Dear Almighty God above, please guide me with your wisdom as to which way I should go. To the left, or to the right? Please make me know the way. I'm so cold and so tired and I need your help to carry on. Please keep me safe. Amen!'

She looked up at the brilliant shining moon in the night sky and gazed at it just floating there, suspended upon nothing in the pitch of black night. As it shone down on her, a tear fell out of her eye and rolled down her cheek.

Just then, a voice from behind her asked, "Are you lost?"

Alexa immediately turned around and to her absolute surprise before her very eyes, stood an elderly gentleman with a walking stick, carrying a small cloth bag.

"Oh yes Sir, I am, I'm lost, and I don't remember which road I was supposed to take!" Alexa exclaimed.

"Well don't worry young girl, I'm sure I can help you. Where is it that you are trying to get to?"

"I'm trying to get to the St. Clemens Convent in Kreunsberg. They are expecting me."

"Aha, yes I know where that is and it's on the road that I am taking. We can walk together if you'd like?" Suggested the old man.

"Oh yes please Sir, that would be wonderful. Thank you ever so much," said Alexa, who was so relieved that she just wanted to hug the old man.

"Shall we go?" asked the man pointing his walking stick to the roadway on the right.

"Yes, and would you like me to carry your bag for you Sir?"

"That's very kind of you to offer, but no, you have your own load to carry and mine is not too heavy."

"Ok, if you're sure Sir,"

They began walking along the road together and strangely, the old man seemed to have such a calming effect on Alexa so that after a short while, she could no longer feel the pain in her feet and legs nor the cold temperatures of the freezing night.

"My name is Alexa."

"Well, I'm very pleased to meet you Alexa, it's nice to have some company on my walk."

"And I'm so very pleased to meet you Sir, I don't know what I would have done if you hadn't have come along when you did."

"Well I'm glad I could be of some assistance, it's not very often that an old man like me is of any use to young people these days it seems."

"Oh, I'm sure you know many useful things Sir and I'm ever so grateful that you know the way and are able to help me tonight," reassured Alexa.

After they had been walking for about fifteen minutes, the old man suggested that they take a short rest on a nearby log. The old man sat down and reached into his bag and from it, he first pulled out a bar of chocolate.

"Do you like chocolate Alexa?"

"Oh yes Sir, I do."

"Good, let's have some then. I find that it always gives me a little boost of energy and it will help us on our journey."

"That's a great idea Sir, thank you very much," said Alexa as the old man opened the chocolate bar and gave her some. She took a square and popped it in her mouth, letting it slowly melt as it sat on her tongue. It was delicious. Alexa hadn't had chocolate in a very long time and sat in silence as she ate it.

"Here, have some more."

Alexa took another square and again said thank you. Next the old man reached down into his bag and he pulled out a bottle of fresh milk, he took off the lid and handed it to Alexa.

"Would you like some Alexa?"

"Oh yes, I would, if you are sure Sir."

"Yes, I'm sure, go ahead drink."

Alexa took a nice refreshing drink of the milk, which went great with the flavor of the chocolate, but she was careful not to take too much and handed it back to the old man.

"Thank you, Sir for sharing with me."

The old man took the bottle of milk and had a drink himself, put the lid back on and put it back in his bag. Then he reached for the chocolate once again and with a big smile on his face, he told Alexa to take a whole row of squares this time. Alexa snapped off a row of chocolate and gave him a great big smile back. They both sat and finished their chocolate and then the old man put the remains of the bar back in his bag. Alexa put her arm around the old man and said thank you for his kindness towards her. Then they both stood up, picked up their bags and carried on with their journey along the road. It had been the most ideal little refreshing rest for them both and Alexa was still savoring the taste of the chocolate, long after she had swallowed it and it was gone from her mouth.

They continued on walking along a few more roads, with the old man leading the way and after a half hour of walking they came to another intersection. The old man stopped and turned to face Alexa.

"Okay this is as far as we go together. I'm taking the road to the left, but you are going to go along the road continuing straight. You will carry on going straight for about three kilometers, then when you cross over the bridge you will go left and pass through a small village with a row of houses. Once you pass by the last house, you will see a sign that says St. Clemens Church and Convent. You will turn right again and walk up the long driveway and then you will be there," instructed the old man.

"Ok, thank you so much for all your help, your generosity and your company too," said Alexa as she leaned forward and gave him a big hug.

"You're welcome child. It was a pleasure walking with you. God bless you," he said, then walked off towards the roadway on the left.

Alexa had felt so safe walking with the old man and had enjoyed his company immensely, but now she was alone again. She stopped walking and turned around to look at the old man once more, but there was no sign of him. He was gone from sight and her eyes couldn't find him anywhere. Alexa thought it was very strange as it had only been about ten seconds since they had parted, and the old man hadn't walked at great speed when he was with her. Nonetheless, the old man was gone.

'I didn't even ask his name.' She thought to herself. *'Did I imagine him? Was he an angel?'*

Alexa continued walking straight along the road just as the old man had instructed her to. The freezing winter's night seemed darker and so much colder now that she was traveling alone again. The snow had begun falling heavily once more from out of nowhere and quickly became blizzard-like. After a few kilometers, the houses came into view which the old man had mentioned but by now the young girl was exhausted beyond tired as well as frozen through to her bones. She felt as though she couldn't go on any further and so decided that her best option would be to knock on the doors of the houses to see if anyone would kindly let her rest there for the night. She hadn't yet mustered up the needed courage to approach the first house so, as she continued closer to the second house, she told herself to be brave. The house was dark with no visible lights on inside, but she approached it and knocked on the front door anyway, while pondering to herself what there was to be afraid of? But there was no answer at the door. So, Alexa continued to the third house, as the wind picked up blowing and swirling the snow around her.

Finally, at the third house there were signs of life and the downstairs windows had light shining through the curtains. Alexa made her way down the snow-covered garden path and began knocking on the door. After a moment or two, the door was opened revealing a short German woman roughly in her mid-fifties. Alexa wasted no time introducing herself and explaining her predicament.

"Good evening, I'm sorry to bother you so late but I'm journeying to visit my old sick aunt and I'm still far away from her house. It's so late at night now, I'm cold and tired and just wondered, if I might be able to rest somewhere for a little while?" Alexa petitioned.

The woman seemed very sympathetic and motioned for the girl to step into her small hallway. "It's ok dear, come in out of the snow," she said.

Just then the woman's husband appeared, to see what was going on at such a late hour of the night. As Alexa looked up at the tall dark-haired man, just behind his back she could see a wooden coat rack fitted against the wall. Her heart seemed to stop on the spot while she subtly tried hard to catch her breath and disguise both her shock and her horror. There hanging on the coat rack, was the decorated uniformed jacket of a German special police officer along with his leather gun belt. Just above on the shelf, sat his police hat decorated with the eagle emblem. Alexa couldn't believe it. Of all the houses along the row that she could have chosen to try, she had picked the very one where a German special police officer lived. She had willingly walked straight to his door. He hadn't even had to find her. She thought she would die. She thought this was her end.

"You see? Look what this war has done! Look at this poor young German girl trying to get to visit her sick aunt. It's late at night, it's freezing outside, and bombs are dropping everywhere," said the woman to her husband, "what is the point of this war?"

"The war is the war!" He replied as he waved his hand in the air in front of his wife, then uninterestedly, he quickly disappeared back into the room out of which he had come from.

The woman invited Alexa to come into the main house and sat her in front of the warm log fire in her living room. Then she hurried into the kitchen and made some hot cocoa and some sandwiches for the girl to eat, along with a slice of home-made cake and placed them on the table for her. As hungry as Alexa was, she couldn't eat anything. Her heart was still in her mouth and her nerves were shot over the identity of the woman's husband. The woman could see that Alexa wasn't eating anything and put it down to her being tired, so she encouraged her to drink up her hot drink and showed her to a downstairs bedroom where she could comfortably sleep for the night in a clean warm bed. Alexa agreed but as she sat in the bedroom worrying, her discomfort would not subside. She lay in the bed but could not sleep as hard as she tried. Alexa began to pray as was her routine.

'Dear God, almighty, here I am in the trap once again, with the bird catcher just outside of my door, this time by my own hand. But this time no one will know my fate, how will I ever be found? Help me I pray...Amen!'

An hour went by with Alexa still wide awake and unable to relax. She heard a set of footsteps come down the stairs and go into the kitchen, then the noise of dishes clattering in the sink. Alexa straightened herself up and cautiously made her way through to the kitchen. Thankfully, it was the woman of the house whom she found there. Alexa began explaining to her that she just couldn't sleep, as she had to get to her sick aunt's house who was all alone awaiting her arrival. The woman tried to talk Alexa into staying until the next day but eventually listened to her reasons. She insisted that Alexa have one more hot drink before setting off again, then she wrapped up the sandwiches and cake for her to take away. Alexa thanked the woman for her kindness and hospitality then left the house. The snow had stopped falling and Alexa walked up the garden pathway, stepping back in her very own footsteps as she made her way out of the gate and back onto the roadway.

CHAPTER -12-

Alexa continued walking in the direction that the old man had told her to go and soon saw the signs for the convent. She felt such a relief that Herr Klauss had gotten the convent information correct and she began walking up the long driveway towards the large main stone building. As she approached the front of the structure, the moon lit up the entrance which had several arches casting long curved shadows across the ground before her. There were two huge wooden doors which were framed and over-laid in cast iron. Alexa wasn't sure what time of night it was exactly, but she figured that it had to be well after 1 am or even later. There were no visible lights on in the building and she was reluctant to start banging loudly on the doors. She looked around and began exploring the perimeter of the building in search of another entrance. She noticed that the property appeared to be in three sections. The first seemed to house an old rectory with its own garden, the second section looked like a traditional church building, a purpose-built house of worship with large arched stained-glass windows and, attached at its rear, a nunnery with a separate yard of its own. Behind that was a much larger and newer-looking brick building consisting of several floors reaching up high off the ground with tall windows which resembled a large school or residential complex of some kind. Alexa decided that the second building would be the best place to try and get someone's attention, so she walked around into the yard and searched for a side door.

She found one at what she guessed was the nunnery and gently began knocking on it but there was no reply. She knocked again several times harder, then a little louder. A few minutes passed by but there was still no answer. Then suddenly from the rear of the nunnery came the sound of a bolt being unlatched and soon after appeared a woman from out of a side gate.

"Come," she said, "Round this way, quickly!"

Alexa followed her and disappeared through the side gate after her.

"Are you Alexa?" the nun asked her.

Alexa nodded yes.

"You are late girl! Follow me," instructed the nun sharply.

She led Alexa into the convent closing the door firmly behind her then picked up a lit lantern and led her down some stone spiral stairs into a cold, damp, eerie and unwelcoming basement. The woman didn't fit the preconceived idea which Alexa had in her head of what the nun would be like. She did wear a black habit which covered her from head to toe but her character seemed to be just as dark as her cloth. Alexa had assumed that when arriving at the convent, she'd be greeted by warm and kind little old Catholic nuns, helpful women who'd welcome her and make her feel at home for the night, but realistically she couldn't have gotten things much more wrong.

The nun walked Alexa along to the end of a long corridor past many closed doors until finally stopping at the very end one. She opened the solid heavy wooden door and walked inside, beckoning Alexa to come in after her. The nun rested her lantern on a small wooden table and reached into her pocket, from which she took out a candle and proceeded to light it from the flame in her lantern. The flame illuminated the small room, which looked more like a dungeon, then she placed the lit candle on the table which she secured in some hot melted wax that she had dripped from the burning candle. There were no windows in the small space and the walls were constructed of cold bare stone which were full of cobwebs and large amounts of dust. In the room was a single metal bed with an old pillow on it, a table, a chair and two buckets on the floor, one empty with a dirty towel draped over its side and one half filled with cold water. Alexa quickly realized that this was where she was to sleep for the night and cringed at the very thought of it. The nun pointed to some sheets and blankets lying in the corner on the ground and told her to make up the bed for herself and that someone would come for her in the morning. Then she picked up her lantern, turned and walked out of the room closing the door behind her. It happened so fast, that Alexa didn't even have time to ask her any questions and then suddenly, she heard the nun put a key in the door from the outside and lock it. Alexa panicked.

"Oh no, please don't lock the door sister," she shouted out as she quickly ran towards the door, but the door was already locked and there was no reply as she heard the nun's footsteps become more distant as they disappeared off down the long corridor.

Alexa was exhausted on all levels. Physically, she could feel the pain of her wounds and the throbbing of both her feet from all the many kilometers of walking she had done that night. She had gone through a real mix of emotions and her nerves were shattered. She had gone from excited to terrified, elated to deflated, scared to relieved, lost to found, from freedom to captured again and everything in between, all within less than a twenty-four-hour time scale. Alexa reached for the bedding, threw it up onto the uninviting bed and climbed under the blanket, curling up into a ball with all her clothes still on her. She kicked off her shoes, left the candle burning and pulled the blanket up over her head. *At least it's only for one night,'* she thought to herself. Then she tried to recall the instructions given to her by Herr Klauss for the next part of her journey home. Being as exhausted as she was, she soon drifted off to sleep.

At some point through the night, the candle had burned itself out, but Alexa was oblivious to that fact as she slept soundly through the entire night, mainly due to exhaustion and fatigue rather than feeing relaxed and comfortable. She hadn't even heard the key go into the lock the next morning when two nuns came to unlock the door and entered into the room.

"Wake up girl! Get up!" ordered one of the nuns abruptly while she shook Alexa who was still fast asleep on the bed. Alexa opened her eyes immediately, sat up, then swung her feet out from under the blanket and round to touch the cold stone floor. She began feeling for her shoes with her feet, but the nun nearest to her kicked the shoes away and out of her reach.

"Here, put these on," ordered the other nun and threw a pair of heavy wooden clogs over to her. They made a loud and familiar noise as they landed at her feet, on the cold stone floor.

Alexa thought that she must be in the middle of a nightmare, she rubbed her eyes hard, but the picture in front of her didn't change in any way. She reluctantly placed her feet into the clogs.

"Okay, up you get and come with us," said the nun nearest to the door. Alexa got up and followed them as they headed down the long corridor and up the stairway at its end. Then they walked towards a large kitchen where there was a group of about thirty nuns sitting eating breakfast together.

"Sit down here," ordered one of the nuns, as she pointed to a spot on a wooden bench next to the long table. Alexa did as she was told while she felt each pair of eyes from the nuns' stare at her and look her over from head to toe. She was still in the clothes that she had arrived in the previous night except for the black shoes. Her blood-stained pajama trouser leg was still tucked into her dirty sock and was pushed into the ugly clog. She then became aware that only she was wearing the wooden clogs. She knew she must have looked a sight but didn't really seem to care about that. A younger nun walked over to where she was and placed a cup of warm milk in front of Alexa and a few seconds later, she put a plate of warm lumpy porridge and a spoon down in front of her also.

"Thank you," said Alexa as the nun turned her back on her and walked away. Alexa reached for the milk and drank half of it down then wasted no time beginning on the porridge. She was famished. She hadn't eaten or drank anything since her short respite with the old man on the roadway the night before, when he had shared some of his milk and chocolate with her, apart from the hot cocoa at the German police officers house. The porridge was lumpy and didn't taste as good as she could make herself, but she ate it anyway. Once she had finished eating, the mother superior came over and stood next to her. She snapped her fingers and two younger nuns came running over to where she was.

"Sisters Mariska and Julia will take you to get cleaned up and give you fresh clothes to wear. Go with them now and report straight back to me when you are done," she ordered, "and don't take all day about it! "

Alexa stood up and the two nuns led her out of the kitchen. After a while of walking along corridors, turning corners and walking upstairs, they arrived at a bathroom and the nun named Julia told Alexa to get undressed while they filled up a metal tub with several buckets of water from the sink. Alexa was reluctant to take her clothes off and was also embarrassed, not to mention that the bathroom was cold and, by the looks of things, so was the water. However, it didn't appear that the matter was up for discussion, as Sister Mariska moved closer to her and began to undo her coat buttons.

"Okay, okay!" Alexa said, "I can do it myself!"

As she began to climb out of her clothes, she slowly stepped into the bath and let out an uncontrollable shriek, as her skin plunged into the cold water. She naturally tried to step back out, but the two nuns pushed her back down into the water and shoved a bar of soap into her hands. Alexa decided that it would be better in the long run for her, just to do as they told her. So, she washed her wounds clean and finished the cold bath as fast as she could. Sister Julia had a towel waiting for her, which was rough and scratchy, but it was clean, and Alexa quickly dried herself off with it shivering all the while. Next, she was handed a small pile of clothes to put on. They were not her own clothes and didn't look like they were particularly her size, but they looked clean and she began to put them on.

Sister Julia pointed to her neck and said. "What is that? Take it off!"

Alexa reached her right hand up to her necklace and took hold of the cross part.

"Oh no, please don't make me take it off, it was my grandmother's," she tried to explain.

"Take it off!" she said again.

"No, you don't understand, I've had it on every day since I was a little girl. I just can't take it off! Please don't make me!" Alexa begged.

"If you don't take it off, we will pull it off. Is that the way you want it? Do you want us to break it off?" Sister Mariska threatened.

Alexa shook her head "No," and slowly reached her hands up to the clasp part of the necklace and gently opened it. She held it in her hand and took one last look at it, before reluctantly handing the necklace over to Sister Julia.

"If you behave and do as your told, you might get it back," announced the nun who seemed to be enjoying bullying the young girl.

Alexa felt tears welling up in her eyes, but she was determined not to show her weakness and fought them back, flipping her inner switch activating the masking of her true emotions, becoming the person that she needed to be. She put her feet into the clogs, tied back her hair and said, "I'm ready!"

The two nuns told her to pick up her dirty clothes and follow them, then they led her back down to the kitchen and stood her in front of the mother superior. Sister Julia handed her Alexa's necklace, which she took a good look at then said to Alexa,

"It's very nice, I'll take good care of it for you and, if you do a good job maybe I'll give you it back one day." She then placed it around her own neck and had Sister Julia fasten it securely for her.

Alexa tried to look unaffected by the nuns' actions, but deep down she hurt so bad. This was the one thing that she had of her grandmother's, the one precious item from her childhood, from her home life which she had managed to keep all of those years. This was the priceless item that had saved her life in her mind, the thing which had attracted the Klauss's to her when they had first selected her from the line-up. Even they hadn't been so wicked as to take it from her. She'd get it back, she'd do whatever it took, but she'd get it back somehow, someday she resolved.

"Time for you to get to work now girl," announced the mother superior, "You will be doing laundry duties this week to start with. Sisters Julia and Mariska will show you where. Go with them."

"But I thought that I was only to stay here overnight?" Alexa queried, "and then continue on my journey home to Poland!"

"Well you thought wrong, didn't you? Now go," ordered the nun.

Having no other choice and being greatly outnumbered, Alexa followed Sisters Julia and Mariska as they led her to a large laundry area and set about putting her to work. The piles of dirty laundry were huge, mountains of white sheets and towels filled one entire corner and black clothing another. For the first time, Alexa wished that she was back working at the Klauss's farmhouse. But she made a start on the mammoth task which lay before her and concentrated all of her energy on working hard towards getting her grandmother's necklace back. She couldn't give up hope, not now. Nor could she allow her thoughts to become dark and negative. Again, she reminded herself that this situation was only temporary and that she'd be free from it soon. She made the choice to rise above the suffering and not become a victim of the circumstance she now found herself in. She had done it before, and she'd do it again.

After her first full day of work at the convent, Alexa was taken to a different room where she was to sleep at night from now on. This room was a lot bigger than the first room which she was placed in when she had first arrived. It looked a little more comfortable, although not by much. This room had four single beds in it and so it quickly became apparent to Alexa that she would likely be sharing with others, although she didn't know who the others would be. It wasn't too long before her new room-mates arrived, escorted by two of the nuns. They too had experienced a long day of hard forced manual labor. They were three girls who all spoke German, but it was apparent that German was not their mother tongue. The three girls were also blonde and seemed to be from another part of Europe and as their individual stories unfolded, it became clear that they had also been taken from their homes against their will, some years prior, just like Alexa. The nuns locked the room door as was their routine and the girls were left alone together inside of the room. One of the girls introduced herself first to Alexa.

"Hi, my name is Marta and I'm seventeen-years old, originally from Holland. What's your name?"

"Hello, my name is Alexa and I'll be nineteen in March, I'm originally from Poland." Alexa answered.

"Nice to meet you." Said Marta.

"This is Henrietta, she's eighteen and also from Holland." Marta pointed to the tall blonde girl sitting to her right and Henrietta said hello in response. Marta then pointed to the other girl in the room.

"This is Greta and she is from Denmark originally but lived in Holland also, she's nineteen and the oldest out of the three of us."

Greta looked towards Alexa and smiled at her, as she leaned forward to shake her hand. Alexa extended her hand to meet Greta's and now the four girls had all been introduced to one another. Alexa realized quite soon that they were all in the same boat, with the same goal: they had all been taken against their will from their families, and they were now all desperately trying hard to get back to their own individual homes. They were also all wearing the heavy wooden clogs on their feet. Henrietta pointed to one of the beds closest to her and told Alexa, that it was where she slept.

"Marta sleeps on that one and Greta on this one, so that one there will be yours." Henrietta pointed to one of the beds.

"Ok, thank you, but I really don't intend to be here for very long." Alexa replied.

"Ha, that's what we all thought when we first arrived here too." Marta said.

"How long have you all been here?"

Henrietta answered first, "I've been here since the beginning of September this year."

"It was two weeks into October when I was brought here," said Marta.

"I got here the first week of November," said Greta.

Alexa thought that if she shared her story of when and how she was taken, it might encourage the others to speak out about their experiences too. "I was thirteen-years of age when my mother and I went to buy me a new pair of shoes. The Nazis drove into town and started rounding everybody up. We were separated into groups, loaded onto different trucks, put into boxcars and transported to Dachau. I got to spend one night with my mother there, before she was beaten and knocked unconscious, the next day I was separated from her. It's been more than four years since I last saw my mother! I have no idea what happened to her. I was taken to Frankfurt, where I was selected and sent to work as an unpaid house slave for a German Gestapo officer and his family at their farmhouse. I was freed by them only yesterday and have journeyed to this place, where I was only supposed to spend one evening. That's my story up until now, what's yours?"

Greta was first to speak after Alexa had related her experience. "I was fourteen years of age when I was taken. I was fast asleep in bed in my family home, when all of a sudden at 3 am our front door was forcefully and violently kicked in and then a bunch of Nazi soldiers with rifles charged into our home. We had no time to run or hide. Immediately we were pulled out of our beds and were rushed outside into the streets without any of our belongings. I was separated from my mother, father, brother and sister. I was sent to Germany as an unpaid domestic slave for four years and now I find myself here with you three girls."

The three girls looked at her empathetically, as they knew how it felt to walk in her shoes, for they had all tread on similar paths to the point which they were now at.

Next up was Marta's history. She began by speaking of her happy childhood in Belgium and then led into the circumstances of her capture. "I was twelve-years old and it's a day that I will never forget as long as I live. My father had just said the prayer as we sat down to dinner, me and all six of my immediate family. Just as my father passed me the bread, we heard the engines of trucks outside in the street followed by the heavy footsteps of German soldiers and their barking dogs. My father told us to quickly go and hide in the places which we had often rehearsed, for a day such as that. We all scampered from the dining table and I hid with my brother, in the secret loosened panel behind the kitchen cabinet and we crawled inside the tiny space. Then I heard our front door burst opened and soldiers running into our house, shouting and then shooting. I heard my father shout out in protest, but very quickly he was silenced mid-sentence with a direct bullet, then we heard a great thud as he fell to the floor. My mother was holding my baby brother and my four-year old little sister was standing together with her in the dining room. The soldiers screamed at her, asking if there was anyone else in the house? And said that if there was anyone hiding, she and my siblings would be shot. So, my brother and I crawled out of our hiding places so that my mother and the others would not be killed. We were all marched outside onto the street and separately loaded onto different trucks. I haven't seen any of my family since that day. My father was left lying for dead, alone on the cold, hard ground. I was selected by the Nazis' with some other blonde, blue-eyed youngsters like me and brought here to Germany as a slave and the rest I'd rather not talk about. I just want to get back home to try and find any of my family who might still be alive."

Greta, being the oldest of the girls took it upon herself to take the lead, summarizing that they had all individually been through horrific nightmare ordeals which bonded them all together, but that they also shared a common goal.

"We have all survived up till now and there must be a good reason for that. I'm sure that if we stick together and do our jobs here as the nuns expect of us, we will make it out of here alive and get back to our homes and find what's left of our families. Somehow, we will find a way together," encouraged Greta.

The girls all agreed and seemed to be empowered by Greta's words. They took some comfort in the fact that they all had shared similar ordeals and that they were also not totally alone anymore. The exhausted girls all got settled into their beds, said goodnight to one another and lay silently with their own thoughts as they drifted off to sleep. Alexa said her prayer silently to herself.

CHAPTER -13-

Over the national radio broadcasts, came news reports that the Second World War was finally coming to an end with Allied troops trying to capture as many Nazi soldiers, Gestapo officers and high-ranking SS officials as possible - those responsible for so many of the atrocities which had occurred since the start of the war. Towards the end of January of 1945, some of the Nazi concentration camps and forced labor camps were beginning to be liberated throughout Germany and Poland and the world then got its first photographic evidence, film-footage and first-hand accounts of the terror that had actually taken place in these horrific and hellish places on earth. Accounts of the undeniable, unimaginable, brutal and inhumane treatment, torture and murder of millions of innocent Jewish men, women and children, and others at the hands of Hitler's Nazi army, Gestapo and evil henchmen.

The nuns had an old radio which they kept in a large wooden cabinet in the main dining room of the convent where they would sit and eat dinner together. After they ate their main meal, they would turn the radio on to listen to the latest news updates being broadcast. The four workhouse girls were always seated at the same small table in the far corner of the dining room to eat their meals together, away from the group of nuns but always remaining within their sights. It was now the beginning of April and Alexa was nineteen. She had been kept there against her will for four months, being forced to slave away in the laundry room every day.

That evening after her meal, Alexa lingered to hear the radio broadcast which gave warnings of bombing campaigns by the Allied forces in one town after another as they aimed to take out key German army targets around Berlin. Reports also told of Nazi soldiers running for cover across the country, trying to cover up their long trail of evil. At the end of the update it was reported that there was a mass of freed innocent prisoners, mainly Jewish but also others who had been taken from across Europe, who were now on foot, refugees trying to make their way back to their various homes. The broadcaster said that the German civilian population in general should assist these unfortunate people in any way that they could, that it was their duty as human beings. The mother superior looked over at Alexa and the other three girls at the table and on seeing that they were listening intently to the radio broadcast said out loud, "That doesn't apply to you girls, now get back to work!"

Then two of the nuns got up from their seats and took them all back to the laundry room. They were never permitted to go to, nor leave by themselves and were never left in the laundry room alone either. There were always eyes watching over them. Someone came and took them to morning prayers and then to breakfast afterwards. Next, they were escorted to work in the laundry rooms and the same at dinner time and after they had finished their work for the day, two nuns would escort the girls back to their room in the basement. Alexa had tried to think of ways to escape, they all had, but there really weren't any opportunities that she could think of. That night as she lay exhausted in bed in the girl's shared bedroom, as she did every night, Alexa prayed hard but this time out loud, for all the girls to hear.

"Dear Almighty God in heaven, we desperately need your help to escape this prison which we now find ourselves in. Please hear my pleas and make a way out for me and my friends. So that we may continue on our journey's home and find our families. Guide and protect us dear God we beg of you. Amen!" The other girls said Amen too. Alexa closed her eyes and soon fell asleep.

When morning came, she and one of the other girls were collected by two of the nuns and taken upstairs to breakfast. She had fast become familiar with her new routine. Then the other two girls were collected and escorted upstairs separately by two other nuns. After prayers and breakfast was over, they were all taken to the laundry room area and guarded over as they began slaving away scrubbing and washing, rinsing and hanging up the never-ending piles of laundry. Henrietta and Marta were ordered to collect the large pile of black clean and dry, nuns' clothing and were then led out of the main room through a door in the corner into the next room, where their duties consisted of ironing the nuns' habits and white linen sheets. While Alexa attended to her monotonous chores, she heard overhead what sounded like airplane engines flying low in the vicinity and immediately continued her work with caution. The airplanes seemed to pass over them and go off into the distance, but after a few minutes they came back and the hum of the airplane engines grew louder, followed by the whistling noise of a fast approaching falling bomb. The nuns began to scream in sheer terror and Alexa immediately ran towards the large stained-glass window on the far, left side of the room and crawled under the large solid wooden table which was directly underneath it, burying herself in a mass pile of dirty sheets for protection. The bomb hit its target and a tremendous explosion erupted as it hit the rectory at the front of the property. Then immediately after, a second bomb began to fall, and this time hit the rear of the convent building. The entire stone structure shook violently as a mass of bricks and mortar began to crumble and fall in, all around the interior. The stained-glass window shattered with the impact of the second explosion, while Alexa was still taking shelter underneath the table, and large sections of glass landed and shattered everywhere. The large table had split in half at its middle from the weight of the falling debris above it, but fortunately Alexa had been cowering under the rear legs section, which still provided her with some protection.

After about thirty seconds had passed by, Alexa was aware of the relative silence that now existed in the laundry room where she was, except for the loud ringing in her ears. There were no more screaming nuns, nor any of them crying out for help that she could hear but more importantly, she couldn't hear Greta either. Alexa slowly crawled out from under the broken table and kicked off the laundry sheets that she had wrapped herself up in for protection. She seemed to be uninjured, apart from the knock to her head which she received when the table snapped in the middle, just above her. She stood up, squinted her eyes and looked around the room to assess the damage. Through the unsettled dust that filled the air like a white mist, she saw that part of the roof had fallen in on the right side of the room and that it had damaged the adjoining room also, knocking down part of the wall and blocking the doorway. She looked for any signs of life and then discovered the bodies of the two nuns who had been standing guarding her and Greta in that area before the bomb had hit, who were now buried under a large pile of rubble. Alexa looked around the room desperately trying to find Greta who had been working nearest to her, calling out her name. Greta's image finally came into her view.

"Greta! You're okay," yelled Alexa as she hugged Greta.

"Yes, and you are too my friend. Who would have thought that these dirty sheets, would actually end up saving my life," said Greta, in amazement. Alexa pointed to her ears, shook her head and gestured that she had a problem hearing. Greta saw that the nuns' deceased bodies were lying on the ground under piles of rubble and quickly became aware that, for the first time there was no one guarding them anymore, nor watching their every move.

"Let's go and try to find Marta and Henrietta," said Alexa. Greta nodded in agreement and the two girls carefully made their way over the debris and out of the destroyed laundry room and on into the next damaged room.

There were no immediate signs of any life in the next room that they reached. This was where Alexa believed that Henrietta and Marta had been taken to work that day, in the area where the ironing was done. The extensive bomb damage was obvious and there were few to no areas that weren't covered with fallen bricks, mortar, wooden beams and piles of large stone. Eventually they discovered the shoes of one of the nuns, just showing out from under one of the large stone piles. It was obvious to them that there was no way she could have survived and was most likely buried alive. Alexa and Marta assumed that the other nun, most likely suffered the same fate!

"I'm glad we weren't in their shoes!" Greta said.

Finally, as satisfied as they could be that their friends were not casualties there, the two girls began looking for an exit out, and carefully tried to make their way back to the kitchen area, while continuing to search for their two friends. Alexa's ears were still ringing, but she couldn't hear any recognizable voices or cries for help. Neither could Greta. They eventually made their way to the kitchen, which was at the rear of the building, only to find that it had been totally destroyed and no longer existed as a room with any purpose inside the structure. It was now part of the outside with its roof completely blown off and gaping holes in its walls. Greta said she'd take one side of the room to search and began looking. Alexa climbed over some of the debris and looked around for any signs of life but quickly realized that the kitchen area was where the second bomb had directly hit and was probably where the most fatalities were. It had only been about twenty minutes since she had actually left the breakfast table that morning, where all of the nuns had been sitting eating. There were fires burning in several places and Alexa decided it was probably best for them to get as far away from the scene as possible. As she turned to locate Greta to suggest that they leave the kitchen area, she heard a voice cry out in pain from underneath the large pile of fallen stone. She turned back around and tried to get close to where the source of the voice was coming from.

"Where are you? Let me hear your voice again louder," Alexa shouted out.

A few seconds later the voice cried out again. Alexa couldn't clearly make out any of the words but could sense the direction where the sound was coming from and climbed over towards where she thought the person might be. Alexa heard the voice again and this time could tell that the injured person lay just below the large pile of stones and rubble where she now stood. She could see only the shoes of one of the nuns and slowly began lifting the heavy stones one by one from on top of her.

"Greta, come over and help me, there's someone under here! Just hold on, I'll get you freed." Alexa said reassuringly as she continued to slowly and carefully remove some of the bricks. Finally, Alexa removed the last few bricks from around the trapped person's face area and to her surprise, discovered the nun's identity. It was the mother superior who had been so nasty to Alexa when she had first arrived at the convent. The nun opened her eyes and looked up at Alexa's face, as she stared back down at her.

"Oh good, thank you girl. Now hurry, get me out of here," the nun ordered her as she gasped for breath.

There was a large wooden beam across the nun's chest area with more heavy stones and bricks still piled high on top of it. When Greta reached where they were and saw who it was, her whole demeanor changed from that of a rescuer, to that of a judge and jury.

"It's up to you Alexa, but I wouldn't help her out if I was you! Not after all that she has done to us and what she has put us through."

Alexa thought for a second, then leaned in and reached down to the nun's neck area. She placed her hand under the nun's white neck covering, then feeling around, she pulled out her grandmother's silver necklace into view, which the old nun had taken from her so nastily when she had first arrived. The nun looked up at Alexa and again ordered her to get her out.

"You did take good care of my necklace and I did do a very good job here, but now I'm taking my necklace back and going home!" Alexa announced confidently. Then she undid the clasp and took her necklace from off of the nun's neck. Alexa estimated that from the injuries the old woman had received, her chances of survival were slim to none. There was no way Alexa could lift the heavy wooden beam from off of her chest by herself and even with help, it would be a near impossible task. Then finally from beneath the rubble, the nun took her last draw of breath and rattled death. Alexa knew there was nothing more she could do there, so slowly and carefully she made her way down from the pile of stones and onto the ground where she put her grandmother's necklace back on around her own neck. Greta leaned over and fastened the clasp for her friend.

"Let's get out of here Alexa!"

Once they were outside it became apparent to Alexa and Greta that they were the only two survivors left standing, out of roughly thirty nuns. They seemed to be the only ones who had made it out of the building alive and in one piece. Then in the distance they heard the return of a single airplane. The girls quickly ran as fast as they could away from the building structures and made a dash for the surrounding trees. Then from behind them, they heard the familiar sound as they had done before, the whistle of a fast falling bomb and they quickly dived for cover in some nearby bushes. The powerful bomb hit its intended target and landed right in the center of the third residential building of the convent which was at the very rear of the property. The largest newer residential building which had several floors to it was being used secretly by the Nazis', with the German Catholic nuns' permission, as a makeshift hospital to care for and nurse wounded Gestapo officers and German soldiers. Obviously, the Allied forces had intelligence as to this fact and when they learned of this location, decided that bombing the three buildings in one swoop, would be the most effective way to bring it to its end.

Greta and Alexa once again were not seriously injured and had only a few scratches each from the bushes they had dived into. They both felt relieved however, they were still worried and anxious over the whereabouts and the wellbeing of their two friends. When they were sure that the bombers were gone and the coast was relatively clear, they carefully made their way back towards the convent.

"Our clogs are gone and we both have no shoes on! We won't get very far bare-footed!" Greta pointed out.

She was right. They hadn't paid much attention up to that point, but their work clogs were gone from off of their feet since after the explosion. The mix of adrenaline combined with their survival instincts had kept their minds focused on their moving to safety and not on the comfort of their own feet.

"You're right Greta," agreed Alexa. "Let's head over to the other side of the convent. We can look for some shoes on our way. No one here will need them there anymore."

The last building to be hit was engulfed with flames and badly damaged. The two girls headed towards the nunneries kitchen area and as they got closer, they heard some movement coming from inside of its walls. Then heard muffled female voices and suddenly became filled with fear at the thought that maybe there were some nuns who had survived after all and would try to keep them enslaved again. They moved back slowly in the direction which they had come from, watching from a distance. Then a female appeared out of the derelict structure who was covered in grey dust from her head, all over her clothing and down to her feet. She sat on the ground and began putting on a pair of lace up boots.

Alexa turned to Greta and said, "It's Henrietta, I think it's Henrietta!"

Greta jumped up and shouted, "It is Henrietta, it is her, she's alive!"

Greta had already began running towards her before Alexa could tell her to wait to make sure it was safe first. Henrietta looked up and spotted Greta running towards her. She hadn't finish lacing up the boots, before she too jumped up to her feet and began running towards her friend. The girls ran into each other's arms with Alexa joining them a few seconds later.

"Marta, get out here! Look who's alive," Henrietta shouted out.

A few seconds later Marta came out of the building's ruins carrying a pair of boots in her hands and couldn't believe her eyes at the sight before her. The four girls were alive. They had all survived and were relatively unharmed. They all embraced for a moment or two then agreed that they couldn't waste any more time, that they had to get as far away from the convent, as fast as possible. Alexa and Greta began looking for a pair of the deceased nuns' boots each, that they could wear to make their escape in. Henrietta disappeared around to the back courtyard and there, found two bicycles that were still in good working condition and decided that it would be their best means of transportation out of there. Two girls on each bike. One would cycle while the other would sit on the saddle, then they could switch over she suggested. Henrietta sold the idea to the girls who were all in agreement.

Alexa came to the realization that there was no way that she could get back to their room where her things were, due to the extensive damage which the building had received. Then sadly she became all too aware, that she wouldn't be able to retrieve her blue shoes either. That saddened her immensely as she had wanted to take them back home with her so that when she eventually found her mother, she could show her what good care she had taken of them. That same pair of shoes which they had gone to buy together, the day when they were both taken. However, she had managed to get her grandmothers necklace back and she still had her life intact, both commodities which were of a far greater and irreplaceable value to her than the blue shoes, she reasoned to herself. Miraculously, they were all still alive.

The girls tied up their boot laces, shook off some of the dust from their clothes and hair, and then climbed onto the bicycles. They steered around the fallen masonry which lay strewn all over the grounds and headed off down the hill out of that hellish place as fast as they could. They never looked back.

CHAPTER -14-

The girls cycled for almost an hour, switching positions on the bikes, taking turns at steering and stopping a few times for short rests along the roadway. Except for Alexa. She said that she wasn't the best cyclist, so Greta peddled their bike for them both. They weren't really sure of where they were heading to, after all nothing was planned. The girls had no idea when they woke up that morning that it would turn into the day when they would gain their freedom back once again. It could also have turned out very differently and indeed, so much worse for them all. The four girls had all come so close to being killed in the bombing raid, so the day was a God-send, a real blessing and each felt as though they had a protective force around them, keeping them safe and shielding them from harm. Alexa was convinced beyond any shadow of a doubt, that her God had indeed heard her prayer the night before and had acted on their behalf. Her faith was already strong, however this just anchored it, making it even firmer.

As they cycled along the uneven roads, they passed by many damaged buildings. Many of which had no doubt been intentionally bombed and targeted specifically by the Allied forces in air raids. However, it seemed obvious that many homes had been unintentionally caught up in the air strikes, with many structures left derelict and abandoned in a severe state of disrepair. There didn't appear to be many people around in the area which they travelled through. It seemed more like a ghost town, totally deserted and deadly silent.

The bicycle that Henrietta and Magda were on had got a flat tire, so the four girls all stopped on the open roadway and took the opportunity to rest up a little. They had no supplies with them, nothing to eat or drink and hadn't had anything since early that morning when they had eaten breakfast at the convent. Greta suggested that they rummage around some of the abandoned damaged houses in the hope of finding something that they could eat or drink, some kind of nourishment. Although they all weren't too over enthusiastic at the prospect of searching through the dangerous structures, they agreed that they had no other options from which to choose. About two hundred yards ahead of them, they saw a large house which had received extensive damage with part of its roof blown off. Several windows were also blown out and part of the exterior wall on its right side had collapsed. They cautiously approached the house then Henrietta suggested that she and Magda look around the back of the property towards the garden while Greta and Alexa take the front side. They carefully began to climb up the mound of rubble which resembled what was once a doorway, to try and find a way inside of the house.

Greta was first to reach the top of the brick pile and Alexa followed close behind her. Greta turned around to look back at Alexa, when suddenly into her view came a large army truck driving along the road which caught sight of them. It came to an abrupt stop directly outside of the house. Immediately four soldiers jumped out of the truck with their rifles pointed directly at them. They yelled at the two girls to stop in their tracks exactly where they were and to slowly climb down. Alexa's heart was in her mouth as she froze with fear, but Greta panicked and decided to carry on into the house, fancying her chances of escape. Two soldiers ran after her inside of the building. Alexa began her descent from the pile of rubble onto the ground below with her hands held up high and walked over to where the two other armed soldiers were waiting for her. They wasted no time in loading her into the back of the truck, while the other two soldiers soon emerged from the building with Greta at gun point and marched her over towards the rear of the truck, then ordered her inside. Once inside, the two friends looked at each other but never said a word. In the blink of an eye, their freedom was stolen from them once more. They were captured again. However, the soldiers had been rather hasty when they had taken the two girls, because while they directed their attention to guarding Alexa at gunpoint and chasing after Greta, they had failed to search the rest of the property thoroughly, so therefore, hadn't discovered Marta or Henrietta. They were both still hiding at the rear of the house in the trees at the bottom of the garden.

The military truck drove for a relatively short distance and eventually came to a stop and parked outside of what appeared to be an old school building. On the other side of the road was a schoolmaster's house and an old church, both of which had received some structural damage. The other prisoners inside of the truck along with Alexa and Greta were ordered to get out of the vehicle, then marched in single file across the schoolyard and into the large school building by the soldiers who kept their weapons aimed intently on them. They were marched along the guarded corridors and guided into a large room where a mix of close to two hundred or more, German men and women were being forced to sit on the wooden floor, all at least a body length apart. The new prisoners were added to the group, who were all being kept against their will. The men were separated to one side of the room and women to the other. Down the hallway, there was another room with young children being watched over and kept separate from the adults. It became clear to Alexa that the soldiers were actually Allied troops. They spoke with

American, English and French accents but seemed at first to be just as stern and mean as the German soldiers had been. Alexa sat on the floor with all the others as directed and could see Greta about three rows in front of her, to her left. She looked around for signs of Marta and Henrietta, but thankfully there was no trace of them in the large group. They had evaded capture. Everyone was kept quiet - no one was allowed to talk. It was made crystal clear to all of the prisoners that they were not permitted to get up for any reason and so, time passed by very slowly for everyone in the large room which intensified their uncertainty.

There was no food provided for anyone to eat and water was in small supply. Toilet breaks were not given very often, so sitting in quiet contemplation was all there was to do. The war was speedily coming to its end, but peace had not yet been declared. There were still bombs being dropped and rifles being fired on the front by both sides. Alexa sat contemplating how happy she was that the war was finally going to be over, that she was still alive and would now be a survivor. She hadn't let on to the soldiers that she was Polish but then again, they hadn't asked. They just assumed that she and Greta were German because they had answered in German. Time ticked by very slowly.

Every few hours a group of ten German women were selected at random and taken out of the room at gunpoint. There were being forced to work on extensive cleaning duties at the nearby damaged church and schoolhouse. Alexa's thoughts changed and turned into ones of frustration as it dawned on her that she was being held prisoner with the large group of Germans as if she were one of them when in actual fact, it was the Germans who had kept her prisoner for over five years. First the Klauss family and then the nuns at the convent. Alexa suddenly found the courage within herself to no longer be victimized and suddenly jumped up to her feet.

"I won't sit here anymore, I am Polish! I'm not a German! Why do I have to sit here with all these German people?" Alexa demanded loudly in her best Polish, "it's not fair."

One of the main American officers who understood Polish and heard her announcement walked over to her.

"Come with me," he said and led her out of the room. He then took her to his commanding officer and allowed Alexa to explain her situation. Alexa told them of her experience, of how she'd been taken by the Germans at age thirteen and been kept as a slave for five years by the Klauss's, then of being imprisoned by the nuns at the convent again as a slave for four months more while trying to get home. The commander asked Alexa if she had been beaten or physically abused by her German captors, but Alexa told the truth that the family had been reasonably decent to her, apart from working her very hard as their unpaid slave and keeping her against her will for so long.

The commander had empathy for the young woman after she explained what she had gone through and decided that she deserved freedom and empowerment. First, he had her taken to a quieter smaller room where there was another Polish family of four and a young Ukrainian woman. He then told Alexa to sit and ordered a soldier to bring her something to eat and drink and when she had finished, they gave her two bars of chocolate to keep for herself which she placed in her pocket. After an hour had passed the commander spoke privately to the soldier and afterwards, they told Alexa to follow them and brought her back into the large room of Germans, but not as a prisoner this time.

The soldier told Alexa to choose the next ten German women from the group, who were to be taken out for heavy manual labor duty across the road at the schoolmaster's house. It was to be used as the new officers' barracks and he said that Alexa would be their boss and supervisor. She was to direct them, to tell them what to do, where to do it and to make sure that they did it properly under her watchful eye. Alexa seemed somewhat uncomfortable with the whole idea and humbly told the commander that she couldn't do it. But he insisted that she pick her own ten workers from the German women and march them out of the room and put them to work. He wouldn't take no for an answer. He reminded her that these were the German civilians who did nothing to help out other young girls taken as slaves just like her, in homes all across Germany during the war years. Some of whom no doubt worked innocent girls as their house slaves. Alexa began her selection and couldn't help but feel slightly empowered as she chose them. The ten women stood up and formed a line, then along with Alexa, they were marched out of the room under the guard of four armed soldiers.

When they all reached the schoolhouse across the road, the extent of the buildings damage became clear as did the amount of heavy clean-up work necessary to make the premises livable for the officers. Alexa was told to give the order for the women to begin work and to start cleaning, washing, scrubbing and sweeping and to make sure they put real effort into the tasks. Alexa was no slave driver, but she made sure that the women did as they were told, while she somewhat relaxed and supervised them. After an hour, two soldiers came over to the schoolhouse looking for Alexa and ordered her to follow them. Alexa was apprehensive and a little scared, as they didn't explain why, or say where they were taking her to. However, Alexa followed them, and they led her down the street into the church.

"Have I done something wrong officers?" Alexa asked.

"Please be quiet and just follow us," one of the officers told her.

Inside the church was deserted and a little dark as the sun was beginning to set outside and didn't allow much light in through the stained-glass windows, which were still mostly intact. The soldiers led Alexa to the back of the church, then down some stairs behind the alter towards a small door. They opened it and brought Alexa into the room. Alexa could not believe her eyes at the sight before her. She had never seen anything like this in her life. In front of her were several wooden trunks full of priceless treasure, gold necklaces, pearl bracelets, diamond rings, earrings, watches, decorative broaches, and precious stones of all kinds and colors. In one trunk was gold coins and solid gold bars. On the floor stood many pairs of silver, golden and precious gem-encrusted candlesticks along with ornate goblets, cups, frames and statues. The loot of priceless treasure was mind-blowing and an awesome sight to behold. Next, one of the officers turned toward Alexa and said, "Take what you would like. You were kept in Germany to work as a slave. Here, take as much as you want."

Alexa looked back at the officer and replied, "But this isn't mine! No, I can't. No, I don't want anything, I don't want any of it, because it's not mine to take!"

The two American officers looked at each other and burst out laughing at the young woman's response, then they said to her again that she must take something otherwise their commander would be angry at them. They explained that it was his wish and orders that Alexa be brought to the room and allowed to pick whatever she wanted for herself from the bounty, as some small kind of compensation for all that she had gone through. Again, Alexa said that she could not take anything from the trunks of treasures for she knew in her heart that it had all belonged to many others and her conscience wouldn't allow her to.

"Well perhaps there is something else here in the room that you could have of lesser value but please, you must take something because my commander won't be best pleased with me if you don't," suggested one of the soldiers.

Alexa looked around the room again and over in the corner, leaning against the wall, she spotted several rolls of exquisite fabrics the likes of which she had never seen before.

A beautiful delicate pink flowered patterned material with gold threads and embroidery on a green background. Alexa pointed to the roll of fabric and asked the soldiers if she could perhaps have some of it, from which to make a dress. The soldiers were happy that the young woman had finally chosen something and said she could have the entire roll. But Alexa being the person that she was suggested that they just give her twenty-five or thirty meters, as that was all that she would need. After some more persuasion from Alexa, one of the officers took out his knife and cut the material after they measured out roughly how much she thought she would need, plus a little extra. Then they neatly folded it up and carried it back towards to the school building for her. They placed it in the quieter room for her where the other Polish family and the Ukrainian woman were. Alexa spent the rest of her time there planning out and making a dress for herself. She saved an extra length for another dress and gave the remaining material to the other two women and their young daughters, so that they too could also make some new clothing for themselves.

Upon hearing that Alexa didn't choose any of the jewels or valuable gold, the commander later asked her why? to which Alexa answered, "For it was not mine to take!"

The commander formed a great respect for Alexa and noticing this, she plucked up the courage to ask for one special favor. She explained to him that her friend Greta from Holland had been picked up with her that day after they had escaped from the convent and was still being held down the corridor in the large room with the other Germans. Alexa asked if she could give her one of her chocolate bars to eat, knowing that she'd be hungry. After listening to her, the commander immediately sent one of his officers through to the large room of prisoners in search of Greta.

"Is there a girl named Greta from Holland in here? A friend of Alexa's?" asked the soldier.

Greta raised her hand and then stood up.

"Come with me please, you don't belong in here! There has been a mistaken identity," he said. Greta quickly followed him out of the large room, down the corridor and into the smaller room where Alexa was. The girls embraced and Greta thanked Alexa for not forgetting about her.

"How could I possibly forget about you? You're my friend," said Alexa.

For the next three days the girls concentrated on making their new dresses out of the material which Alexa had chosen. They were given pairs of scissors, needles and threads to use from the school supplies and were allowed to relax making themselves as comfortable as they possibly could be, with enough to eat and drink. Now all they were missing was Marta and Henrietta. They both couldn't help but worry about where they now were.

CHAPTER -15-

After the third day of being kept in the school, the soldiers' told Alexa that she and the others who were not German and who had also been innocently taken against their will from other European countries, were to be moved out from the school the next day. A large army truck would be arriving to transport these casualties of war on the long drive to France. They would be safer there than they'd be in Germany and would be re-settled into a displacement camp until they could eventually return safely to their homes.

In total there was a group of close to twenty mainly young women, who were loaded onto the truck with Alexa and Greta. However, none of the others looked as pretty as they did in their newly made dresses, as basic as they were. The Commander decided to do one more favor for Alexa before she left on her journey and that was to give her and Greta a nicer pair of shoes to wear than the ones which they had on. He first asked them to remove both pairs of their clumpy old lace up boots, which they had taken from the deceased nuns and put on before leaving the convent. Then he had one of the soldiers take the boots back into the large room of Germans and from the women sitting there, he selected two females who wore the same size of shoe as Alexa and Marta, to give up their pretty pairs of shoes. The soldier took the two pairs of nicer shoes and handed them over to Alexa and Greta to try on. The young women did as they were instructed and found that they fitted just fine and really made their new dresses look even more elegant. The commander winked at them and smiled in approval and both women thanked him for all that he had done for them. Then they climbed up, into the back of the open truck with the others.

"You're a beautiful young woman Alexa inside and out and I hope that you eventually get back to your home safely and reunited with your family. God speed," said the commander as he banged on the side of the truck, to signal for the driver to move off.

"Thank you for everything," said Alexa, as she waved goodbye and the truck drove off along the road into the distance.

It was far from being a comfortable ride sitting on the floor of the open top truck and to also be piled in with a group of strangers, but the two friends took comfort from the fact that they had each other. After the truck had been journeying for about two hours, it pulled off the road at an Allied military fuel-loading area. As the truck rolled in, it caught the attention of many of the military personnel and Allied soldiers there. The passengers were allowed to get out of the truck and stretch their legs for a time, while the truck parked up next to the diesel pump to have its tank filled up. Most of the young women were pretty Europeans in their late teens and early twenties, with perfectly trim figures and stunningly good-looking features. It became apparent to them that they hadn't gone unnoticed and that they had the attention of the young enamored soldiers. But one female seemed to be attracting more attention than the others. In a rather short amount of time, Alexa and Greta had a small group of Allied soldiers hanging around them and showing a definite interest towards them. But it became clear that Alexa was drawing the most attention, due to her natural beauty and strikingly good looks.

Some of the American soldiers began offering them small gifts of US stockings and some French officers gave them bars of chocolate. But by far the most impressive gesture came from a young Italian soldier who dropped to his knee and began serenading Alexa on his guitar as he sang an Italian love song to her. Alexa blushed as all attention and eyes stared directly on her and on the entertainment being performed for her enjoyment. When the song ended, the soldier gained a rapturous round of applause and whistles, to which Alexa continued blushing as she thanked the young soldier for his musical serenade. Appearing totally smitten by her, he stood up, leaned forward and kissed Alexa's hand. He then continued to sing her another song in Italian.

Once their truck was filled up with diesel and ready to go, the driver told the group to climb back onboard and as Alexa was settling down into where she would sit, the Italian soldier ran over looking for her.

"For you! Bellissimo," he shouted out, as he reached up and handed his guitar over to Alexa.

"But I don't know how to play it," Alexa tried to tell him.

"Don't say that," said one of the other girls on the truck sitting near her, "Just take it and maybe you can trade it for other things when we get to the camp in France!"

The engine revved up and the truck pulled off. It was back on the road again for the long drive heading towards France. Sitting in the truck with all the others, Alexa couldn't help but have flashbacks to five years earlier when she was originally taken from Poland. In her mind, her thoughts travelled back to being loaded onto that very first military truck with her friend Karolina, when they were both torn away from their mothers' in the square. In the early days of her capture, she thought about that horrific day a lot. In fact, she couldn't get the nightmare out of her head for the longest time and the whole ordeal would replay itself over and over like a movie in her head, stuck on repeat. However, through time it replayed less and less in her mind although it was never further than a thought away. The journey in the back of the truck triggered those memories once again and they all came flooding back to her.

Just as she had done that very first day in the back of the truck, Alexa began to pray. She recited the 91st Psalm that she knew so well silently to herself. However, this time with much less anxiety and terror than she had felt on that first truck ride at the hands of the Nazi soldiers and without the blood-thirsty barking Alsatians viciously snapping at her. This truck ride was far more relaxed, and Alexa felt so much safer, knowing that she was being protected by the Allied troops and was being taken to a place of sanctuary out of Germany. However, there was still a great amount of uncertainty ahead of her. Alexa added her own personal petitions at the end of her prayer and asked that she be kept safe from there on in and as always, that she make it home one day soon to be reunited again with her family. She left it in God's hands.

After one more stop along the eight-hour journey, the truck finally reached its destination at Mourmelon in the North East of France, about ninety miles from Paris. It was an abandoned military airbase which was now being used as a camp for displaced European civilians, run by the US army and the Allied troops. When they first arrived, the group was led over to a large grey canvassed tent. Inside were soldiers sitting at a desk with bundles of white forms and paperwork in front of them, waiting to register the new arrivals and record all their pertinent information. Next, they were directed over to a large solid brick building which was home to the camp's kitchen and cafeteria being run by the Red Cross. There they could get something basic, although very bland to eat and something to drink while they waited to receive their assigned residence barracks where they would be living temporarily. Greta and Alexa lined up together to register at the desk in the hope that they would be placed together in the same barracks. They were near the front of the line of new arrivals and were processed fairly quickly, due to there not being a large mass of new arrivals that day when they got there.

They walked over to the Red Cross building where they got some watered-down soup to eat, along with a piece of bread and a lukewarm cup of mild coffee to drink while they waited. An hour went by before their names were called out by a French female soldier who then escorted them to their assigned barracks. There were two sections to the camp, with about twenty long solid brick buildings in each. Previously these barracks had all been used by the soldiers of the air force base when it had been operational. The larger front section of the camp now worked reasonably well as a temporary shelter and sanctuary for the many displaced Europeans, as if stuck in limbo, while they all waited to eventually get back to their homes. The rear section of barracks was used to house the American and Allied troops.

Once taken to their assigned building which was for females only, they were shown into a room with about twenty bunkbeds in it and told that they would sleep in the second bunks from the end at the very far corner of the room. They were metal army-issue bunkbeds, so they were far from being the most comfortable. This was by no means a five-star hotel, nor could it even rank close to a one, but they were provided a place to rest their heads and lie down for the night in relative freedom and safety compared to what they had been used to. They were given a set of clean white sheets, a pillow and one grey blanket each from the Red Cross, along with a clean towel to use and told that every two weeks they would be refreshed and laundered. Alexa and Greta went over to their assigned beds and made claim to them. Greta took the top bunk, placing her bedding on top of it. They were both pleased that they would be together, for as long as they were to remain in the camp. Alexa placed her gifted guitar from the Italian soldier underneath her bunk. The female soldier handed them some ration cards which allowed them to get some minimal personal toiletries and clothing from the Red Cross supply store, then she pointed out where the bathroom and wash area was that they could use.

"I wouldn't leave that there if I were you. It'll disappear very quickly around here," said the officer pointing to Alexa's guitar.

There was little to no privacy in the barracks, being that they had to share the large open room with up to forty other women of various ages, sizes and backgrounds. Trust and honesty were not common traits which were automatically shared between them all. The female soldier suggested Alexa might be able to trade or sell her guitar to one of the soldiers who might be interested in it, although she wouldn't get much for it. She reasoned that it'd be better to get something for it, rather than it being stolen from right under her and be left with nothing to show for it. Alexa told the female soldier that she couldn't even play it, then agreed that her suggestion would be a better idea. The soldier then led her out of the barracks with the guitar to where she could trade it with the American soldier whom she knew. The soldier was happy to give Alexa a few American dollars for the instrument and Alexa was happy to sell it.

After returning to her barracks, Alexa and Greta decided to take a walk outside and explore the perimeter of the camp to get familiar with their surroundings. There were lots of displaced people just like them walking around the grounds of the camp. They were obviously trying to come to terms with having been liberated from the various hardships and imprisonments which they'd had forced on them, as well as now being relatively free again. The looks on their faces told stories of torture, great suffering and deep sorrow. At this point in their lives' journeys, they were indeed relatively free, but they would in actual fact never be free from the memories etched into their minds, nor the ordeals that they went through, nor the horrific things which they had witnessed and experienced during their war years.

As Alexa and Greta walked through the camp, they could feel the eyes of some of the other women staring at them intently. Alexa figured out that it must be due to their very different clothing. Everyone else mainly wore the old dull clothes which they had arrived in, or plain army-issue work uniforms, with worn-out old shoes and looked far from attractive. Whereas both Alexa and Greta wore the dresses which they had made out of the fancy colorful material Alexa had chosen, along with the pretty pairs of relatively new shoes that the American commander had sourced for them. They became even more aware of the stares that were upon them and heard the loose talk of jealous lips as they passed by the women.

"Who do they think they are?"

"I wonder what they had to do to get those dresses?"

"I wonder which Gestapo officer they slept with?"

"I bet you they stole them!"

Those were some of the comments which they overheard being unkindly directed at them. Greta seemed to be getting more affected by the mean comments than Alexa was and grew more irritated and angered by each one.

"Ignore them," said Alexa as she linked her arm through Greta's, "They're just jealous."

Greta knew they were, but she had less self-control than Alexa did and was easily wound up.

Suddenly from behind them, they heard a woman's voice shout out to them, "Hey Princesses, where's your castle?"

Alexa said to ignore her, but Greta couldn't. She stopped in her tracks and quickly turned around on her heels, to see who and where this woman was who owned the comment. As she did, all of a sudden, she spotted what she thought was a familiar figure just behind where the woman was standing.

She couldn't believe her eyes and firmly grabbed Alexa's arm as she began pointing with her other hand.

"Look! Is that who I think it is?" Greta asked.

Alexa looked in the direction of the figure and caught sight of a blonde woman's back, just as the person had walked into the Red Cross building. They both quickly ran over to the building's door entrance and went inside. To their absolute amazement and complete joy, Greta's suspicion was proved correct. There before their very eyes stood Henrietta, their dear friend whom they hadn't seen since the Allied soldiers had picked them up and taken them from the derelict house four days prior in Germany. They both shouted out simultaneously "Henrietta!"

Henrietta looked up towards both girls and did a double-take. She too seemed to be overcome with emotion upon hearing the familiar voices of her friends and seeing their happy faces. The three friends hugged each other tightly and let out giddy laughter like excited little girls. Just then Marta appeared inside the building on her way to join Henrietta and spotted her three friends locked in their ecstatic embrace. She wasted no time and ran over to where they all were, throwing her arms around them all.

"Marta! You're here too! Thank God you're both okay!" exclaimed Alexa. In an environment where there was little or nothing to celebrate, or to be overjoyed at, these four friends were overjoyed that they were all reunited once again, together in the same place.

"We are survivors, all of us!" Henrietta said, "We survived being taken as children. We survived being worked as slaves by the Gestapo. We survived that convent, those nasty nuns and even the bombings and here we are together again."

They all agreed that they had indeed been more than fortunate and took great comfort and strength from their survival.

"...And we survived being captured by the Allied troops and being brought here to France," added Greta.

"Yes, we did! God heard my prayers each time and made a way out for us and brought us all back together again," said Alexa.

"Well whatever it was, I'm grateful and from here on in, let's stay together until we all get home, no matter what," said Marta.

The four friends mutually decided that it would be best for them all to stay together in the same barracks and to select bunks next to each other. Alexa suggested that they quickly all go over to the registration tent and explain to the French female soldier on duty, whom she already knew from helping to sell her guitar, that they were all best friends and request if Henrietta and Marta would be allowed to take the other empty bunkbed next to theirs. When they explained the reason for their request to the soldier, she said it would be alright and that she would change the records but that they would have to go and inform the two newly assigned women to those beds, to move to another bunkbed on the end of the opposite side of the room. They thanked the soldier and quickly made their way back to the barracks. The two women were already there but agreed to move when Henrietta insisted that it was an order from the soldier.

None of them had any belongings to their name, except for Greta and Alexa. They both had their old clothes rolled up and tied in a small bundle which they had changed out of when they had put on their newly made dresses. Alexa no longer had the guitar in her possession, but she did have a few US dollars now in its place. Greta began telling Henrietta and Marta all the things that had happened to them since they had last been together at the derelict house. Marta and Henrietta were amazed at the schoolhouse story and about Alexa's bravery and boldness. They were shocked to hear about the priceless treasure which Alexa had turned down and especially the compassion and generosity which the American commander had showed towards Alexa. They all laughed together over the Italian soldier instantly falling in love with Alexa and giving her his guitar, but, were not puzzled as to why.

The hours passed by and turned into days, which became weeks and then months, while they remained living in the camp. Everyone there was given a job of some kind by the American troops and had daily duties to perform in return for food, clothing, shelter and army protection. Alexa and the three other young women were back doing laundry duties again on a large scale which they were very good at by that point, having had lots of practice when being in German captivity. They could pretty much remove any stain or stubborn marks from a piece of fabric. Although they weren't being forced to work at hard manual labor, washing piles of laundry wasn't their prime ambition in life, nor was it an easy job. However at least this time working with the American and Allied soldiers, they were doing so on a more voluntary basis, for the good of themselves and all the displaced people in the camp and they were in actual fact, relatively free for the first time in close to five years. It was unclear to Alexa and her friends when they would actually be able to return home as it was still very much dangerous terrain throughout Europe, with many German soldiers and Gestapo officers running for cover and being chased and hunted down by the many Allied troops and the Russians who were seeking revenge. So, the residents at the displacement camp all stayed put, awaiting safer days ahead.

In return for their hard work, the workers were given smart American uniforms to wear as a form of identification along with guaranteed food and shelter. They also got to have some down time to relax and unwind when they were not working or performing camp duties. On one warm Sunday evening, in the heat of the French July summer of 1945 Henrietta suggested that she, Alexa and Greta try to borrow three bicycles from the French army and take a bike ride around the surrounding area nearest to the camp. There was a little French village called Mourmelon-Le-Petit close to where they were, in which the American and Allied troops were made very welcome by the French locals. The three friends decided that going for a cycle together would be a welcome distraction and a great way to unwind a little. Marta had caught herself a summer cold and choose wisely to stay in her bunk at the camp, to rest up and skip the bike ride. Henrietta asked one of the young American soldiers whom she had gotten to know quite well, if she and her two friends would be permitted to borrow some bicycles for a few hours to go for a ride into town together. It wasn't something that was generally done as the bicycles were primarily for the use of the army personnel but since the soldier had taken a real liking to Henrietta, he gave his permission and said that he would square it up with his commander if anyone asked and gave them special passes to leave the camp for a few hours.

As the three young women climbed onto the bikes, Alexa made it known to her friends once again, that she had only been on a bicycle by herself once before when she was a very young girl about seven-years of age and hadn't been very good at it. Undeterred, Alexa decided to try again. After all she thought to herself, *'...how hard could it be?'* She placed one foot on the ground and her other foot on the highest pedal, and then following Henrietta's lead, she pushed off and attempted to ride the bike. Her first try wasn't successful at all and very quickly the bike toppled over to the side forcing Alexa to land on the ground with a crash. Greta and Henrietta couldn't help but laugh at the funny sight before them and encouraged Alexa to try again. Alexa rose to her feet, wiped herself down, then once again mounted the bicycle for a second attempt. She was a little more successful and managed to get the wheels to move forward with both of her feet on the pedals this time before losing her balance and falling off, landing again on the ground. The other two women laughed again at their friend and Alexa too this time couldn't help but join in, finding it quite amusing herself. But she was determined to ride the bike and got back on it several times. Her final attempt was far more successful and after a little more practice, she was riding along with her friends and had gotten the hang of it. The three of them headed off slowly at a steady pace, down the dirt road which led out of the camp and towards the village. The road was bumpy and full of pot holes, but all three young women managed to steer their way safely around them without too much effort or difficulty. They all seemed to enjoy the surrounding scenery of the beautiful French countryside as they rode past open fields taking in nature's breathtaking views - a much welcomed change of scenery than being in the displacement camp all the time.

After cycling for roughly fifteen minutes, they arrived at the village of Mourmelon-Le-Petit and decided to use their American ration cards to each get themselves a cool and refreshing bottle of Coca Cola to drink. Just ahead of them at the bottom of a fairly steep hill was a small French restaurant which had tables and chairs outside of it, where some American officers as well as some locals were sitting chatting together in the late summer sun. Henrietta suggested that they stop there for a little while, so being in the lead position she steered her bicycle down the hill and over towards the restaurant, followed closely behind by Greta and finally Alexa a little further back. Henrietta and Greta came to a stop and pulled their bikes off the road, resting them along the side wall of the restaurant. They had caught the attention of the American soldiers who were watching them approach with pleasure. As Henrietta looked up towards where Alexa was on her bike, she caught the entertaining sight unfold before her eyes just in time. For as much as Alexa had quickly mastered the ability to ride a two wheeled bicycle, she hadn't learned how to stop one, and before she could even let out a panicked scream, she went head first over the handle bars. Alexa and her bike crashed into a giant bundle of hay which was positioned at the bottom of the hill. It cushioned her landing as she tumbled head over feet and disappeared into the center of the giant haystack.

The American officers sitting outside the restaurant had a front row seat at the live comedy show which had just played out before them and spontaneously erupted into laughter at what they had just witnessed. Henrietta and Greta were also laughing hysterically at their friend's comical misfortune. Then they both ran over to the pile of hay to try and assist her.

"Are you alright Alexa?" Henrietta asked, while trying to hold back her laughter.

"Yes, I'm fine!" Alexa answered, as she tried to climb her way out of the straw pile. Rather than a pretty young blonde woman neatly dressed in her American works uniform, what emerged resembled something that looked more like an old scarecrow with straw everywhere.

"What happened?" Greta asked.

"I didn't know how to stop the bike! I've never done it before," Alexa told them.

Henrietta found that to be even more hilarious and laughed even harder.

"Are you serious?" she sniggered, "All you needed to do was to pedal backwards to brake and the bike would have slowed down and stopped, you, silly goose!"

One of the American soldiers had gotten up from his table and had made his way over to where Alexa had crashed into the hay to see if he could be of assistance.

"Are you alright young lady?" He asked.

Alexa was rather embarrassed and quickly tried to brush off the loose straw from her hair and clothing and make herself look more presentable. She couldn't speak English, but kind of guessed what he was saying.

"I no speak English," said Alexa, "Sprechen Sie Deutsch?"

The soldier then enquired in German, if she was okay.

"Yes sir, I'm okay thank you."

"That was quite a trick you performed! Would you like me to recover your bicycle from inside the hay?"

"Yes, thank you, if it's not too much trouble."

The soldier began moving the straw apart and burrowing his way through, in search of the bike. It didn't take him long to find it, then he proceeded to pull it out onto the road and shake off the straw.

"There you go, it seems to be undamaged. What's your name?"

"I'm Alexa and these are my two friends Henrietta and Greta."

He shook their hands and said hello then shifted his attention back onto Alexa. "I've seen you around before, back at the camp and hoped that I'd get the chance to meet you in person one day."

Alexa blushed as she looked down to the ground. Her two friends turned and began walking over towards the restaurant where they had left their bikes, leaving Alexa and the American soldier to chat alone.

"My name is Mark and I'm from Brooklyn, New York in America. Where are you from originally?"

"I'm from Poland," she answered, "But I have been away for five years now."

"That's a long time, you must really miss your family and I'm sure that they really miss you too."

"Yes, I can't wait to be reunited with them again."

"I'd like to buy you a coke, may I?" Mark asked.

"Yes, that would be nice, I'm rather thirsty after my bike ride."

"Yes, I'm sure and it'll help get the taste of straw out of your mouth."

They both shared a smile. Greta and Henrietta had sat down at a table outside and were waiting for the waitress to come and take their order. They too had attracted the attention of a few soldiers. From time to time, they glanced over at their friend across the road with the handsome American soldier, happy for the attention that Alexa was getting. After a few minutes, Mark wheeled the bike over to the restaurant, rested it against the wall with the other bicycles and invited Alexa over to a table to sit with him. The waitress went over to their table first and took their order.

"Two cokes please, unless the lady would like something stronger."

"No not for me, a coke would be nice thank you."

"Has anyone ever told you how very beautiful you are?" Mark asked.

Alexa blushed. The man's comment had made her feel pleasantly uncomfortable and she wasn't sure how to reply to his question. She really hadn't had many compliments directed her way before and had never been alone with a man who had a romantic interest in her. This was all new to her, but his tall, dark handsome good looks hadn't escaped her attention. She was also quite interested in him.

"No," she answered, "But thank you."

The waitress returned with their drinks and placed the two cool bottles of coke on the table along with two glasses. She then proceeded to pour Mark's drink first into his glass. Mark thanked her and told the waitress that he'd take-over, reaching for Alexa's bottle of coke he poured it into her glass for her, then placed it in front of her. Alexa thanked him and the conversation began to flow naturally between them both. There was an obvious chemistry between them and a strong mutual attraction that didn't go unnoticed by both of Alexa's friends sitting close by.

"I would love to see you again and perhaps take you out on a date." Mark stated.

"I'll think about the date part but will also look forward to seeing you again as well."

"Which department do you work in at the camp?"

"I'm assigned to the laundry department."

"Ah, good now I know where to find you."

After they had been chatting together for thirty minutes or so, Alexa thanked him for the coke and got up from the table. Mark said it had been his pleasure and that he looked forward to seeing her again soon, then he reached for her hand and gently kissed it, as he stared adoringly into her eyes. Alexa's could feel her heart beat a little faster, then after a few seconds she broke away from his stare but couldn't help trying to hide the large smile that was on her face. They said goodbye and Alexa walked over to Henrietta and Greta's table. The women had large smiles on their faces at seeing their friend being given such attention from the American soldier.

They finished off their drinks then got up from the table, then headed over towards their bikes. They wheeled them out onto the road and then Alexa looked back towards the restaurant. Mark still had his eyes firmly fixed on her then he raised his hand in the air and waved goodbye to her. Alexa waved back, then the three girls rode off on their bicycles back in the direction of the displacement camp as the sun began to set.

CHAPTER -16-

Monday morning brought the start of a new work week to the camp and after eating their breakfast rations, the workers all began making their way to their various appointed work stations. Alexa and her three friends reported as usual to their positions in the camp's laundry department and began their duties with the other women assigned there, as they had done for the previous six months. It was like being in a Turkish steam room all of the time. Intense heat rose from the vats of boiling water filling the air, like a heated fog, or a train's released cloud of thick white steam. Besides the high temperatures, the workers had to manually beat the huge piles of never-ending laundry in the massive vats stirring and thrashing them with large paddles, then scrubbing on large metal scrubbing boards. Once rinsed off from all traces of the laundering soap suds, the women had to feed the laundry manually through the heavy-duty jaws of the hand-wound mangles, to squeeze out the excess water before then hanging all the items individually up to dry. Once hung up, the collection of many white sheets resembled a sailing regatta. The laundry building never shut down and workers were rotated on twelve-hour shifts, so that the mass piles of dirty laundry were always being cleaned round the clock. It was physically exhausting work. However, the women did receive a small wage for their efforts and were a vital and necessary part of the camps functionality, as well as its hygiene.

Just after mid-morning, two American soldiers made their way into the laundry department and began visibly scanning the area, looking at the workers. Henrietta nudged her friends arm pointing them out to Alexa who popped her head up from what she was doing to look over in their direction. One of the soldiers began speaking with the female supervisor of the department, who was also an American soldier, then he handed her some paperwork. After reading the document she looked down at a list on her desk and then pointed over in the direction to where Alexa and her friends were working. Next the three Americans shared some words, then turned and walked over to where the women were. The supervisor stopped in front of Greta and told her to stop what she was doing and asked her to please follow them. Next, she walked with her over to where Alexa was and told her also, to stop what she was doing.

"You have both been selected to work at the camp's supply store so you will no longer be needed here in the laundry department as of today. You will go now with these two soldiers and they will take you to your new positions," instructed the supervisor.

Henrietta was close by and overheard what had been said to her friends. As pleased as she was for her two friends to be leaving the hard and tedious work of the laundry department, she couldn't help but wish that she too had been selected to go with them. But unfortunately, both she and Marta had not been picked to go to the new jobs and would have to remain where they were.

"We'll see you later," said Alexa to her friends, as she and Greta followed the two American officers who led them outside, through the camp and over to the supply store.

"How lucky are we?" voiced a smiling Greta.

"Well just hold on a minute, we don't know what we'll be doing yet," Alexa reminded her.

"Sure, I know but it's got to be better than doing laundry all day long. My hands will be glad of the rest and to be out of the water. That I do know."

They arrived at the Red Cross supply store and the soldiers took them inside and over to a main registration desk where their names and details were written down in a large book. Then they were taken to the back of the main supply storage area where an American female officer took over and began showing Alexa and Greta where they would work and what their new duties would be.

"I hope you can both count and write," said the officer to them.

"Yes," they both replied, "We can."

"Good, then you shouldn't have any problems here."

She directed them over to a large shipment of army blankets which had just been unloaded from the back of a French truck and told them to make a start on counting them. Then they had to check the totals off with the shipping list and log the numbers into a ledger which she gave to them.

"See, I told you this job was going to be much better than doing laundry," confirmed Greta and Alexa had to agree with her.

The task of counting and recording all of the army issue blankets took them a few hours to complete and once they were finished, they began stacking them on storage shelves. Once their work was checked over by the supervisor, they were free to go for lunch. They made their way over to the large Red Cross building where the main canteen was and joined the line of other hungry workers waiting for food. Each person received a bowl of warm watered-down, vegetable soup and a buttered bread roll, which they ate wherever they could find a space at the many long wooden tables in the large dining room.

Alexa and Greta looked around the room for their two friends but were surprised that they couldn't see them. After they had finished eating their lunch, they began making their way back to their new place of work. Once back inside the supply store, their supervisor gave them the details of their next job assignment and showed them over to the area where they'd be working. A large crate of soaps had been offloaded from one of the trucks and Alexa and Greta were instructed to count and log them all into the ledger, then proceed to place them into smaller boxes, with one hundred bars in each box. They got started right away and both seemed to quite enjoy their new task.

After about twenty minutes, the supervisor escorted two young men dressed in plain American workers uniforms who were carrying a toolbox and stepladders over to an area close to where Alexa was. There was an obvious electrical problem in the building and several of the overhead lights weren't working. The two men were electricians. They immediately began investigating the root of the problem. One of the men was particularly handsome. Tall, blond and blue eyed, which both women hadn't failed to notice as he had first walked past them.

"Hey Alexa, he could easily pass for your brother," joked Greta.

"Very funny, I don't have a brother."

"Well if he was your brother, I'd be wanting you to introduce me to him."

While up on the ladder, the handsome electrician glanced over to where the two women were from time to time. He seemed to be rather distracted by one of them in particular. Alexa's beauty hadn't escaped his notice and he seemed to do a double-take every now and again, just to make sure that his eyes weren't deceiving him. Alexa subtly kept an eye on him also while she continued working but made a conscious effort not to catch his eye or let him see her obvious interest in him. After a while, he came down from the ladders and began searching through his tool box, but he couldn't seem to find what he was looking for, so he told his assistant to go off and fetch the parts which he needed to complete the repairs. While he waited for the other man to return, he casually strolled over to where Alexa was working and confidently introduced himself.

"Bonjour Mademoiselle, my name is Antoni. May I ask what your name is?" asked the man in German.

"Hello, my name is Alexa."

"I haven't seen you here before and believe me when I say, I would definitely have remembered you if I had!"

Alexa felt the need to look away from his captivating stare, but her eyes were transfixed on his and she couldn't disconnect. She was amazed at just how handsome he was up close and even more amazed at how her heart seemed to have skipped a beat when he spoke to her.

"So how long have you been working here in the supply store?" Antoni asked her.

"Today is my first day here. I was working in the laundry department until this morning."

"Then today must be my lucky day, Alexa," he replied, smiling a flirtatious smile at her.

Alexa didn't say it out loud, but she was thinking the very same thought to herself. Greta continued counting the soaps nearby, while Antoni flirted with her friend. He came across as very confident and rather sure of himself, which no doubt stemmed from his handsome good looks. Greta assumed that he was probably used to having women fall at his feet, hanging on his every word and doing exactly what he wanted, with minimal effort on his part. But Alexa seemed different to him somehow than the women he was used to, and he was more than willing to put in the extra effort to keep her interest as he tried to win her favor.

"You smell like a garden full of fresh roses," he complimented her.

"It's probably just all these soaps that you can smell."

"Would you like me to lift up those boxes of soap for you? They look far too heavy for the likes of someone as pretty and delicate as you to be handling?"

"Thanks for asking, but it's okay we don't have to move them ourselves. We've just to leave them all packed and stacked."

"Okay, if you're sure."

Antoni spotted his assistant on his way back with the parts that he had sent him to go and fetch.

"I have to get back up the ladder now Alexa and fix the lighting, but why don't I meet you outside of here after you've finished work and we can chat some more and get to know each other a bit better?"

Alexa wanted to say yes but didn't want to appear too eager. So, she made up the excuse that she had to meet up with her two other girlfriends straight after work.

"Well, what about tomorrow then?"

"Maybe."

"No maybes just say yes for definite. I will wait for you outside of here after work ends tomorrow, Okay?" Antoni insisted.

"Yes, okay then," agreed Alexa.

"Good, I look forward to getting to know more about you."

Antoni winked his eye and smiled at her then turned and made his way back over to the stepladders to complete the electrical repairs. Alexa got back to the job assigned to her but couldn't take the grin off her face.

"Well look at you, two men swooning over you in two days. It's like you put them in a trance or something," noted Greta. "...and let's not forget the poor young Italian soldier that serenaded you and gave you his guitar, he's probably still pining over you. What is it with you Alexa?"

"They all came over to me, let me remind you. I didn't go looking for them, nor did I give out invitations," she replied. "I can't help it if they like me."

Greta knew that what her friend was saying was true and even she couldn't deny Alexa's natural beauty. She knew Alexa hadn't instigated in any way all of the attention, which was being directed towards her and in reality, deep down Greta was a little envious that such interest hadn't been aimed in her direction.

As the afternoon ticked away, the two women concentrated on completing the tasks assigned to them in their new jobs and did so with relative ease and little distraction. There was roughly an hour left to go in their work day and as the clock approached 4 pm, a familiar face appeared in the supply store and made his way over to where Alexa was working.

"Good afternoon pretty lady," said the tall, dark and handsome man as he stood behind Alexa.

"Good afternoon Sir."

"Please don't call me Sir, just Mark will do fine. So how do you like your new job?"

"I like it very much, it's a nice change from being in the laundry department."

"Oh, good I'm so glad. I heard they were looking for two new female workers here, so I thought of you and your friend after meeting you both yesterday and was able to pull some strings...and here you both are."

Just then the sound of clanging metal fell to the ground with a loud crash distracting their attention, bringing their conversation to an abrupt halt. Antoni had dropped one of his tools while up the stepladders, which shifted their attention from off of themselves and onto him. The dropped tool didn't seem to be entirely accidental or unplanned and Antoni seemed quite pleased that he had caused the distraction as he waved over to Alexa, while he waited for his assistant to hand the wrench back up to him. However, it only caused a brief pause between Alexa and Mark, and they quickly resumed their conversation again.

"So, it was you who suggested us for this job! Thank you very much Mark, that was very thoughtful of you."

"You're very welcome, I thought this work would be easier on you both and that you'd be good at it too. I also knew it'd be a good way for me to see you more often as I regularly stop by here on a daily basis." Mark said while smiling at Alexa. "So, did you think any more about going out on a date with me?" Mark asked her.

Alexa could see that Antoni was staring over at her intently from up his stepladders while Mark, standing right in front of her, was awaiting her reply.

"No, I'm sorry but I haven't really had the time to, I've been too busy today with my new job."

"No problem, I'll let you think it over some more, then I will ask you again tomorrow.'

Greta walked over to Alexa's aid and used the excuse that she needed her help to check over her numbers. Alexa was happy for the diversion and politely excused herself from the conversation with Mark. They said goodbye and Alexa went to check over Greta's total count with her.

"Thanks for that."

"No problem, but what are you going to do now? You can't go out with both of them!"

"I know," said Alexa. "Now I have a real dilemma on my hands, they are both good looking and both seem really nice."

"Well here comes the tall blond one again, so you better think fast," suggested Greta.

Antoni had finally got all of the main overhead lights to work and his assistant was now packing up their tools getting ready to leave. Antoni wasted no time and quickly walked over to where Alexa was, then enquired once again whether she would be able to meet him after she finished work that day instead of the next one. Alexa sensed he was being somewhat more determined with her this time which she put down to his seeing her chat with Mark. However, she stuck to her story of having to meet her friends after work but agreed that she'd still meet him the next day instead. Alexa felt butterflies in her stomach when she spoke with him and seemed very smitten with the handsome young man, much more so than she did when speaking with Mark. Antoni said goodbye then he and his assistant left the supply store. The two young women completed their work for the day.

After their work had ended, Alexa and Greta headed back to their barracks and waited there until Marta and Henrietta returned. Then they all made their way to the cafeteria building together for their main meal. The conversation centered around Alexa and Greta's new jobs and why it was that they were selected for the two new positions over everyone else at the laundry station. It was Greta who filled her two friends in on the reason behind it.

"Well, it seems that getting our new jobs today was all thanks to the American soldier that Alexa met yesterday after her bicycle acrobatics. It was he who suggested us for the jobs as he wanted to get in Alexa's favor and probably be able to see her more easily, as well as more often," said Greta.

"Well aren't you two the lucky ones? But hey, didn't he see that you had another friend with you yesterday?" Henrietta asked Alexa.

"I'm sure he did, but I think there were only two new people needed at the supply store."

"Maybe tomorrow Alexa will be moved once again to another even easier job," said Greta sarcastically.

"Today she got another new handsome admirer, tall, blond and even better-looking than the American one yesterday."

"Really, another one?" said Marta.

"And she has a date to meet with him tomorrow after she finishes work," added Greta.

"But aren't you supposed to be going on a date with the American too?" Henrietta asked, "You better be careful, else you'll start another war!

"Well I never! Asked out on her very first date and she's got two dates in twenty-four hours with two good looking young men. You're so lucky Alexa!" Marta said.

"Ok, enough already, let's change the subject," urged Alexa.

"No let's not, we're all actually quite enjoying this one," laughed Greta.

They sat finishing their food, while they continued to tease and quiz Alexa about her two suitors.

"So, who is this latest man?" Henrietta asked, "Tell us more about him."

"His name is Antoni and he's an electrician," answered Alexa.

"Where is he from?"

"I don't know. I never asked him, but I think he's also displaced like us. He spoke in German to me."

"So, who did you like more out of the two of them?" Greta asked her.

"If it was up to me, I'd pick the American, then you could marry him and go off and live in Brooklyn with him, and start a whole new, safe and easy life away from Europe," suggested Henrietta.

"Well they are both very handsome and seem really nice, but I did feel my heart beat a little faster when I spoke to Antoni," said Alexa.

"Ooh, was it love at first sight? Did you get butterflies in your belly?" Marta asked jokingly.

"I think I did actually, I just didn't know what they were at the time."

They all giggled like giddy little schoolgirls, then exited the building and took a leisurely walk around the camp before retiring for the evening while giving Alexa advice for her date with Antoni.

Sunrise brought on the dawn of a brand-new day and while the majority of the workers in the camp were preparing themselves for just another boring work day no different from all the others prior to it, for Alexa this day held great excitement. Although she felt quite nervous and apprehensive about her first ever date at the end of her work shift, she was very much looking forward to it and could think of little else the whole day. Finally, the last hour of her work shift arrived and she found an old mirror in front of which she spent a little time straightening her clothes and fixing her hair in order to look the very best that she possibly could for Antoni. However, being such a natural beauty, very little effort was needed which was just as well, being that there were no cosmetics, no makeup nor fancy beauty products available to assist any of the women in the camp. Greta looked her friend over from head to toe and gave her a nod of approval and after her own final inspection Alexa said, "Wish me luck."

"You don't need any luck my beautiful friend! Any man would be lucky to have a date with you."

"Thanks Greta, but I don't feel so beautiful."

Alexa took a final look at the clock as the hour hand reached the five. The two friends left their work station together and headed towards the exit. As they walked outside of the door, just across the way, smoking a cigarette and leaning against a tree, was Antoni waiting patiently for his date. Alexa said goodbye to Greta and walked over to where Antoni was.

"Hello beautiful, how are you today?" Antoni asked her.

Alexa immediately felt a kaleidoscope of butterflies fluttering away inside of her stomach and her heart again, skipped a beat. Antoni dropped his cigarette to the ground and extinguished it under his boot. Then from behind his back, he produced a single yellow rose surrounded by a bunch of wild flowers which he had hand-picked from a nearby field. He handed them over to Alexa who excitedly reached out her hand to take them from his. Their hands touched briefly for the first time and their eyes locked. They shared a moment.

"Thank you so much, they are lovely," Alexa said with a delighted expression on her face.

"Lovely flowers for a lovely young lady. Come on let's get away from here."

They began walking away from the buildings of the busy camp and headed off towards the surrounding fields. The picturesque French countryside surrounded them, making the perfect backdrop for their first date. After walking together for a while, Antoni led them through a meadow, over to a nearby stream and suggested that they sit by the large oak tree, under its canopy of leaves. Anthony took off his uniform jacket, placing it inside out and facing downward on the grass, then invited Alexa to sit. Alexa sat down, still holding her bunch of flowers in her hand.

"I wish I had some fresh baguettes, French cheeses and some fine red wine to serve you Mademoiselle, but alas I do not."

"Not to worry, I'm happy just to be here with you and you've picked a most charming spot for us to enjoy."

Antoni reached into his pocket and retrieved a bar of dark chocolate, "Well, I do have something nice for you to eat." He opened the paper wrapping and lay the bar of chocolate on top of his jacket, next to Alexa. He then broke it up into small squares and invited Alexa to help herself. Alexa appreciated that he had obviously put some thought into their date, even though he had very little resources.

"Thank you, I love chocolate."

Her mind immediately travelled back to the last time she had had some. The memory of being held in the old schoolhouse with all the Germans, when she had stood up for herself and declared that she was indeed a Polish citizen and had actually been taken prisoner by the Nazis', years prior. The kind American commander, who had empathy for her story and had given her much needed food to eat, followed by several bars of chocolate. Then in an instant, her memories shifted to the old man who had appeared on the dark road on that cold winter's night when she was lost trying to find her way to the convent. He had appeared like a guardian angel out of nowhere, an answer to her prayers, keeping her company, showing her the way and sharing his bar of chocolate with her.

"What are you thinking about?" Antoni asked her.

"Oh, just about the last time I had chocolate to eat."

"Tell me about it."

So, Alexa began telling him of the last two times she had chocolate and then rewound her story back to its nightmare beginning, telling Antoni of how she was originally taken away from her mother in Poland, almost five years earlier. Antoni listened to every word of her story and several times during it, seemed visibly uncomfortable. He smoked two cigarettes while she spoke which Alexa put down to the stressful nature of her story.

"...and then I got moved to the job in the supply store on Monday, met you and here we are on our first date."

"That's quite a story Alexa. You have been through a lot."

"Yes, but I always tell myself, it could have been much worse. There are so many people who have suffered horrifically during the war and have perished. Me, I've always had God on my side, and he's kept me safe. I'm still alive and soon I will make it back home and hopefully find my mother and sister there waiting for me."

"You have a very positive attitude despite what you've been through. That's good! You also don't seem to hold hatred or malice towards the Germans'."

"Well I suppose I don't really. Don't get me wrong, I despise what the Nazis have done to millions of people under Hitler's direction, but I don't hate all of the German people because if it. I believe that when hate is encouraged, supported and allowed to run loose in society, the stronger it becomes. Hate is like a poison, that can infect and quickly spread becoming pandemic. Look at the influence that Hitler's hatred of the Jews' has had on such a mass scale. His toxic hatred became so divisive, so destructive and so deadly."

"You are right Alexa, what you're saying is so true."

"Just look at how the Jewish race has been treated, terrorized, tortured and almost totally annihilated across Europe and for what? What did they ever do that was so terrible? They raised families, worked hard and worshipped their God. Is that not what we all should have the right to do?"

"You're right Alexa, I agree with you."

"Good, because it's very clear that through hate and peoples' indifference and intolerance, hate spread like wildfire. And look how it then spread throughout Europe to non-Jews. Look at my life and that of my mother's. We were Catholic and look at how our lives and the lives of so many others, have been forever changed all because of the spread of Hitler's hatred. So, No Antoni, I will not allow a breeding ground for hatred in my life. Love is the answer, only love! And my trust I place in God, the true source of love. He promises that everyone will answer to him on judgement day and that he will repay the wicked for their evil deeds."

"You have very strong faith for a woman so young, I wish I had such faith!"

"Tell me your story Antoni, where are you and your family from?" Alexa asked while she reached for another piece of chocolate, "How did you end up here in France at the displacement camp?

CHAPTER -17-

Antoni took out another cigarette and lit it up. "My family are from Gryfów Śląski in Poland. I was born there."

"So, does that make you Polish or German?"

"It was originally Polish land and then in the 1740's, Prussia ruled over it. Years later it reverted back to Polish territory and now it is back under German jurisdiction, but I don't think it will remain that way now that the war is over. It was German land when I was born there, so technically and geographically I'm German. But I tell people that I'm Polish. My family moved to Lodz when I was a small boy, where I went to school. I grew up in Poland, speaking Polish and living Polish! I'm as good as Polish!" Antoni said nervously.

"Oh, I see," said Alexa in a surprised voice.

"Please, you must keep this between us, no one here can know that I am geographically German. Please promise me Alexa! You're the only person I've told."

Alexa admired his honesty for she knew how easy it would have been for him to lie about that fact to her and she would have been none the wiser, but she wanted to know more about him, before committing to keep his secret.

"What have you been doing during the war?"

"My family were very wealthy at one point. My grandfather was the owner of five large and very successful fabric factories in Poland. Unfortunately, he was killed in a tragic car accident and my father and his siblings had to take over running the businesses. We lived very well in our large family home in Lodz. We wanted for nothing and had the best of everything. My parents were very happy." Antoni paused for a moment and reached for another cigarette while he paced forward towards the edge of the stream from the oak tree and then back again, looking down the whole time. "Then the Nazis' came! They took our factories from us and all that we owned. They took our stately home and threw us all out onto the street with nothing. My father was forced to go and work for the German army handing out ration cards to the nearby Poles, who were starving and given very little to survive on."

Alexa was riveted to Antoni's story and hung on his every word. She could feel the deep emotion pouring out from the young man.

"My father was such a good-hearted man and was so deeply distressed by the plight of the desperate Polish families whom he saw lining up in front of him. The German army placed him in the job of handing out minimal ration cards to the Polish citizens who qualified for them. He was so determined to help the Polish people that he began stealing extra ration cards and would give them out secretly to the Polish people with small families. That was until someone, an informant, reported him to the Gestapo one day and then he was immediately removed from his post. I've never seen him again since that day and as I tried to search for any trace of him, there was no further information. Rumors spread that he had perhaps been sent as a prisoner to a concentration camp that very week. So, I don't even know if he's still alive."

"That's awful, I'm so sorry Antoni."

Antoni could feel that Alexa was filled with compassion towards him and he moved closer to her, sitting down on the grass next to her on her left. Alexa reached her left hand over and placed it gently on his right forearm. Antoni abruptly pulled his arm away, which startled Alexa, as if she had done something wrong. Antoni then proceeded to unbutton his cuff and to roll up his sleeve, exposing his bare right arm.

"Look, you see this?" Antoni pointed to his arm. It was heavily scarred over a large section, from the tendon at his right thumb, all the way up through his wrist, along his veins and almost up to his elbow.

"What happened to you? Who did this to you?" Alexa asked him, visibly saddened by the physical pain which she could only imagine that he must have gone through.

"I did it!"

Alexa was shocked at his reply, "What do you mean you did it?"

"I knew that the Nazis were going to force me to join the German army and I was determined that I would not be placed in the position to kill innocent people. So, I took a sharp knife and hacked away at my own right arm, so they would hopefully find me unfit for military combat. It was the most painful physical experience I've ever endured and took a long time to heal, but it worked because I was trained as an electrician instead." He turned and stared into Alexa's deep blue empathetic eyes. "...and that training brought me to work in the supply store yesterday and brought me here to you today! Electricity brought me to you Alexa!"

Alexa's eyes were fixed firmly on his. There was a moment of silence and then Antoni leaned in and kissed her gently on the lips. It was Alexa's very first kiss and she wasn't quite sure what to do, but she didn't want to pull back. Secretly, she had wanted him to kiss her from the very first minute they had met. The kiss lasted a few seconds and then Antoni pulled back.

"So, you see, you must keep my secret. No one can ever know that I am German. They wouldn't understand."

"I will keep your secret, I'll tell no one, I promise!"

Antoni had gained her trust and leaned in once again to kiss Alexa. This time he reached his arms around her, holding her close to him in a tight embrace. The kiss lasted considerably longer than the first one had done, and Alexa hopelessly melted into Antoni's arms. She could have stayed there all day, absorbed in the comfort and safety which she felt wrapped in Antoni's arms - something she had never felt before. *'This must be love'* she thought to herself. Antoni peeled his lips from Alexa's and, releasing her, he reached for her hand.

"I want you to be my girlfriend. Will you be my girl?"

Alexa was still trying to catch her breath and felt quite light-headed after her second kiss, but she didn't need much time to think about the question, nor to reply with her answer.

"Yes, I'll be your girl Antoni."

The warm July evening was drawing to a close as the sun began gradually sinking down from the deep crimson sky, getting itself ready to set. Antoni suggested that they start heading back to the camp, realizing that it was getting quite late and they had missed dinner already. Neither of them seemed too bothered by that fact, nor were they very hungry which was just as well. Antoni stood up and then helped Alexa to her feet. He handed her the remainder of the chocolate bar and picked up his jacket, shaking off the loose grass. He took another cigarette out of his pocket and raised it up towards his mouth, then stopped and instead, pulled Alexa close to him and laid another kiss on her soft lips. By now she was getting the hang of it and she kissed him right back. Antoni lit his cigarette holding it in one hand while he took Alexa's hand in his other and led them through the tall grass and out of the meadow.

Alexa felt like she was walking on clouds, *'This must be what love feels like,'* she thought to herself and happily held on to Antoni's hand.

When they arrived back at the camp, Antoni said he'd meet her again the next day after work outside of the supply store. Alexa agreed and they shared one final lingering kiss goodnight before leaving each other's company.

"Don't forget your promise Alexa. Tell no one that I'm German. Okay, my beautiful girlfriend?"

"Ok, I won't forget, I promise. It's our secret."

"Goodnight."

Alexa turned and walked toward her barracks where she knew her friends would be waiting for her return and waiting to hear all about her date. She'd tell them about most of it, just not about Antoni's history or where he was born. She'd keep his secret. As she entered their room, Greta was the first one to notice her and announced her arrival to Marta and Henrietta. They all noticed the glow radiating from her and how absolutely over the moon and happy she appeared to be.

"Alexa's in love," sang Marta. "Alexa's in love."

"So, what if I am?" Alexa replied with a large smile on her face, not denying it.

"Tell us all about it," said Henrietta, "How did your date go with the electrician?"

"It was great and he's now my boyfriend," announced Alexa as she lay down on top of her bed.

"Does that mean that you kissed?" Marta asked as she walked over to Alexa and sat down next to her on her bunk.

"Maybe it does. We sat by a stream and talked for a while. He brought me a bar of dark chocolate and even gave me flowers. Oh no!" Alexa exclaimed.

"What is it?" Greta asked.

"I forgot to pick up my flowers, I left them behind where we were sitting."

"You must have had your mind on other things," joked Marta.

"Don't worry, if you're his girlfriend now, I'm sure he will be giving you plenty more flowers," suggested Greta.

"So, does that mean you'll not be interested in a date with the American soldier now?" Henrietta asked.

"That's right, I'll have to tell him that I'm not interested in going out with him. But you three are very welcome to go on a date with him if you wish."

They all laughed at Alexa's sarcastic comment. It was getting late and Alexa was tired from her long day and all of its excitement. She just wanted to climb into her bed by herself and reflect on her date with Antoni and drift off to sleep daydreaming about him. But she knew her friends wouldn't be able to leave her in peace. Not until their curiosity was satisfied. So, like the good friend that she was, Alexa answered their questions as best as she could. However, she remained conscious of her promise to Antoni to keep his secret.

The following morning the girls headed off to work after they had finished breakfast. Alexa was especially hungry since she had missed dinner the night before. She ate two helpings of watery scrambled eggs that morning. Soon after Marta and Henrietta arrived at work in the laundry building, an American and a French officer appeared asking to speak to Henrietta. She went off to speak with them then returned back to her work station, about half an hour later.

"What did they want with you?" Marta asked.

"Well, it seems that there is an Allied truck which is going to transport some people from here back to the Netherlands. They say it should be safe now to return and since I'm Dutch, I have been selected to go home."

"When?"

"Tomorrow!"

The two friends stared at each other for a moment, as the reality of her words sank in. Then they began hugging one another. For as much as Henrietta had wanted to go home for so long and had been her ultimate goal, knowing that she'd be setting off the next day was rather overwhelming. For Marta also, it was a shock and hard to process. She was happy for her good friend to be finally returning home to find her family, but she felt a pain in her heart at the realization that they'd soon be parted, after being so close like sisters for so long.

"I'm going to miss you more than you know Henrietta! My days will be empty without you," Marta tried hard to fight back her tears but some escaped and trickled down her cheeks.

"Please don't cry Marta, I'm trying to be strong right now. Anyway, you'll probably be next. We'll all be going home soon. We knew the day would eventually come."

"What about Greta? Is she going back home with you?" Marta asked.

"Oh, I never thought. I don't know. They never mentioned her to me. We will have to find her and ask."

They carried on working for the rest of the morning shift and when lunchtime came, they went off in search of Greta and Alexa to tell them the news. They all seemed to lose their appetites and were filled with sadness. Henrietta tried to be the strong one as usual and insisted that she needed a sweet black coffee for the shock, so they all got themselves one and sat drinking them together at a nearby table. Greta had heard nothing about the transportation arrangement that morning, so they assumed she wouldn't be included in it.

"Let's not go back to work, this afternoon," suggested Greta, "Let's just spend our last afternoon together!"

The four friends looked at each other and nodded in agreement. It seemed to be the best idea and just the thought of it made them all feel a little bit happier under the circumstances. They'd take advantage of the situation and make the most of the limited time which they had left together. They finished drinking their coffee, then grabbed a fresh apple each to take with them and all headed off together out of the displacement camp. They made their way towards the nearby French countryside and found an open field to go and rest in. The four friends spent three hours relaxing there in the tall grass together, chatting and laughing as they spent their last afternoon together in each other's company lying in the hot

July sun. They all agreed that no matter where they ended up, or whatever paths their lives took them down, they would always remain good friends. They vowed that they'd all find each other again somehow and that they'd keep in touch until they were old and grey.

The hours went by very quickly and the women eventually made their way back to the camp in time for dinner. They decided to return to their barracks to clean up first before going to eat. On Greta's bed there was a note which had been left for her attention, ordering her to report to the main army office as soon as possible. The four friends looked at each other in silence as if they knew already what the reason for the note was. Just as they had suspected, Greta was informed when she went to the main army office, that she too had been selected to travel back to Holland on the same truck as Henrietta, leaving first thing in the morning.

The four friends made their way to dinner for their last meal together. While they were sitting eating, Antoni came over to their table to speak to Alexa. She introduced him to Henrietta and Marta whom he hadn't yet met. Both women were glad to meet him and became aware of just how handsome he actually was in person. Alexa and Greta hadn't exaggerated about his good looks. Antoni asked Alexa to come and speak with him alone, so she got up from the table and walked outside of the building with him.

"I waited for you after work today. Why didn't you meet me as we had agreed?" Antoni enquired.

"I'm so sorry Antoni, but at lunch we discovered that Henrietta has been selected to be transported back to Holland tomorrow morning. We all skipped work this afternoon so that we could all spend our last afternoon together. Now we've just found out that Greta is leaving with her too."

"Oh, I see, but that's good news, right? That they are finally going home?"

"They are my best friends and we've all been together every day since the convent. We are family now. We are all going to miss each other so much and who knows what they will find when they return home?"

"I don't suppose you want to spend some time with me after dinner, do you?" Antoni asked.

"I'm sorry, but I want to spend my last few hours with my friends tonight."

Antoni understood, but selfishly hoped for a different reply from Alexa. Antoni persisted, "Can I see you tomorrow after work then?"

"Yes, I will meet you outside of the supply store when I finish."

Antoni leaned over and kissed her cheek then Alexa said goodbye and headed back to her friends to finish her meal.

"So that's your handsome boyfriend! He's a good looker alright. I'm glad I got to meet him before I left here," said Henrietta.

"Are you going to marry him Alexa?" Marta asked her.

"Well he's not asked me yet!"

The women smiled and Greta said, "Don't let that stop you." Then they all began to laugh. After dinner they made their way back to their room in their barracks for their final night together. They tried to write down a reliable address where they could be contacted when they got back home, however since they did not know the situation at their homes, it proved difficult. They were full of mixed emotions. Alexa suggested that she say her prayer for them all out loud, to which her three friends were in agreement. They kneeled together, closed their eyes and clasped their hands. As she recited Psalm 91, she changed some words from singular to plural, using us and our, instead of me and I. Once she got to the end, she said "Amen" followed by, Henrietta, Greta and Marta. The three of them said it this time with more conviction and hope than they ever had before. Then they slept.

The morning arrived all too soon and the young women awoke to grey overcast skies with light rainfall. They got washed and dressed, then Henrietta and Greta packed together their small bundles of belongings, which didn't amount to very much, and they all made their way to get breakfast one last time together before their two friends headed off on their journey home. The mood was somber, and the girls were visibly saddened. It was time for Greta and Henrietta to get on board the truck and bid their friends au revoir. There was a small group of people gathered around the truck. Reluctantly, they started saying their final goodbyes and hugged each other tightly before heading off on their six-hour drive.

One of the French soldiers asked out loudly, "Okay, so who's traveling to Belgium and Holland on this truck?" His question caught Marta's attention as she was after all from Belgium, but she hadn't been told that she was to go on that truck with the others.

"Ask if you are to go with us," said Henrietta.

Marta asked the soldier, telling him that she was from Belgium. The soldier checked his list for her name and said that yes, she was indeed on it and was supposed to be traveling on the same transport also. Marta panicked and told him that no one had informed her and that she didn't have her belongings ready to leave. The soldier told her to go and get them quickly, that the truck would wait for her for ten minutes only. He told her to hurry up. Alexa went with Marta back to their barracks, running all the way there and back. They hardly had time to process the reality of the situation. Alexa however, understood clearly what it meant for her. She was going to be alone. Her three friends were all leaving together on the truck to return to their homes, but she was staying behind. Alone again.

The engines of the truck revved up with all the passengers on board, except for Greta, Henrietta and Marta. They all hugged Alexa one last time as they tried to fight back their tears. They climbed into the back of the truck and it pulled off as they waved and blew kisses to Alexa, with tears rolling down their faces. Alexa was left standing in the rain, watching as the vehicle disappeared out of the camp gates and off into the distance. Her friends were gone, gone too soon!

Alexa made her way to the supply store where she was due to start work. She hadn't had to work alone since she was at the Klauss's farmhouse. Her American supervisor came over and inquired as to where Greta was and as to why they both hadn't showed up for work the previous afternoon. Alexa began to explain what had happened with her friends the previous day, trying hard to keep her emotions in check, but failing miserably. Alexa couldn't hold back the tears that were streaming from her eyes, as she told her story. Thankfully, the female supervisor was empathetic to Alexa's version of events and sympathized with the sadness she was displaying as best she could.

"Look, I'm sure you'll be going home soon too Alexa, back to Poland. I hear that it's safer there now. You'll probably be reunited with your family and friends too, that you haven't seen for so long. Then you can get in touch with Greta and your other two friends again when you're settled. How you're feeling now is only temporary, believe me," she tried to reason. The woman's positive words did help to calm Alexa down somewhat. She stopped the tears from falling, composed herself and got ready to start her days work. '...I've gotten through tougher days than this,' Alexa thought to herself, as she shifted her mind onto her work.

CHAPTER -18-

Alexa's work day finally came to an end and she headed outside of the supply store. Antoni was waiting there for her, just as he said he would be.

"Hello beautiful! How are you today?" Antoni asked as she walked over towards him.

"I'm glad to see you, but it's been a really tough day. All three of my best friends left the camp this morning and I'm all alone again."

"You're not alone Alexa, you've got me and I'm not planning to leave you anytime soon." He reached out his hand and pulled her close, holding her in his arms. She felt comforted and reassured by his words, as she nuzzled her head into his chest. Antoni held her tightly and began stroking her pretty blonde hair, "Don't worry. You've got me, I'll look after you darling."

They headed off towards the canteen building and ate their first meal together, which would be the first of many. Eating together became the young couple's new routine and from then on, they spent almost every spare moment in each other's company when they weren't working. They were inseparable.

Antoni regularly brought up the subject of leaving the displacement camp in his conversations and of finally returning home to Poland with Alexa. Since before the official end of the Second World War on the second of September 1945, many of the displaced Europeans gradually began trying to make the long and difficult journey back to their homes by any means possible. Searching for what they had lost, for what had been left behind and for what was violently and horrifically stolen from them. For the familiar, for their families, their friends, their homes, their belongings...their lives.

Antoni had managed to save up a small amount of money by doing some private electrical repair jobs in a few of the local French homes and businesses. It wasn't much, but it was something. He had also won some money from gambling in occasional card games with both the American and Allied troops, being that he was quite good at poker. He had a great poker face. He started making plans in his head for Alexa and him to leave France and make the long journey back to Poland together. Alexa told him that she didn't have any money, or really own anything of value besides her grandmother's necklace with the cross but that it wasn't probably worth much except sentimental value to her. To her it was priceless.

Antoni figured out that when they were ready to leave, it would be best for them to get a ride into Paris on one of the Allied trucks and from there catch a train to Berlin. They'd have to change trains in Berlin, but from there they could get on a train that would take them to Warsaw, which was in the center of Poland. Once there, they could travel relatively easily by train or bus to Lodz where Antoni's mother and father lived and where he had grown up. Hopefully once there he would locate his father Fritz, or at least, be able to begin the search for him. Next in their plans would be to travel to Alexa's home town of Lublin, in search of her mother Sophia and her sister Asha. After that, there was no plan. They would go day by day and try to rebuild a new life for themselves.

It was now nearing the end of September. Alexa and Antoni had been dating for a relatively short time. Although they'd only been together for almost two months, they were completely in love with each other. Antoni decided that he was going to ask Alexa to marry him. It wasn't uncommon in the displacement camp for marriages to take place since many people were alone, abandoned, stripped of their families and desperate for love. For a feeling of closeness with another human being who understood their trauma. For a connection with someone of the opposite sex. A partner. When they found someone to share intimacy with, they'd fall into each other's arms quickly and marriage was entered into lightly, with big expectations. There was a priest from the Red Cross who performed simple ceremonies for young couples, who had met each other in the camp and fallen in love, or in like. The celebrations were by no means elaborate but they were happy occasions where vows and rings were legally exchanged. The brides often borrowed a simple second-hand white lace dress to wear which the Red Cross would loan out for such occasions and they'd also have a small bunch of fresh flowers to hold. Beyond that, depending on how popular the couple were, not much else. Their friends would throw them a small party with whatever supplies they could gather together. Antoni decided that he would propose to Alexa that weekend and as long as Alexa said yes, which he was sure she would, he'd waste no time in arranging the nuptials. Then he'd put the plans in motion as soon as possible for their journey back to Poland together.

The last Friday of September arrived and at the end of the work day, Antoni waited outside of the supply store for Alexa to finish work. When she came out, the young couple made their way to dinner and ate their meal together as usual. Antoni suggested that they take a leisurely walk to the meadow where they had gone on their first date. It was a beautiful warm evening out and he suggested, they go and watch the sunset together. Alexa loved that romantic idea so after they finished eating, they made their way out of the gates and away from the camp, arm in arm. Antoni took her back to the same tree by the little stream, where he had first taken her almost two months earlier. Alexa began looking around the base of the tree, as if she had lost something and to her surprise, she came across what she was looking for. Extremely withered and far from how they had looked when she had first received them, lying scattered on the ground where she had left them, were the remains of the bunch of wild flowers which Antoni had first given her.

"What are you looking for?" Antoni asked her.

"Look, do you remember these?" Alexa pointed down to the remains on the ground.

"No, what are they?"

"Those were the flowers that you gave me on our first date. I was so upset when I got back to the barracks that night and realized I had forgotten them."

He once again lay his jacket inside out on the grass and told Alexa to sit down.

"Don't move. I'll be back in a few minutes!"

"Where are you going?"

"It's a surprise! Just sit here until I get back, Okay?"

"Okay."

Antoni lit up a cigarette and walked off into the tall grasses of the meadow. When he returned a few minutes later, he had a large bunch of pretty wild flowers in his hand with a red rose in the center. He appeared from behind the tree and sat down next to Alexa.

"Oh Antoni, they are beautiful."

"I wish I could give you something even more beautiful right now but I'm afraid this is all I have." He handed her the flowers and took hold of her right hand, "Alexa, I want to marry you. Will you be my wife?" Then Antoni reached his hand into his shirt pocket and from it pulled out a white cotton handkerchief. He opened it up and from the center, lifted out a round shaped piece of metal.

"I know it's not much, but it's the best I could do for now."

Alexa looked down at the simple ring, which was made from a metal piece of wire that had been bent round by hand twice. Threaded through the wire were two glass beads, one clear smaller one and a red colored one next to it. It became obvious to Alexa that Antoni had made it himself, she looked up and starred into his eyes, then spoke the words that he wanted to hear.

"Yes, I will. I will marry you Antoni." Those were also the words that she had wanted to hear herself say to him. She was head over heels in love with Antoni and had dreamed about sharing her life with him since soon after the very first day she had first met him. Antoni leaned over and took her close in his arms. They locked lips and shared a long and passionate kiss.

"I love you Antoni."

"And I love you too Alexa and when we get back to Poland, I promise you I will buy you a beautiful, more precious ring that you can be proud of." He placed the ring on her finger, then tightened it to make it secure. They both leaned back against the tree and watched the setting sun, as it filled the sky with deep reds on its descent. Overhead passed a flock of geese in flight, a beautiful sight against the sunset. The geese let out their collective cries as if making a public declaration of their approval for the young couple. Antoni began telling Alexa the plans which he had come up with. Of how he wanted them to get married as soon as possible, so that they could then get ready to leave the displacement camp at Mourmelon and begin part one of their long train journey from Paris. Alexa didn't need much persuasion. She was in agreement and onboard with his plans.

"Okay, I will go into town to the jeweler who I did some electrical work for and buy our wedding rings. Then I'll speak with the priest at the camp to see how soon he can marry us. After we do that, then we can get set to leave and I'll buy us tickets for the train to Berlin from Paris."

"Wow! It's really happening."

"Yes beautiful, we're getting married and we're going home."

Antoni sat with his arm around Alexa, while she lay her head against his chest and they watched the sun completely disappear from the horizon. As darkness filled the sky, the newly engaged young couple slowly made their way back to the camp, walking hand in hand. The stars sparkled in the sky above, like diamonds against a blanket of black velvet. Antoni walked Alexa back to her barracks and kissed her goodnight. Alexa wished more than anything at that point, that she could go inside and share her wonderful news with her three best friends. But they were gone.

On Saturday morning Antoni rose early and kept to his word of searching out the Catholic priest to discuss the possibility of his performing their marriage ceremony. He was willing and said he could marry them the following Saturday morning in the small chapel inside of the camp. Next, Antoni hitched a ride into the nearby town of Mourmelon-Le-Petit and visited the local jewelry shop. He knew the owner Robert from when he had completed some electrical repairs for him the month before. He told the owner of his plans to marry his beautiful Polish girlfriend and purchased two basic gold wedding bands, which he was given at a reduced price. Robert told Antoni that his wife Sonia was a hairdresser and said that if Alexa wished, he'd arrange for his wife to give her a new hairstyle for free, the day before the wedding. Antoni said he'd tell his girlfriend about the kind offer and maybe he'd arrange for her to come back on Friday if she was interested.

At the local station, He asked for the train schedule to Paris and from Paris to Berlin. It was only an eighty-minute train ride into Paris, so if he was unable to get them a ride directly into Paris on one of the army trucks, the train from Mourmelon-Le-Petit would work out fine. Then he made his way back to the camp to share the good news with Alexa. On hearing Antoni's updates, Alexa was ecstatic and couldn't wait to be his wife. However, she did wish that her three friends were still around to witness them saying their vows on their wedding day. Neither of them would have any family members there, nor would they have any really close friends attending to help them celebrate the occasion. It didn't bother Antoni too much, but it did make Alexa sad. Never once had she imagined that her wedding day, would play out in such a non-eventful, no frills way. Antoni reassured her that when they got back to Poland and reunited with their families and friends, they would have a proper wedding celebration. That made Alexa feel a lot better and she viewed their upcoming nuptials, more as a formality and as only part one of their union.

The following week sped by quickly and Alexa counted down the days until she was to marry the handsome young man with whom she was so in love. She agreed to go into town and have her hair done by the jeweler's wife, so Anthony walked there with her. The women were introduced and were happy to make each other's acquaintance. Sonia was an elegant and very pretty blonde woman who seemed genuinely excited and happy for the young couple. She welcomed Alexa warmly and the first thing she did, was make a fresh pot of coffee for them both at the back of the shop. Antoni and Robert made themselves scarce and left the shop together, saying that they'd return in a few hours' time. That seemed to suit the women just fine and they began getting to know one another better and discussing various hair styles.

Sonia mentioned that she had got some brand-new hair dyes to try out and that they were all the rage in Paris. Alexa decided a new hair color would be a welcome change for her, a nice change from looking like a perfect blonde German woman. After all, the war was over now she reasoned and so being blonde and Arian looking wouldn't have to be her saving grace any more. She chose the dark brown dye to try out, from the three available colors and the jeweler's wife seemed only too happy to oblige her. When the process was complete, she looked in the mirror at her new hairstyle. Alexa was happy with her new image even though it was only temporary. The blonde Alexa was gone. A little over two hours later Antoni and Robert returned to the shop and there, they got their first look at Alexa's new hair style.

"Wow! What have you done?" Antoni asker her in a shocked voice.

"I decided I needed a change, so I got rid of the blonde. Don't you like it?" Alexa asked him disappointedly.

"I'm just surprised that's all! I love blondes!"

Robert nudged his arm and quickly said, "He meant to say that he loved your hair blonde, didn't you Antoni?"

"Yes of course I did. I loved your hair blonde Alexa, that's who I fell in love with."

"So what? Now you don't love me with dark hair?"

"Don't panic! It's only a temporary dye, it will wash out in a few weeks and she'll be back to blonde again," reassured Sonia.

"Of course, I still love you Alexa, we're getting married tomorrow, aren't we?"

"Yes, but..."

"But nothing, tomorrow you'll be my wife and when the dye washes out, you'll be blonde again."

Alexa thanked Sonia for doing her hair for free and for the pleasant few hours they had spent together in each other's company. Robert and Sonia wished them all the best and congratulated them in advance for their wedding day. Antoni and Alexa left the shop and headed back to the camp.

"Are you sure you still love me Antoni?" Alexa asked, looking for reassurance from him.

"Of course, I do, I love both of you," he laughed.

"That's not funny!"

"Sure, it is, it's like getting two wives for the price of one. What more could a man ask for?" He laughed even louder.

"You better behave Antoni, or you'll end up with none," then Alexa laughed.

"You're more than enough for me Alexa. I'll be so happy to have you as my wife." Antoni leaned over and kissed her on the cheek. Then he took a second look at the new Alexa and cracked a half-smile. "But please don't ever dye your hair dark again. For our second wedding in Poland, I want you blonde again, Okay?"

"Okay," she replied, and they continued on walking hand in hand.

Alexa opted not to wear the basic Red Cross white lace dress which was loaned to all the young brides who wished to marry in the displacement camp. Instead she wore her smart army-issue uniform which matched Antoni's attire. She had decided to wait for their second wedding, their proper celebration to dress as she'd really like to. The ceremony was over very quickly and after they exchanged their vows and placed the wedding rings on each other's fingers, the priest pronounced them husband and wife. They sealed the proceedings with a kiss, and both signed the necessary official documents. One of the Allied army soldier photographers in the camp, took a photograph of the newly married couple and once he developed it, he gave it to the newlyweds as a souvenir. It was their first photograph together.

Antoni had informed the Mourmelon camp army office that he and his new wife would be leaving the displacement camp that weekend, to make their own long journey back to Poland together. The camp commander arranged for them to be driven on the Sunday morning into the center of Paris to the main railway station and authorized for them to be given some supplies for their journey, as well as some extra ration cards. The commander also gifted them a bottle of French wine to celebrate the beginning of the young couple's new life together. They spent their wedding day in the camp and were congratulated by several of their fellow camp-mates and a few of Antoni's friends. They ate in the Red Cross building as they did every day, but word had spread about their marriage and halfway through, a couple of the Allied troops came over to their table. They brought a bottle of vodka with them to celebrate, and the soldier who had bought Alexa's guitar from her, played some songs and serenaded the happy couple. The impromptu party went on for a few hours with singing and dancing. Antoni and Alexa had their first dance together and one of the French cooks brought out a small cake that she had made for them, which helped to make their wedding day just that little bit more special.

As the evening approached 9 pm, the newly-weds thanked everyone for celebrating with them and for all their good wishes on their journey the next morning. Since Alexa's three girlfriends had left the camp, there had been no new women assigned to share her bunk with her. The camp at Mourmelon had served its purpose for over a year, as a safe haven for many displaced people. Many had started to leave the camp over the previous month, to return to their homes and there weren't any new arrivals coming anymore. The camp had notified everyone in it that it was going to close as a refuge for the displaced so, those who were still there were making plans with the Red Cross to leave.

Antoni gathered the few belongings together from his barracks that he'd be taking on their journey and brought them over to Alexa's room. He packed them along with Alexa's things into an army issue duffel bag ready for their morning departure. Antoni carried their packed bag to a room where he had been granted permission for them both to sleep. It was to be their last night in the camp and their first night together as a married couple. They spent the night together sleeping in each other's arms.

The morning was a beautiful one, bright and sunny with blue skies. Antoni and Alexa ate breakfast together then after collecting their belongings, they made their way to the army truck which would be driving them to the train station in Paris. They both took their last look behind them at the place which had been their home for the past six months. They said their goodbyes then climbed on board the truck, and for the first time, they got to sit up front next to the driver.

CHAPTER -19-

fter an hour and a half of driving, the truck arrived on the outskirts of Paris. As they drove through the suburbs on route to the capital, it was clear that many of the working-class areas of Paris had suffered from several bombing raids. Primarily, parts of Paris were bombed by the Germans at the start of the war, but towards the end of the war, the Allied troops caused much of the structural damage as they targeted French factories taken over by the Nazis during the German occupation. Although Paris was not as heavily bombed as many of the other major European cities, the scars were still very visible. However due to Hitler's fascination with Paris, his desire was to keep the city in its state of architectural beauty, and it had pretty much remained intact.

The truck driver was a French soldier and he took the scenic route as a little treat for the newly-weds and drove them around the Arc de Triumph, down the Champs Elysees, then South towards the Eiffel Tower. Alexa was in awe of the world-famous landmark and got a sense of its tremendous height, even though they were on the opposite side of the river from it. They drove along the banks of the river Seine where the beautiful architecture of Paris was unspoiled and on display before their eyes. They passed by the stunning and ornate Louvre museum and the Notre Dame cathedral, both of which remained unspoiled. Then the driver turned left heading North towards the Gare Du Nord, Paris's main train station which was another architectural gem in its own right. The truck came to a stop outside of the station and the driver let Antoni and Alexa out with their belongings and wished them Bon Voyage. The couple thanked the soldier for driving them and for the scenic tour, then headed into the station to find out the departure times of the trains to Berlin. They approached the main information booth inside of the station and found out that the next direct train bound for Berlin was due to leave at 1pm from platform five. Antoni purchased two second-class tickets at the ticket counter and located the platform from which the train would be departing. The station was a tall structure with lots of large arched windows high up on both sides and had a massive glass roof supported by long ornate, cast iron beams and pillars.

The station was a bustling hub of constant activity, with a variety of people coming and going in all directions. A real tapestry of humanity - French, American and Allied soldiers arriving and boarding trains carrying duffel bags, civilians too - a mix of young and old, rich-looking, neatly dressed Parisians, both business men in fine suits and elegant ladies in fine French fashions complete with matching heels, hats and handbags. Noticeable too were those far poorer people, in rough-looking, old tattered clothes and also those who were injured and wounded, all struggling to get back to their homes. Liberated prisoners from labor and concentration camps, a shadow of their former selves, refugees, men and women from various displacement camps. Gaunt-looking shells, protruding bones, hollow faces with sunken eyes, blank stares and empty expressions. Each face with a heartbreaking story etched into it, but each remaining silent, unable to form the words to relate their horrific experiences with others.

It was almost 10 am and since they had a few hours to spare before boarding their train, Antoni decided to take his pretty new wife to a Parisian café. They walked back out of the main entrance and onto the streets of Paris. Alexa had never been on the streets of such a large and beautiful city before and was loving the experience. There was so much to see and take in. Alexa scanned the sights before her eyes, soaking it all up. There were multiple blocks of elegant five and six story stone residential buildings, some with ornate balconies overlooking the streets below, with painted wooden window shutters for privacy and flower boxes full of color. The tall elegant street lamps had one or two large white round glass shades on each pole and although they were all switched off during the daytime hours, Alexa could imagine that they'd illuminate the streets at night with a magical glow. They passed by multiple shop windows with colorful artistic displays, accompanied with fancy unique hand-painted signage, freshly potted floral arrangements and hanging baskets accenting the doorways. Inviting French café's, with small outdoor tables and two matching chairs strategically placed on the pavements, to welcome the patrons who sat comfortably enjoying freshly brewed coffee and pastries, while reading their newspapers or chatting with a friend. Life in Paris seemed vibrant and most definitely worth living.

While she walked arm in arm with her new husband, she glanced down at her wedding ring and it suddenly dawned on Alexa that they were in the city of love and technically, they were actually on their honeymoon. Antoni spotted a quaint little café across the street which he liked the look of and suggested that they stop for a while and order something there together. The morning sun was still shining brightly, so they picked a table outside and sat down at it. Antoni lit up a cigarette and waited for the waitress to bring them a menu and told Alexa that he had enough money for them to order a hot drink and a small snack each. So once the waitress arrived, Antoni ordered two strong black coffees in his best French. Then he asked for a croissant with jam for himself and Alexa selected a fresh pastry from the selection on display inside. For the first time Alexa felt truly free, a free citizen of the world. She felt safe in the protection and love of her handsome new husband. This was a new chapter in her life. She wasn't just an actor in this romantic movie, she was the new leading lady in it. Made over and ready to embrace life, Alexa felt happier than she had ever felt before.

The time was approaching noon, when Antoni said it was time for them to leave the café and head back to the train station. Antoni paid their bill to the waitress, gathered their belongings and began walking with Alexa back to the Guard du Nord, the same way that they had come. Along the way, Antoni stopped at one of the bakers and purchased some fresh baguettes, using the French ration cards which he had been given by the Mourmelon camp commander. Then at another shop he bought some smoked sausages, sliced ham and two local cheeses for their journey. Using up the majority of the French ration cards which he had remaining, Antoni bought two bottles of milk, some butter, a small pot of jam and some chocolate.

As they continued walking through the streets, Alexa caught sight of an old book shop and stopped to take a look in the window. She noticed an old Polish Bible on display, which was just like the one that she had when she was a child and pointed it out to Antoni. Antoni was not religious himself, but he could see how interested Alexa seemed to be in the small black book.

"Oh Antoni, could we buy it, please?"

"It depends how much it costs darling."

"My German Bible was lost when the convent was bombed at St Clemens and I haven't had one since, but this Bible is the very same kind as the one I had growing up in Poland."

"Ok, let's go inside and ask how much it is."

When they went inside, they found an elderly French gentleman sitting behind the counter. Alexa lifted the Bible from out of the window and flicked its pages a few times back and forwards, then brought it over to the counter. Antoni asked the old man how much he wanted for it, as Alexa opened the Bible to Psalm 91. She began reading the chapter that she knew so well, from off the page in an undertone. The old gentleman encouraged her to read it louder so that he could hear her too. She did just so, and her native Polish words reached his ears.

"Are you Polish, my grandmother was Polish?" The old gentleman asked.

"Yes, we both are, and we are returning back home to Poland today for the first time in five years since the war," answered Alexa.

"My wife and I are actually heading to the train station just now, for the one o'clock train, to Berlin. How much do you want for the Bible Sir?"

"Since your wife reads it so beautifully, she should have it."

"I had the very same Bible when I was a young child in Poland, my grandmother and my mother would always read it to me." Alexa told the old man.

"Well now it is yours again. Please take it as a small gift from me. Take it back to Poland with you on your journey home and read it often."

Alexa was overcome with emotion at the old gentleman's kind gesture, so she leaned over the counter reaching out her arms and kissed his cheek.

"Oh, thank you so much Sir. This means more to me than you could ever know."

"You're very welcome. Bon voyage and may God be with you Madame."

Antoni thanked the man and shook his hand. The young couple walked out of the old book shop, with Alexa carrying her new Bible in her hand. She was delighted with it, as well as touched by the kindness of another stranger towards her.

When they arrived back at platform five, the time was 12:40 pm. The whistle blew as the inbound Berlin train pulled into the station and as it slowed down to a complete stop, the brakes screeched, and a large blast of steam bellowed out from the front engine engulfing the air. Once all the passengers arriving in Paris alighted from the carriages, Antoni located an empty second-class carriage and climbed on board, helping Alexa up the few steps and led her to their compartment. The train compartment sat six people, but they were the first to arrive. Antoni lifted their duffel bag up onto the overhead storage shelf above them, placed their food on the seat next to him and pointed for Alexa to sit in nearest to the window. Antoni said he was going out onto the platform for a smoke before the train left, which was alright with Alexa, since she really didn't like the smell of cigarettes and secretly hoped he would stop one day. Once he had finished smoking, he climbed back on board and joined Alexa in the compartment and closed the sliding door to give them some privacy. The station master blew his whistle and the train released a blast of hot steam, then gradually moved off away from the platform out of the station, rolling down the tracks slowly picking up speed. Antoni put his arm around his wife's shoulder, as the train pulled out of the Paris station and began its long journey to Berlin.

"We're finally going home darling," Antoni said to Alexa and kissed her cheek while she looked out of the window.

"At long last," she said and kissed him back.

After about twenty minutes into the journey, the sliding door of their compartment opened, and the train conductor appeared asking to see their tickets. Antoni handed them to him for his inspection. He tore the corner of the tickets and then gave them back saying thank you, then exited and slid the door closed behind him. Seeing the conductor triggered Alexa's memory which rewound to her last train journey when she was leaving the Klauss's. She recalled the fear that she felt that day as the conductor yelled at her, telling her that she didn't have a first-class ticket and shouldn't be there in the first-class carriage. The terror and anxiety that she felt, in case her true identity was discovered by the Nazi soldiers and Gestapo officers who filled the entire train carriage, had almost paralyzed her with fear. Antoni asked what she was thinking about, noticing the serious expression on her reflective face so Alexa shared her story with him. Antoni got a good sense of just how terrifying it must have been for his wife that day as she related her frightening experience to him. He told her that he was proud of her for fooling the Germans and keeping her Polish identity concealed. Then he laughed at the fact that she had even managed to get the Gestapo officer to feel bad for her predicament and pay the balance of her ticket to make it into a first class one. Alexa also laughed at that part of the story for the very first time. She had never looked at it that way before. Having Antoni by her side, seemed to make everything that much better and all the more bearable. She also pointed out to him that her belief in the power of prayer and her unshakable faith in Psalm 91, had gotten her through many difficult times since she was taken from Poland. Antoni had never been convinced by the idea of prayer and God's saving power, but he seemed to respect Alexa's belief in them.

Antoni suggested that they get comfortable and take a nap since they'd had a very early start that morning and still had another nine hours train journey ahead of them until they arrived in Berlin. Alexa agreed and stretched out on one side of the compartment, snuggling her head into Antoni's chest. The sound of the train speeding along the steel tracks made a relaxing repetitive melody of four beats to the bar, which soon soothed the couple into a deep relaxed sleep.

After roughly five hours into their journey, the train had crossed the border at Strasbourg leaving France and was now traveling North through Western Germany approaching Frankfurt. Alexa was first to waken and open her eyes. As she sat up, Antoni also wakened. She reached for the bag of food supplies which they had bought and began preparing something for them to eat. Luckily Antoni had a pen knife in his pocket which he used to cut open the baguettes, slice some cheese and sausage, then used it to spread some butter. They opened one of the bottles of milk to drink and shared it between them. Soon after they had finished eating, the train pulled into the station at Frankfurt. Antoni took the opportunity to stretch his legs down on the platform for a few minutes and smoke a quick cigarette. Alexa stepped out of their compartment into the corridor of the carriage and lowered one of the windows near to where her husband was smoking and leaned out of it taking in the view. A few minutes later, after all the new passengers had gotten on board, the station master blew his whistle and waved his flag, signaling the train driver to depart. Antoni climbed back onto the train then it sped up once again continuing on its journey to Berlin.

They walked back towards their compartment and once there, discovered that they were not alone anymore. A young woman had boarded the train at Frankfurt and had chosen their compartment to sit in, perhaps thinking that it was an empty one. She took Alexa and Antoni by surprise, but they said hello to her and sat back in their seats across from her. The woman seemed very withdrawn and didn't appear to want to engage in a conversation. She had her head turned all the way to the right, with her face almost touching the window as she stared out of it, avoiding direct eye contact with the young couple. She sat quietly and still, tightly clutching a brown paper bag on her lap. It was obvious to Alexa that the woman was filled with fear. She recognized that look and knew it all too well.

Alexa estimated that the woman was roughly about twenty-five years of age. She had what looked like dark hair, but it was hard to tell its length or style, as she wore a head scarf which covered most of her hairline. Her clothes looked well-worn and very shabby, almost as though they belonged to someone else. As Alexa glanced down at her shoes, she could see that they were slightly too big for the woman's feet and seemed as though they'd be more suited to an elderly woman instead. As she looked over at the side of her face, she noticed her predominant bone structure and became aware of how thin she actually was. Alexa surmised that this woman was a poor soul and that she must have gone through a horrendous ordeal.

About half an hour after leaving Frankfurt, Alexa began reading her new Bible to herself. It gave her such comfort to be able to browse through its pages and to read it in Polish once again. She revisited some of her most favorite scriptures and re-read them, losing herself in the verses. After a while, Antoni said to Alexa that he was going to the toilet and asked if she minded if he took a walk to the restaurant carriage to see what was going on there. Alexa said it was okay with her, that she'd be happy reading until he returned. He took his cigarettes with him, kissed her cheek and said he'd be back in a little while. Alexa continued reading and the woman continued staring out of the train window, as if in a trance.

Antoni walked along the narrow corridor of the moving train and through two more carriages then arrived at the restaurant car. There were a few tables with people sitting eating and drinking and at one table sat a group of American soldiers playing poker. At the restaurant bar there were some stools where Antoni sat himself down on one of them and asked the bartender how much it cost for a beer. He figured that he may as well use up the remaining Francs that he had left and lit up a cigarette as the bartender served him his beer. Once he had finished smoking, he decided to go over with his beer and sit at the empty table next to the American soldiers, in hope of striking up a conversation with them. Antoni wasn't shy and it wasn't long before he wangled his way into their poker game. They dealt him a hand of cards and he started putting his plan into action. He bluffed that he was a relatively new beginner at the game and that he fancied his chances with his last few Francs. He said he had just gotten married the day before and was feeling lucky. The Yanks were more than willing to win his money from him, so Antoni deliberately lost his first two hands, as he cast his hook. Then on the third hand he began slowly reeling them in. He put on his familiar winning poker face and the next few hands were his. He reached for his winnings from the center of the table, thanked the soldiers for letting him play and announced that he had to get back to his wife. The soldiers were none too happy and wanted Antoni to continue playing, so as to give them the chance to win their money back. Antoni calmed them down and promised that he'd go check on his wife, tell her where he was and then return to their poker game. Eventually the soldiers agreed but told him to hurry back. Antoni had them right where he wanted them. They hadn't realized that they had fallen into his trap and that he'd soon return for the sting to clean them out.

Antoni made his way back to the train compartment where Alexa was. The scene hadn't changed at all since he had left. Alexa was still reading her Bible and the woman was still clutching her paper bag, staring out of the window. Antoni sat down and explained to Alexa about the poker game that he had gotten into with the American soldiers in the restaurant car and how he was winning money that they would need to continue on with the next part of their journey. Alexa understood and agreed that he could go back and play for another hour and assured him that she'd be okay reading her Bible until he returned. Antoni said he'd wait another ten minutes as part of his plan, so that the soldiers wouldn't think he was too eager. Alexa took the opportunity to go to the toilet on the train while Antoni kept an eye on their belongings. When she returned Antoni kissed her again, then left the compartment sliding the door closed behind him and made his way back to the restaurant car.

Before Alexa continued reading her Bible, she reached for their bag of food and took out a bar of the chocolate as well as the bottle of milk which she and Antoni had started drinking earlier. She tore open the outer wrapping of the chocolate and broke a few pieces off. Alexa looked over at the young woman sympathetically and asked her if she would like some, but the woman didn't respond. Alexa figured that the woman must not understand Polish and asked her again in German this time, but still she didn't respond. Alexa leaned over and placed her hand on the woman's shoulder and this time, she got a reaction. The woman flinched nervously and then burst into tears, taking Alexa by surprise.

"Please don't cry. I was only trying to be kind and give you some of my chocolate." The woman turned and looked at Alexa directly for the first time with her sad eyes full of tears. "It's okay!" Alexa said reassuringly, "I won't hurt you. Look I'll go back over to my own seat." Alexa placed the chocolate down next to her and moved back over to where she had been sitting.

"No one's been that kind to me in such a very long time," said the young woman in a Polish accent through her tears.

"Look it really is okay. You are more than welcome to share my chocolate with me, and I have some milk too if you'd like some?" Alexa reached for the bottle of milk and passed it over in the woman's direction.

"Wait," said the woman as she reached her hand into the paper bag which was on her lap. Out of it she pulled an old metal cup which was dented in several places, with most of the outer enamel coating chipped off of it. "I have my own cup," she said, very matter-of-factly. She held it out towards Alexa with both hands, who filled it up halfway with the milk. The woman's hands were shaking as she quickly raised the metal cup up to her mouth and began drinking. Alexa then reached down for the bar of chocolate and handed it to the woman.

"Please, take as much as you like."

The woman carefully rested her cup with one hand on her lap and with her left hand, reached over and took the piece of the chocolate from Alexa, then slowly lifted it up to her mouth.

"You are Polish?" Alexa asked her.

"Yes," she replied after she finished her mouthful of chocolate.

"We are too. My husband and I are returning home for the first time since the start of the war." The woman finished off the rest of the milk in her cup, wiped it clean with her sleeve, then put it back in her bag. "Wait, you can have some more if you'd like."

The young woman began to cry again. Tears trickled down her face. Alexa felt so bad and was moved with pity for her. She reached over and put her arm around the woman's shoulder who at first pulled back then reluctantly, fell into Alexa's arms sobbing, in real need of some human affection.

"There, there, it's okay you're safe now!" Alexa tried to reassure her.

After a few minutes the woman composed herself and reigned in her emotions.

"My name is Alexa, what's yours?"

"Teressa," she answered and slowly the two young women began talking candidly to one another. For the next half-hour the two strangers spoke to each other honestly, as if in a confessional. The young woman began to confide in Alexa and opened up to her as much as she possibly could, about the nightmare through which she had survived. Alexa was a good listener and displayed real compassion and empathy as the woman spoke. Teressa told her harrowing story of how when she was twenty-three years of age, she was taken by the Nazis from the ghetto in Kraków along with her two small children, her husband and her parents and sent to Auschwitz concentration camp. She told how at gunpoint, they were all crammed into boxcars like animals, huddled together with strangers and transported to hell on earth. She told of how she was separated from her family on that first day when they had arrived at the concentration camp and that she had never seen her son or daughter ever again after they were torn from her arms. Nor did she ever see her parents, or her husband again either.

Teressa spoke of how she believed that she was the only one who was kept alive in her family, but that she couldn't understand why. "Why did I not die?" She kept asking out loud, over and over again. She related how all humanity was stripped from her on that first day. "They took my belongings. They took my clothes. They took my shoes. They took my wedding ring. They took my hair, by shaving it all off of my head. They took my dignity and my identity." She told Alexa that her name was stolen that day also, then she lifted up the sleeve of her left arm and showed her number on her forearm. The ink tattoo that was etched into her skin on the first day when she arrived by the tattooist, a fellow Jewish prisoner. Her only means of identity in the camp from that day onwards. Teressa spoke of how desperate and demoralizing the living conditions were for all of the prisoners in Auschwitz and Birkenau. How they were crammed together to exist in dismal unsanitary barracks, packed full beyond capacity with hundreds of desperate prisoners in each, with six or more people lying on each bunk. No bedding or blankets, no heat in the winter, and no food or drink. How they were starved and beaten and worked like dogs, less than dogs even. She said that the Nazis' Alsatian and German Shepherd dogs had a far superior life than the prisoners had there. Teressa explained how worthless a human life was inside of the camp and how insignificant a prisoner with a tattooed number actually was. How quickly someone could become a target for death and of just how quickly a bullet could find its next random target, within a split second for any reason, or no reason at all. "An unexpected bullet was the best way to go," she said in her opinion. That's the way she had wanted to go, "A much better way than being piled naked into the gas chambers with a group of desperate people all clambering on top of you, trying to get your very last breath of air." Teressa went on to tell that in the end it made no difference how you expired, as once you were dead, by gas or by bullet, you were thrown into the ovens anyway and up through the chimneys you'd go.

She spoke of how she prayed and prayed so hard to God so many times to help her and her family, but that God didn't listen to her, so she eventually gave up. There was no God, there was only living hell in Auschwitz. She said that if you were really lucky, you'd die in your sleep and not see the next morning, but that she was never that lucky. Then she spoke of how one morning she was selected and put on a transport out of Auschwitz and journeyed by train to Germany where she was forced to slave in a labor camp. Once the war ended and the camp was liberated, she spoke of her being too ill and too weak to travel home and of having no family to return to, nor anywhere really to go.

Alexa had tears trickling down her face the whole way through, as Teressa related her horrific experience to her. Now it made complete sense as to why the woman was so withdrawn and was the way that she was, *'how could you be anything different after going through all of that?'* thought Alexa to herself. Alexa decided to tell Teressa her story, in the hope that it might take her mind off of her own nightmare slightly for a little while. Teressa listened to Alexa's personal experience with compassion and at the end of it said, "I hope that you will find your mother and sister and that they are still alive."

Alexa hadn't ever allowed herself to think that they wouldn't both be alive. She had always entertained the idea that she'd return to Lublin one day and find her mother and sister there waiting for her. However, Teressa's words now made her think realistically that there was a real possibility, it might not actually be the case. *'Well I'm almost home now and I'll soon find out the truth...'* Alexa thought to herself, then she refused to give any more fuel to that fire.

After the two women had shared their stories and had expended a flood of emotions, they both seemed rather fatigued by it all and returned once more to silence. Teressa stared blankly again back out of the train window as she had done before, and Alexa immersed herself in the comforting verses of her Bible. Only a short time had passed by, when Teressa suddenly stood up and said that she had to go. Alexa looked up from her book and said okay, thinking she was going to the toilet, but Teressa never returned to the compartment.

Antoni's plan worked, just as he had wanted it to and he left the poker game with the American soldiers, the big winner, with a large amount of the winnings. He now had a bundle of US dollars in his pocket, more than enough to get him and Alexa back to Poland and enough to last them at least a month to live on, he figured. He returned to the train compartment to tell Alexa the good news. She closed her Bible and cuddled with Antoni for the rest of the journey to Berlin.

"What's the chocolate doing over there and where's that woman gone?"

"Don't ask," replied Alexa as she tightened her hold of him.

CHAPTER -20-

When the train finally arrived in Berlin, it was after ten o'clock at night. Wanting to spend as little time in Germany as possible, Antoni wasted no time in finding out when the next train to Warsaw was. When he asked, he was informed that the train would not go all the way into Warsaw's main station, due to extensive bombing and damage on the train line. He inquired where he should depart from the train, pointing out that he wished to travel to Lodz. The station-master told him where he should get off but couldn't suggest alternative transportation to Lodz at that time. Antoni bought two tickets for the overnight train which was due to leave at midnight. They sat in the station until it was time to board the train. Alexa made them up another baguette with some of the sliced ham and cheese which they still had left. There was nothing to buy in the station at that time of night, but Antoni promised Alexa that once they got on board the train, he would take her to the restaurant car for a hot drink. Midnight fast approached. They climbed up onto the Warsaw train and as promised, Antoni took his wife to the restaurant car where they sat down at a vacant table. Once the train had pulled out of the station, Antoni ordered them some hot coffee from the restaurant bar.

The journey to Warsaw was a rather uneventful one. It was peaceful and quiet, and the train didn't seem to be too full of passengers. Antoni found them an empty compartment in one of the carriages which they had all to themselves. They settled down comfortably into their seats and slept for the majority of the train ride through the night, with Alexa nestled in Antoni's arms. The journey to Warsaw took over seven hours and as daylight broke, they got their first look at their native Poland. They both had mixed emotions although they were glad to be almost home. However, they were mainly filled with anxiety and worry upon seeing the massive destruction that was everywhere.

As the sun began to rise, it illuminated the view outside of the train window. But it did not shine on, nor reflect any fresh vibrant colors. Rather, it poured light onto row after row of ruins, dull, grey and burnt-out skeletons of derelict buildings. It was then that the large-scale destruction and extensive damage which the city of Warsaw had suffered, became visible to them. Half-standing, bomb-blasted buildings remained. Empty shells with windows, walls and roofs blown out. Piles of debris everywhere. High mounds of bricks and concrete mangled together with twisted metals and splintered wood filled the landscape as far as the eye could see. It resembled a biblical apocalypse of catastrophic proportions. Hitler's original plan to totally annihilate the city by bombing it, as well as everyone in it was almost a complete success. The Nazis and the German Luftwaffe had demolished about eighty-five to ninety percent of Warsaw, almost razing it entirely to the ground. Very few buildings were left intact. All significant buildings of importance were first plundered then set alight with flamethrowers, then finally blown up by specialized German troops. Warsaw's historic old town and castle, its museums, government buildings, churches, schools and libraries, its beautiful architecture, homes and residential buildings were all destroyed. The Nazis had even destroyed Warsaw's main train station in January that year before their retreat, which meant the trains could no longer go all the way into the center of the city.

Antoni had read a few newspaper articles and had heard some reports over the radio about the damage which Warsaw had suffered at the hands of Hitler's army, but he hadn't ever imagined that it would be as devastated as it was. Alexa was beyond shocked at the destruction she was seeing out of the window and had not been prepared for what she saw, on such a large scale. She began to pray silently over the desolation and obvious loss of life which her mind told her must have occurred, but she also prayed that the rest of their journey be a safe one. The train began reducing its speed and the conductor came along the carriages telling all those passengers onboard that the train would come to a complete stop in roughly fifteen minutes at the Zachodnia Station, on the outskirts of Warsaw. Antoni and Alexa gathered their belongings together and made their way out into the corridor. When the train finally stopped, unable to go on any further, everyone exited the carriages and climbed down onto the platform. Antoni scanned the area to get his bearings. The station was roughly eighty-five miles from Lodz, the town where Antoni's family lived and the first destination for where they were bound. They headed out of the small station and made their way onto the streets of Warsaw, where the true scale of the devastation and destruction was clear to see.

They walked along the main roadway, heading West out of the city. On their journey they passed several civilians also walking along the roadside in one direction or the other. Many were pulling small carts or pushing old damaged prams to help them carry their few belongings, or some salvaged furniture which they had picked up on their journey. Most walked alone, although some were in groups of twos or threes. Each seemed to have a definite destination to which they were heading, no matter how long it would take them to get there. On either side of the roads were groups of Polish work crews, made-up of both civilians and army soldiers, who were attempting to clear the piles of rubble and debris from the bombed-out buildings. The Varsovian men and women from all walks of life and backgrounds, rolled up their sleeves and got stuck into the mammoth clean-up task before them. People from other towns and cities across Poland also volunteered and came to help. They formed long human chains, passing filled-up buckets of rubble from one to another, brick by brick, from hand to hand, moving the chunks of concrete down the line to fill up the awaiting trucks. 'The entire nation builds its capital!', became the city's rallying cry. It was obvious that the clean-up task would take a great deal of effort, but it was well on its way. Warsaw's people were determined to rebuild their beloved capital. Firstly, for life to be lived there once again by the living and the future generations to come and secondly, as a tribute and a mark of respect to the hundreds of thousands of Poles who were murdered there at the hands of Hitler's henchmen.

After walking for roughly half an hour, Alexa suggested that they sit down and eat something, then they'd have one less thing to carry. They found a small patch of nearby grass and sat down under the morning sun to finish off the rest of their food which they had remaining from the day before. They didn't rest for very long before continuing on their journey once again. Antoni carried their duffel bag on his back and lit up one of his cigarettes. Not long after they began walking again, an Allied truck pulled up alongside of them and asked where they were going to. The soldiers had recognized Antoni and Alexa's American army issue uniforms and offered them a ride to Lodz which was in the direction they were headed. The couple were grateful and jumped up into the rear of the truck and settled in for the bumpy ride.

Well over an hour later, the truck finally reached the center of Lodz. Alexa had never been there before, but for Antoni, he was home at last. His first thought was to make his way back to the home where he had lived and grown up in with his parents. The last place he had lived before being taken to

Germany to work. There he hoped he would find them waiting for him. Antoni led the way and after a twenty-minute walk, they arrived at his home. Sadly, there were no visible signs of life. The front door was locked, and no one was home. Antoni knocked on the door of the neighbors' house, but the people he used to know that once lived there, were gone and the new people didn't seem to know who his parents were, or anything about them at all. He decided to make his way to his grandfather's villa to see if there were any other family members still living there. He knew the Gestapo had taken over his deceased grandfather's five fabric factories and mills in Lodz at the beginning of the war while Antoni was still living in the city as a teenager. However, he now prayed that his family had got their businesses and villa back and perhaps, he'd find his mother and father safely living there together, now the war was over.

As they approached the road where the villa was located, Antoni had to try and catch his breath. The location looked far different from the way he remembered it. The villa had been bombed and lay in complete ruin. He hardly recognized the remains of his grandfather's once stately home. This was the place where he had spent many hours as a young child playing and enjoying life. He had many happy memories there but now it was destroyed. There was no roof, no walls, no windows. It was just like the buildings they saw in Warsaw. Only large piles of rubble remained - bricks and mortar, broken glass, twisted metal mangled with broken wooden burnt-out and charred beams. Antoni was shocked and in a state of disbelief. He lit up a cigarette as he stared at the sad state of his family's derelict villa before him, shaking his head. He set down their duffel bag and sat on the ground in shock. Alexa tried to give some comfort but couldn't reassure him of anything. She didn't really know what to say for the best.

Antoni took a final look at the villa then after about fifteen minutes, headed back into town with Alexa trying to figure out what to do next. They found a cafe on their way and decided to stop at it. They went inside and sat at a table where they ordered some coffee to drink. Things hadn't gone the way Antoni had expected them to. He had been so sure that his mother would have been waiting for him at home. He had only been gone for three years since he had been forced to join the German army. But, in reality, three years was a whole life-time for some people.

"Antoni! Is that you?" Asked a female. Antoni looked over in the direction of the voice and his eyes found a pretty young blonde woman staring back at him.

"Elena! Is that you?"

The girl ran over to Antoni and hugged him and was so obviously delighted to see him.

"I knew you'd make it back here safely one day, I just knew it!"

"This is my cousin Elena. Elena this is my wife Alexa."

"Your wife! Wow she's pretty and you are all grown-up my little cousin."

"Where is my mother? Is she still alive? I just went to the house but was told she doesn't live there."

"No, she doesn't live in that house anymore but yes Auntie Stephanie is still alive. She'll be so happy to see you and meet your new wife. I will write down her new address for you."

Antoni was relieved to hear that his mother was still alive, but also wanted to know about his father. "What about my father? Where's Fritz?"

Elena sat down on one of the chairs at their table and the happy smile quickly disappeared from her face. "You remember he was arrested for giving out extra ration cards to the Polish families? Well they also accused him of giving them to the Jews in the Lodz ghetto. Two of grandfather's factories were within the ghetto's walled area and the Nazis claimed that your father used them to smuggle in ration cards to the Polish and Jewish families with children. They transported him to the Stutthof labor camp near Gdansk and no one has ever seen him again." Antoni said nothing but became overwhelmed with emotions. He got up from his chair and walked outside of the cafe and immediately lit up a cigarette.

"I'm sorry to have to share this awful news with him now, but what else could I say?" Elena turned to Alexa with a hopeless expression on her face.

After roughly ten minutes had passed Antoni came back into the cafe and said that he must go and find his mother. Elena wrote down her address and said she'd pay for their coffees. They said their goodbyes and the young couple left the cafe, promising to see Elena again soon. Antoni made his way with Alexa to the address on the piece of paper and knocked on the door, a few seconds later a woman opened the door.

"Hello Mama!"

The woman looked in amazement at the tall young handsome man standing before her.

"Antoni! Is that you my son?"

"Yes Mama, I'm home!" Antoni said, as he threw his arms around his mother and embraced her tightly.

"Oh, thank you God," she said out loud as she wept tears of joy. Then, after a few precious moments in each other's arms, Antoni pulled back and introduced Alexa as his new wife to her. His mother was surprised but greeted Alexa warmly and brought them both into her home. She couldn't believe the wonderful sight before her eyes. Her boy had finally come home.

They spent the next few hours catching up on each other's lives, their personal experiences during the war and the lives of Antoni's friends and family members. Antoni's mother filled them in on the events that caused the loss of the family business and his grandfather's destroyed villa. They spoke of Antoni's father's imprisonment by the Gestapo and of his being transported off to Stutthof, at which point his mother began crying. Once she had composed herself, the woman began getting to know Alexa and insisted they stay with her at her home. She had no desire to let her newly returned son out of her sight anytime soon. The couple stayed with Antoni's mother and she took great pleasure in fussing over them and making them as comfortable as she possibly could. She gave Alexa some of her nice clothes and shoes to wear, instead of the army issue uniforms they were wearing. She opened a trunk in her bedroom where she had stored some of her husband's clothes and gave Antoni his father's clothing to wear, as it was almost a certainty that Fritz would never return home now.

Three weeks had gone by and as much as Alexa was enjoying living with her mother in-law and getting to know the other members of Antoni's family nearby, she longed to see her own mother and sister again. After she and Antoni discussed the matter privately, they told Stephanie that they'd be making the journey to Lublin to track down Alexa's immediate family and from there, they would decide their next move. Stephanie wasn't thrilled for them to be leaving her, but she understood the reasons for it and hoped that Alexa would also be reunited successfully with her family. She gave them a generous amount of money which she had saved and hidden and packed their clothing into a small suitcase each, then prepared some food for them to take on their journey.

The next day they headed for the main train station in Lodz and bought tickets to take them to Lublin, Alexa's home town. The train ride took them seven hours and finally by late afternoon Alexa was back in Lublin. Although she was in her home town, it didn't look quite like she had remembered it. Just like Warsaw, Lublin had suffered severe structural damage, first from the Nazi army during the war and secondly at the end of the war, from the Russian army as they marched in to liberate Poland. Lublin suffered at least seventy percent destruction to its city and, although not as many as Warsaw, the death toll of its Jewish population was extremely high, with many Polish Christians losing their lives too.

Alexa wasted no time in making her way back to the home where she had lived with her family as a child. Antoni told her to slow down but as she got nearer to her neighborhood, she felt a strong desire to start running, as though she couldn't wait a minute longer. She just wanted to throw open the front door of her house and run into her mother's arms as she had done as a child. For her mother to embrace her tightly, the way that Antoni's mother had greeted him, with tears of joy. To hear her mother's voice, say her name again after all these years and tell her that she was finally home and was safe now. To be reunited with her adoring little sister Asha who wouldn't be all that little anymore. But she was sure their love for one another would be just as strong as it used to be. All those thoughts raced through her imagination, then finally they had arrived outside of her house.

Alexa straightened her clothes and fixed her hair then walked up to the door and went to reach for the door handle, but Antoni told her it would be better if she knocked first. Alexa knocked on the front door and then took a small step backwards, readying herself for her family reunion. Twenty seconds later the door opened and there before her, stood a middle-aged man whom she'd never seen before. He took her by surprise, and she stuttered to find her words.

"Is my mother home?"

"Who is your mother?"

"Sophia! Sophia is my mother, and this was our family home with my little sister Asha. Where are they?"

The man stared at Alexa and then at Antoni standing next to her. "Look I don't want any trouble! I don't know where your family are, but they don't live in this house. I live here and have done for almost four years. I'm sorry but I can't help you." The man went back into the house and closed the door firmly behind him.

Alexa's heart sank and tears slowly began to well up in her eyes. She turned to Antoni who took her in his arms and told her to be strong, that they'd keep looking, just as he had done to find his mother back in Lodz. Alexa then thought of trying at their dear old neighbors' house next door - Magda and Michael's, with their twins Eva and Peter. She knocked on the door which was opened by a woman who was clearly not Magda. Alexa asked if she knew the family or where they were. The woman looked at the young couple suspiciously.

"Well they're definitely not in my house. I'm sure they are back in Germany somewhere with all the other murderers, from what I've heard."

Alexa had forgotten that Magda and her family were German and had moved to Lublin from Berlin when she was eight. Their being German had never been a problem before the war, but Alexa could understand why it would have become one during and definitely after the war had ended.

"Are you Germans too? Because if you are, you're not welcome around here," said the woman in a hostile manner.

"No, we are Polish. I used to live next door with my family, but my mother and I were captured in the market square by the German soldiers over five years ago. My mother and I were then transported to work in the forced-labor camp in Dachau, Germany and that was the last place where I saw my mother. I was taken as slave labor for five years and today is my first day back home. My little sister was left in this house that day with the neighbors and I'm trying to find her too."

The woman seemed to soften up upon hearing Alexa's situation and that she was Polish.

"Well I have no idea where your mother and sister are. I'm sorry for what you went through, but I can't help you. I'm glad you're not German, but I'm glad that the German family are gone from this house. People in this town won't tolerate Germans here you know!"

Antoni took Alexa's hand and said thank you to the woman for her time and that they'd continue their search elsewhere. Then he led his wife away from that place and all of its memories. Alexa was crushed at finding out that Magda and her family were gone and that she was no closer to finding out what happened to her mother, or the whereabouts of her sister.

Alexa tried to think of her next move, of what she could try next to help her get closer to finding her family. She suddenly thought of her best friend Helena, whom she had last seen five years earlier, on the day before Alexa and her mother were captured. She remembered that last Friday afternoon when they were walking back from school, after the Germans had ordered all the pupils and teachers to leave the premises and march on the long roadway back into the town. In her mind's eye, Alexa could see the final image of Helena, who once they had parted, had turned back before reaching the street where her home was and waved goodbye to her. Alexa recalled vividly how she had responded by waving back and blowing a kiss to her and then, all too quickly she was gone from sight.

Alexa told Antoni that she wanted them to go to Helena's house next. They began walking there together. They didn't have too far to go, only a few streets. Alexa approached the front door of her friend's home, took a deep breath, then began to knock. The door opened and there before her eyes stood her best friend.

"Helena!"

"Alexa! Oh, thank God you're alive."

The two girls, now both young women, hugged each other tightly as though they were two little girls again. They were completely overjoyed to see one another and were filled with emotion. Helena's mother appeared at the door behind her daughter and was also delighted at the surprise of finding Alexa standing there and joined them in their embrace. Alexa introduced Antoni to them as her new husband and the excitement levels grew. There had been very few occasions over the past five years of war for them all to experience such joy and happiness, but this was truly a time for them to celebrate.

"Where is my mother and Asha, do you know where they are?"

"You better come inside." Helena's mother said.

Helena's mother began preparing some coffee for them, then Alexa braced herself and asked if they knew what had happened to her mother and sister again. They looked at each other apprehensively and then, with one of them sitting on either side of Alexa, they both reached for and held her hand. Alexa could sense the tension coming from them and dreaded their next words.

"We are sorry to say that we have never seen your dear mother again and she has never come home," Helena's mother told her.

Alexa burst into tears, broken by the news that she was hearing about her dear mother. After a few minutes of sobbing, she enquired through her tears about her little sister Asha. They began explaining that when she and her mother never returned home that day, their neighbor Magda continued to look after Asha. They told Alexa that Magda and her family had taken her in and raised her as one of their own. Alexa seemed happy and comforted to hear that. However next they told Alexa, that about a year after they both still hadn't returned home, her mother's sister-in-law had come to visit from Katowice and, upon hearing about the situation, had made arrangements for Asha to go back and live with her. They said that they hadn't seen Asha in almost four years.

Helena stood up and left the room and when she returned, she was carrying a parcel wrapped in brown paper and tied with string. She handed it to her friend and told her that Asha had left it in her safe-keeping, for her to give to Alexa whenever she returned home. Alexa's eyes began to tear up again as she held the parcel in her hands. Written on the outside, in her little sister's hand writing were the words 'For my sister Alexa.' She ran her finger slowly over her sister's words as if somehow, she could touch a tiny part of her.

Helena asked Alexa what had happened to her the day that she was taken away with her mother. Alexa started at the beginning, when she was trying on the blue pair of shoes. She filled in all the facts that she could and finally, told them of working in the displacement camp in France for six months, where she met Antoni and married him just the month before.

Helena and her mother hung on every word of her story and were moved to tears several times during Alexa's account of her ordeal. At the end, they both hugged Alexa with such depth of feeling and real empathy for all that she had gone through.

CHAPTER -21-

Alexa carefully opened up the parcel and found inside that her little sister had enclosed a change of clothing for her, along with their family Bible. Alexa was touched by her little sister's thoughtfulness. She knew the clothes would never fit her now, but she appreciated the gesture and was moved by it. When she opened up the bible, she discovered that inside were some family photographs of them all. She hadn't seen her family in person, nor a picture of her mother or sister in so long. They had existed only in her mind's eye and in her precious memories. Looking at the photographs was like holding a carbon copy of her memory. They were both just as she remembered them to be. Looking at the photos warmed her heart but broke it at the same time. There were photos of her father and grandmother too and she took pleasure and comfort in seeing their faces once again. There was also a piece of paper on which Asha had written down the address of where she had been taken to live with her uncle's wife, Isabella. Alexa's uncle had died when the girls were young, so neither of them had known him or his wife very well at all. The address was somewhere in Rzeszów which was almost a three-hour journey away from Lublin by train. Alexa was determined to find her sister again so the following morning, she and Antoni boarded a train to Rzeszów and made their way to the home of Alexa's aunt in the hope of finding her little sister there.

They eventually arrived at the address and knocked at the front door. After a short pause, a woman answered and asked what they wanted. Alexa began explaining who she was and that she was searching for her younger sister. She asked if Isabella was home, at which point the woman said that she was Isabella, her uncle's wife and invited them in. As she led them into the lounge, it was obvious that Alexa's aunt had a taste for the finer things in life. The room was spacious and looked very grand with its expensive decor, antique furniture and collection of elegant ornaments. The woman obviously had money or was left a significant amount of wealth from her deceased husband, whom Alexa recalled her mother once telling her about him being a rich man.

"I have just returned from visiting my old home in Lublin yesterday, where I went to try and find my mother and sister. I haven't seen them since the day my mother and I were taken in the street by the Gestapo, over five years ago." Alexa began explaining her dilemma to her aunt as best as she could in the hope that she would be empathetic and give her the answers which she was desperately seeking. "There was no sign of my mother or sister in Lublin. Not at our old home and not at our neighbor's home either. I did visit my best friend from school, and she gave me a small package which she told me Asha had left behind for me and it was in that package where she wrote your address down telling me she was being taken to live with you. So, we came straight here to find her."

The woman's whole demeanor suddenly changed completely and there was an obvious agitation and uneasiness that seemed to come over her face. "Well, yes I did bring her here to live with me but she's not living here now."

"Where is she? Is she okay? Please I need to find her! It's been so long since I last saw her, when I was taken away to Germany."

Isabella looked extremely uncomfortable as she prepared to deliver her next words. "Well, your sister Asha didn't like living here in my fine house in Rzeszów. It seems it wasn't good enough for her. She kept crying and begging to go back home to Lublin to wait for you and your mother to return. So, I eventually arranged for her to go and live at the home of a wealthy Polish woman in Lublin, where she was offered room and board, in exchange for some help with the lady's four young children."

Alexa couldn't believe what she was hearing. Not only was Asha not being cared for by her own family, but it now seemed as though she was working in return for a roof over her head. Alexa couldn't help but draw the parallels with her own situation, having been worked like a slave in Germany for all those years, and now finding out that her young sister had perhaps been forced to do something similar, but in their very own home town. Alexa couldn't understand why Helena and her mother hadn't seemed to have known anything about Asha living and working in Lublin. Something just didn't seem right to her. "Do you have the address where she is?"

"Maybe, I think it's written down somewhere in my bureau. Wait here. I will go and look for it," Isabella left the room. Alexa turned to Antoni in hope of some comfort and reassurance, but even to him, things didn't sound very good. Alexa's aunt returned a few minutes later with a piece of paper on which she had scribbled down the address and handed it to her.

"How long has my little sister been living there at the woman's house in Lublin?"

"I don't know, I haven't been keeping count," said Isabella in a short and impolite manner.

Alexa was taken aback by her response but decided it was best not to push her on the matter. However, there was one more question which she had to ask before they left.

"Do you know where my mother is?"

"No, I have no idea. Nor do I have any interest in finding out! I never really liked your mother anyway," she declared abruptly.

Alexa who was always calm, suddenly became incensed and inwardly her blood began to slowly boil. *'How dare this woman say such things about my lovely mother',* she thought to herself. She tried to keep her emotions in check, but it was no good.

"How dare you speak about my mother that way. She never really liked you either, but at least she had manners enough to give you respect!" Alexa's face was turning red with anger.

"Get out of my house you, ungrateful child you! You're no better than that nasty little sister of yours! Your mother was probably glad to be rid of you both. No wonder she's never come back!"

"Don't talk to my wife that way! There really is no need for you to be so cruel and hurtful!" Antoni interjected.

Alexa was proud of her man for standing up for her and for coming to her defense, but as mild tempered and peaceful a person as she was, even she wanted to lunge for the mean old woman.

"Get out! Leave my house I said. Immediately!"

"Don't worry we are going!" Alexa replied. She and Antoni headed out of the room, along the hallway towards the front door, with the irate woman following close behind as she continued to hurl abuse at them. Antoni reached to open the door and they stepped outside.

"...and don't come back!"

Alexa had no intentions of ever going back and hoped that she'd never set eyes on her nasty aunt ever again for as long as she lived. As she stepped over the doorstep and out onto the garden path, she became overwhelmed with a desire to throw one more deserved, unkind comment back to the woman. "You would have made a very good Nazi!"

"...or a Gestapo's wife!" Antoni added, then he reached for his wife's hand and they hastily made their way, away from that place.

As they began making their way back to the train station, Antoni spoke of his surprise over how unexpectedly nasty Alexa's aunt had been. Alexa told him that she vaguely remembered overhearing a conversation between her mother and grandmother when she was young, about her aunt Isabella being an unpleasant woman who was sore and bitter over the fact that, in her opinion, she had married the wrong brother. That seemingly she had really wanted to marry Alexa's father and had only settled for his brother, after he had married Sophia, Alexa's mother. They agreed that it was no wonder she was so bitter and cruel, even though it didn't excuse her poor behavior.

They redirected their thoughts to the more pertinent issue of Asha's whereabouts. Neither of them could understand why Helena hadn't known that Asha was actually living in Lublin. Surely, Asha would have gone to visit them and to enquire if there was any word on Alexa and her mother. It made no sense to them. It just didn't add up. They stopped first for some refreshments before their long return journey at a small cafe, then they boarded yet another train in Rzeszow and headed back to Lublin, with their attention firmly fixed on locating Asha. After the train finally arrived in Lublin's main station, the young fatigued couple asked some locals for directions to the address which Alexa's aunt had given her. After a long walk on the late October evening, they finally arrived at the large property where Asha was supposedly staying. Alexa was anxious and more than a little apprehensive, but it was the only possible lead that she had left to try. She mustered up the courage and moved towards the front door. Before she could raise her arm, Antoni knocked his knuckles firmly against the solid wooden black door and patiently waited with his wife for a reply. Eventually a short slender brunette opened the door and asked if she could help them, before stopping mid-sentence.

Alexa hadn't seen her little sister for over five years, but it didn't matter at that point. She would have known her anywhere. She could have picked her out from amongst a crowd of a thousand young girls and from a mile away. Before she could form the words herself, her little sister beat her to it.

"Alexa! Oh my God! Is that you?" shrieked Asha.

"Yes! My darling little sister it's me! At last I've found you!"

"Thank God, you've finally come for me! I've prayed and prayed for the day you'd come for me!" The two sisters threw themselves into each other's arms and hugged one another tighter than they had ever done before. Tighter than they had ever hugged or been hugged by anyone ever before. Then streaming floods of tears, those of sheer joy, began to flow uncontrollably from them both. The tenderness of their reunion was abruptly cut short, as the silhouette of a tall woman approached the door from inside of the house and stood behind them.

"What is going on here? Who are you people?" asked the woman. Suddenly a small child appeared at her side wrapping itself around her leg.

"I am Alexa, and this is my little sister. I have come to take her home!" Asha stood by Alexa's side, as they both faced the woman in front of them together. Asha still had tears rolling down her cheeks while she clung on to Alexa's arm.

"Well you can't just take her away, she works for me."

"Not anymore she doesn't!"

"The war is over, haven't you heard?" Antoni added in a convincing questioning manner.

"The war may well be over young man, but money is money and I paid good money to this girl's aunt for her!"

"She's not an object, she's a human being and she's my little sister. My aunt had no right to trade her to you for any amount of money. How would you like it if someone did that to your children?" Alexa stared at her with utter disgust, "My sister has worked her very last day for you! Now we are going to collect her things and she is leaving your house with us this very minute."

"You'll have to wait until my husband gets home."

"Actually, no we won't!" Antoni replied in a firm and authoritative voice.

"Come on Asha, show me where your things are," said Alexa, then pushed past the woman and went into the house holding her little sister's hand to locate them, while Antoni followed and stood guard in the hallway. The woman of the house continued to complain, but after a short while, seeing that she was wasting her breath, finally went quiet.

It didn't take very long for Asha to pack all of her things together, she didn't have very much. Then, she and Alexa made their way down the long hallway with her belongings, followed by the woman close behind them, who tried once again to air her grievances. But it was no use, a few more steps and Asha, was finally out of the house and free. Antoni took her bag and introduced himself to her, as her sister's husband. Asha still had tears streaming out from her eyes. She was extremely emotional, and her body was shaking. She was still in shock at the fact that her sister had finally come for her and at what had just occurred. She had always hoped and prayed that one day her sister and she would be reunited again but had almost given up hope that it would ever happen. She couldn't take her tear-filled eyes off of her big sister. Alexa walked with her arm around Asha and was also in a state of disbelief herself. It was a dream come true for them both. Well, part of the dream at least.

Alexa suggested that they all go to Helena's house. There weren't too many people or places in Lublin that Alexa knew, where they could still go to visit but she knew they'd all be made welcome by Helena and her mother. As they approached the house, they could see that the lights were on in their front room. Antoni knocked on the door and Helena's mother answered, delighted to see the young couple again and even more excited to see that Asha was with them.

"Oh, dear girl, you're safe. Where did you find her?"

"We've only just found her in the last hour," said Alexa. "It's a long story!"

Helena's mother invited them all inside and they all got reacquainted and caught up as best they could on each other's lives over the previous five years. Asha told them of how her aunt Isabella had been very mean to her from the start and had never let her leave the house alone. She told of episodes when Isabella would beat her and how eventually she announced one day, that she was tired of her presence and then basically sold her to the rich woman in Lublin. Asha related how she had a long list of heavy chores to carry out daily, taking care of all the household duties as well as looking after the woman's four young children and of how she wasn't allowed out of that house alone there either and was locked in a room at night and whenever the family went out.

Alexa couldn't believe the parallels between both of their lives. At least Alexa was five years older than Asha when she was forced to work for the Klauss's but Asha was just a little girl. It was so unfair. Alexa was visibly upset upon hearing her sister's horrendous life ever since she and their mother were taken away. Alexa and Helena tried to console Asha, who was even more upset as she related her story and continued to sob long after her words had stopped. Asha had always been a gentle and emotional little girl, but now she was a broken soul. "What happened to Mama?" Asha next asked.

"I wish I had the answer to that question," replied Alexa, "All I know is that the last time I saw her, was the day after we left you with Magda. Remember when we went into town to buy my new shoes? Well, while I was trying on the blue shoes I wanted inside of the shop, the Nazi troops pulled up outside in the street and started rounding everyone up."

"Where did they take her to? Where did they take you?"

"Mama and I were transported to a work camp called Dachau in Germany. There we were separated, and I never saw Mama again after that. I was sent to Frankfurt, where I was lined up in front of Gestapo officers and their wives and finally selected by one of them, because I was wearing grandma's necklace with the cross on it. One of the Gestapo wives saw it, pointed to it and asked if I was Catholic, to which I said yes. So, they selected me to be their unpaid slave. They took me to their large farmhouse, and I worked all day from 4 am to 11 pm seven days a week, taking care of the house, their farm, all the chores and their three children for five years."

Asha started to wail uncontrollable tears again and hugged her big sister tightly. "Don't cry Asha, it wasn't as bad as what you went through. I was never beaten."

Alexa then fast forwarded on in her story to being at the displacement camp in France and told of how she had met Antoni and of how they had gotten married there, only just over a month before. That part of the story seemed to lighten the mood up a bit and Asha finally stopped crying.

Asha looked at her sister's hand and asked to see her wedding rings. Alexa sheepishly moved her hand towards her sister to show her unpretentious rings. Antoni spoke up and explained how he had made the engagement ring himself from some old wire and glass beads as a temporary substitute until he could afford to replace it with something more valuable in the future. He proudly pointed out that Alexa's gold wedding band was real and that he had purchased it, along with his own in France. As Helena and her mother looked on, they agreed that it was very thoughtful and meaningful of Antoni to have made the token engagement ring and added that it was very romantic. Asha stood up and walked over to where her bag of belongings sat on the floor. She opened the bag and pulled out a pair of well-worn, lace-up brown shoes and proceeded to pull out a pair of rolled up white socks from the toe section. She brought the socks back over with her to where Alexa was sitting and began to unfold them, then she placed her small hand inside one of them. Alexa curiously watched her and asked her what she was doing. Asha then pulled something out and reached over for her sister's hand.

"Here Alexa, this is perfect. You can use this as your engagement ring."

"Oh, my Goodness! It's Mama's rings! But how did you get them?" Alexa was mystified.

"Don't you remember? The day you and Mama went to buy the shoes, she let me wear her rings while I lay ill in bed until she came back. But as you both never came back I've kept them safe all this time."

Alexa felt a tear form and fall from the corner of her eye, then roll down her cheek. She took the rings and examined them closely then, held them tightly in her hand and placed them firmly against her chest close to her heart.

"My fingers are too small to wear them, and I've always been afraid of losing them, so that's why I've kept them hidden in my shoes. But you're married now, so you should have them Alexa."

"Thank you so much Asha, I can't tell you what this means to me."

"I know what it means to you."

Alexa took off Antoni's wire ring and placed it down on the table in front of her, then placed her mother's engagement ring on her wedding finger, on top of her own gold wedding band. She looked down at her hand with great satisfaction and with a feeling of completeness and contentment. The ring was made of yellow gold and had four claws holding a rectangular cut amethyst in place, which was raised from the surface. Alexa could vividly remember her mother proudly wearing it and now, she would wear it with even more pride. This was indeed the most perfect ring that she could have wished for. Sentimentally its value was priceless, and Alexa was delighted to now have it as her own. She reached for Asha and threw her arms around her little sister, kissing her cheeks and forehead repeatedly.

"I have something for you in return darling." Alexa sat back and reached both of her hands up towards the back of her neck. She unclipped the clasp on her necklace and took off her cross. "Do you remember this?"

"Of course! It's grandma's cross! And you still have it."

"I've worn it all these years and it's kept me safe, from when I was taken away from home at thirteen until now and has brought me back home again safely. Now it will be yours and it will protect and keep you safe." Alexa reached over and fastened it securely around her thirteen-year-old sister's neck. Asha reached up and took hold of the cross in her hand, looking at it with a mix of pure delight, disbelief and sentimentality. Then she in return, reached for her sister and hugged her tightly.

"Thank you so much. I'll always wear it. I'll never take it off."

"I'll wear Mama's wedding ring on my other hand and keep it safe until you get married one day and then it will be your wedding ring, so Mama will always be with us in a small symbolic way.

It was too late at night for them to go anywhere else and, as they had nowhere else to go, Helena's mother made up beds for the three of them and they all stayed the night. The next day, Alexa and Antoni started discussing their best options for the future. They were now a family of three. Antoni said he'd start looking for electrical work and, as the town of Lublin was rebuilding, he didn't think it would be too hard for him to find employment of some kind. After breakfast he headed off in search of work and as he asked around, he was told that he'd have to register his name and skills at the town hall. When he got there, he was asked his full name, town of birth and work history. The Polish man who was taking down his details, became suspicious of him and started asking him more probing questions. "What kind of name is Methner? It's not Polish. In fact, it sounds German to me. Are you German?"

"No, I'm not German, I'm Polish! I grew up in Lodz."

"You may well have grown up there, but you were born in a German town with a German surname. That's the kind of people who we don't want here in Lublin! Don't you know what your people did here and throughout Poland?"

"They are not my people, I'm not German!"

"Tell that to your parents. You even look German. There is no work for you here! I'd suggest you leave Lublin immediately, because I'm going to spread the word about you and that kind of word travels fast."

"Look you've got it wrong."

"No, you've got it wrong! Go back to Germany and clear off out of this office before I call the police on you."

Antoni had no choice but to leave the office. Of course, even though he didn't feel like he was German and had grown up in Lodz, the truth was that by birth, he was born in Gryfów Śląski, a part of Poland which was under German occupation at the time. So technically, whether he liked it or not he was German, and his surname was definitely a German one. He quickly made his way back to Helena's home to tell Alexa what had happened and to discuss that maybe it was better that they rethink living in Lublin, for it was going to prove very problematic for them there.

They didn't have too many options to choose from, so Antoni decided that it would probably be best for them to make their way to Gryfów Śląski, which was in the German part of Poland where he was born. Polish newspapers had begun to report that there was an abundance of large spacious apartments for rent, as well as plenty of work available there, being that it was so close to the German border and not a lot of native Poles particularly wanted to live there. All of the remaining German soldiers living there, had been chased over the border by the Russian troops. It was after some long deliberations that Antoni and Alexa decided that it would be a good place for them to try, at least for a few years until the raw wounds of the war began to heal and they got back on their feet.

They planned to leave Lublin and make their way there with Asha within the next few days, in search of a new life. Helena's mother allowed them all to stay with her until they were ready to leave. She went into town and bought their three one-way train tickets for them, then she purchased some fresh loaves of bread, some meats, cheeses, and drinks for their journey. She wouldn't let Antoni reimburse her for what she had spent. It was her way of doing a little to help them out. She had great empathy and imagined how it could easily have been her daughter Helena who'd been taken by the Nazis in 1940 and separated from her. How Helena could now be the one motherless, with no family, no home, no employment and the daunting task of trying to rebuild an entirely new life from scratch. She felt it was the very least that she could do and knew beyond a shadow of a doubt, that Alexa's mother would have done the very same for her child, had she been in her shoes.

Early the following morning Antoni said that he, Alexa and Asha would make their own way to the train station. Alexa knew the way and Antoni didn't want anyone to connect him to Helena and her mother, on account of his being German, just in case anyone gave them any trouble. They packed their belongings, took the food which was prepared for them, said their heartfelt goodbyes, then began the walk to the station.

They reached the station in time to catch the 7 am train. The train ride would roughly take fifteen hours as it journeyed from Lublin in the East of Poland to Gryfów Śląski all the way to the far West of the country. They were all relieved to be leaving Lublin. Alexa had the horrific memories of being taken by force with her mother from there and never seeing her again after Dachau. Asha had heartbreaking memories of being abandoned there, of losing her mother and sister there, then being sold by her evil aunt and returned as a kept house slave there. As for Antoni, his run in with the man at the employment office, gave him an idea of the levels of hatred now felt towards Germans by the Poles. They all hoped that life would improve for them in a new town.

CHAPTER -22-

When they finally arrived in Gryfów Śląski, it was just as Antoni had heard. There was plenty of work and lots of vacant places to live. Antoni quickly got himself a job as a full-time electrician and rented a furnished apartment for them all in the center of town. It had two rooms, a spacious kitchen and a bathroom. It didn't take long for Alexa to find employment as a cook in a local restaurant and she also managed to get Asha some afternoon shifts in the same establishment, clearing tables and washing dishes. They were all working and bringing home their wages, which the three of them put together to pay their rent, food and bills and any money that was left over each week, they saved up in a jar. This was really the first time that both Alexa and Asha had received payment for their hard work, and they took tremendous pride and satisfaction from it.

Almost a year had gone by and in the August of 1946, Alexa gave birth to her first child, a baby girl whom they named Stashia. The following year in September Alexa gave birth to a baby boy, her first son whom they called Henry. Alexa was a wonderful and very loving mother and was delighted to be raising a family of her own. Antoni continued to work hard and was the main source of income for his family. He worked long hours and earned a good wage from an electrical company installing street lighting, for which there was a great need after the war. Alexa stayed home to look after her children which was a full-time job in itself, while Asha continued to work at the restaurant and was eventually promoted to a full-time waitress.

At the end of her third pregnancy in September of 1948, Alexa gave birth to another son who she named Richard. But tragically the baby only lived for three short weeks and died suddenly in his sleep. Alexa was devastated and heartbroken over the loss of her tiny infant as deep sorrow once again touched her life. She was only twenty-two years of age at the time and couldn't understand why such a tragedy had befallen her. Fortunately, she had her two other children who needed her care and full attention at that time. Her deep sadness was often interrupted by her son and daughter's needs, who brought her great joy and reminded her of happiness again.

Alexa however, disliked living in the same apartment after Richard's death. It reminded her far too much of discovering his tiny little cold, lifeless body, not breathing in his crib. So, Antoni eventually found them a bigger home to live in just outside the center of town which had three bedrooms in it. The change of location was very beneficial for Alexa, and although it didn't take away all of her pain and heartbreak, the new surroundings were a welcome distraction. Since the bigger apartment was more expensive, Antoni had to work even longer hours which often meant him having to work away from home and he was often gone for a few days at a time. Asha moved with them to the new place and continued to help Alexa with the children, but she had met a young Polish man and their romance blossomed. They had started dating seriously, so her attention lay elsewhere.

Four days after Christmas in 1949, Alexa gave birth to her second daughter Sofia. She was blonde-haired, blue-eyed and beautiful just like her mother and thankfully, she was healthy and lived past her first year. In the summer of 1950, Asha married, and she moved out of Alexa and Antoni's home and into her own apartment with her new husband. As promised, Alexa gave her younger sister their mother's wedding ring, which she had looked after since Asha had given it to her for safe keeping. Asha was delighted to wear her mother's wedding ring as her own and it gave her the sense that a part of her mother was always close to her. Asha still lived close to her sister and visited Alexa several days a week and also helped her out regularly with caring for her nieces and nephew, until her husband was offered a better job in the town of Kraków, and they moved away. Alexa went on to have two more children with Antoni over the next four years. A boy she named Stefan and then a girl she called Krystina.

Alexa had a full house filled with five small children to look after, which was like having several full-time jobs at once. Her hands were always busy and there was little or no time for anything else besides childcare, cooking, laundry and housework. But she was young and healthy, and she was happy to be working to raise and nurture her own young family while her husband provided for them. To her it was never a chore, but rather, something which she took great joy in; caring for the needs of her own family. Stashia was seven years old, Henry was six, Sofia four, Stefan two and Krystina only a few months old, when Antoni began working away from home more and more. Alexa was still very much in love with Antoni and appreciated him working so hard to put a roof over their heads, food on the table and clothes on their backs. Alexa was a loyal wife and an adoring mother, she had good morals and was a beautiful young woman who took pride in her appearance. She never smoked or drank as some of the young women did after the war and she was always well-spoken, polite and very well-mannered.

Antoni was very good at his job and after a relatively short period of time, he was promoted to senior electrician. He had learned to drive and was given a company work truck to get around from job to job. Antoni told Alexa that he had a big installation job on in Jelenia Gora, roughly thirty kilometers away from where they lived and that he'd be gone for at least three days. Alexa had gotten used to him having to work away and her being left at home alone with the children. She always looked forward to his return.

After only the second day that Antoni was away on the job out of town, one of his colleagues arrived at their home by himself. When Alexa answered the door to him, she panicked at first thinking the worst, that perhaps Antoni had been in a serious accident at work. However, Antoni wasn't hurt, he was more than fine. The colleague appeared to be a decent man with a good moral compass and said that his conscience had forced him to come and tell her what he was about to divulge to her. Alexa never expected for one moment, what she was about to hear from his mouth.

"I'm so sorry to tell you this, but your husband is not working far away from home on a long installation job as he told you. He is actually only ten kilometers away near Luban."

"What do you mean?"

"He's met an attractive young eighteen-year-old woman and is with her now at her home. He's been having an affair with her for months and has told her that he'll marry her. There have also been other women he's been involved with over the past few years, way before her. I'm sorry to be the one to tell you, but I couldn't stay quiet about it anymore. You are a beautiful young woman and Antoni is crazy to even look at anyone else. He's so lucky to have you as his wife and the mother of his children. I felt you should know!"

Alexa stared at the man with a shocked expression across her face, as though the bottom had just been ripped out of her world, and it had. She couldn't believe the words she was hearing. She felt a stabbing pain in her heart as the man spoke, and her mind began to automatically search through the recesses of her memory. Dates, times, discrepancies, for holes in Antoni's stories that hadn't or didn't add up, or that might have sounded suspicious at the time. Now she doubted everything. The trust which she had for her husband, was now shattered and everything was tainted by the liar's brush. So many thoughts raced through her head. The older children were running around inside of the house and the younger ones were making loud noise and being boisterous. Alexa suddenly screamed at the top of her lungs for them to be quiet, something she had never done before, and which was so out of character for her. The children were startled and stopped in their tracks. Alexa didn't know what to say to the man after his delivery of such devastating news, but she thanked him for confiding in her and told him that, as hard as it was to hear, it was better that she knew the truth.

On the third day, Alexa awaited Antoni's return back home, to confront him face to face with the information she had been told. She had rehearsed over and over again, what she was going to say to him when she saw him again, but she worried that her emotions and feelings of anger would take over. She had always been a peaceful person, but this news about Antoni's infidelity and betrayal not only broke her heart, but it infuriated her and made her blood boil.

Antoni eventually arrived home and when he walked through the door, he as always, approached his wife to kiss her. As he leaned forward towards Alexa, she pulled away from him and told him not to kiss her with his cheating lips. Antoni wasn't expecting such a response from her and it caught him off guard, but he quickly put on his poker face and asked her what she was talking about. Alexa informed him that she knew he had been with another woman for the past three days and that she also knew that there had been others before her too. He kept a straight face and accused her of being crazy while trying to laugh it off. Then, he jumped on the defensive and protested his innocence which he tried to back up with his having to work so hard to provide for their large family.

Alexa wouldn't give up her stance and asked him how he planned to marry the young eighteen-year-old girl, when he was already married to her with five small children. She suggested that he take their children over to her house and see how long she would remain interested in him, knowing he was actually already a husband and a father. Alexa raised her voice and let out a barrage of accusations directly at him, which she had never done before. Antoni lost his temper and for the very first time, lifted his hand to Alexa and slapped her hard across her face. The older children saw him hit their mother and began to cry. It was as though a flame had been lit igniting Antoni's temper, then he completely lost control. He continued to strike Alexa a few more times with his hands and finally pushed her down to the floor, then uncaringly, he stepped over her and headed back out of the front door slamming it behind him and drove off in his truck.

Alexa was in shock and as the tears ran down her face, they stung as they reached the open cut on her right cheek. She was shaking in fear and she was hurting. The children were scared. Her oldest three were visibly upset. After Alexa got back up onto her feet and tended to her wound, she looked in the mirror and made up her mind. She would not tolerate such treatment and certainly not from someone who supposedly loved her. She began packing a suitcase, with a few changes of clothes for her three youngest children and herself. She then began to explain to Stashia and Henry that when their father came back home, she would be going to visit their aunt Asha in Kraków overnight and that they'd be staying with their father, but the children didn't welcome that information and Alexa realized that she couldn't leave without them. Antoni arrived back home a few hours later with a bunch of flowers in his hands and apologized profusely for his behavior, begging his wife to forgive him. Alexa switched on her old defense mechanism and became who she needed to be in that situation; the wounded but forgiving wife. But internally she refused to be treated that way, or to live with someone who was unfaithful as well as violent towards her. The following day when Antoni left for work, Alexa finished packing her suitcase with a change of clothing for each child and took all the money from their savings jar. Then with all five of her children, she left the apartment and headed for the railway station. She boarded a train to Kraków on the journey to visit Asha.

Alexa stayed at her sister's home for five days, then eventually returned back home to Antoni again. The break had done her good, but she missed her husband, despite what he had done to her. She still loved him. Antoni seemed to have learned his lesson and was on good behavior after that, but unfortunately, he didn't have a complete change of character or habits and before long, he was back to his womanizing and cheating. However, he never lifted his hand to Alexa ever again.

Alexa tried to handle his unfaithfulness as best as she could, but it wasn't her idea of a happy marriage and she knew deep down that she deserved much better. When Stashia her youngest daughter had finished attending her first school at age eleven, she had finally built up enough courage and strength to leave Antoni and was determined to provide for and raise her family on her own. However, Antoni had other plans and he told Alexa that she was only allowed to take the three girls with her and that he would be keeping his two sons, Henry and Stefan with him. Alexa was not in agreement, but Antoni insisted that she wasn't taking his sons away from him, so Alexa left taking her three daughters with the full intention of returning for her boys, when she had settled down in a new apartment and had her own income, which she eventually did.

CHAPTER -23-

Many years had gone by since the days of Alexa's servitude, when she was first taken and enslaved by the German Gestapo family at the tender age of thirteen. Alexa continued to be a hard worker throughout her life, as she had been in her youthful years. Holding down four part-time jobs at one stage when she was a single parent, in order to support and provide for her young family.

She'd begin her days back then by first baking fresh bread every morning at the local bakery. After that shift was ended, she'd then work a full shift in a laundry house where she'd wash, hang, iron and fold large piles of laundry. Next, she would work in a nearby cafeteria, where she'd prepare and cook large meals to be served to a steady stream of hungry customers. Then finally at night, she'd collect large buckets of coal and carry them for five kilometers on foot and deliver them to customers near where she lived. During the span of her work day, her oldest son Henry would stop by the bakery and she'd give him fresh bread to take back home for all of her children to eat for breakfast. While she worked in the laundry house, she would take care of her own family's laundry needs as well, so her children always had clean clothes to wear. After school, Stashia would bring her siblings round to the back of the cafeteria, where Alexa would give her children some food to eat. Stashia would then take the children back home, where she'd look after them until their mother came home at night. After school her son Henry would carry home the clean clothing for the family. After Alexa's long day of hard work, she'd eat some food herself before leaving the cafeteria and would then collect her two heavy buckets of coal for delivery and walk the long road back towards home. That was her daily routine for the years while her children were still young, her only means of providing for them all.

In an attempt to better herself and her income, she studied hard at night while her children slept, to qualify to become a crane operator at the large Gdansk ship-builders yard and port. She had faith and determination that she could achieve the goal which she set herself. She was delighted to finally learn that her efforts and sacrifices had paid off and that she had passed the exams with flying colors. She became the very first fully qualified female crane operator in Gdansk, a job usually carried out by men only. This great achievement allowed her to earn herself a greater wage and a whole new level of respect. She was eventually moved to a management position and offered a larger apartment with extra bedrooms to live in with her family.

Years later, when Alexa was fifty-three years of age and was the proud mother of her six beautiful grown children. She loved having a vibrant family of her own to love and care for, but she unfortunately chose badly when it came to love. She and Antoni were finally divorced and several years later, Alexa met the man who would become her second husband. Once again, she loved him very much, although not quite as much as she had loved Antoni. They built a future together and had a daughter whom they named Violetta. Unfortunately, however, as time went by in their relationship, it became apparent that he had more of a love for alcohol, than he did for her and their daughter. One day he went out drinking and never came home again. Alexa found herself single once more and looking after her young children alone.

As the years had gone by in Poland, Alexa had regained contact with and kept her dear friendships with her three European girlfriends Henrietta, Marta and Greta long after the war had ended. They kept in touch by writing to each other endearing letters and made regular phone calls to one another, when they'd update each other on their young children's progress and the various paths which their lives were taking. They had all individually visited Alexa in Poland with their children and their friendships grew even stronger with the passage of time.

Alexa had also kept in touch with the Klauss family of her own choice. She had written to the family a few years after the war had ended, thanking them for freeing her and to inform them that she had been successfully reunited with her younger sister, but sadly not her mother. She asked after their children, whom she still had a genuine fondness for in her heart, after caring for them full-time for five years of her life. Alexa was delighted to receive a warm reply back from the family in the form of a letter, which was then followed soon after by some gifts. The Klauss's began sending large cardboard boxed parcels every few months, packed full of goods to Alexa's home for her and her family. Alexa was surprised to receive these large parcels and upon opening them found inside such things as, coffee, tea, chocolate, sweets, biscuits, cheese, tinned meats, medicines, shoes, leather jackets, all kinds of clothing for both adults and children, shoes, small ornaments and always a couple of hundred marks safely hidden inside one of the items.

Poland had taken a long time to recover after the war had ended and there was much poverty spread throughout the country. Life was not easy in Poland and times were indeed hard. The rebuilding of many lives took great effort and inner strength and was a very long and painful journey of recovery for most. Alexa much appreciated the packages that came from Germany for her and her family and enjoyed sharing them out. She was a giver and kept very little for herself. Not that they ever could, but in a small way the packages were like a form of compensation, a way of making up for all the years that Alexa had slaved and worked so hard in Germany never being paid by the Klauss's. The packages continued to arrive at her home for many years to come and Alexa collected the German marks enclosed within saving them all up, depositing them into her bank account. Alexa eventually received some payments from the German government too, for the five years during the war that she was kept and worked against her will. The German government had begun a restitution program of its own in which they made monetary payments to many Europeans who had been taken by the Nazis from their homes, losing all of their belongings and who were imprisoned or used as forced German labor. The payments to Alexa were a minimal amount and they continued sporadically every six months for a couple of years, as a form of compensation for all the time that she had been kept by the Klauss's. Of course, these payments could never make up for what Alexa had lost and sacrificed during the war years and although it wasn't a small fortune, it did allow Alexa to buy some larger house-hold items and a few extras. However, they were issued only for a limited time and eventually the payments came to an end. However, the parcels from the Klauss family continued to arrive for decades.

During the years leading up to and especially through the 'Solidarity movement' in the 1980's, life became even harder in Poland and many basic general items became unavailable to buy in the shops. Daily items that were once taken for granted, became highly sought after and whenever news of an incoming shipment or delivery was due to arrive at a local store, word travelled quickly, and a mass of people stood in long lines for hours in advance outside of shops in the street, in the hope of making a successful purchase. During these tough times, several of Alexa's good friends living in wealthier parts of Europe whom were better off than she, also began helping out by kindly sending parcels of goods to her and her family. Around the spring of 1978 Alexa received a letter from the Klauss family inviting her to travel back to Germany, but this time on vacation as their guest. Since her children were all grown up, Alexa decided to take them up on their offer and to bring her oldest daughter along with her on the journey. Plans were set in motion for the trip and travel was booked by airplane and paid for them by the Klauss's.

Alexa was a little anxious about returning to Bitburg, the old town in Germany where she had been forced to live and work for the Klauss's during the Second World War. Although she had been terrified as a young girl when she was first taken and was initially really scared when she had first arrived at their home, once she got familiar and used to the Klauss's, she wasn't terribly afraid of them anymore. Although they had demanded much labor from her on a daily basis and had given her a full list of chores to carry out, they weren't terribly mean to her or physically abusive. The family had grown fond of Alexa over a relatively short period of time and so they were not as wicked to her, as unfortunately was the case with many other Gestapo-run households with their cruel treatment of innocent young teenagers who had also been taken from European countries against their will. They had trusted her, even to the point of allowing her to cross the border each Sunday into Luxembourg during her last year with them, to go spend the day at the shoemaker's home and then to return alone. Alexa, although naturally a little apprehensive to revisit her past, was quite looking forward to seeing some of the people she'd grew fond of and the place once more, where she spent those years of her life.

Alexa and her daughter boarded the plane in Gdansk. It was their very first time on an airplane and the excitement of the flying experience, was a good distraction for Alexa. The flight took less than two hours, then landed safely in Frankfurt.

From the airport, they took a bus into the city's main station and boarded a train for the journey back to Bitburg. Alexa couldn't help but reminisce about her train rides in the past. From the very first one when, after being captured by the Nazis when she was horrifically forced at gunpoint into a train wagon as a teenager, not knowing where she and the other boys and girls were destined for. When they were all crammed together in the unpleasant dark and dingy boxcar, with the foul smells that made her feel nauseous and made others around her vomit.

Then Alexa's thoughts skipped to her second train journey, the one towards her freedom. When she had entered the first-class carriage full of Gestapo officers and soldiers, only to discover that she didn't actually have a first-class ticket and shouldn't in fact be there. She recalled the vivid scene and the mixed emotions of panic and fear which she had felt, as she concealed her true identity and pretended to be an eighteen-year old German civilian. She thought of the Gestapo officer who came to her aid by paying the train conductor the rest of the money needed in order to make her ticket into a valid first-class one.

Alexa couldn't help but be convinced by the power of her prayers. She had lost count of how many times she had actually petitioned God on her own behalf for his protection and help, but she became very much aware of the many times that God had heard her petitions and had in fact answered her prayers. Alexa's faith had been strengthened by what she felt was God, figuratively taking hold of her right hand and guiding her through the dangers which she faced. So that no matter what situation she found herself in, she never felt truly alone and never became completely overcome and paralyzed by fear.

Alexa's daughter interrupted her mother's thoughts and asked if she could go and buy something from the restaurant car. She gave Stashia some money and told her not to be too long. Stashia left their compartment and slid the door closed which triggered Alexa's thoughts back to the memory of her first train journey to Berlin from Paris with Antoni, just after they had married and finally left the displacement camp. Pleasant images flashed up in her mind of the few hours they shared together in Paris on their honeymoon before boarding the train. Of them walking through the Parisian streets hand in hand. The cafe that they sat in together drinking coffee. The Polish Bible which the elderly French man had given her in the old book store. Then, their catching the train to leave France as they began their long journey home. She recalled how good it had felt to snuggle into her husband's chest as they slept on the train and then how Antoni had gotten himself invited into the poker game with the American soldiers and had won a nice sum of money off of them in the restaurant carriage. Antoni had been the true love of her life and those earliest years spent with him had been amongst her happiest ones. It broke her heart when she found out that he was unfaithful and even though she had chosen to leave him and eventually obtained a divorce, deep down in her heart, she still held a torch for him and knew she always would. Stashia returned to the train compartment to join her mother and after roughly five hours, they finally approached Bitburg.

As they departed from the train, Alexa looked around scanning the faces of the people on the platform and then spotted a tall blond man in his forties, whom she recognized as Richard, the Klauss's oldest son. He was no longer the young teenager whom she remembered when she had last seen him, but she couldn't mistake his facial features. He was the spitting-image of his father when he was that age. Alexa waved to him and he walked over to them and re-introduced himself, kissing her on each cheek and welcoming her. Then he introduced himself to Stashia, took their suitcases from them and led them out of the station towards his car. Alexa was surprised at just how much he looked like his father.

Herr Klauss had been in his early forties when Alexa had first met him and to her, Richard was now his double. She hadn't seen the family for over thirty years so she knew that everyone would have changed and aged. Herr and Frau Klauss still lived at their same farmhouse and as Richard drove them through the town towards it, Alexa began to recognize the familiar surroundings of where she was. Richard turned into the gates and drove up the long driveway and soon stopped outside of the Klauss family home. The outside of the property wasn't as well kept as she remembered it used to be and as they all got out of the car, Herr and Frau Klauss came out of the house to greet them.

"Alexa, it is so good to see you again. Welcome," said Herr Klauss. "And this must be your daughter."

"Hello Herr Klauss, it's good to see you again."

"Please Alexa, call me Fredrick," he shook her hand and kissed both of her cheeks, as was the German custom, "and please my wife is Emilie." Alexa had never been permitted to call them by their first names when she was a teenager and had worked for them, so it seemed a little odd and un-natural to her at first, but these were different times and she was no longer a young girl, nor was she their slave. She was a woman to be respected in her own right.

"Alexa welcome! It's wonderful to see you again, How, was your journey?" Frau Klauss asked as she also greeted Alexa, but she did so without the handshake and instead warmly hugged her and kissed her cheeks.

"Thank you, our journey was just fine Emilie. This is my oldest daughter Stashia."

They greeted her also, acknowledging what a pretty girl she was and then invited them both into the house, followed by Richard who carried in their suitcases. Frau Klauss served some coffee, sandwiches cakes and pastries in the lounge for everyone to enjoy while they all caught up on each other's lives and news. All of the Klauss's children were married with children of their own and no longer lived at their parent's farmhouse, but they didn't live too far away, and Alexa was assured that she would get to see them all during her visit. After over an hour of chatting together, Richard excused himself and said he had to be going. He promised he'd come by soon to take Alexa and Stashia out in his car, to visit some of the sites and also some of the other local people who remembered Alexa and were looking forward to seeing her again.

Alexa began to clear off the table and to gather the used plates and cups together, but Frau Klauss said there was no need and that she was their guest. However, Alexa insisted that it was no bother and began carrying the tray full of dishes, through into the kitchen. It was all very surreal and as she walked through the kitchen door, her memory flashed back like a time machine to when she was a teenager and had to slave away after the Klauss's. The kitchen hadn't changed all that much. It was still the same layout and even the kitchen furniture was the same. Only the color of the walls had changed, but that was only the paint color, and only a cosmetic change. Alexa placed the tray on the large kitchen table, but instead of washing all the dishes and cleaning up as she had always had to do all those years ago, she left the full tray sitting on the table and turned to leave the kitchen behind her. It wasn't her job anymore.

It was getting late and Alexa and her daughter were tired from all their traveling that day, so Herr Klauss carried their bags upstairs, while Frau Klauss showed them to their bedrooms. They took Alexa to Richard's old bedroom which had been redecorated since he was a child and told her to make herself at home. Alexa was relieved they hadn't expected her to sleep in her old room, she felt as though that might have been too much emotionally for her to handle. Next, they showed Stashia to their daughter Anna's old room, which had also been redecorated and looked warm, comfortable and inviting. The Klauss's told them to make themselves at home and to help themselves to anything they needed. Alexa was grateful for the kindness they were showing her but couldn't help but compare just how very different things had been some thirty plus years before, to how they were now.

Alexa really didn't hold any malice towards the Klauss's, nor was she a person who was filled with hatred, nor one to harbor resentment. However, she was human and remembered all too well just how hard and long she had to work on a daily basis, all year round. How depressed and alone she had felt having no family of her own around her and how desperate she was to be reunited with her own family again in Poland. Also, the fear factor that had always haunted her daily, knowing that she was an undesirable Polish girl in the eyes of the Germans and could easily be taken off to a concentration camp or killed at any time. These feelings had been prominent ones, every day of her captured life since the age of thirteen. However, she was also well aware that her experiences could have also been so much worse and even more horrific for her than they actually were living with the Klauss's. She remembered how she had made certain choices, conscious decisions to keep herself and her frame of mind positive, as difficult as it was at times. To keep her faith and her hope fueled and alive, in the firm belief that her situation was only temporary and that one day she would be free. As Alexa reflected, she realized that this had been her blueprint for survival, her escape from tragedy to triumph and how she had chosen to live her life rather than just survive it.

Alexa made sure that Stashia was comfortable in the guest bedroom. As she left the room and turned out the light, she again reflected on how ironic the scenario now was. There she was wishing her own daughter goodnight, some thirty plus years later in the Klauss's daughter's old bedroom, where she once used to look after young Anna. She could never have imagined that scene ever happening way back then. Alexa said goodnight to the Klauss's and retired for the evening with mixed emotions, closing the door to Richard's old bedroom behind her. As had been her unbroken routine since she was a young child, Alexa began to pray and recite Psalm 91, as she did every night before going to sleep. That was the one constant, the one thing that had never changed. Her belief and faith in God had never faltered and she trusted without a shadow of a doubt that God had indeed protected her throughout her life and trials, ultimately delivering her to safety.

The following day Alexa took Stashia for a walk into the old part of town. It was very familiar and nostalgic for her, even though it had been so long since she had last walked on those very streets. Some of the same old buildings which Alexa remembered still remained. However, there were many that were no longer standing in their original places anymore and new taller and more modern buildings now replaced them. Alexa recognized the home where her old friend Elizabeth used to live and work all those years ago and decided she would knock on the door just to see if it was still owned by the same family. The home looked old and uncared for, with its front garden overgrown high with weeds and neglected with broken and missing fencing. Alexa approached the front door and knocked upon it. There was no answer and just as she was about to walk away with Stashia, someone slowly opened the door. It was a short, elderly, white haired woman, but as Alexa looked into her eyes, she recognized her as being the wife of the family whom her friend Elizabeth had worked for long ago. The woman didn't recognize Alexa at first, so she told her who she was which triggered the woman's memory and then she warmly welcomed her and invited her into her home. The woman now lived in the large house all by herself and explained that her husband had died many years prior and that her children were all married with their own children and lived in East Germany. She seemed very happy to have some visitors and warmly invited Alexa and her daughter to come and join her for some coffee. Alexa asked after Elizabeth, as to where about she might be living now, but the woman said she had no idea, nor did she have a contact address for her. Alexa was polite, however that was actually the only reason why she had stopped at the house in the first place. To ask what had happened to Elizabeth after the war had ended. After she drank her cup of coffee, she made her excuses and told the woman they had somewhere else they needed to be and that they had to leave. The woman told them to come back again anytime they were passing, but Alexa had no intention of returning there.

Alexa stayed in Bitburg at the Klauss's home for a week in total with Stashia on their vacation. Richard came back to the farmhouse the next morning as promised and took them out on a tour of some of the local places of attraction and interest. Along the journey around noon time, he drove them to visit an old family friend and neighbor of the Klauss's, the Klien's. They remembered Alexa very well as a lovely young teenager and were genuinely delighted to see her again. They had her, Stashia and Richard join them for lunch and had prepared quite a feast for them all to enjoy. They shared their various memories and stories from the past together, from when Alexa was a young girl, through her teenage years when she had lived at the Klauss's. Then they caught up on events from when she had left the town of Bitburg in 1945, right up to the present day.

The Klien's also showed a sincere interest in Stashia, asking her questions about her life in Poland, her siblings, her likes, her hobbies and her ambitions for the future. They made Stashia feel very welcome and she got to see first-hand, just how well respected and well-liked her mother was. The fondness which they felt for Alexa was very obvious and most endearing, even after the passage of such a long period of time and them not having been in touch for decades. Stashia couldn't quite understand what made her mother so special to them. She of course loved her own mother very much, but they were mother and child, it was natural, they were blood relatives. But these German people, as nice as they came across, were all strangers in Stashia's eyes. She had never heard of them before and really couldn't understand the true affection that these people seemed to have for her mother.

After they had spent a few hours at the Klien's home enjoying their hospitality, they gave both Alexa and her daughter some small gifts and souvenirs to take home with them. Richard said it was time that they left, as they had another few stops to make that day around town. They hugged goodbye and got into Richard's car. He then drove them for a further fifteen minutes to another house they were expected at. Alexa didn't recognize the house, but it was quite pretty and well-cared for. Its gardens were full of vibrant colorful flowers, which filled the air with sweet perfumes. Alexa asked who lived in the house and who it was that they were going to visit. But Richard wouldn't say and told her it was a surprise. They all got out of the car and walked towards the front door of the house. Richard knocked on the door, which was opened by a neatly dressed older woman whose eyes smiled at Alexa with delight and sheer joy. Alexa looked at the woman who had aged gracefully and was equally delighted to recognize and see her again too.

"Oh, my goodness, is it really you Alice?" Exclaimed Alexa, then before even waiting for a reply, she lunged forward and wrapped her arms around the now elderly woman. The two of them hugged each other tenderly, then pulled back to look at each other.

"Oh Alexa, how wonderful it is to see you again. I've prayed and prayed for your safety all of these years...and here you are standing in front of me."

They embraced again and Alexa's eyes filled with tears of joy as she became overcome with emotion. The woman was the shoemaker, originally from just over the border in

Luxembourg. The very woman who had figured out that Alexa was being kept and worked as a Polish slave by the German Gestapo officer and his family, when she had come to collect their newly-made shoes. She was the woman who had gone out of her way to make the then young seventeen-year-old girl feel welcome, wanted and cared about. She was the woman who invited her into their family as their special guest. Alice and her husband, who was a high-ranking town official, had challenged Herr Klauss when he came looking for Alexa and demanded that Alexa be allowed to come over the border to visit with them in Luxembourg every Sunday, so that she'd get to have a day off to relax and spend with their family. Alexa had never forgotten the generosity and kindness extended to her by Alice and her family, even though they had lost touch after the wars end. It had restored her faith in humanity and had reminded her, that not all people were bad and abusive. That not all people should be labelled the same. That, she was indeed worthy and of value and was very likable. They had even made her a pair of her very own shoes as a gift.

Alexa introduced Alice to Stashia, who was delighted to meet her daughter. She kissed her on both cheeks and then invited them all into her home. Alice prepared fresh coffee for them all, which she served in her finest set of bone china. She brought out a tray of fresh cream cakes and a selection of pastries for them all to enjoy. There was also a plate of fine Belgian chocolates and biscuits, which she placed on the table before them and invited them all to help themselves. Stashia once again could see just how admired and highly thought of her mother had been all those years ago and evidently still was, and again it surprised her. They caught up on the void of the years which had passed. Alice updated Alexa on her family, of her two grown children and their individual lives, and proudly showed photographs of her grandchildren and shared stories of their achievements. Alice had left Luxembourg a year after the war had ended and made the move to live in

Bitburg with her husband and family, after their home had been destroyed by an accidental fire.

Next Alice asked Alexa about her journey back to Poland when she was just eighteen and had left the Klauss's farmhouse near the end of the war. Alexa hadn't ever really talked about her story all that much to people since the end of the war years. She knew what she had gone through, but she also knew that many others had gone through far worse experiences. She had kept it privately to herself for all those years and concentrated on raising her children and working hard to support them. However, being back in Germany again after all this time, she had now told her personal story of the long journey she had made to get back home to Poland, three times already. Telling Alice would be her fourth time, but these were people who genuinely cared about what she had gone through and what she had returned to find, so it seemed easier to share it with them.

She told them a detailed account of her boarding the first-class train carriage and almost fainting out of fear, as she found it full of Nazi soldiers and Gestapo officers. Then of her long walk at night through the snow-covered forest. Of arriving at the convent and there, being kept against her will again and being worked by the nuns for a further four months until the bombing by the Allied forces. She spoke of her escape with her three friends until she was picked up by the Allied troops and taken to the abandoned school with all the local German civilians. Then of her standing up for herself and declaring that she was actually Polish and that there was a mistaken identity. The empathetic US commander who had her select ten German women to supervise and then of being offered treasures beyond her wildest dreams. Alice hung on every word of Alexa's story and listened intently as it progressed onward with her journey to the displacement camp in France and her time spent there, reunited with her three girlfriends. Then she spoke of her first love and of marrying Antoni and their journey back to Poland together, to find their families.

Alexa told of the heartbreak she felt of never finding her mother alive and eventually learning that she had actually been hospitalized after serious beatings and either killed there or marched to a concentration camp. Even at the age of fifty-one, Alexa still became emotional when she thought of the senseless murder of her beautiful mother and of the last time, she had ever seen her, when they were in Dachau separated by the Nazis. She then talked about the joy she had upon finding and being reunited with her little sister Asha and how inseparable they then became. Alice went to her drinks cabinet and brought out a crystal decanter which was filled with cognac and asked Richard to pour each of them a glass. Alexa's story evoked deep emotions from her listeners as she spoke, especially from Alice and in some way, it had proved to be very therapeutic and somewhat of a release and healing process for Alexa, as she talked about her personal experiences.

There was a knock on the door and Alice excused herself to get up and answer it. When she returned to the lounge, she was accompanied by another older woman, who had heard that Alexa was visiting with her friend Alice and asked if Alexa was still there. The woman had never known Alexa personally however, she was anxious to meet her. Alice introduced her to Alexa and to her daughter Stashia. Richard seemed to already know her, and they greeted each other warmly. Once they were introduced, the woman invited Alexa to come to her home for some refreshments and said that her husband and family really wanted to meet her too. Alexa thanked the woman, but politely declined her invitation. She explained that they had already been shown so much German hospitality that day, that they couldn't possibly eat or drink anymore. The woman seemed very disappointed and begged Alexa to please reconsider. Alexa could see that the woman was very anxious and that it seemed very important to her for some reason. Alice even began to join in, encouraging Alexa to go to her friend's home which was close by, even if just for a short visit. Eventually, they managed to persuade her into going to the woman's home although Alexa did make it clear that she wouldn't be able to stay for very long. Stashia was again amazed at the way people were reacting to her mother, with such admiration and true affection for her.

Richard went out to start the car and Alexa said her goodbyes to Alice and promised to return to see her again two days later, when the rest of her family had arranged to visit. Alice promised them a hearty home-cooked German meal together. Alexa and Stashia headed out of the house and into the car with the woman and Richard. As they drove off, Alexa and Alice waved to one another.

CHAPTER -24-

After a short distance, Richard pulled his car over off from the roadway and parked it outside of a small white cottage, which was where the old woman apparently lived. They all got out of the vehicle and made their way into the woman's home. There was a man sitting in a high-backed comfy-looking leather chair, who Richard greeted first by calling him uncle Hans and hugging him in a manly way. He stood up from his chair and Alexa became aware of his height. Although he was an older man, well into his seventies, he had retained his tallness and was a rather elegant, good looking gentleman, with a full head of grey, almost silver hair.

"Hello Alexa!" He said looking straight into her blue eyes.

"This is my husband Hans," said the woman introducing him to Alexa.

Alexa looked back at him, but she didn't recognize him as someone whom she had ever known from her past. Hans extended his hand out to shake Alexa's.

"Do you remember me?" He asked.

Alexa felt bad and slightly embarrassed that she had no idea who he was.

"I'm sorry Sir, but it's been so long since I was in Germany. Please forgive me, but I'm afraid I don't remember you." As she reached out her hand to shake his.

"Do you remember our train ride together?"

Alexa looked puzzled and somewhat confused, as she began to search her memory for a match.

"I'm the officer who paid your ticket on the train!"

Alexa couldn't believe the words that she had just heard the man speak. However, she now made the connection immediately and recognized him clearly from that day in the first-class train carriage, all those years ago. He was the tall blond Gestapo officer who had smiled pleasantly at her and who had been so kind to her. It was something that had always puzzled her, she had never been able to figure out exactly why he did what he did. He was the one who had come to her aid when the train conductor was giving her a hard time over her ticket discrepancy. He was the one who asked the train conductor how much it was to upgrade her incorrect train ticket to a first class one and had then kindly paid the amount, so that she could remain seated in that carriage. Now after all those years, the pieces of the puzzle were slowly beginning to fall into place.

"Wow! I remember you now!"

Hans leaned over and gave Alexa a gentle hug, but she was hugging him back far tighter now that she knew and remembered who he was. A genuine sense of immense gratitude for his very kind gesture all those years ago, overwhelmed her. Alexa was in sheer amazement at this unexpected revelation. The surprised expression continued to show upon her face as the others looked on with contentment and excitement.

"Oh Sir, thank you ever so much. I don't know what would have happened to me that day, if you hadn't paid the rest of my ticket. Herr Klauss had told me that it was a first-class ticket which he had bought for me and said specifically that I was only to sit in the first-class carriage."

"I know he did. Frederick is my cousin and I told him that it would be better that we set things up that way for you. We knew that I'd be traveling on that very train, in the first-class carriage that day and I agreed to look out for you and make sure no one hassled you and that you'd come to no harm on my watch."

Alexa stared at Hans in disbelief over the fact that Herr Klauss and he, had gone to all that bother to ensure her safety.

"We decided it was better that you didn't know about our plan. So that there was no way you could give the game away or blow my cover. As you know, at that time you, being Polish, could very easily have been killed and believe me when I tell you, there were plenty of blood hungry soldiers in that carriage who wouldn't have thought twice about shooting you."

Alexa was very well aware of the dangerous situation that she was actually in back then in the train carriage but now it all made complete sense to her. She began thanking Hans profusely, over and over again for making sure that she was safe.

Hans's wife brought a tray full of fresh coffee into the room and placed it down on the table in front of them. Hans asked Richard to bring over his crystal decanter and some brandy glasses from the sideboard and to pour them all a drink.

"How did you get on, once you finally got off of the train? Hans asked her. "I remember watching you from the window as you walked away with your little suitcase. Did you reach the convent safely?"

Alexa told him she had walked through the snow-covered forest in the dark for several hour's but didn't go into great detail about just how difficult a journey it had actually been for her on foot. She told him she had eventually reached the convent very late at night and that the nun there wasn't very pleased to receive her, nor was she very nice to her. That in fact she was placed in a locked, cell type brick room in the basement and then kept in the convent for four months and forced to work hard labor with three other European girls, who were also being held against their will.

"That was not the plan! You were only supposed to stay there for two or three nights. That nun was another cousin of ours and it was Frederick who arranged that part of your journey with her. I never liked her, not even when I was a young boy. I knew she was mean but that was really wicked of her to do what she did. What happened in the end? How did she eventually let you go?"

"Well she didn't really let me go. The convent was targeted by the Allies in several bombing raids and unfortunately, she was killed with most of the other nuns who were there."

"Good, that serves her right!" Hans said, "Well at least you got away alright and you weren't killed."

"No, we were very lucky. My three friends and I, all made it out of the convent ruins together uninjured, with only a few scrapes and cuts. We were finally free from that nightmare and able to escape, after all those months." Alexa didn't go into all of the details of her long journey to get back home, but at least now she knew the important part that the Klauss family had played in planning her escape journey. Now Hans also knew the details of his and Frederick's attempts, to help assist Alexa to get away safely. The risks they had taken had all been worth it.

Hans raised his glass and made a toast. Everyone else joined him and also reached for their glasses, as he said out loud, "Here's to surviving!" Then he knocked back his cognac in one go and placed his empty glass back down on the table. Then he stood up and walked out of the room and said, "Wait here!" He was gone for about ten minutes, then he returned carrying an empty medium-sized, solid black suitcase. He walked over to Alexa and handed it to her. "Here, this is for you. It's the same suitcase which I had with me in the first-class train carriage that day, all those years ago. I want you to have it as a souvenir from my family to yours."

Alexa was surprised at his kind gesture and humbly said, "Thank you very much Hans, that's very kind of you, but it's okay, you keep it."

Hans wouldn't take no for an answer and insisted that Alexa keep the suitcase to carry her belongings in and take back home to Poland with her. Realizing how insistent Hans was that she accept his gift, Alexa finally agreed to take it and thanked him for his generosity. Hans said she was very welcome and told her that he was sure that she'd need the extra luggage to carry all the gifts and souvenirs that he was sure she'd accumulate during her visit.

"It seems like a very good and strong suitcase, that will carry all of our things safely and keep them nicely protected. Thanks again, I'll take good care of it."

"It's getting late and it's time I drove you both back to my parent's house. I still have another two hour's drive home after I drop you both off." Richard said to Alexa and Stashia.

Alexa agreed that it was time they left. She stood up and thanked Hans's wife for her hospitality and for insisting that Alexa come to her home to meet her husband. Then she turned to Hans and again thanked him for what she now knew he had done for her all those years ago on the train. "I will never forget what you did for me! Thank you."

"I'm just glad that you were safe and that you survived. I'm also really happy I could help in some small way to get you back home!"

Alexa picked up the suitcase and handed it to Richard to put into his car, then she moved towards Hans and hugged him goodbye. Alexa knew she'd probably never see him again but was so grateful that she'd gotten the chance to meet him and to also thank him in person after all those years. Stashia climbed into the back seat of the car and Alexa sat up front with Richard who started the engine and drove off. Hans and his wife waved, until the car was gone out of sight.

As Richard drove, Alexa continued to be overwhelmed by the new revelation that she had just learned. "That was quite an unexpected surprise!"

"Yes, we knew you'd be surprised and would never expect it."

"But I don't remember your Uncle Hans living in the village back when I was here, all those years ago."

"Well, no you wouldn't, because he didn't live here back then. He lived in Berlin."

"Ah, that's why I wouldn't have known him. When did he move here?"

Richard paused and didn't answer right away. Then he began to explain. "Well sometime after you left our farmhouse and the war finally came to an end, the Allied troops began hunting down, how can I say? Well, anyone who served as a Gestapo officer and arresting them. They started conducting extensive investigations, to discover who had played which roles during the war." Richard appeared to be visibly uncomfortable as he spoke, but he had started, so he carried on.

"So, what happened, can you tell me?"

"Well, one day some British soldiers arrived at our farmhouse and searched it thoroughly. Father was arrested and taken away on that very day. He never came home for a very long time. At about the same time, uncle Hans was also arrested in Berlin. So, his wife, my aunt Danka packed up all of their personal belongings and came to live with us."

"I had no idea." Alexa voiced in surprise.

"No, of course you wouldn't. My parents don't talk about it, ever, so please don't mention to them that you know, or that I have told you."

"No, don't worry, I won't."

"My father was tried at Nuremberg, where they sentenced him and sent him to prison. They found him guilty of war crimes - they called it, but my father didn't kill anyone. He didn't work at any of the concentration camps. He was a good man, a good father, a good husband."

"I never knew what he did, or what his job was. Never in all of those years and I never asked." Alexa said.

"He had an office job, where he kept records to protect Germany's precious art collections during the war, so they would not all be destroyed. He didn't visit concentration camps and he certainly did not kill any one. He wasn't responsible for prisoners, nor was he involved with anything bad that happened to the Jews, or the Poles or the Europeans."

Alexa heard Richard's words and silently to herself thought, '*but I was Polish, I was a European and your parents selected me to be their unpaid slave for five years.*' Part of her wondered how Richard could say such a thoughtless, insensitive thing to her. He was no longer a young boy, after all. He was a grown German man, who knew the facts about the atrocities which had actually gone on under the Nazi regime. The whole world knew how, many millions had suffered and been killed, tortured and enslaved - yet he seemed to be defending part of that very regime, at least the part his father was responsible for.

"My father had to spend five years in prison. It was very hard for my mother and our family. I had to become the man of the house. Uncle Hans was sentenced to three years in prison, it was not easy for him or for my father."

Alexa could no longer hold back her words, as she listened to Richard's.

"Well, it wasn't very easy for me, being rounded up and taken away from my home and family at thirteen-years of age and imprisoned to work as a slave for your family for five years, let me tell you."

Finally, the penny had dropped. Richard seemed to have grasped the reality of the situation that Alexa had actually been forced into all those years ago, at the hands of his own people. At the hands of his own parents. He seemed to realize just how insensitive and selfish his words had come across. "Yes, I'm sure it was very difficult indeed for you. I'm sorry, I didn't mean to be so insensitive. I didn't think, please forgive me. There is no comparison Alexa with what you went through."

"It's okay, apology accepted Richard."

"Thank you, Alexa." Richard stopped talking and continued to drive. He reached his hand over towards the round knob on his car radio and turned it on. The music began playing instantly, on a pre-set station and as if on cue, the words of the current song played out. 'God bless the child, whose got his own, whose got his own…' A Billie Holiday song was playing on the local German radio station. Stashia began to sing along to the chorus, from the back seat of the car and Alexa pondered to herself, on just how ironic that very moment in time now was to her. *'Herr Klauss got five years in prison after he freed me from my five years as his prisoner. An eye for an eye. I wonder what he actually did?'* But she didn't ask. Alexa stared out of the window on her side of the car, silently trying to process all of the new information, that she had now been given. Stashia didn't speak German, so she hadn't understood their conversation. She continued to hum along to the melody and Richard drove them the rest of the way back to the farmhouse.

Alexa spent the remainder of her week in Germany meeting a few more people from her past. Everyone remembered her fondly and most gave her little gifts or souvenirs to take back to Poland with her to remember them by. As it turned out, the suitcase which Hans had gifted to her, came in very useful indeed. When Alexa returned home, she had more than double the amount, of belongings that she had originally set off with. Once she unpacked the suitcase, she placed it on top of her wardrobe and kept it as one of her most treasured possessions, which she'd glance up at during some point of her day. She never used it for anything, except for keeping it as a permanent reminder of her harrowing journey back to freedom and as a reminder to be grateful for each day of life that she lived since. She never forgot.

The trip back to visit Germany had been a very beneficial journey for Alexa on many levels. She had been warmly received by the Klauss's who treated her as though she was part of their own family. Although, they never discussed the fact that they had actually chosen her out of a line-up of Aryan looking teenagers, who'd all been taken away from their families and forced to work as unpaid house slaves, all those years ago. There was almost an unspoken apology, a silent remorsefulness which Alexa sensed from them. The words 'I'm sorry!', were not really necessary for Alexa to hear, and the Klauss's never actually said them to her. But through their actions, they showed they really had cared about her. That in itself, gave her a sense of healing and closure.

The many years of their sending her large parcels of goods as well as money, was the way they presumably chose to handle their feelings of guilt. Deep down they knew that they could never make up for the impossible situation which Alexa had to go through, but at the same time they knew and understood Alexa could have been treated so much worse by another Gestapo family, as many other young girls were. Some young European girls were regularly beaten violently by their captors and even raped, so in comparison to them, Alexa had been in a far better position. After all it wasn't the Klauss's own doing or choice, that these teenagers were forcibly taken from their homes and made to work for German households. Unfortunately, it was just the way it was during the war. Alexa was one of the many casualties of Hitler's war.

The Klauss's continued to send parcels to Alexa and her family for the rest of their days. They also sent her letters and cards and they'd telephone her from time to time. When the elderly couple finally passed away at a ripe old age, their children continued the tradition of sending parcels to Alexa. Although not quite as frequent, they still generously sent them and every few months, made phone calls. They never forgot Alexa.

Throughout her long life, Alexa's home was a constant hub of activity. Her telephone was always ringing and was an important means of international contact for her. On a monthly basis, friends from her past across Europe would call her to enquire how she was and remind her that she wasn't forgotten by them. They'd have uplifting conversations sharing their news and hearing hers. Especially Marta, Greta and Henrietta right up until their deaths. Alexa's family members were also regular callers, especially those in her family who lived abroad in various countries and who couldn't visit as much as they would have liked to.

Alexa's five children which she had with Antoni all married and all gave birth to a girl, so Alexa had five granddaughters, all of whom were a year apart in age. They were all born and grew up in Poland, except for Stefan's daughter. He had married a pretty young Scottish woman named Rebecca, whom he had met while she was visiting her father's family in Poland. Stefan proposed and within a short time they were married. Alexa loved all of her children, but always had a special unconditional love for Stefan who was a handsome hooligan and the prodigal son of her family. He could do no wrong in her eyes. He took after his father in so many ways, including his looks. His mother was delighted that he was going to settle down, so much so that she gave Stefan her amethyst engagement ring which had once belonged to her mother and her gold band from his father Antoni, for him to give to his bride. Stefan had no desire to remain living in Poland with his new wife and instead moved over with her to live in Scotland, seeking a new life for himself with better opportunities. However, within the early years of their daughter Rochelle being born, Stefan was unfaithful, following in the footsteps of his own father. Rebecca decided that she had no other option but to divorce him and raise their young daughter alone. Although Stefan had never held his family in a very high regard, nor kept in regular contact with them or his mother, his ex-wife now did. Rebecca would call Alexa from time to time and update her on Rochelle's progress as her young daughter grew up, but unfortunately, she could never update her on her son Stefan's life or his whereabouts which saddened Alexa greatly. She always wondered where he was. Rebecca became like a daughter to Alexa and their relationship became a special one.

Rebecca took her daughter Rochelle over to meet Alexa for the very first time when she was only two-years old. She was the middle child of Alexa's five granddaughters. Naturally Alexa fell in love with her granddaughter at first sight and was delighted to get to spend time with her. Rebecca would take her over to Poland every summer on vacation for four weeks during the school holidays and so, Rochelle was able to get to know her grandmother from a very young age, and she grew to love her very deeply. As a young child Rochelle learned quickly to speak Polish and so could communicate with her grandmother easily, they understood each other very well.

CHAPTER -25-

In her later life, Alexa had developed the creative skills which she had learned early on in her childhood and, over the years, became a very talented artist. She had a special aptitude for painting flowers, especially poppies and sunflowers and sold several original pieces in various art galleries in Poland and received many commissions throughout Germany and Europe over the years. Alexa took pride in her art and was proud of the fact that her talent had come from her father and ran in the family genes. When Rochelle got a little older, Alexa would spend time drawing pictures for her granddaughter when she'd come to visit her during the summer months. When Rochelle was about seven-years old and on vacation in Poland, her grandmother taught her how to paint and with practice and perseverance, she eventually became rather good at it in her own right. The artistic gene was a common one shared by five of Alexa's children. They were all very artistic except for Stefan, the gene had seemed to skip him and instead, passed on straight to his daughter. Only Rochelle was the artistically talented one out of the five granddaughters, which gave her and Alexa an extra special bond and shared talent in common. When Rochelle turned thirteen years of age, her mother gave her the gift of her amethyst engagement ring. Being that she had been divorced from Stefan for a long time and due to the fact that it had once belonged to both Alexa and Sophia, it seemed appropriate that Rochelle have it next. From that day on, Rochelle never took it off her finger and it became one of her most treasured possessions in life.

When Rochelle was eighteen-years of age and working for a newspaper, she answered a call to place an American job vacancy in the sheet. After some deep thought and debate, she decided to take the job in New York herself, where she lived for twelve years. During those years living in America, Rochelle called her grandmother every other month, long distance and they continued to share an interchange of mutual and unconditional love. Alexa would always ask her granddaughter the same question, 'When she was coming back to visit her in Poland?' And always made it known that she wanted Rochelle to leave America, as it was just too far away from her and Europe. Their relationship was always very special to Rochelle, who showed her love for her grandmother by sending her cards and gifts, always keeping in regular contact with her and finally she made the long trip over to visit Alexa in Kraków. After the nightmare that was September eleventh in New York in 2001, and the horrific attacks of evil terrorism that occurred on that day, Rochelle reluctantly decided to move back home to Scotland to live. From there she booked a long overdue, seven-week vacation to visit with her grandmother in Poland for some quality time together and a much needed catch up. Alexa still lived in Kraków at that time, which was a beautiful town, one which Rochelle loved very much and had visited often during her teenage years when spending time with her grandmother and family.

They both enjoyed and made the most of their precious time spent together and Alexa spoiled her granddaughter just as she had always done, when she was much younger. They spent most of their time talking in conversations for hours on end about the family, life in Poland and art. Alexa would always begin a discussion on how important and great God still was in her life. Alexa read her Bible daily and every morning when she woke up and every night before she fell asleep, she'd recite her life-long prayer of Psalm 91. She said it aloud every night while she had her granddaughter with her, before they both went to sleep.

"Where did you learn this prayer, Babcia?" Asked Rochelle.

"My grandmother taught me it when I was a little girl. You know, the version I say is actually a Polish rhyme that young children used to learn in school. An old Polish poet from the sixteenth century by the name of Jan Kochanowski wrote it based on the original verses of Psalm 91. But you know it was God who wrote the original, right?" Alexa smiled.

"Can you say it out loud for me now Babcia?" Rochelle smiled back. Then as if pushing play on a recorded cassette player, Alexa began reciting the 91st Psalm on cue, that she knew off by heart.

Rochelle shared many stories of her adventures over her twelve years living in New York with her grandmother, who hung on her every word, as if walking in her shoes across America with her. Alexa asked if she had ever been to Brooklyn New York? Rochelle told her that she had and began explaining what it was like there. Crossing the Brooklyn bridge and looking back over the East River to Manhattan, at its amazing skyline view. The ornate brownstone buildings with their metal fire escapes climbing up the outside and bright colored fire hydrants on the streets below. The wide mix of cultures, the variety of international foods for sale available on most blocks and the tempting aromas that filled the air, especially in the warmer months. Summers at Coney Island with its amusement park rides, boardwalk and packed beach.

"Yes, indeed I have been there several times. Remember the tee-shirt which I sent you Babcia a few years ago, the white one with BKNY on it? Well that's where I bought it for you. In a store in Brooklyn."

"Ah yes my darling, thank you, I loved it and I still have it. It's somewhere in my closet, tucked away safely to keep it good."

"I remembered that you always had a thing for Brooklyn and that's why I bought it for you. What was that all about anyway?"

Alexa paused for a moment and smiled, then began to tell the story of Mark the American soldier, whom she had met at the end of the war. Alexa told her granddaughter, that life could have been so much different, if she had only chosen Mark from Brooklyn to marry, instead of Antoni." Then she remarked, "But if I didn't marry your grandfather, I wouldn't have had you as my granddaughter and all my beautiful children."

"Then thank goodness you did marry Antoni I couldn't live without you in my life. You're my number one, my sunshine, my bright diamond, my heart and I love you so much Babcia!"

"And I you, my darling. You're my brilliant, my balsam, my princess."

Rochelle directed her grandmother's attention to her left hand and there on her middle finger, she proudly displayed her amethyst ring, "Do you remember this Babcia?"

"Oh my, how could I forget it. I haven't seen that in a very long time," Alexa said pensively as she stared down fondly at the ring, "It looks good on you, it was my mother's you know?"

"I know Babcia. It was your mother's, then yours, then my mother's and now it's mine."

Alexa reached over and squeezed her granddaughter's hand. Then Rochelle asked her grandmother if she'd like to try the ring on again.

"Yes okay, it has been a very long time. My fingers are fatter though now, it might not even fit me."

Rochelle slid off the amethyst from her middle finger and passed it to Alexa, who slipped it on to her wedding finger. It would only go on so far and not passed her knuckle, so she placed it on her little finger. Alexa raised her hand toward her eyes and looked closely at the invaluable ring, with a sentimentality, and took a deep breath. Rochelle then asked her to please share her war story with her.

"It's a very long story my darling."

"Good, we've got plenty of time."

Alexa asked her to first make a fresh pot of tea and get them some cheesecake. Then she sat down next to her granddaughter on the couch, took a deep breath and began to tell her story from the very beginning, while she continued to wear the ring. Rochelle gave her grandmother her undivided attention.

Alexa first began talking about her parents then she gradually led up to that day in September of 1940, when she and her mother had left her younger sister behind with the neighbors, wearing her mother's rings. Of her mother taking her to buy a new pair of shoes and then suddenly, her world being turned upside down and life as she knew it was wrenched from her, when the Nazis drove into the town square and tore them apart.

Rochelle was engrossed in her grandmother's story and was filled with such deep empathy, feeling Alexa's emotions as she narrated her story. As her grandmother related her traumatic experience as a young teenage girl, Rochelle could imagine herself in Alexa's shoes. Tears welled up in her eyes and as Alexa recalled the last time, she had ever seen her mother, when she was struck in the head in Dachau and knocked to the ground unconscious. Tears trickled down Rochelle's cheeks. "Oh, Babcia that's just awful, I'm so sorry," said Rochelle, as she tried to fight back her tears. She wrapped her arms around her grandmother and told her that she loved her. "What happened to your mother?"

"It's hard to say for definite. I wrote to the Red Cross for many years in the hope of finding out what happened to my Mama, but the trail kept growing cold. There was information pointing to her being sent to slave for the Gestapo, but it must have been really bad for her, as she was listed as admitted to a German hospital in 1944 with serious wounds, after multiple beatings. That's the last solid piece of factual information I have. The hospital was liquidated near the end of the war and if she was still alive then, she'd have been a victim to one of two horrific endings. Many of the patients were shot and buried in a mass grave outside on the hospital grounds and those still able to walk were taken on a death march or transported to concentration camps to be finished off. Many years ago, I went to the location of the old hospital and took some of the earth from the sacred ground there, where the killings took place. There is a monument to all those people killed there you know. But I'll never know for sure if that was her final resting place." The room went silent. Neither of them said a word. There was a long pause. Both women wiped the tears from their eyes and Alexa looked down at the ring on her finger. "My poor Mama."

Alexa told her granddaughter her entire wartime history from start to finish uninterrupted. She also stressed just how important Psalm 91 had been throughout her nightmare and how it had given her inner strength, courage and faith, and how she was never really alone, because God was always with her. How he always rescued her, guided her in some way and kept her safe and had granted her a long life. "We're made in God's image out of love and we must always choose love over hate my darling. Never allow breeding room for hate. Hate is a toxic poison, always remember that."

Once she got to the part in her story about her visit back to Germany for the first time with Stashia in 1978, she then talked about Hans. Rochelle was in complete amazement and totally gripped by the story. Especially when Hans had revealed that he was the Gestapo officer in the first-class train carriage all those years before and was the one who had paid the remainder of her train ticket.

"Wow! That's amazing. I'm speechless."

"I know, I was shocked, stunned and in a state of total disbelief, when he introduced himself that day and told me why he had done what he had done for me."

"Babcia you should write a book. Your story is incredible! As you've sat and told me it today, I can see it all play out vividly in my mind as if I'm watching a movie!"

"Darling, I see my whole life's movie replaying over in my mind's eye every day of my life and yes, I'm sure it would have made a great book, but I'm far too old to write it now. Look how my hands shake. But you my darling Rochelle, you could write it for me."

"I will one day Babcia, I promise you I will!"

Alexa then told her of how Hans had given her the gift of his black suitcase to keep and bring back home to Poland with her. How he had told her that it was the suitcase which he had carried with him on the train all those years ago. Alexa pointed to the top of her wardrobe and said, "That's it up there!"

"Really? Can I lift it down and look at it Babcia?"

"Yes, if you want, but it will be covered in dust my darling. I don't use it for anything, and it's sat up there for years now. I have always stored it up on top of the wardrobe as a souvenir, so that I never forget Hans and what he did for me."

Rochelle grabbed a wooden chair, placed it in front of the wardrobe and climbed up on it to reach up for the suitcase. She carefully took a hold of its handle and lifted it down, placing it on top of the table in front of her. It did have a thick coating of dust on it. It had a hard, black exterior with two brown wooden strips that went all the way around the case, on the top and bottom. Its dimensions were roughly 24 x 16 x 8 inches and it had two small locks on the front. Rochelle tried to open the case, but it was locked.

"Do you have the key to open it Babcia?"

"Yes, I think it's in the top drawer over there, in the little red heart box," Alexa pointed to her dresser, "But there's nothing in it darling. It's empty."

Rochelle opened the drawer and located the little red heart box. Inside she found two small keys threaded together with a piece of red ribbon. She took them over to the case and tried them in both of the locks. The clips sprung free and she opened up the case. Inside the walls of the case was an elegant burgundy velvet lining, but due to the age of the case, it gave off a fusty aged odor. Rochelle noticed something that seemed visibly odd to her. Inside of the case seemed to be a little shallower than the depth of the walls on the outside of the suitcase. She began feeling around the bottom of the inner part and to her, it seemed different from the lid of the case. She wanted to explore it more closely but was afraid that her grandmother wouldn't want her to investigate thoroughly inside. However, the case belonged to Alexa and her grand-daughter would never have done anything that might upset her, so she said to her. "Babcia, I think there could actually be something in the bottom of the case."

"What do you mean?"

"I'm not sure, but I think there might be an empty space below the bottom panel, under the lining as it seems much shallower than the outside of the suitcase. Can I please cut along the edge of the lining and take a look beneath it? I promise, I'll sew it back up again when I'm finished."

Alexa was a little hesitant at first but eventually agreed that her granddaughter could investigate it inside. Rochelle got a pair of scissors and carefully began to cut the stitching, of the lining at the near sides right hand corner. Once she had it undone, she looked through the opening and saw that there was a piece of hardwood the same size as the bottom of the case, which was attached and seemed to be screwed in place at the four corners. Rochelle slipped her hand underneath the velvet lining and used her knuckles to knock on the wood. The sound echoed a hollowness.

"What are you thinking darling?" asked her grandmother.

"I'm not sure, but I'm thinking that there may be something hidden underneath Babcia." Rochelle asked Alexa where she could find a screwdriver and then proceeded to release the rest of the velvet lining from its stitching. Once she found the screwdriver, she began to release the four screws and the piece of hardwood eventually became loose. Rochelle slowly and carefully lifted out the flat piece of wood which revealed a folded piece of paper inside, sitting on the bottom of the case. Alexa could see it and asked her granddaughter to hand it to her. Rochelle placed the piece of wood down flat on the table and handed her grandmother the piece of paper. Alexa carefully opened it up and read it to herself.

"What does it say Babcia?"

"It says, 'THIS IS FOR YOU ALEXA, FROM THE KLAUSS FAMILY!........SORRY!',"

Alexa was more than surprised to be holding the handwritten note in her hand. She'd had the suitcase in her possession for so long, for all those years, but had never known or even thought that there might be anything hidden inside of it which was meant for her. She wondered if the note had been there since her train ride when Hans had paid her train ticket? Or, had Hans and the Klauss's put the note there when she visited in 1978? She wondered why they hadn't told her, or why they hadn't just said the word "Sorry!" to her directly? She would never know for sure because, Herr and Frau Klauss has passed away several years before, as had Hans. Alexa had outlived them all.

Rochelle still had a puzzled look on her face, "Babcia, I think there is something else still hidden here for you. It doesn't make sense to go to all that trouble, just to hide a simple note that you might never have found." Rochelle began examining the rest of the interior of the case. She looked in the walls of the case and the lid, but eventually had to admit that there was nothing else concealed within the suitcase for her grandmother. She reached for the piece of hardwood and lifted it up off of the table, so she could put it back into the case the way it was when she had taken it out, just as she promised to.

As she tilted it backwards towards her, Alexa said, "Look, what's that on the back of the wood?"

Rochelle turned the hardwood over to the other side and saw that there was something attached to it. There before their very eyes, was a large piece of what looked like old artist canvas, without a frame. It was held down in place by its four corners, so Rochelle quickly went into the kitchen and got a clean blunt butter knife, to try and release it with. Very gently, she began to loosen the first corner which didn't take too much effort to become unstuck. Next, she loosened the second, third and fourth corners, one at a time, until the canvas sat loosely on top of the hardwood faced down.

"What is it darling?" Alexa asked.

Rochelle slowly and carefully reached for two of the adjacent corners and lifted them up at the same time, to reveal an unframed oil painting. She flipped it over and laid it back down on the piece of hardwood, facing upward this time. It was of a young male in a straw hat, walking by open fields with two large trees casting shadows on the ground on a sunny day. He was dressed in casual blue clothing, carrying a bag on his back and what looked like an artist's canvas under his left arm, with paintbrushes and paints in his right hand. The oil colors were bright, mainly blues and yellows, with visible raised brush strokes.

"Wow! I can't believe you have discovered this! I never knew it was there all this time," Alexa exclaimed. "It's beautiful."

"Oh, my goodness! Could it really be?" Rochelle who was dumbfounded, asked.

"Could it really be what darling?"

"Look at the style of the painting Babcia, does it remind you of any one painter's style in particular?"

Alexa had stood up by this point and was hovering over the painting, examining it closely.

Rochelle reached for her laptop and powered it on. She opened up her search engine and then she typed into the search box, 'second world war stolen paintings,' and after a few seconds, the results showed a list of the ten most famous paintings that had still not been found or recovered since the days of Hitler's pillaging and stealing of priceless art masterpieces across Europe for his planned super museum. Rochelle couldn't believe her eyes as she scrolled down the list of paintings. There it was in front of her, displayed on the screen of her computer, a detailed description and photo of the very painting which they had just discovered. Vincent van Gogh's 'Painter on his way to work' dated 1888! And there it was, what appeared to be the original oil painting, sitting on her grandmother's table in front of them, in all its splendor. One of the great missing masterpieces, by one of the great masters.

"Babcia, this is a Van Gogh! Do you have any idea what this is worth?"

Alexa had to sit down. She couldn't believe her eyes and she couldn't believe that she'd had this masterpiece in her possession for all those years without even knowing it. In her head she could hear Hans's words to her now, after he had given her the suitcase. 'It's from my family to your family.' Now his words made sense to her, as did the note with the apology from the Klauss family.

"I cannot keep it!" Alexa said to her granddaughter without any hesitation, "Because it's not mine. It rightly belongs to someone else and has been stolen from them and their family. Just like the room full of treasure in the church all those years ago, at the end of the war when I was offered whatever I wanted, the same principle applies, it's not mine to keep! We will have to see that it's returned to its rightful owner. I can't keep it!"

Rochelle knew her grandmother was right. Firstly, her fine-tuned conscience would never allow her to even think about keeping it. If word got out that she had it sitting in her small apartment, it would be targeted to be stolen by every thief in the country, it was far too valuable. It was far too famous to ever be sold to a collector or buyer, without causing a tremendous media frenzy world-wide. And finally, this was a priceless beautiful work of art, by the great Vincent van Gogh that deserved to be appreciated by art lovers around the world. So, Rochelle completely agreed with her grandmother and told her that she would begin researching on her computer, where and who to get in touch with about returning the painting to its rightful owners and how to go about it.

"Darling, first can you go make us a fresh pot of tea and bring through the special box of chocolates up in the cabinet. For now, the painting is ours and we are fortunate enough to get to sit alone with this great masterpiece of Vincent van Gogh's. Let's sit and enjoy it and truly appreciate it for now together, before we have to give it away. You know that he's my most favorite artist, don't you? Why do you think I painted so many sunflowers?" Rochelle agreed that it was a splendid idea. She quickly made her way into the kitchen and returned a little while later carrying a silver tray which had her grandmother's best China teapot full of freshly brewed Earl Grey tea, two clean glass cups and saucers, along with sliced lemon, a sugar bowl and fresh milk jug, accompanied by a plate of fine Belgian chocolates. She placed the tray down on the glass coffee table and positioned the painting across from them on the larger wooden dining table at eye level. Alexa told her to lock the door, so that no one could come in and disturb them. Rochelle turned the key in the door, then poured them both a hot cup of freshly brewed tea. Alexa told her to open her display cabinet and bring out the small bottle of Spirytus Polish vodka which she kept for medicinal purposes and had her pour them both a small crystal shot glass each. She did just so and then she joined her grandmother on the sofa.

"Here's to Vincent!" Rochelle said and they both raised their glasses, took a sip of their drink and smiled the biggest smiles, as they turned their eyes towards the masterpiece. They both could not believe what they had uncovered as they feasted their eyes on the priceless oil painting before them.

"Here's to you, me and Vincent," toasted Alexa, "Three artists in the one room!"

The End

PHOTOGRAPHS

Alexa 1965, Gdansk, Poland.

Alexa & Antoni's
wedding photo.
Paris, France 1945

Antoni's Grandfather is in the center
with his family & his father Fritz is
the one on the left.

Alexa & Asha 1992
Kraków, Poland

Rochelle & Alexa
1989 Kraków, Poland.

Asha, Rochelle & Alexa 1993 Kraków, Poland.

Alexa wearing Rochelle's gift of the BKNY tee-shirt.
2004 Kraków, Poland.

Alexa 2008, Slupsk, Poland.   Alexa 2008, Slupsk, Poland.

Alexa's amethyst engagement ring
which was stolen in Glasgow,
Scotland in January 2012.

Alexa's final resting place in Slupsk, Poland.
18th April 2019
Finally laid to rest next to Antoni who
Died on 11th November 1994.

Rochelle Alexandra at Alexa's grave.

ACKNOWLEDGEMENTS

First and foremost, my thanks go out to my grandmother Alexandra for sharing her story so openly with me. For her unconditional love and her fine example of not holding onto malice or hate. Secondly, a massive thanks goes to my mother Caroline for always taking me to Poland on vacation as a child, so that I could grow up knowing and loving my grandmother and for her 110% enthusiasm on this project and many others of mine. I couldn't imagine my world without you in it, thanks for all that you do for me.

Next my thanks go to my great friend Dorothy Robertshaw for her continued support, encouragement, love and wonderful friendship. Thanks also to her family and NY/CT tribe who have all received and encouraged this novel with much excitement from the very beginning. Thanks to Ruth Griggs for my bio pic and her precious and priceless friendship and helpful contacts in Massachusetts, especially Janice & Sarah.

To Magdalena, Cece and Anita for Polish translation assistance. Thanks to the very talented Heywood Gould for his writing advice. Special thanks to Paul Yilmaz for copy edits. To Euan Girvan for his editorial assistance and to Gina Fiserova for her final editing skills. Big thanks to Kristin Bryant for her creative talents in producing such a wonderful book cover design. Thanks to my beta readers, whom all gave great feedback, valuable input and genuine excitement for my manuscript. Wilma Voois your support has been fabulous. Thanks to the many people whom I have shared this story with verbally over the years, mainly at dinner parties, who have all listened intently and encouraged it's reaching a larger audience one day. Finally, that day is here.

Thanks to the team and tribe at AAE, Niccie Kliegl and especially Kary Oberbrunner for his wisdom, advice, coaching and encouragement on the publishing, marketing and business side of producing this book and making it become a reality. I'm now going to thank Google. I'm so very grateful for the valuable time which that clever little search engine has saved me and the easy access to research material, which it provided me with.

Last but not least, thanks to everyone who accommodated, tolerated and assisted me during the years process of my writing this novel. There were so many. I began writing the first chapters in Scotland, then travelled with it on my iPad and continued writing in Paris, Poland, and Spain. It neared its completion in New York and Massachusetts and was finished in Westport, Connecticut. On trains, planes, buses and in cars. Hotels, restaurants, cafes and at bars. In trendy apartments and fancy houses, at office desks and on comfy couches. So, to all of you friends and strangers that helped along the way.

Thank-you all.

ENDNOTE

The reference to Psalm 91 at the end of chapter 1, is a mix of all the verses in the chapter combined and written out into one long verse. It should be noted that this version is not a direct quote from any one source. Rather, I have combined parts from several Biblical versions which include The King James, The New World Translation and The American Standard Version, for easier understanding and comprehension throughout the story.

The 91st Psalm which Alexa recites and refers to throughout the novel, is actually an old Polish Church song taken from the renowned (16th Century) Polish poet Jan Kochanowski, which was widely learned by young children in school. This version translated into English is written below, which Alexa up until 92 years of age, continued to recite off by heart as her daily prayer.

Who will give himself up to His Lord,
And trust in Him sincerely from the bottom of his heart.
Can say boldly: I have protection in God,
No scary awe will ever come at me.

He sets you free from the traps
And saves you from infected air,
In the shadow of His wings He'll keep you forever,
Underneath His feathers you will lie safely.

IN ALEXA'S SHOES

His stable shield and a solid buckler,
Standing behind them, neither about a night mare,
About a fright nor about any arrows don't you care,
Which we are lavished in on the way in broad light.

A thousand heads turn to You from here,
The imminent sword will not reach You,
And You, amazed by what Your eyes saw,
You will live to see the unavoidable revenge over the sinners.

If you say to the Lord, You are my hope,
If the Highest God is your escape,
No bad experience will ever come your way,
And no damage will happen to your home.

He made His angels watch over you,
Wherever you step, they will care about you,
Will carry you in their arms, wo while you're walking,
No sharp stone can hurt your feet.

You will tread on impatient
Venomous snakes and slow worms safely.
You will mount the vicious lion without fear.
And you will ride a giant dragon.

Hear the Lord speak: "Anyone who loves me
And honestly walks along with Me,
Then I will love him back in all his trouble.
And I won't forget and will indeed help him.

His voice won't be condemned in Me,
I will protect him in the fight,
Let him be sure of happiness and good heartedness,
And of long lifetime and of My thoughtfulness.

Visit www.RochelleAlexandra.com
OR www.InAlexasShoes.com
and share your families uplifting, inspirational and
encouraging true life stories.

Inspirational   Stories   Photo Gallery   World Map   Share   Writing Assistance   Comments

Share Your Inspiring Family
Life Stories with the World.

We all have a grandparent or a relative who is either living or deceased, who has a great life story or experience which is inspirational. Many of these stories unfortunately don't leave the perimeter of their families ears and so therefore don't reach a greater audience, where they could be inspiring other people out there and keeping their memories alive.

f   y   P   @

© 2024 by Rochelle Alexandra. Proudly created with Wix.com

CPSIA information can be obtained
at www.ICGtesting.com
Printed in the USA
LVHW101712020719
622875LV00022B/47/P